BREAKDOWN

By Katherine Amt Hanna

Breakdown

ISBN 9781461093794

Acknowledgements

Much love to my dear husband who put up with all of this for so long and works so hard. Hugs to my mother, for all her help and support. Special thanks to Laura Symons, the first person to convince me of my potential, and my steady cheerleader. Many thanks to my critique partner, Cindy Borgne, for all her help and hard work. Kudos to my dad for proofreading.

Breakdown

Prologue

January 10, 2000 New York

I've been waiting to die, but I'm not even sick yet. I tell myself I want to die. What's left to live for? Sophie, my heart, my love, my life, is dead. Rosie, my sweet little baby, my joy, my second love, is gone, too. What's left? A house full of memories.

And a world gone to hell. What's left to go on for? I've gathered all the pills in the house and put them in a plastic bag, but so far I haven't taken them. How much worse does it have to get before I can take them? They sit on the counter in the bathroom, with a bottle of water. I look at them each night before I go to bed alone. But I can't take them.
I want to get sick. I want this to be over.

If you find this, if you know me, and you care, and I'm dead, can you send it to my brother Jon? I've taped an envelope with his address into the front cover. Just tear out the pages with writing and mail them to him. If you can. If there's still mail going overseas. If there's still mail at all.

Jon, I hope you are okay. You and Mum and Kevin. The phones don't work anymore, and the electricity is off now. I heard on the news before it went off that Britain was hit hard. Riots in London where Kevin is. I tried to reach him, and you, but I never got through.

I was at the airport when it all started, two days after Christmas, on my way to see you and Mum. There had been some talk of the flu, but they hadn't banned travel yet. We didn't think it would come to much. It was just the flu. How many flu scares have there been that never came to anything?

So Sophie drove me to the airport. We took the baby along. Why not? If she'd been older we all three would have come to visit, of course. I said goodbye to them and got on the plane. I didn't know I'd never see my baby again.

The plane didn't take off. The computer problems had started, but they didn't tell us that then. I got a different flight for the next morning. If I'd known what was happening, I'd have gone home, given up the quick trip to see Mum. The plane actually took off, but then turned around and went back to La Guardia after two hours. That's when I knew that things had gone bad, and I had to get home, but they wouldn't let us leave the airport.

They held us there for three days. They said we'd been exposed. What a nightmare. They kept us in one of the lounges, over a hundred of us. They had police with guns outside the door. They passed out masks for us. The television had CNN on. They were talking about the computer problems and the flu thing getting worse. Finally a doctor came and gave us all a shot, and they let us go.

That was New Year's Eve. Everything had been cancelled, of course. Everyone was supposed to stay home. All the buses and trains were stopped. There were no taxis on the streets. Hardly any cars. I had to walk home. No one would give me a ride. Everyone I saw was wearing a mask. There were lines outside the grocery stores. Some places had boarded up windows. All the restaurants were closed. I couldn't find a place to eat. I got in a line and got a sandwich at a deli, but it cost nearly all the cash I had. There were police with rifles all over the place. I didn't get home by dark, and there was a curfew, so I had to hide out in someone's garage or risk getting shot by police.

And then when I got home, Rosie was gone. My poor little baby. They had already taken her away. I never got to hold her one last time. I never got to say goodbye.

Sophie was dying. I got to see her before she died, but she didn't wake up. I sat with her, then got in bed with her, and held her while she died. My sweet, darling Sophie. There was nothing I could do. I hope she knew I was there with her at the end.

Sophie's friend Elaine had come when Sophie got sick. She tied a black shirt to the front gate when Sophie died, and a truck stopped. Men in biohazard suits took away my Sophie. No funerals. Too many people sick and dying. I think Elaine was sick when she left. I guess she's dead by now.

How could this happen? How could everything go bad so fast? God, I miss them. I find myself planning how to keep warm and eat and wait it out, but then I wonder if I even want to. And then at night, when I'm alone in bed, I know I don't want to. What's to go on with now that my Sophie and Rosie are gone?

In the mornings I eat something and plan out how to get through the day. I think about Archie's cabin on the mountain. It must be safer there. I could take all the food and go there. But I don't want to leave the house and all the things that still have Sophie's smell. I sleep with one of her sweaters. I sit in the nursery and hold one of Rosie's little blankets and rock it like it's her. I can't leave them.

I guess there's no chance I'll ever get back to Bath, now. I wonder how it is over there. I wonder if Mum is okay, and Kevin, and you, Jon. God, I hope you are okay.

Last night I dreamed about Brian. Not a good dream, we were screaming at each other, like the last time I saw him. I think about all of the people I left behind in Britain. I guess it will be a long time before I ever find out what's happened to them. Maybe it's better if I don't know. Then I can pretend that everyone there is okay.

Bath, England – August, 2006

Chapter 1

It was easy to forget, Brian reflected as the bus bumped along bad roads, the hardships and struggles that had brought him to this point. He wondered when he had become happy again. Like a child's growing up—something that seems impossible to a parent holding a newborn baby—happiness had grown in him, day after day, in unnoticed increments. He glanced down at his son, Ian, dozing against his arm. Fear for his boys' futures no longer burned in Brian's heart with hot intensity. It had faded to a glowing ember that flared only if he poked at it.

Beyond the dirty window, the morning sun lit a landscape hardly changed by the desperate winter of six years ago. The changes were more visible in the cities, where panic and rioting had left their mark. Brian had managed, with the help of his brother Simon, to keep his own family safe—his two boys and Fiona. Not many of the people he knew could say that.

He sighed and shook Ian gently as the buildings of Bath came into view.

The bus pulled into the station just before eight o'clock. Ian shuffled impatiently in the aisle in front of Brian as the other passengers disembarked. They'd had to sit at the back of the crowded bus, and to an eleven-year-old the wait seemed long. Brian cradled a carton of eggs in one hand, and rested the other on his son's shoulder. Ian turned to look at him briefly with his big, dark eyes. A strand of pale hair fell across his forehead,

11

and the boy shook his head a bit to shift it. Brian was struck by the maturity of the look. Since he had started coming into Bath with Brian on market day, Ian had grown more serious, and Brian wasn't sure how he felt about it. He missed the silly laugh that used to bubble out of his son so easily.

At last they were down the bus's steps. Ian pushed through the crowd to claim their rucksacks as the driver pulled them from the luggage compartment. He brought both packs to where Brian stood.

"Ta." Brian hefted his pack onto his back while Ian held the eggs. They set off with the others from the bus toward the open market.

The first stall they stopped at was busy, and they had to wait while two women haggled over dried beans, flour and cornmeal. When it was their turn the owner greeted them by name and began to lift the eggs carefully out of the carton. Assured that none were cracked, he handed over the usual paper sack of sugar. Brian gave it and the egg carton to Ian, who put them both in his rucksack.

They spent a good part of the morning in the busy market, trading for the things on Fiona's list or paying cash if they had to. Brian let Ian barter for some lined writing paper, standing behind him with an eye on the stall's proprietor.

The list finished, they took an alley through to the next street and got in the queue at the grocery store. It was half an hour before they made it inside. Ian disliked the place and always scowled as Brian shopped, but to spend the ration coupons they had to visit the grocery. Brian handed over the coupons and counted out the money exactly.

"I'd heard there might be coffee?" he asked the clerk.

"Nar, not 'ere." She said it as if she'd heard it many times. "Bristol, maybe, but I doubt it."

Brian thanked her, then packed the groceries into the rucksacks, leaving out the small bag containing the lunch his wife had sent along for them.

"Shall we eat in the Parade Gardens?"

They walked up Pierrepont Street past boarded-up hotels and coffee shops. The window boxes that used to overflow colorful flowers late into the fall now held scraggly weeds. Paint flakes and crumbling mortar littered the sidewalk; larger junk and rusting cars sat in the street. They settled themselves on the stone steps leading down to the overgrown gardens. Before the Bad Winter, meticulously manicured flowerbeds had bordered the open green, and on fine days striped lawn chairs invited you to be lazy for a while. Now tall grass hid the stones marking three long trenches and dozens of smaller graves.

Fiona had packed sandwiches, apples, and a biscuit each. They drank water from a plastic bottle they had brought along, and relieved themselves against the stone wall at the bottom of the stairs. Then they climbed back up to street level and set off for the Distribution Center, where the old covered market used to be.

Brian had noticed how much of Ian's socks showed between his trouser cuffs and shoe tops. Ian admitted that yes, his shoes had got too tight again, so they started with the racks of used shoes. Ian found a pair of sturdy leather work boots with the soles hardly worn, and near-perfect Wellies. Brian nodded his approval.

They visited the clothing racks next, checking for jeans and cords in good condition, finding two pairs of each. Brian added three flannel shirts. He chewed his lip as he counted out the coupons, but smiled when he saw Ian watching him.

"You're growing too fast, old boy," he said. "We'll have to wait 'til next month to get you a jacket. C'mon, let's go do the books."

The used book shop was located in a small side street near the abbey, still run by an old man with a fuzz of white hair whom Brian had always known only as Flynn. He had somehow managed to carry on through the worst of times, hardly leaving his flat above the store, or spending his days in the narrow aisles between shelves, sorting and cataloguing, or wrapped in a blanket in an armchair by the door, reading to escape the harshness of the changed world. The place was more of a library now, with no tourists to spend their holiday money on quaint old volumes. Brian visited nearly every week. He had brought two books back to trade in. Ian picked out an adventure about a young American cowboy, and Brian got a mystery novel. He gave Flynn a tin of meat, a squash from the garden, and a selection of leftover ration coupons.

"Oh, I say, Brian," Flynn said as they were about to leave, "your old mate Chris was looking for you earlier this week."

Brian stopped dead in the doorway. The name jolted him. He stared at Flynn, who sat reading the fine print on the tin's label, apparently unaware that he had said anything unusual.

Brian gulped, thinking Flynn had to be mistaken. "Um, are you sure?"

Flynn looked up. "What? Of course I'm sure. Hardly knew him at first, it's been so long. But yeah, he asked after you, said he'd been round to your house, but you'd gone and did I know where to. I told him you live out in Hurleigh, now."

"Chris Price, was it? You're sure, Flynn?"

"I'm not dotty yet, Brian. He looked different, you know, but it were him, I tell you. He stayed a good few hours, asking about folks what used to live here. He'd brought some lovely muffins and jam, and we had a bit o' tea. I told him you were out Hurleigh way."

Good memories battled with bad ones in Brian's head. The long childhood friendship had ended with hard feelings and harder words. He remembered the last horrible thing he'd uttered with such contempt, nearly ten years ago, and felt his face grow warm with shame.

Ian was watching him, clutching his bundle of clothing.

"Uh, thanks, Flynn," Brian said, and went out. He headed down York Street. It couldn't be Chris. It was impossible. Chris had been in New York. By all accounts, New York had been hit hard.

"Dad?"

Brian stopped and turned around. "Sorry."

"Did he mean Uncle Jon's brother? Chris, from the band?"

Ian didn't know how the partnership had ended. All he knew was that his dad and Chris Price had been famous rock stars before he was born. He had seen and heard the CDs kept stored in a cabinet in the sitting room.

"Yes."

"Wow."

Brian shook his head. "I think Flynn must be mistaken. How could he have got here?" *Even if he survived.* "He lived in New York, remember? There aren't many ships, and hardly any planes."

"But Flynn said it was him, for sure. Maybe he got on a ship."

"I doubt it." Brian stood looking into the distance, his eyebrows drawn together. "C'mon, let's go."

"Where?"

"We'll go to the Government Center. He'll have to register there if he wants to get his coupons."

They queued for half an hour at the information desk, then watched as a pale girl searched through a box of cards. Not too many years ago she would have punched the information into a computer and had their answer in seconds. But, despite all the public assurances six years ago that the experts were confident, nearly all the computers were junk, now.

The girl finally told them she did not have a card for a Chris Price. She suggested they try the Health Center, two floors up.

"Sometimes the cards don't get filed right. But he'll have to have a blood test to relocate here, and they'll have the record of that."

The queue for the Health Center was even longer. The man on the end said he didn't know if he would get in before the place closed at six.

"Well, that's out then," Brian said to Ian. "It's nearly time for the bus."

They walked back toward the bus station.

"Uncle Jon never talks about him," Ian said.

Brian sighed. "No. I don't talk much about Uncle Colin, either, do I?" In the beginning it had hurt too much to even think about his dead brother Colin, and how Colin's stubbornness had doomed him and his family. Brian thought maybe he should make the effort at some point, so his sons would know about their uncle, aunt, and cousins.

"Did I know him?"

Brian thought Ian meant Colin, then realized he meant Chris.

"No, you were just a baby when he moved away. When we get home I'll show you some pictures, okay?"

"I've seen the pictures," Ian reminded him. "And Uncle Jon has some in his room, too. Y'know, if he wants to get to Hurleigh he'll have to take our bus."

"You're right," Brian said, his mouth gone dry, as they turned the corner into the station. Brian scanned the place.

Most everyone in the bus station lingered near the stalls. Three people had already queued for their bus. Brian caught sight of a man sitting on a low brick wall in the afternoon sun. He wore a bulky brown jacket, his hands stuffed into the pockets and his head down. At this distance, there wasn't much to distinguish him from any other stranger in the street. But Brian stood rooted, staring with his mouth open. He put a hand out in front of Ian.

"Stay here," he said. He walked forward, breathing as if he'd run the last two blocks. "Chris?"

The man on the wall looked up, saw him instantly. Brian stopped, choked on guilt. *Not dead...*

Chris eased himself off the bricks, and came forward a few steps. He wore his brown hair long, pulled back into a tail. A few pieces had come loose and hung down around his face. He hadn't shaved, and

17

his clothes looked like they needed a wash. His eyes had a haunted, uncertain look to them. Brian knew that look; he'd seen it in his wife's eyes occasionally as she gazed at their children during the Bad Winter, when so many were dying.

Chris glanced down. When he brought his eyes back up the haunted look was gone, and he seemed suddenly unburdened. His mouth formed a silent word: *Brian*. He took a deep breath. His voice came out relieved.

"You look good."

Chapter 2

"Chris—" Brian gasped. He started to move forward, but Chris took a quick step back. Brian's stomach balled up. He tried to keep his voice steady. "Have you had a blood test?"

"Of course. Negative."

Relief flooded through Brian. "Then you're good," he said, but he stayed where he was.

"Yes, I suppose." Hands still in pockets, Chris stared at Brian.

"It's good to see you," Brian said, thinking it was a phrase more appropriate for an acquaintance at a party, not someone you thought had been dead for six years. But no other phrase came to mind.

"It's good to see you," Chris returned. It sounded automatic. His next words were barely audible. "I didn't think I'd find you."

"How did you get here?" Brian asked.

Chris was looking past Brian at Ian. "Is it safe to bring him here?"

"He has to know. He has to learn how to go on, doesn't he?" Brian had been through this with Fiona, over and over.

Chris nodded. "Well, you haven't seen what I've seen, but maybe it's different here."

Brian's answer came out harsher than he expected. "How do you know what I've seen?"

"You look like you've got it easy."

"Better than most," Brian agreed. "But nothing is easy anymore."

Chris drew himself up, his face hardening. "Yeah, I know."

It occurred to Brian all at once that Chris shouldn't be alone. He should have a wife and child with him, but he didn't. Guilt hit him again.

Brian turned to Ian. "Go queue for the bus, old boy."

Ian shuffled off, looking back several times.

Brian swallowed hard. This wasn't going well. Chris's sudden appearance had unbalanced him. The whole thing had an unreal, dreamlike quality to it. He hadn't really believed Flynn, even though he'd gone through the motions of checking at the Government Center. Until Ian had suggested it, he never thought Chris might be waiting at the bus station.

"Chris, what happened? We thought you were dead."

"No, not dead. Almost, a few times."

"How did you get here?" Brian prompted when Chris said nothing else.

"I walked, mostly."

Brian did not understand. "Walked? I thought you were in New York."

"No, from—" Chris said, then stopped. He seemed to be thinking hard. "It's a long story." He did not go on.

At a loss, Brian did not know what to say, what to do. It was starting to sink in: Chris was alive, standing here in front of him, and he had done nothing to show he was in the least bit happy about it. He felt he should make some gesture, but at the same time it was as if Chris didn't particularly care. Or maybe Chris was taking cues from him, Brian thought. Had he come across as indifferent? Was it too late to change the tone of the conversation?

"Look," Chris said suddenly, making Brian flinch. "Except for Flynn I've not found anyone. He told me about my mother. Is Jon dead, too?"

"No," Brian said, glad to have some good news for him. "Jon's all right. He's well. He's with us out in Hurleigh."

Chris took a deep, ragged breath and let it out, closed his eyes, looked like he might fall down. His shoulders sagged, he put a hand up to rub his face, then looked at Brian again.

"What does he know about Kevin?"

Kevin, the middle of the three Price brothers, had been living in London with his girlfriend and her daughter. Brian shook his head. "We've never heard. He rang Jon, back at the start, and said they were coming. But they never did."

"He's dead. They're all three dead." Chris's face went hard again.

"Can you be sure?"

"I've been there, to London, to his flat. The door was marked."

"Oh. I'm sorry." It all came back to Brian, the enormity of it, symbolized by rows of stone markers in the parks where children used to play. At times it still threatened to overwhelm him, and he had to focus on those who depended on him, not on those who were gone. Now a familiar grief trickled past the dam he had built to hold it, grief he usually felt only late at night in the dark, or as he trimmed the weeds around three small graves in the Hurleigh churchyard. He took a few deep breaths and shored up his dam, and the spillage drained away.

"But Jon's with you?" Chris asked. He looked at Brian as if he hardly dared to believe it.

"Yes, he's fine."

"Sandy?"

Brian hesitated; he didn't know the name. "Um, I don't—"

"Jon's girlfriend."

"He never mentioned a girlfriend," Brian said. Chris took it in with a curious expression, then a resigned shake of his head.

"Fiona?"

"She's fine, and Preston. Simon is with us, and Alan, and Laura—"

"*Laura?*"

Chris and Laura had been engaged and lived together for three years when the band was at its most popular. They'd called it quits without getting married.

Brian nodded. "I found her here in Bath, took her out to Hurleigh."

As close as they'd been once, Brian had hardly recognized her. She had lost her husband, her sister, and her job. She had burst into tears when Brian asked if she needed help.

The haunted look passed across Chris's face again. "All this time," he said, "you were all here, safe. And I—" He stopped and squeezed his eyes shut.

Brian didn't know what to say. Chris shook himself and got his composure back. Brian glanced over to where Ian stood. "Look, the bus will be along soon. Do you have any money?"

"Yeah, I've got money."

"Right, then. If we want a seat, we should queue."

Chris nodded, but did not move. "Is it okay?" he whispered, not looking at Brian.

"Of course," Brian said. "Yes, of course! God, why wouldn't it be? Chris, I—" Brian had to stop, swallow. "We've missed you. I always hoped you were okay." But as he said it, he knew it wasn't completely true. Maybe since the crash, since he'd had to reevaluate his life, but before that, for years, he had nursed a festering resentment, and New York was not far enough away to suit him. He had argued with Fiona about Chris's few visits with Ian, and put a stop to them. When the crash came, he had felt a sort of remorse, a sense that there was a small, ugly part of his past that could never be changed, never put right. He had mentally put Chris in the same sad category as so many others, whether they were in the Hurleigh churchyard or somewhere unknown and far away, with nothing to be done about it. He took a breath, forced a smile. "Jon's going to be over the moon."

Chris nodded again, but still he did not move, seemed uncertain.

Brian hesitated, took another breath. "Um, are you hungry? I have food—"

"No, I just ate, actually," Chris said tightly. "I'm not some skinny."

"That's not what I meant," Brian said, taken aback that Chris would use that word. "It's just that..." He stopped.

"I look like shit, I know." Chris leveled a stare at him. "I've been on the road. I washed when I could. Not much chance for laundry. Sorry."

Brian figured the best thing to do was ignore the subtle hostility. He probably deserved it, but it still felt like a slap in the face. He thought back to the last time he'd had a conversation with Chris. It hadn't really been a conversation; it had been more of a screaming match. It was the last thing he wanted now.

"Let's go home, Chris," Brian said, trying to sound welcoming, sincere. He gestured with his head toward the bus line where Ian stood, holding their place.

Chris blinked and looked away. "I have some things." He stepped back to the wall were he'd been sitting, pulled a duffle and a blanket roll with a strap of some sort out from behind a small bush, and slung them over his shoulder. He joined Brian, walked beside him, keeping a distance. His face was not as hard as it had been. He seemed to be trying to think of something to say.

It was only a short distance to the queue.

Chris was looking at Ian. "I wouldn't have known him."

Ian watched them approach. As they reached him, Brian saw his son clench and unclench his fists.

"Hi, Ian. You were a baby the last time I saw you," Chris said quietly.

Ian ducked his head. "Hi."

The line had grown, and the regulars cast suspicious looks at Chris. Chris stood next to Ian and did not look at anyone. The bus pulled into the station, swung around to its stall, and stopped with a hiss and a squeal. Brian took all of their various packs and bundles and stowed them in the luggage compartment. He counted out the bus fare for himself and Ian, and found his hands were shaking a bit. He turned to tell Chris how much the fare was, but Chris was already counting out coins from his pocket. When it was their turn Brian and Ian got on first. Chris followed.

"Hold on," the driver said. He waved Brian and Ian past, but his eyes narrowed as he looked at Chris. "I want to see your card." He held out his hand.

Chris reached into his pocket and pulled out an official green card, dated and stamped. The driver scrutinized it with a frown, then shoved it back at Chris, took his money, and waved him on. Chris pushed past Brian and went all the way to the back, scrunching himself into the corner by the window. Brian sat next to him, giving him as much room as he could, and Ian sat across the aisle. Chris remained tense, drawn in on himself, his mouth a tight line. Ian shot defiant glances at the other passengers. The seat in front of them remained empty as everyone else boarded; two people stood at the front, rather than sit there. Ian got up and took the seat as the driver slammed the door closed.

The bus lurched out of the station, and Brian glared at the backs of the other passengers. They all knew him and Ian, and their suspicion of Chris angered him. But then he had to admit to himself that they had every reason to be wary, in spite of a current blood test card. The cards were a formality, renewed every six months, but everyone knew they didn't mean much a week after they were issued. Incubation time could be days to weeks.

Brian glanced sideways at Chris. He realized he would have given anyone who looked like Chris a wide berth. He felt a niggling apprehension begin to grow. He had not thought this through. Of course he would not have left Chris there in the bus station, but bringing

25

him into their group was going to change things. Jon would be ecstatic, but what about Laura? There was bound to be some tension there...

Wondering about that made him wonder about himself. Now that he had looked at Chris and seen him as the others on the bus would, he realized that he did not really know Chris any more than they did. He himself had changed in the past six years. Those years must have changed Chris, too. *I don't know him at all.* His head began to ache as his thoughts churned around in circles. Chris sat staring out the window. *I have to talk to him.*

"How did you get to Britain?" Brian asked, keeping his voice low. Ian looked around at him, then at Chris.

Chris kept his gaze on the back of the seat in front of him. "There are some ships. They don't take passengers, unless you have a hell of a lot of money, so I worked my way over. Came in at London."

"Did you walk here from London?" Brian asked, startled.

Chris shook his head, finally looked at Brian. "No. I spent a short time in London, then got another ship to Portsmouth. They—" He bit off what he was about to say, started over. "I worked there for awhile, then at another place near there. That's where I walked from."

"Weren't there any buses?" Ian asked, keeping his voice down, too.

Chris shrugged. "Might have been. But I didn't mind the walk." His face softened whenever he addressed Ian, Brian noticed.

"That's a long walk," Ian said.

26

"It is. I found a bicycle, thought I might ride, but the tires had gone bad."

"We could have got tires for it," Brian said.

"But I would have had to push it here on the rims, wouldn't I? I pushed it to the nearest town and traded it."

"I hope you got a good price for it," Brian said without thinking.

Chris looked at him straight-faced. "I think so," he said, in that flat tone he had that carried weight. *You're not the only one who knows what he's doing*, the tone and the look together conveyed.

Brian kept his mouth shut and nodded once, conceding. Chris hadn't changed so much after all.

"What's London like?" Ian asked.

Chris glanced at him briefly, then back at Brian. "You've not been to London, have you?" He meant since the crash, Brian knew, and this time his voice held a hint of something else—not quite superiority, but something close. *You haven't seen what I've seen*, Chris had said. Brian shook his head. "You don't want to go to London," Chris continued, swiveling his head back to Ian to answer his question. Ian was smart enough not to ask "Why not?"

The bus reached its first stop and several passengers got off. The man and woman who had been standing took the seats, with a peek toward the back.

"So how did you end up in Hurleigh?" Chris asked once the bus was underway again.

"Bought an estate there, before the crash. Well, Simon did, really, though I paid for most of it. Simon was fixing it up. We left Bath that first winter, just after Christmas. Just in time."

"Estate? Big place?"

"Big enough. Land to farm. We do okay."

Chris nodded. "Farms are safer. Are there many outbreaks?"

"Nothing in the last year, that we've heard of. Rumor is the small ones go unreported."

Chris turned his head to gaze out the window at the countryside. Brian and Ian exchanged looks, stayed quiet. Brian felt that some of the tension had eased, but he was wary of asking Chris too many questions. The bus made its scheduled stops and the seats emptied.

"How is Laura?" Chris asked, breaking a silence.

"She's well. She had a bad time of it. Lost her husband..." Brian trailed off, uncomfortably aware that he had made no mention yet of Chris's apparent loss. For some reason, it seemed impossible to ask.

"It'll be good to see her," Chris said, and took up watching out the window again.

Brian berated himself for not saying anything. He felt nearly sick with the strain of the whole thing, and was glad that the ride was nearly through.

The bus pulled over by an old stone shelter. Ian was down the aisle in a flash and had the cargo bay open by the time Brian and Chris joined him. In spite of the long day he was full of energy. He pulled out their bags and bundles, and held Chris's out to him.

"Ta," Chris said, and Ian almost smiled. The bus pulled away.

Chris looked around him as he slung his bags and adjusted the straps over his shoulders. The shelter stood at a crossroads. On their right the road curved away up a hill, on the left it continued down. A petrol station stood on the opposite corner, and a few stone houses across from it.

"The village is down the hill." Brian pointed. "We're up this way. We've got a bit of a walk from here."

"Lead on," Chris said. "Can't be all that far."

Brian turned and started up the road. Chris followed. Ian hurried to take the lead, in spite of his heavy pack, head down, determined not to lag behind. Usually, Brian took his time going up the hill from the bus, especially if Ian was with him, but today even Ian knew this was no time to dawdle, and they all three set a quick pace at the edge of the disused tarmac.

"Not much further," Brian said. The top of the chimney became visible past the trees on their left, and shortly after the little attic window under the peak of the roof glinted with the reflection of the sinking sun at their backs. Brian realized the house would soon be alerted. He wondered if he should tell Chris. The road straightened out some. They could see the gate in the high wall that surrounded the house and yard.

"Nice place," Chris said. Of the three, he was breathing the easiest, but he seemed tightly wound, anxious.

"Yeah, plenty of room," Brian said.

He turned a bit, and Chris slowed, shoving his hands into his pockets.

"Maybe you should go on ahead," Chris said. "Tell them."

"They'll know anyway. Likely we've been spotted from that window. Preston takes his binoculars up there and waits for us on Saturdays. He won't know you, but he'll tell them someone is with us."

Chris nodded, his face a mask.

"You okay?"

Chris nodded again. "Doesn't seem real, after so long."

They reached the gate. Ian grabbed it and pushed. It swung inward on squeaky hinges. Brian and Chris followed him through into the yard.

To their left stood the small gatehouse, then another section of stone wall. Beyond that the garage, the barn, and other outbuildings ranged around the left side and back of the yard, casting long shadows now as the sun continued its fall. The big house rose up on their right, the end wall of the kitchen with its tall windows facing the yard. Fiona was already coming out of the kitchen door, with Preston right behind her. She stopped on the step, saw them, and came out through the small walled garden. She had her blond hair pulled back and clipped, the way she wore it when she was working in the kitchen all day. She rarely wore an apron, but she had a small towel tucked into the front of her jeans. She stared at Chris. Her hand went up to her mouth, and she quickened her pace, meeting them only a few steps from the garden.

"Hello, Fiona," Chris said, his voice low.

"Oh, Chris!" she gasped, and stepped forward to hug him. Brian was surprised at how readily Chris accepted the hug, how he put his arms around Fiona, his face against the side of hers. "Chris, this is wonderful! It's so good to see you!"

"I'm so glad you're all okay," he rasped.

Fiona pulled back to look at him, bit her lip. "Sophie?" she asked in a whisper, and almost immediately, with a look of pain, "Rosie?"

Chris shook his head, blinked a few times.

"Oh, I'm so sorry!" she said, reaching up to wipe at her eyes.

"It's okay."

She hugged him again, sniffed, put a kind of smile onto her face. Preston had been hanging back, shy and wary, but wanting to be in on things anyway.

"You've not met Preston," Fiona said, motioning him forward. "Preston, this is your Uncle Chris, Uncle Jon's brother." At nine, Preston was generally more adventurous than his older brother, and therefore needed closer supervision. He had a more rugged build than Ian, and his hair was dark like Brian's. He had his mother's grey eyes. At the moment they were wide and curious.

"Hi, Preston," Chris said, and the boy echoed a shy "Hi."

Brian glanced off toward the Dealy farm, saw Jon just opening the gate in the gap between the machines shed and the henhouse. He was watching the group of them, but obviously hadn't recognized Chris yet.

"Here's Jon," Brian said to Chris, pointing, and Chris froze for an instant, then moved, stepping around Fiona and the boys, pulling the bedroll off his back and letting it drop.

Chapter 3

Jon scowled as he scuffed along the path between the two farms, his jeans leg rubbing unpleasantly against the raw spot on his shin where that bloody beast Queen Anne had got him with her hoof, *again*. What a silly name for a cow. *I've had it with that animal.* He vowed to stop trying to make nice with her. It did no good; it never had. He wondered idly what supper would be as he reached the gate and unlatched it. He glanced into the yard as it swung open, saw that Brian and Ian had got home, realized that there was someone with them, hugging Fiona. Whoever it was he had a bag of some sort over his shoulder, but his face was hidden from Jon's view by Fiona. She seemed to be introducing Preston to the man.

Brian looked over and saw him, pointed, said something. The man took a step, and Jon saw his face.

It's Chris—

It took his brain a moment to catch up from the shock that jolted him, as if someone had thrown a bucket of ice water full onto him. *It can't be*, was his next thought, and he tried to think rationally around the dizzying rush: *swing the gate closed, listen for the click of the latch, step forward... look again, see who it really is...*

Chris was thinner, his hair longer, he had a stubble of beard, but there was no doubt now. Jon had given up the forlorn hope, had stopped going into Bath to check for messages at his flat or the telegraph office, had ceased scanning faces in the market-day crowds in

Frome. He'd never even dreamed that his brother would someday walk right into the yard, alive and well.

Chris stood frozen for an instant, then started to move, pulling a bedroll off his shoulder and letting it drop, almost running toward Jon, who had not stopped moving, only slowed, staring, still taking forward steps in a kind of daze.

Chris didn't have time to get the duffle off over his head, he'd nearly reached Jon, seemed out of breath, said "Jon!" and they both stopped and faced each other for perhaps three seconds before grabbing each other tight and holding on.

"I should have come sooner," Chris was saying, "I thought you'd be dead. I'm sorry, I should have come..." in a voice that cracked. Jon could feel him shaking, or maybe it was himself.

"I thought you were dead," was all Jon could come up with. "Oh my God. Chris. Chris, it's you—" He had to pull away to wipe his eyes and look at his brother again. "I thought I'd never see you again." He kept a grip on Chris's sleeve.

"I thought you'd be dead," Chris repeated.

A thousand things, a thousand questions, all rushed into Jon's head, damming up there, catching in a logjam in his tight, tight throat. "Mum's dead," he said, watching Chris's face.

Chris nodded, his eyes bright. "I know."

"Kevin never made it here, he rang, said they were coming, but—"

"Kevin's dead," Chris told him.

"He was in London, but I don't know, maybe—"

"He's dead, Jon. I was in London. I went to his flat."

The revelation was another jolt. Jon had to breathe in, then out. "You were in London? When?"

Chris didn't answer right away. His mouth opened, he looked down. "Last year."

"Last *year?*"

"I'd just come in on a ship from Canada. Came into London, went to his flat, to see if I could find out anything. The door was marked, for all three of them, deceased."

"Charlotte. And Penny," Jon said, his mind shoving their names forward amid the conflicting emotions. "They were engaged. He'd told me a few weeks before Christmas. He was going to tell you, when you came. He'd finally popped the question."

"Huh," Chris whispered, "good for him."

Something broke through the jumble in Jon's mind. His stomach turned over. "Sophie—"

Chris shook his head, swallowed. "No, they're both gone. Right at the start. Long time ago, now."

"Oh, God, Chris, I'm sorry."

"It's okay," Chris said. He put up a hand to wipe at his eyes, then put his arms around Jon again and hugged him hard. "It's okay now, right? I've found you."

"Where have you been?" Jon said then, hugging back. They parted, and Chris adjusted the bag over his shoulder. "Here, let me take that," Jon offered, reaching for it.

"No, it's okay, don't worry about it."

"Where have you been, Chris?" Jon asked again, for an instant jealous of Brian and his long bus ride back from Bath with Chris, and wanting to hear all the things Chris must have told him during the trip. They started to walk back toward the others waiting in the yard.

Chris seemed to be thinking. "Different places. It was a few years before there was any way for me to get over here, of course. I finally made it to London in June of last year. I've been a few places since then."

"Where?"

"It's a long story."

"When did you get to Bath?"

They reached the others. Fiona was smiling, but Brian's expression was guarded.

"Wednesday, I suppose it was," Chris said. "I've been staying at your flat... had to get a blood test, then went looking for whatever I could find out. Found Flynn on Thursday."

"He said you'd been there," Brian put in. "I'm afraid I didn't quite believe him."

Chris eyed him, and shrugged.

"We checked at the Government Center," Brian went on. "They didn't have you registered."

Chris shook his head. "No, I didn't register. That can be tricky."

Jon noticed the tension between his brother and Brian immediately. Every time Chris looked at Brian, it took him two tries: his eyes shifted in Brian's direction first, then to his face. Brian was not smiling. Jon nearly chided them both, but stopped himself. It was all in the past; they would figure that out soon enough, he was sure.

"Let's all go inside, so Chris can sit down," Fiona said. Jon bent to pick up Chris's bedroll from where it had fallen. Chris put out a hand for it, but Jon waved him off, slung it over his shoulder.

"This is nice," Chris said as they went inside. He stopped just inside the door. Jon could see him glancing around, taking in the Aga, the light fixtures, the long table, the row of fresh bread loaves on one counter. "Um, is Laura here?"

"She's not back yet," Fiona told him. "She should be here in time for supper. Simon, too. You know Alan, right? You'll meet Vivian, his wife. They live in the gatehouse. I'll have them over for supper, as well."

Chris nodded, put his hands in his pockets, then took them out again. He stepped away as Brian came in the door, as if they were opposing magnets, unable to touch, repelling automatically.

"Do you want to sit down, have a drink or something?" Jon asked him.

"If there's time, I'd like to have a wash. I'm a bit grotty, I'm afraid."

"Plenty of time," Fiona assured him. He nodded, stared at her face, as if needing to reassure himself it was really her.

"Come on up, then," Jon said, "and you can shower."

Jon led him out of the kitchen and up to his own room. Chris surveyed the bed and bedside tables, the bureau with its framed pictures, the desk and chair in the corner, the bookshelf full of books, the electric lamps.

"Posh," Chris said.

"Is it?" Jon asked, and Chris shifted his eyes over.

"Compared to some places, yes." He made a quick gesture toward the bedside lamp. "You've got lights."

"Yes. Not awfully reliable. We lose them if a good wind blows. For years we didn't have any. But we can get news on the radio most nights. And we have the solar, of course. That runs the well-pump and the Aga, and we can charge batteries for torches and the like. One of Simon's extravagances that turned out to be invaluable." He put Chris's blanket roll on the bed.

"And a shower?"

"Sure." Jon shrugged. "Or a bath, if you'd prefer."

"No lugging pails up the stairs," Chris said quietly. He moved into the room, pulling his duffle bag off over his head.

"You had to do that? Where?"

"In Breton, a little town near Portsmouth. I worked on a farm there. If it was warm enough we washed outside, in a little room built against the house. But Grace never liked—" He stopped, did not look at Jon, put his bag on the bed and unzipped it. "Showers in London, though," he said, as if to change the subject.

"How long were you in London?"

"Couple of months." Chris rummaged in his bag, pulled out some clothes. "None of this is really clean."

"I've got clothes you can borrow."

"I couldn't carry much, so I left some stuff behind. I've got coupons, though."

"Don't worry about it," Jon said. He opened drawers and gathered everything Chris would need.

Chris stood still, watching Jon. "I didn't expect to find you."

"Why not?"

"You were reckless. Kevin was careful. I guess he was too careful, stayed where he was, like he was told to do. He should have tried to get out of London."

"That's what he said, when he rang me. He said, 'they told us to stay put.' I told him to pack what he

37

could and get out. I told him it would be safer in Bath."
Jon shook his head. "It wasn't much safer, really. But
he said he was coming. I think he just needed someone
to tell him what to do. He said he'd been trying to ring
you, but couldn't get through. He wanted you to tell
him to get out."

Chris took a long breath and let it out slowly.

"It's not your fault," Jon said.

"Yeah, I know. But if I'd made it here, after
Christmas, he'd have come out from London."

"Maybe." Jon waited, holding the clothes, and
when Chris didn't go on he asked, "What happened, on
your end?"

Chris straightened with a little shudder. "Sophie
drove me to the airport. We took Rosie along. There'd
already been some flight cancellations, but not mine, so
she left me and went home. They cancelled my flight
after that. I stayed the night, got on a plane the next
morning, but it turned around after a few hours and
went back. Then they held us at the airport for days.
Things were starting to go to all to hell. By the time I
got home Rosie was gone, and Sophie... died that
night." Chris pulled a few pieces of clothing out of his
bag without really looking at them, then glanced at Jon.
"Do you know where Mum is buried?"

"Yes. There was still a bit of room left at her
church. Some of the members helped me dig her
grave." The memory of that hellish day, hacking blindly
at the frozen ground for hours, remained jagged-edged.
"I'll take you, if you want."

Chris nodded, pulled another shirt from his bag. "It
all happened so fast, within days. If my flight had been

just one day later, I might never have gone to the airport. Everything would have been different."

"What if I'd gone to New York for Christmas?" Jon said. "You'd invited me, do you remember? I've always wondered what would have happened. Maybe Kevin would have come out to take care of Mum."

Chris balled up the tee shirt in his hands. "'What if...?'" he whispered. "That's a phrase I've beaten myself with the past six years, Jon. What if I hadn't tried to come here after Christmas, hadn't ever gone to the airport? What if I hadn't let Sophie go to the airport to see me off? Maybe she wouldn't have caught it. What if they hadn't cancelled my flight, and I made it here? Would I have spent the past six years trying to get back there, going the opposite direction?" He sighed, shook his head again. "It's a bottomless black pit, that phrase, those two little words. And what if I'd got here and found out you were all dead?"

Jon's stomach felt hollow. "Is that what kept you away? Since London?"

Chris did not look back at Jon, but he nodded. "I was afraid I wouldn't find anyone. I didn't know if I could stand that." He sat down hard on the bed, reached into his duffle and pulled out a plastic bottle a quarter full of water, and drank it down.

"What made you come, finally?"

"I decided that I could stand it. I had to know."

"Well, you're home now, finally," Jon said. Chris's head jerked up at him. Jon could hear him pull in his breath, and saw a flash of uncertainty in Chris's expression. Then Chris stood up as if to cover it, tossed the bottle onto the bed.

"I'd better have that shower," he said, and reached for the clothes Jon was holding.

Jon got him a towel from the cupboard in the hall, showed him the soap and shampoo, how to work the shower to get the optimum temperature, and then left him to it. He went into the empty room next to his, the room that was supposed to have been Colin and Emily's room. Over the years it had been used for storage. A few boxes were piled on the bed and stacked on the floor, but it was a good-sized room, bigger than his own, and even after Jon had pushed all the boxes against one wall there was plenty of space. He found bedding in the closet and set about making the place comfortable for Chris.

Brian stuck his head in the door. "Do you need anything? Fiona wanted me to ask."

"No, thanks. It's okay, isn't it, to put him in here?"

"Of course," Brian said. "I can clear out those boxes, if you'd like."

"No, don't worry about it," Jon said. "They're not in the way."

"Right, then," Brian nodded, and glanced toward the loo. "Supper soon, Fiona says."

"We'll be down as soon as he's ready," Jon said, and Brian went back downstairs.

The bathroom door opened soon after. A shave and clean clothes made a world of difference in Chris's appearance. Jon wondered why he wore his hair so long; he never had before, always kept it short and neat, but he didn't say anything about it. Jon was back in his own room, gathering up Chris's dirty clothes into a laundry basket. He held it out and Chris dumped the stuff he'd been wearing into it.

"I've got you set up in the next room," Jon said. He picked up the blanket roll and motioned for Chris to follow.

"This is nice, thanks," Chris said, coming in, carrying his duffle, coat, and shoes. "The whole place is nice," he went on. "How long has he had it?

"He bought it about a year before the crash," Jon said. "Took most of the year to get it ready, too. It was rather a wreck, I hear. Needed lots of remodeling and upgrades."

Chris shook his head ruefully and tossed his stuff onto the bed. "Brian's private little kingdom," he said softly.

"What?" Jon said, taken aback. "It's not like that at all. Brian hadn't much to do with it. It was all Simon's idea. He used up all his own money first, then convinced Brian to give him more. He saw it coming long before the rest of us. If it weren't for Simon we wouldn't be here."

"Huh. Good old Simon. He always was a few steps ahead of the rest of us." Chris sat down on the bed to put on his socks.

"Supper's about on. We can go down as soon as you're ready," Jon said.

Chris nodded, reached for his shoes, pulled one on and began to lace it slowly. Jon watched him, saw how stiffly he held himself, saw him fumble with the laces.

"What's wrong?" Jon asked.

Chris shook his head. "Nothing," he grunted. But he sat for a moment after he'd finished the first shoe, then reached for the second.

"Smells good, doesn't it? I'm starved," Jon tried.

"It does," Chris agreed, then glanced up at Jon. "I'm not very hungry, I guess," he said, his face blank.

It struck Jon then, and he could have kicked himself. "You look tired."

"I haven't slept well the past few days. Wondering, y'know? I'm guess I'm—I don't know—just overwhelmed." He dropped his head down, rubbed at his eyes.

"You don't want to go down, do you?"

Chris shifted on the bed. "I don't want to be rude."

"It's all right, they'll understand. I'll tell them. You can just rest." Chris looked up at him, his eyes pleading. "It's all right," Jon repeated.

"Thanks," Chris whispered.

"Sure," Jon said. "Get some rest."

Chapter 4

At supper, mindful of the small ears at one end of the table, they spoke of what a good, happy thing had happened. Jon grilled Brian about everything Chris had told him on the bus ride. Brian made it clear that Chris hadn't said much, but related the main points. It seemed that Brian was being careful to say only neutral things about Chris, and Jon thought Fiona might get a different version of the story later that night. Jon wondered how much of Chris's reluctance to come down to supper was because of Brian. He couldn't believe that the two of them would let something that had happened so long ago cause problems now. He wanted to say something, get it out in the open, but he couldn't do that with Ian and Preston at the table.

When they finished eating Brian took the boys off to read in the sitting room, and the rest of them rehashed and speculated in low voices until Jon felt ill. He kept quiet, and finally they noticed his glowering face and ended their discussion. He helped clear the table, and put together a plate of food for Chris. Laura laid a hand on Jon's arm as he was about to leave the kitchen.

"Tell Chris we'd love to see him," she said, "but if he just wants to sleep 'til tomorrow, we understand."

Jon nodded, and went upstairs. He knocked softly and opened the door. Chris jerked awake and sat up with a gasp.

"Sorry," Jon said. "I didn't mean to startle you."

"Wow. I was dreaming." Chris swung his feet over the side of the bed.

Jon used his elbow to flick on the light switch. "I've brought you some supper. I thought you might be hungry now."

"Brilliant," Chris said, squinting a little at the light. He balanced the plate on his knees. "I guess I am, a bit." He took a few bites.

"Everyone said to tell you they understand if you just want to sleep until tomorrow. But of course they'd love to see you, if you're up to it."

Chris nodded noncommittally as he chewed. "So, how many are there?"

Jon leaned against the doorframe and counted them out on his fingers. "Brian, Fiona and the boys, Simon, me, and Laura. And then Alan and his wife Vivian are in the gatehouse. Nine. You make ten. Oh, and David is here quite a bit. He's Laura's fellow—" He broke off at the sudden thought that maybe Chris would try to re-kindle things with Laura.

Chris glanced up at him. "Laura has a fellow? Good for her."

"I thought maybe you—"

"No," Chris said, with a firm shake of his head.

"Right, sorry," Jon said, and felt his face getting warm. "I just…"

"What about you? Do you have a girl?"

Jon had been afraid he would ask. His stomach clenched up. Chris was watching him.

"Not anymore."

Chris nodded a little, chewed, swallowed. "I asked Brian about Sandy, but he didn't know the name. I'm sorry, Jon. I liked Sandy a lot, you know that."

Jon realized he was staring with his mouth open when Chris's eyebrows drew together. Sandy had been so long ago, it was hard to feel anything about her, to remember how he'd once felt about her. It was hard to remember that Chris wouldn't know that. "Uh... yeah, thanks..." he muttered.

"Not Sandy," Chris said, more as a statement than a question. "Tell me." He took a bite, kept his eye on Jon.

"Nothing to tell," Jon said, his heart thumping in his chest. "Didn't work out." He clenched his teeth, angry that after a year he still felt nearly as raw as he'd been that day, stumbling home with the ring in his pocket, having to face everyone and tell them what had happened. He knew if he let himself he could still cry over it, over her, and he wondered if he'd ever get to the point where he could leave it behind.

"Okay," Chris said, and went back to eating. He finished the food, drank the water, set the plate aside. "That was good, thanks." He sat with his eyes down, and Jon could see Chris's left thumb caressing his wedding band.

"Has there been anyone since Sophie?" Jon asked him, not sure what he wanted the answer to be. Chris tensed, clenched his left hand into a fist, studied the floor.

"No."

"Do you still miss her?"

Chris paused, as if he were trying to decide what to say. Jon was starting to get used that.

"Of course I miss her."

Jon felt a stab of regret. "I'm sorry, I ... that's not really what I meant." He shifted his feet on the floor, stuffed his hands into his armpits. He didn't know how to ask what he really wanted to know.

"Go on, then," Chris said, his voice softer.

"Um. How long was it before—well, before it didn't hurt so much anymore?" He managed to look at his brother, and saw understanding in Chris's face, and sadness.

"Is there still a chance—?"

"No," Jon interrupted, his voice coming out harsh.

"Then let it go. Don't torture yourself."

"You didn't answer my question," Jon pointed out, a little miffed that Chris would resort to the same overused statements he'd already heard too many times.

Chris took a breath, but didn't look away. "Part of me died with her," he said. "It's just been this past year that I've been able to—to start—to move on."

Jon's heart sank, but he wasn't sure if it was more for Chris or for himself. He didn't know how to respond. Chris went on before he could.

"Don't end up like me," he whispered, shaking his head.

"What do you mean, 'like you'?" Jon asked, taken aback. He'd never had any reason not to admire his older brother.

"Don't make the wrong choices," Chris muttered. "God, I've made so many wrong choices. I have so much to regret."

"Don't say that!" Jon pleaded. "Chris, please, don't say that. I know you, it can't be that bad. Just forget it all, whatever it is, and start over now, here, with us. Everything will be okay."

Chris got that look on his face again, the one he'd had earlier, the uncertainty. Jon wanted to ask him about it, even though he thought he might know the reason—he was pretty sure Brian had something to do with it—but Chris spoke before Jon could.

"Do you ever think about going somewhere else? Finding something different, something with a future?"

"This is a good place," Jon said, feeling suddenly defensive. "It's got a good future. I've seen a lot worse. You're not the only one who's seen things. And of all the places you say you've been, have any been that much better than here? It doesn't seem like it, from the looks of you." Jon made himself stop. Chris's face had gone expressionless, but Jon knew his brother was thinking hard. "Is it Brian? Do you still hate him that much?"

Chris sat back, and a look of hurt washed across his face.

"I've never hated him."

"No one would know that, from the way you're acting," Jon said, trying not to be angry, at a loss. The conversation was veering off into territory he wasn't prepared for.

"The way I'm acting? What exactly did he tell you?"

"Nothing," Jon said, fidgeting where he was. "But I can see it. I'm sure everyone can."

Again Chris fixed him with a stare, keeping his face a neutral mask. Jon found it disconcerting; it was so unlike the Chris he remembered from before.

Voices drifted up the stairs, and the sound of footsteps. Brian's voice, and two smaller answering him. He was bringing the boys up to bed. Jon nudged the door closed with his foot. Brian shushed them as they passed and went into the loo to brush their teeth.

Jon looked back at Chris, who stared blankly at the floor, his arms crossed.

"Are you going to let what happened back then ruin everything now?"

Chris answered him in a monotone. "It's not entirely up to me, is it?"

"But you'll try, won't you, to make it work?" Jon persisted, a bit of desperation creeping in. The thought of the two of them, Chris and Brian, remaining as angry at each other as they had been before made him feel slightly sick.

"Of course," Chris said, reaching for his coat draped across the foot of the bed. "This ought to be washed," he went on, changing the subject. Jon stayed still, watched him empty the pockets onto the coverlet.

It was a roomy jacket with deep pockets, and Chris had put them to good use. Among the junk Jon could see two folding penknives, a spoon, bits of paper, string, candle stubs, a blood test card, coins, keys, and rocks. He thought he saw a bullet, or at least a casing. From a breast pocket Chris pulled a bunch of folded maps and other papers. Lastly, from an inside pocket, he pulled out a black handgun. He glanced up at Jon as he stuffed it into his duffle.

"Where did you get that?" Jon asked.

Again the pause before Chris answered.

"I found it. It's handy if you've got bullets for it."

"Have you?"

"A few."

"Have you used it?"

Chris straightened up to look at his brother with his face hard, then shook his head and turned away. "No," he said, but something about the way he said it made

Jon think he might be lying. Chris dropped the coat into the laundry basket with the rest of his dirty clothes.

Out in the hall, beyond the closed door, they heard Brian say "Goodnight, sleep tight," and pull the boys' bedroom door closed. Chris watched the door as footfalls descended the stairs. Jon kept quiet. Chris began to scoop the debris from his coat pockets into his bag.

"Rocks?" Jon asked, to break the uncomfortable silence.

"Flints," Chris replied. "Handy..." and Jon remembered making sparks when they were children. He glanced over at the bureau, where a small framed picture sat. He'd taken it from his own chest of drawers, put it there earlier, after he'd made up the bed, a small gift for Chris. It was one of the last group pictures taken of their family: their mother and the three boys, she looking happy and proud, the boys all looking a bit annoyed. He didn't remember how old they all were. Teenagers, obviously. Chris looked over and saw it too. He moved tentatively, reached out, picked it up.

"Huh," he said softly.

"I thought you might like to have that."

"Thank you."

"I have some others. I'll show you tomorrow, or whenever."

Chris looked up from the photo, his eyes bright. "I'd like that. I haven't any left."

Chris's tone and what the statement implied wrenched at Jon, and unexpected emotion welled up without warning. "God, I missed you," he rasped, his throat tight. "I'm so glad you're here."

"Me, too," Chris nodded. He put the picture down, seemed to hesitate, then took two quick steps toward Jon and hugged him hard. "It'll be okay," he said, as Jon hugged him back. Jon had to work to keep the tears out of his eyes. He nodded against his brother's shoulder. "It'll be okay," Chris repeated, as he'd done when they were decades younger, reassuring his brothers when their mother had locked herself into her bedroom to cry out her despair alone into her pillow. Chris had promised them it would be okay, every time, and then he would stand at her door, pleading with her until she let him in, and sit with her, rubbing her back, dry-eyed and unflinching while she sobbed. In later years she would tell them that Chris had always given her the strength she needed to go on. Jon pulled away, took deep breaths to calm himself.

"Should we go down now?" Chris said, his voice barely audible.

"You don't have to."

"I know. No reason to put it off."

"Okay," Jon agreed. He put his hand on the doorknob.

"Oh, wait—" Chris said, and rummaged in his duffle. He pulled out a cube wrapped in old gift-wrap and tied with string, about the size of a half brick, but obviously not that heavy. He picked up the supper plate, too. "Okay, lead on."

Jon took the plate from him, and led Chris downstairs.

Chapter 5

Simon had focused on practicality where most of the house was concerned, but the sitting room retained the grandeur of days gone by. Ornate paneling and moldings decorated the walls, dark wood floors showed around the edges of thick carpets. A richly carved mantel surrounded a fireplace in the middle of the far wall, but no fire was lit on this mild summer night. Heavy velvet drapes hung on the tall windows. Even with Brian's grand piano in one corner, plenty of room remained for enough furniture to comfortably seat the whole group. Simon had brought in some of it when he remodeled the house. The rest had come from Brian's house in Bath.

All heads turned toward Chris and Jon as they entered the room. Fiona sat on a large settee, Alan and his wife Vivian on a sofa. Simon had claimed one of the window seats, David the big green armchair on the right. Laura perched next to him, half-sitting on the arm of the chair, her fingers playing with the hair at the back of his neck. Only Brian wasn't seated; he lurked in the far corner behind the piano, pretending to look for a book on the shelves.

Laura was the first to move. She rose with an uncertain smile, said Chris's name under her breath.

Chris's mouth opened as he looked at her, but he said nothing. His expression was as hard to read as it had been since he arrived. He took one step toward her, and she closed the gap.

"Welcome home," she said as she hugged him. His return hug seemed tentative to Jon.

"Your hair is different," Chris said as they parted.

"So is yours," she countered, her eyes bright, and self-consciously put a hand up to push a strand of straight brown hair now touched with grey back behind her ear.

"I'm so glad you're okay," Chris said. "You look good."

"You look thin," she said, and Chris shrugged.

Simon jumped up off the window seat and crossed the room with his hand out. "Chris," he said with a nod, "good to see you again. Glad you've found us." After a moment of hesitation Chris shook his hand—something most people did not do anymore—and nodded back.

"Thanks."

David had stood at the same time, stepped forward in front of Laura, and also put his hand out.

"This is David Rigg," Simon introduced him, and Chris shook his hand as well. David stood a head taller than Chris, with thinning pale hair and small, round glasses.

"Nice to meet you," David said, and then retreated quickly back to his chair, taking Laura's hand and pulling her down onto his lap possessively as he sat down.

"You've not met Vivian, Alan's wife, have you?" Simon went on. He pointed to where Alan shared the sofa with Viv, small and blond. She smiled a warm, understanding smile, and said "Hello," in her high, sweet voice.

Chris nodded at her. "Good to meet you," he said, then, "Hello, Alan."

Alan Frasier had worked with Chris and Brian for many years. After the breakup, he'd formed a partnership with Brian, steering him in lucrative directions.

"Good to see you again, Chris," Alan said.

"Wine?" Simon asked, trying to ease the tension without actually being jovial.

Chris's eyebrows went up. "Yes, please."

Simon moved to the sideboard. "We've an excellent wine maker right here in Hurleigh," he said to Chris. "We always break out a bottle for special occasions."

"Come sit down, Chris," Fiona said, putting her hand on the cushion next to her. Chris turned a bit, and Jon saw the closest thing he'd seen to a smile yet.

"Sorry about supper," Chris said to her as he sat down, leaving as much gap between them as he could. He still had the gift-wrapped cube in his hand. He tucked it into the space between his leg and the arm of the settee.

"Oh, don't worry about that," she said. "You must be exhausted after walking nearly from Portsmouth."

Jon took the armchair closest to Chris, as Simon came over with two glasses. He gave one to Jon.

"So you came over on a ship?" Simon asked as he handed Chris the other wineglass. "From New York?"

"No, from Canada, actually. Halifax. Easier, with a British passport." Chris sipped the wine. "This is nice, thanks."

"But they don't take passengers?" Vivian asked.

"No, I had to work my way over. And it wasn't so easy getting on. I had to work in the shipyards for a year before I got a place."

"What's it like in the States?" Alan asked him.

Chris did the pause-to-think that Jon had already become familiar with. He sipped his wine to cover it.

"Not so different from here, really," he said to the room at large. "Certain areas were hit harder than others, at first, but it all degraded pretty fast. There was this overall sense of outrage that something hadn't been done to stop the whole thing. Sometimes it seemed that to them the loss of convenience was worse than—" He stopped, blinked.

Jon watched Chris take a breath, try to keep his face casual. A short silence in the room threatened to become awkward, then Chris went on.

"I traveled around for some time, after—after I was alone," he said, keeping his tone as even as possible. "I went to Baltimore, a few other places. Ended up back in New York, but it was no good there, so I set out for Canada. Didn't make it. We got jumped on the road by a gang. They nearly killed me."

The women made little noises of concern; Jon found it hard to swallow the wine he'd just sampled. The "nearly killed" part was the worst, but he had caught the "we," and wondered if anyone else had. Chris went on with hardly a pause.

"Luckily, another group came along just in time and rescued me. I ended up at a monastery, of all places, nursed back to health by the monks. They had a nice little commune going. I stayed for nearly two years." He stopped to have some wine. The room was quiet, all of them holding back, waiting for him to go on, having decided at supper that tonight was not the time to grill him about what had obviously been a hard and painful journey. Jon got the impression that Chris had already decided what he was going to tell them. "Opportunity arose to go out with a team heading north," Chris went on, "so I took it. We'd heard there were ships coming over. I left them and made it into Canada on my own. Eventually got on a ship."

"What's it like in London?" David asked. Jon glanced at him. He was watching Chris intently. Laura elbowed him lightly, but he pretended not to notice.

"Yeah, London," Chris said slowly. "Well, it's got its pluses and minuses, but mostly minuses. Half the people you run into would just as soon kill you for whatever they might get off you. Jobs aren't hard to come by, but the work is long and hard and the pay is lousy."

"What did you do? Did you get a job?" Fiona asked.

"Not exactly," Chris said, turning his head toward her without looking at her. Jon could see he'd gone stiff again, the mask was dropping down over his face. He clutched the wineglass with both hands. "I fell in with a group—just, um, lucky. They had a pretty good set-up. The work wasn't bad. They had electricity and running water, plenty of food. But I never really planned to stay in London, of course, so I didn't stay long."

Jon wondered if it was as obvious to everyone else that Chris was lying about London.

"I got another ship to Portsmouth—just a quick hop—and worked there for a couple of months. Met a nice chap, and when I got ill—not the plague—he sent me off to his hometown, where some friends of his took me in. Little place called Breton. I'd only planned to stay the winter, but it was just George, his wife, mum, and sister, so I stayed on to help. They're good people.

It was easy to stay, they needed me, y'know? And I didn't know if anyone was here." He shrugged, sipped at the wine, seemed to be relaxing slightly now that he was nearing the end of his story. "But of course, I wanted to know for sure. So here I am." He turned to look at Jon, and Jon gave him the barest of nods and the hint of a smile, to let Chris know that it was okay. "Please tell me you have cows," Chris said suddenly, glancing around, "because I've got damn good at milking."

Little chuckles all around broke the silence, and Jon grinned at Chris, glad that he was starting to relax, finally.

"No cows here, but the next farm over has plenty, and we help out with them," Simon explained. "As much milking as you'd care to take on."

"Just steer clear of Queen Anne," Jon put in quickly, rubbing his shin.

"Ah, that beast has a bit of the devil in her," Simon agreed.

"I'll leave her to you, then," Chris said to Jon, eliciting more chuckles. He drained the last of his wine, and set the glass carefully on the table next to the settee. Then he picked up the package he had brought down. "Um, I have something," he said, and looked across the room at Brian, who was still hiding behind the piano. Brian was watching him, and they kept eye contact for a few tense moments.

Brian looked away.

Jon scowled. Why would Brian act like that? Why not accept Chris's gift? Fiona made a 'tsk' sound.

Chris did not react. His eyes flicked toward Jon, and he shook his head once with no change of expression. He merely turned toward Fiona and handed her the gift.

"It's for everyone," he said. "You open it."

She took it with a smile, didn't protest with a pointless "Oh, you shouldn't have!" as so many might have. She fingered it lightly, then pulled on the string. The paper wasn't taped, and she undid the folds to reveal a plastic-wrapped tin of loose tea. She stared at it with her mouth open, as if she did not quite recognize it. There were several gasps from around the room.

"It's tea," Fiona said, holding it up, as if she might have said, "It's gold," or "It's diamonds."

"It's old, it's from before, " Chris explained, "but it's vacuum sealed, and the plastic wrap doesn't have any holes, so it might still be okay." In the old days it had been a fairly expensive blend, now it was nearly priceless.

"Where did you get it?" Jon asked.

"I found it," Chris replied, as if to reassure everyone that he had not spent a huge sum on it.

"You don't just *find* stuff like that anymore," Brian said from the corner. "It's hellish expensive. Did you steal it?"

"Brian!" Fiona exclaimed.

Jon jumped to his feet, his hands clenched automatically into fists at his side. "That's a shit thing to say."

Chris stood, too. He put a hand out and touched Jon's arm, caught his eye, and shook his head gently at him. He looked at Brian in the corner. Jon caught a flash of pain in his brother's expression before the hard wall went up.

"I always wanted to fix it with you," Chris said. "You know I tried. Even now, you're still an ass." He shifted his gaze to Fiona, frozen on the settee. "I'm sorry," he whispered, then turned and left the room. Jon shot an angry look into the corner, but Brian had turned his back on the room. Jon followed Chris upstairs without a word.

Chris sat down on the bed, hunched over. Jon closed the door and leaned against it.

"I'm sorry."

"It doesn't matter," Chris said. "It's not your fault."

"No, I'm sorry about what I said earlier. About you letting what happened—"

"I know," Chris interrupted. "It's okay."

"What can I do?"

"Nothing," Chris said, shaking his head. "It'll either work out, or it won't."

Jon stood aching by the door, wanting to help, wanting to do something to make things right. "It has to work out," he said. "This can't go on." He had the ghastly thought that Brian would make things so uncomfortable that Chris would leave, go back to the farm he'd been working on, or somewhere else. It must have showed on his face.

Chris waved a hand as if to dismiss Brian. "I thought that might happen, y'know. Pauline said it might. It's too unexpected. He isn't ready to deal with it."

"Who's Pauline?"

"George's sister, in Breton. She's a psychologist. Well, she was, anyway, before. We talked about it."

"What else did she say?"

Chris turned his head away then, crossed his arms. "She said he'll get over it."

"Are you over it?"

Chris met Jon's eyes, his face neutral. "Yes. Don't worry, he's not going to chase me off. I've lost too much. I'm not going to walk out on you again."

Jon swallowed, almost ashamed that he'd been so transparent.

From downstairs came the sound of muffled voices and the slam of the kitchen door.

"Fiona will set him straight," Jon said.

Chris got a little smile at that. He nodded. "Yes, I expect she will."

"Tell me more about Breton."

"Um, tomorrow? I'm knackered."

Jon shuffled his feet, reached for the doorknob, decided to let it go. "Of course, sure. Goodnight, then."

"Goodnight, Jon."

As he readied himself for bed, Jon realized that Chris's story of how he got to Hurleigh raised more questions than it answered. He wondered about London, Portsmouth, and Breton. What about Breton made it so easy for Chris to stay there instead of moving on to find his family? Jon decided to ask Chris in the morning.

Breton, near Portsmouth, England
October 2005

Chapter 6

Chris trudged along the road, keeping by habit toward the verge, though it was unlikely he would have to step aside for any vehicle. He'd passed the church and rectory, saw no other houses, and was thinking that Cooper's directions and estimate of the distance up from the crossroads where the lorry had dropped him had been optimistic.

The grade got steeper. He had to slow down. His ribs hurt. He paused to cough hard, bent over with his hands on his knees, grimacing at the hammer-blow pain in his chest. He straightened carefully, got his breath back, and walked on.

He wondered if he looked presentable enough. He had taken time to have a thorough wash and careful shave in the cold dormitory bathroom at the Distribution Center that morning, but the face that looked back at him from the mirror was obviously not fully recovered from illness. The dark circles under his eyes and gaunt appearance had startled him.

Another curve and he finally saw it, just ahead on the left: a stone house covered in climbing vines, with a small roof over the front door, just as Cooper had described it. A brick path led down from the door to an iron gate in the waist-high stone wall bordering the road.

Chris walked along the wall until he reached the gate. He found Cooper's letter in his pocket, then fished out his blood test card and held it with the letter. He took a deep breath, which caused a coughing fit that wracked his whole body and hurt his aching ribs even more. When he looked up, he saw a woman coming around the corner of the house. From her auburn hair Chris guessed that it must be Pauline.

She noticed him by the gate, and came a bit closer, a small frown on her face.

"Yes?"

"I have a letter from Michael Cooper," Chris said, holding it up. "For Pauline Anderson."

Her eyes opened wide at Cooper's name. "I'm Pauline," she said, coming down through the garden to the gate. She wore dark green corduroys with muddy knees, wellies, and a heavy brown jumper with a few holes and bits of yarn sticking out here and there. Her hair was pulled back; a few wisps had escaped the fastener and framed her face, gleaming in the late afternoon sunlight. Chris held the letter out to her over the wall, with his blood test card on top. She saw it and glanced up at his face, then took both from him with dirt-smudged hands. She inspected the card, handed it back. "Thank you. He's not with you, then?"

"No, he's in Portsmouth. I'm Chris Price. We were working together. He sent me. He said you might have work for me. It's in the letter."

"Portsmouth?" she said quietly, her eyebrows arching, and Chris nodded. She studied him again, then opened the letter. While she was reading, Chris had another coughing fit. He turned away from her, tried to tone it down. When he turned back, she was watching him.

"You're ill."

"Bronchitis, or something. It's not the plague," he said, trying not to sound too defensive.

"Well, no. You've got a valid card, don't you? Anyway, wouldn't you be in hospital if it were?"

Chris wondered if he was supposed to laugh at the joke, then realized that she wasn't joking. She really thought there were hospitals that would still take you if you had the plague. She didn't get out much, clearly. Or maybe there was one around here that actually would.

"I saw a doctor yesterday. She said I'm not contagious anymore. But I can wear a mask if you want me to." Chris pulled a white surgical mask out of his pocket and held it up.

She looked startled. "No—no, of course not, if the doctor said you're not contagious."

Chris put the mask away with relief. He'd had enough of the damn things. "I've got food coupons, and a little money," he said. She was reading again. She got to the end of the letter and folded it back into the envelope.

"You look like you need to sit down." She unlatched the gate, and swung it open. "C'mon, then. God, you didn't walk from Portsmouth, did you?"

"No, I got a ride on a lorry. Walked up from the crossroads." Chris followed her around to the back of the house. He wished she'd slow down. The walk up had taken more out of him than he liked to admit. His duffle seemed to weigh more than it had at the bottom of the hill. His legs felt rubbery when they came into the partly-paved yard.

To the left stood a small barn, a chicken coop with a dozen or so birds nosing around in a wire enclosure, and several other outbuildings. The large vegetable garden to the right, behind the house, was mostly harvested down to weedy dirt. A man tinkered with a tractor parked in front of the barn.

"George!" Pauline called, and he raised his head. She held the letter up. "I've had a letter from Michael. This is a friend of his, Chris Price."

George got the same wide-eyed look Pauline had at the mention of Cooper's name. He came around from behind the tractor. He dressed more like the history professor he used to be than a farmer. Chris was surprised at how young he looked. Cooper had told him that George was the older brother, and Chris had envisioned an older man, even though he knew that wasn't the case, forming the image of grey hair, a tweed coat with patches on the elbows. Instead, George had thick dark hair and appeared younger than Chris himself. Chris would have thought him the younger brother, the one who'd gone missing.

"George is my brother," Pauline said to Chris. He nodded.

"Good to meet you," George said. "How is Michael? We've not heard from him in quite a while."

"He's good," Chris said, then turned away as he coughed long and hard.

"That's a nasty cough." George put hands on hips, one foot automatically edging backward.

"He's seen a doctor, he's not contagious," Pauline said. "Michael asked me to look after him. He can stay awhile, can't he? We can put him to work when he's better." She turned to look at Chris, a small smile on her face.

"I can earn my keep," Chris put in.

"Well, we can certainly use a hand around here," George agreed. "And I wouldn't turn away a friend of Michael's."

"Thank you," Chris said.

"Do you know anything about these bloody machines?" he said, hooking his thumb back toward the tractor.

"Just the basics, really."

"Ah, well." George shrugged.

"Come in the house," Pauline said, and turned for the back door. Chris followed her in.

The door opened directly into the kitchen, which was bigger than Chris would have thought for the size of the house. He saw that originally it had been two rooms. The wall between them had been removed, and the wallpapers didn't match. Peaceful warmth and the smell of wood smoke and food cooking enveloped Chris, and he was reminded of childhood summers at his grandparents' house in the country, eating blackberry pie in the kitchen after a day of fishing with his brothers. He stopped, rooted, just inside the door, had to drag himself back into the present.

An older woman was straightening up from a black iron woodstove set against the far wall between two windows. She wore a print dress and a cardigan. Her grey hair curled closely against her head.

"Mum, we have a houseguest. Michael has sent us a letter, and a friend," Pauline said to her. "This is Chris Price. He's going to be staying for a while. Michael's asked me to look after him. This is my mum, Grace."

"Hello," Chris said.

"Well, how do you do?" Pauline's mother said, smiling at him. "How is Michael?"

"He's good."

"Marie's not back yet?" Pauline said to Grace.

"Not yet, no."

"Marie is George's wife," Pauline said to Chris.

Chris nodded, coughed some, but not too badly.

"Chris needs something to eat," Pauline said to her mother. She turned back to Chris. "Sit." She pointed to the table and chairs. Chris slung his duffle off his shoulder and did as he was told.

"I had a bit of lunch," he said, but Pauline looked at him skeptically.

"Not much, I'd guess, from the look of you. If you've got food coupons why haven't you used them?"

"I only just got them this morning, when I was let go."

Pauline put her hands on her hips. "Michael said you were on a work detail, at a Distribution Center."

Chris nodded. "That's right."

"You were in jail?"

"They held me until I passed a second blood test, is all." He wondered if she had any idea what sort of bitterness, frustration, tedium, hunger, and discomfort that simple statement minimized. From the piercing look she gave him, he thought she might. Her mother made a disapproving clucking noise by the stove.

"They still do that?" Pauline said, and he nodded. Her mouth went hard. She turned away to get a mug out of a cupboard. She used a padded mitt to pour water into the mug from a teakettle on the stove, then got a jar out of another cabinet, and stirred a spoonful of the contents into the water. She brought it to him. "Hot water and honey. We haven't any lemon, of course, but it should help your throat, all the same."

"Thank you."

"And then they expect you to pay them back for your jail time," she said, as much to her mother as to Chris.

He nodded again, sipping the water and honey. It felt good going down. He put down the mug and opened his duffle. "Cooper—ah, Michael—sent you some things." He pulled out a bag of salt, packets of yeast, a sack of sugar, razor blades, several boxes of matches, and a jar of mixed seasonings, piling them on the table. Grace came over and exclaimed in delight. She picked up the seasonings and unscrewed the cap to smell it. Chris found the bar of scented soap and small bottle of shampoo. "He said these were for you, especially," he said, handing them to Pauline. She smiled, held the soap to her nose, closed her eyes for a moment.

"I'm not always such a mess," she said lightly. "Where did he get them?" She held the soap out for Grace to have a sniff. Chris let the question go, not having an answer for it anyway. He pulled the ration books out of the side pocket of his bag.

"Here, take these."

"Two books?" Pauline put the soap and shampoo down on the table.

"Michael sent one, the other's mine."

She chewed on her lip, took them from his hand, looked at the blank one thoughtfully. "Mum, do we have a pasty left, for Chris?" When her mum had turned away to get it, she looked back at him. "Where did he get it?"

Chris sipped at his mug and shook his head. "I don't know."

66

"I don't want him to get in trouble."

"He's clever. Anyway, it's done, right?"

"Clever, yes." She frowned. "Was he in jail, too?"

"Not with me. I don't know. But I suppose so." He had another coughing session, a bad one, and it hurt his ribs so much he clutched at his chest and leaned over in his chair, his eyes watering.

"You've cracked a rib, haven't you?" Pauline said.

"I expect so."

"You need to be in bed." She dropped the books onto the table, went to the sink, washed her hands. "Mum, I'm going to make up the bed in the spare room. Get Chris fed, would you? I'll be back down in a bit." She kicked off her wellies by the back door, and picked up two buckets sitting there. "I'm taking the water up," she said. She went out of the kitchen in her socks. Chris could hear the stairs creaking as she went up.

Grace brought a pasty over on a plate, and a fork. "It's still a bit warm. She'll take good care of you, dear. I'd advise you do as she says." Chris looked up at her, and saw that her eyes were crinkled up with a smile.

"I will do," he assured her, and managed a smile in return. "Thank you, for everything."

She patted his shoulder, and he took up the fork. The pasty was, of course, delicious.

***

Pauline led him up, and Chris climbed the stairs behind her, gripping the rail. He had to stop to cough halfway. She waited for him at the top.

"Here's the loo," she said at the first door, and let him look in. "Wash up in the basin, there's soap there, and clean water in those buckets. Dirty water goes in the loo if you need to flush, or in the bucket in the tub if you don't, for the next flush. Do you have an old flannel?" Chris nodded, and she went on. "You can hang it here," gesturing to a bar within reach of the toilet that already had four hanging on it. "Paper's a luxury we don't often have, of course... You'll keep your towel in your room. Have you a towel?" He nodded again. "Good." She left the doorway and went down the short hall to the end. "This will be your room."

He followed her in. It was tiny, with barely room for a bed, bureau, and a chair next to the bed. The closet door was half the width of most doors.

"The closet's full, but there's room in the bureau; the top two drawers are empty. You can hang your towel here." She gestured to a short chrome towel bar attached to the half-sized door. She put her hands on her hips. "Do you need anything?"

Chris shook his head. He set his duffle on the bed and looked around the room. Lace curtains framed the window, a tray on top of the bureau held an oil lamp, a drinking glass and a plastic bottle of water. The chair had a crocheted cushion, the bed a white chenille spread and a fat pillow. Two non-descript landscapes hung on the wall over the bed, and a framed mirror over the bureau. The room in his grandparents' house had been only fractionally larger. He had shared the bed with Kevin. Jon, the youngest brother, had slept on a pallet on the floor. "It's brilliant," he said. He sat down on the edge of the bed.

"Is it?" She glanced around her as if seeing it fresh. "How long have you known Michael?" she asked him, out of the blue.

"A couple of months, is all."

"What did he tell you about us?"

Chris wasn't sure what she meant. "Um—"

"I mean about him and me," she clarified.

"Ah. That it didn't work out, that he wishes it had, that you're still friends." He stopped there, it seemed enough.

She crossed her arms, leaned against the doorframe. "We grew up together. He lived just down the road."

"Yes, he told me."

"It's been almost a year since I've heard from him. He always did that, disappeared, for months, or years." She stared off out the window, deep in thought.

Chris was quiet, looking at her. She had changed into jeans and a pale green knit shirt that hugged her curves. She had muscular arms, a slim waist, trim hips. Her face had a strong jaw and a pale wash of freckles, her eyes tended toward green. If he'd had to guess, he might have put her as George's older sister at first glance, but once he had a chance to look more closely, he could see that was only because she had an elegance to her looks, whereas George had a boyishness. She had to make herself look stern; when she didn't think about it her mouth turned up at the corners. He could see why Cooper had liked her. He had to stop looking for a round of coughing. A little groan escaped him.

"Let me get you some aspirin," she said, concern in her voice.

"I don't want to use up your medicines."

"Don't be stupid," she said. She left him abruptly, and came back a few moments later. She poured water from the bottle on the bureau into the glass, and handed it to him with two white tablets. "Take them."

He did. "Thanks."

"We boil the drinking water, of course. Now, have a wash if you want, and get into bed. Stay there. I'll bring you up some supper if you're awake. You need to rest if you're going to get better, right?" She smiled at him a little, or maybe she just wasn't thinking about it.

Chapter 7

Chris huddled in the bed, coughing, ribs aching, unable to fall asleep, watching the light fade and the window finally go as dark as the room. Later, there was a soft knock, and Pauline came in with a plate and a mug, barely visible in the soft light from the hall. Chris coughed and struggled to sit up without hurting his ribs.

"Did you sleep at all?" she asked, setting the plate and mug on the dresser.

"I don't think so."

She lit the oil lamp, then pulled a second pillow out of the closet and put it behind his back.

"Thanks."

"Do you want to eat?"

"Please."

She brought him the plate: two fried eggs, a slice of ham, and a thick slice of bread with butter on it. He hadn't seen food like that since before Portsmouth. The aroma of the food filled his nose. He picked up the knife and fork.

Pauline got the mug from the bureau. "Cider." She set it on the chair next to the bed, and did a double-take. "Is that a torch? Does it work?" she asked, as if she didn't believe it.

Chris nodded, his mouth full. He had got the small black torch before he left Portsmouth. The batteries were the re-chargeable kind. He'd put it on the chair in case he needed it after dark. He swallowed his mouthful. "The chap I got it from said it's a good charge. I don't know how long it will last."

"Does everywhere else have electricity?"

"Only the cities, usually. Some bigger towns." He took another bite. "This is delicious, thank you."

"You're welcome. I'm glad you like it. I thought the eggs would be good for you."

"I haven't had eggs or ham in a long time." He paused to cough.

She fished in her pocket, held out more aspirin. "Here, have these."

"No—"

"I can hear you in here coughing. I know it hurts. Please, just take them."

He did, and she handed him the cider. "Gosh, that's good, too." He took another drink.

"A man in the village makes it. I thought the alcohol might help you sleep." She sat down gently on the end of the bed. "Why didn't Michael come with you?"

"He wasn't released." Chris tried to make it sound casual, so she wouldn't be worried. "He has a few more weeks."

"Is he going to come when he is released?"

"I don't know. We didn't really talk about it. He said once that he kinda thought he'd worn out his welcome." He took another bite.

"That's not true." She shook her head with a distressed frown. "Could I send a letter? To the Distribution Center?"

"I suppose so. He'll get it, I think, if he's still there."

"He didn't say where he was planning to go?"

Chris shook his head, chewed a bite quickly. "He said he had some prospects, but wouldn't say what. He said he'd write to you again."

She took a deep breath, let it out. "I won't count on it. You didn't know him long enough to really know him."

"He seemed a good chap."

"He is a good chap," she agreed. "He's just not, well, for the long-term, you could say. I don't know that he's ever finished anything in his life."

Chris didn't know what to say to that. Pauline roused herself, stood up.

"Well, I'll be back in a bit for the plate." She went out.

Chris ate every scrap of the food, using the bread to mop up the egg yolk and any grease left from the ham. He felt full for the first time since London. He left the plate on his lap, leaned his head back against the pillow, and closed his eyes, occasionally lifting the mug for a drink of the cider. He considered what Pauline had said about Cooper. He could see how her assessment would fit. Cooper had talked a lot about Pauline. He had made it clear they had been occasional lovers for years, but it was also clear that Cooper had never made any firm commitment to her. Chris was nearly certain he never would, and he was glad Pauline seemed to understand that, even if she did still care for Cooper to some extent. When he finished the cider he heaved himself painfully out of the bed and used the loo.

Pauline came back for the plate and mug. "Do you want me to leave the lamp lit?"

"No, don't waste the oil. I have the torch."

"Right, then. You needn't get up in the morning if you don't feel up to it. I'll bring you up some breakfast."

"I might be ready to get up by then."

"Let's just see how you get on. Goodnight." She turned down the lamp until it was out and pulled the door closed, leaving him alone in the dark.

Something was coming for him, something dark and vile and formless, snaking through the house, slipping along the floors, trying the doors, full of pain and grief and loss. He tried to block its way, but it split around him, two foul seething masses, one of them flowing up the stairs, relentless, unstoppable. The other surrounded him, beckoning with desolate blackness. He couldn't get away from it, his legs wouldn't work, and it crawled up his body, dark and anguished and heavy, dragging on him, pulling at him, until he screamed, and it filled his mouth, gagging him...

Chris jerked awake, sat up in the bed in the dark and groaned at the pain in his ribs, gasping for breath, not knowing where he was. The door opened, letting in light from a candle, and someone stood there. Pauline, he remembered.

"Are you okay?" She held the candle down low beside her. "I heard you calling out."

He clutched at the covers, tried to control his breathing, tried to get the dream out of his brain. "I'm okay," he managed.

"Can I get you anything?"

He shook his head, didn't know if she could see it, but didn't know if he could say anything else. He needed a drink of water.

She came into the room, set the candle on the bureau, and poured him a glass of water. His hand trembled as he took it from her, gulped it down. He sat holding the glass until she took it from his hand. His ribs hurt with every breath. He started coughing, and it seemed to last forever, and eventually he sagged back onto the pillows and closed his eyes. He felt her sit down on the end of the bed.

"I'm sorry I woke you," he said.

"It's okay. I could light the lamp, leave it low."

He didn't answer her. She got up and he heard the clink of the glass chimney as she lit it.

"Do you want me to sit here for a bit?"

"No, I'll be all right. Thank you."

"You can call me if you need anything. I'm in the next room."

"Thank you," he said again, and he heard the door shut softly. He opened his eyes and saw the small pale flame of the lamp. It was nearly the same as the lamp at Archie's cabin on the mountain in New York. He remembered watching the flame of that lamp as it got lower and lower, and finally sputtered out in the middle of the night. All of the torches were dead by then, all the candles had been burned down to the last guttering puddles of wax, and it was the last of the oil. He had started sleeping on the couch by the woodstove, the final source of light, little shafts seeping out through the front grate.

It had been a long time since he had felt such a need for light. It had been awhile since he'd had that dream. His eyes hurt, and he closed them, and eventually he slept.

Chris awoke with a shudder, fists clenched. He blinked to clear his eyes, huddled under the covers, and took an inventory of the ordinary room until he calmed. The London dreams, still new and wrenching, kept changing. How long before they became routine? *Too long.*

The window was a pale rectangle of light. Chris didn't hear anything in the house yet. He crawled out of bed and turned down the lamp wick until the flame went out. He pushed back the curtains. He gazed down on the front garden, the iron gate in the wall, the road. Clumps of trees and bushes dotted the field across from the house. Dense grey clouds pressed down, and wispy patches of fog lingered at the edges of the field. Off to the left, down the road, Chris glimpsed the top of a house that might be where Cooper grew up. He heard a bird singing. He left the window and had a long coughing fit, hanging onto the top of the bureau until it passed, then padded in bare feet down the hall to the loo.

When he came out, Pauline was standing by her door, in a long, pale dressing gown.

"Good morning," she whispered. "Did you sleep more?"

"Yes," he nodded as he passed her. He stopped in his doorway. "I don't think I'll get up yet."

"Okay, that's fine. I'll bring you breakfast later."

"Thanks," he said, and closed the door. He drank from the bottle on the bureau, plumped up the pillows, and lay back carefully against them, half-sitting. He thought he might not cough as much if he wasn't lying down. He closed his eyes and tried to clear his mind. He felt he might sleep now that it was light.

76

When he woke next, it was more slowly. The dream lingered, but this one was easier to deal with, it left only a deep sadness, none of the panic of some of the others. He used to wake up crying when he dreamed about Sophie, but not anymore.

Chris sat up carefully. A shaft of weak sunlight came in through the curtains. From the angle, he could tell it was near noon. He rubbed at his face. His ribs still hurt, but he felt more rested than he had in weeks. He eased his legs over the edge of the bed, and saw a note on the chair, a small scrap of paper.

"Decided to let you sleep!" it said, with a little smiley face. Chris picked it up, his heart pounding, his hand shaking. He held it, stared at it. It looked a lot like Sophie's handwriting. She used to leave him little notes with smiley faces on them. But then she would put an "S" inside a little heart. He sat holding the note for long minutes, blinking, then folded it up and left it on the bureau. He took his towel to the loo and had a wash and a shave. He changed out of the shorts and tee shirt he'd slept in. It hurt getting his shirt on, and bending over to lace his shoes, and it made him cough. He went downstairs.

Grace was arranging cutlery and plates on the kitchen table. "Good afternoon, Chris. Did you get some good sleep?"

"Yes, thank you."

George's wife was there, taking a dish out of the oven.

"You didn't meet Marie yesterday, did you?" Grace asked him.

"Hello," Marie said with a smile. She was small and dainty, with light brown, curly hair cut short, and

77

glasses. "Pauline looked in on you, but you were sleeping so soundly she decided to leave you. You're just in time for lunch."

"Can I help with anything?"

"You can ring the bell to call them in," Marie said. "Just outside the door. Give it a good jangle; that will get them in here."

Chris found the bell mounted on the wall beside the door, and swung the cord back and forth a few times. He stood outside, breathing in the fresh air as deep as his aching ribs would allow, but then he had a coughing fit.

"It doesn't sound as bad today," Pauline said, coming around the side of the house. She wore the same mucky clothes as the day before.

"Definitely improving," he agreed.

She took hold of the handle of a pump next to a tub and worked it vigorously. The water came spurting out. "You were so asleep earlier, I didn't want to wake you for breakfast. Especially since you didn't sleep so well last night." She peeled the brown jumper off over her head; she had another shirt on under it, tucked into her cords. She pushed up her sleeves and washed her hands and arms.

"No, not a good night. Sorry about that."

"Don't worry about it." She grabbed a towel hanging on a hook, dried her hands and rubbed it over her face. "I'll get you a candle for tonight. Candles are cheaper than the oil." She worked the pump again, and put a bucket under it. When it was full Chris reached for it. "Don't even!" she scolded. "You're resting, remember?"

"I'm not exactly an invalid. I was unloading lorries the day before yesterday."

"Which is why you're in the state you're in." She turned to keep the bucket out of Chris's reach.

George was coming across the yard from the barn. He grinned at Chris. "I wouldn't bother to argue with her."

"Okay, I give up," Chris said. He opened the door for Pauline and held it.

"Thank you." She smiled and went in, kicking off her wellies as she had the day before.

***

Chris went up to the spare room after lunch, feeling guilty, like he was skiving, but his ribs ached, and Pauline wouldn't let him do anything anyway. He lay back against the pillows, tried to relax. He thought about Pauline and Michael. She was a strong-willed, no-nonsense type, it seemed, and he wondered why she would let herself waste time with someone like Michael. It was clear she cared for him, in the way she asked about him, the disappointed look on her face when he had told her Michael had no plans to come when he was released. But maybe it was just leftover feelings from before, more worried friendship than anything else. For all he knew, there was someone else on the scene already, someone he, and Michael, did not yet know about. It would be interesting to find out. Chris let himself drift off into sleep.

He was standing by the old stone wall in London topped with curled wire. He began to run, but it wasn't fast enough. He could see them in the distance: two shadowy figures, running ahead of him. He called out to them to wait, but they didn't hear. Behind him, the blackness got closer, sweeping swiftly toward him, occluding everything, muffling the gunshots. He tripped and fell, found himself on top of Beryl. He held her in his arms, his back to the wall, watched the blackness creeping toward them while she gasped for breath and then went still. "You have to go," a voice said as the door slid back and bright light assaulted him.

Coughing painfully was a lousy way to wake up. Add regret and despair and guilt, and Chris remembered why he preferred to work himself to exhaustion to limit the dreams. He blinked and shuddered. He heard Beryl's last words in his head, over and over. He coughed more, harder than he needed to, using the pain to kill memories.

The sun hung at about the same place as when he had arrived the day before. Twenty-four hours here, most of it in bed, hard to believe. Time to get up.

At the bottom of the stairs, Chris glanced into the little sitting room. Marie was there, on her hands and knees, sweeping with a brush and dustpan around the fireplace. She glanced up.

"Oh, hello. Y'know, I used to hate hoovering. Now I realize what a lovely, easy job it was." She laughed.

"We never realize how good we have it until it's gone," Chris said. It came out harsher than he'd wanted it to.

"That's true." Marie got to her feet, careful not to spill the dustpan. She smiled. "But then, sometimes we don't realize what we were missing until we find it, eh?"

"Yes, I suppose," he agreed. "Can I help?"

"Aren't you supposed to be resting?"

"I have been. Just woke up. I'm feeling better, really. I'm not used to doing nothing. Let me help, please. I'll sweep." Chris put out his hand for the brush.

"All right, you can do the stairs."

"Brilliant."

When he'd finished the staircase Chris found Marie in the kitchen and asked for something else to do.

"I can show you how to trim lamp wicks."

"I know how to do that. Shall I clean and fill them, too?"

"Lovely." She got him a scissors, rag, and a bottle of lamp oil. He did the lamps downstairs first, then went upstairs.

Marie had told him to do all the lamps in the bedrooms, but he hesitated before he went into Pauline's room. She kept it very neat, like the spare room. There were no clothes lying about, no clutter. It was much bigger than the spare room, of course. There were more pictures on the walls, more furniture, little knickknacks on the bureau and tables.

The lamp sat on the bureau. Chris cleaned and trimmed and filled it, put it back carefully near a group of framed pictures. He stopped to look at them: Pauline and George when they were teenagers, their parents—he recognized Grace—a young Michael lounging in a punt on a river, George and Marie's wedding photo. One picture showed Pauline and Michael together, from

81

many years before, dressed up to go out somewhere fancy. He wore a tuxedo, she a shimmering dark green strapless gown. They had their arms around each other.

The last two pictures showed Pauline and George, both much younger, and another young man together on the couch in the sitting room downstairs, and the young man by himself, seated on a stone wall. Chris looked closely at the three of them and could see the family resemblance. It was the missing brother, obviously. Chris thought that Michael had probably told him, but he couldn't remember the brother's name.

He went into the other two bedrooms to do the lamps there, and saw other pictures of the same young man at different ages.

When he'd finished he went back downstairs and sat with Grace and Marie in the kitchen, doing small jobs at the table while they cooked supper. They told him about various people in the village, but did not ask him anything about himself. He wondered what Michael had put in the letter to Pauline, and was glad he didn't have to answer a lot of questions.

Chapter 8

Breakfast was over when Chris came down the next morning. Grace cooked him eggs and toast in spite of his protests that he could get his own meal.

"Indulge an old lady who's spent her whole life mothering," Grace said with a chuckle. "Anyway, Pauline would scold me if I didn't feed you properly."

Pauline and Marie had gone into town, she told him, and wouldn't be back until lunch. Chris washed up his dishes and went out in search of George.

"I'm supposed to tell you to rest," George said.

"I'm good, fully rested."

George scrutinized him with a critical eye. "If it weren't for Michael's letter I'd have sent you packing. You're not exactly the picture of health."

Chris shrugged. "Short rations at the Distribution Center."

George shook his head. "God, what we've sunk to," he muttered. "Okay, I'll show you around. But no lifting, no chopping wood, no shoveling muck, right? I've had bruised ribs before, I know what it's like."

"I can milk."

"Oh? You've spent time on a farm?"

"Back in the States, yes. It's been awhile."

"Tomorrow, maybe, if you're up early enough."

"Get me up, then. Put me to work."

"I'll ask Pauline."

"I know what I'm up to."

George grinned. "Are you trying to avoid my sister? She's the one supposed to be looking after you."

"I don't need looking after," Chris said, annoyance making his shoulders tense.

George got serious. "No, you've got this far, come all the way across the ocean. Hell, I'm scared to go as far as Portsmouth. I wouldn't think you need looking after. Except Michael said in his letter you'd work yourself to death, given the chance."

"Different situation." Chris stood a little straighter, tried to lose the defiance. "I've had two nights' sleep, and most of a day. I'm—" The rest of what he was about to say was cut off by an insistent coughing fit. He ended up bent over, head down. "Shit."

"Take the day off, for God's sake," George said, putting a hand on Chris's shoulder. "Sit on your ass and enjoy it. Do that, and I'll get you up tomorrow for milking."

Chris found a bench against the wall of the barn. He leaned back, closed his eyes, felt the warmth of the sun on his face. He tried to relax and enjoy the thought of another day of complete rest, but he couldn't shake the *must-work-to-survive* feeling.

"Who are you?" a small voice said.

Chris opened his eyes. A boy stood a couple of meters away, staring at him. It was hard to judge his age. He was small and thin. His right cheek sported a dirty smudge. His disheveled brown hair needed cutting. His clothes were a motley assortment of too-short trousers, worn shoes, a stained tee, and a man's flannel work shirt instead of a jacket.

"I'm Chris. Who are you?"

"I'm Wes."

"Well, it's nice to meet you, Wes," Chris said, and held out his hand.

"That's not safe."

"It is with me." Chris left his hand out.

84

The boy thought about it, then came closer and shook it briefly.

"What are you doing here?" Wes asked next.

"I'm going to be working here."

Wes's expression darkened. "I work here. Are you going to take my job?"

"What do you do?" Chris asked.

"Whatever Pauline tells me to."

"Well, I'll be working with George. I expect there's plenty of work for the both of us."

The boy thought this over and apparently agreed. "All right. Where did you come from?"

"Portsmouth."

Wes didn't answer. Chris thought he probably didn't know where that was.

"Where do you live?" Chris asked.

"In the town. I have my own house." He puffed himself up as he said it.

"Really?"

"Yeah, so I have work there, too. But I come and work for Pauline some days. And I work for the butcher, and the grocer."

Chris found himself smiling. "You're a hard worker, then?"

Wes stuck out his chin. "I'm stronger than I look."

"I bet you are," Chris said, trying to get a serious expression back.

"What are you doing today?"

"I'm not working today."

"Why not?"

"Um, I hurt my ribs," Chris explained. "I'm not supposed to work until they're better."

"I hurt my arm once," Wes said.

"Yeah? So did I. And you know how it hurts if you try to work too soon, eh?"

Wes nodded, then turned around as George came out of the barn.

"Hey, Wes. No school today?"

Wes scowled and scuffed at the ground with his shoe. "Not today."

George shook his head. "Why don't you go clean up the chicken house?"

The boy went off at a trot.

"He's an orphan?" Chris had come across enough of them over the years to recognize the signs.

"Yes. He's quite a character. We all try to look out for him, but he's fiercely independent. He's been on his own since the Bad Winter."

"How old is he?" Chris didn't think he could be more than ten.

"Oh, he's thirteen, at least."

"Really?"

"Yes, he's small, isn't he? He's a good boy." George watched Wes unlatch the gate to the little yard of the hen house. "Won't let anyone take care of him." He shot a look at Chris, and one corner of his mouth turned up. Chris let it pass.

"He hasn't any relatives in town?"

"No, he's not from here. He showed up in the spring, after it happened. We're not quite sure how he fetched up here, but he settled right in to stay."

"He says he has his own house?"

George nodded. "A little place near the Post Office that'd been empty for years. I think Pauline would take him in if he'd let her. But she'd make him wash regularly and go to school. If not for that I think he'd take her up on it. He adores her."

"Huh," Chris said.

"She's always had a soft spot for strays," George went on, sliding his eyes over at Chris. "Michael knows that." He grinned and went back into the barn.

Chris stayed on his bench for as long as he could. Forced idleness gave his mind too much time to wander, he'd found, and he didn't like the "why didn't you" and "you should have" and "what if" scenarios that crept out of the corners of his brain, making his head hurt. He found George and shadowed him for a couple of hours as he did various chores around the farm.

The bell rang for lunch. Wes was washing his hands at the pump. Chris and George took their turns, and went in to eat.

"If you're feeling up to it, I could take you into town to register," Pauline said to Chris as she passed him bread.

"Okay," Chris said. "George made sure I didn't overdo."

Pauline smiled, and turned her face to Wes. "You can walk with us, Wes."

The boy furrowed his brow and tried not to look at Chris. "Nar. I'm going 'round by the bridge."

"Suit yourself," Pauline said.

Wes bolted his food, mumbled a brief thanks to Grace, and took off before the rest of them were finished.

"It's not like him to miss a chance to walk with you," Marie said to Pauline.

After lunch, Chris made sure he had his blood test card in his pocket, and a little bit of money in case there was a fee to register. He waited in the yard for Pauline. She came out, smiled, and led him out through the front garden, the way she had led him in.

"We don't get many visitors," she said as they started down the road. "The town, I mean. So, don't be surprised if –well. Word's out."

Chris wasn't sure what she meant by that, but she went on before he had a chance to ask, as if to change the subject.

"Michael said in his letter that you're planning to go on to Bath, to look up your family."

"That's the plan."

"He said you've been out of the country?"

"I lived in New York for quite a while."

"Why did you go to New York?"

"I moved there for my job."

"Oh, what did you do?"

Chris decided there was no point in avoiding it. "I was a musician."

She turned to him with a little smile while they walked. "Musician? Like a rock star?" she said, pleased with her joke. He took a moment before he answered.

"Yes, actually."

She stopped, mouth open. Chris walked on a couple of steps before he turned back to her.

"Seriously?"

He met her gaze. "Seriously."

"Like, songs on the radio, Top of the Pops, and all that?"

"All that."

"What songs?"

He mentioned the two songs that had first made him and Brian famous, songs found on 'big hits' compilation CDs, songs people had still sung along to years after they were hits. Songs that, like all of them, hadn't been heard by anyone in more than five years. "'Good Match' and 'What Did Milla Say?'"

"I know those songs!" she exclaimed. "You were famous!"

"For a few years. Doesn't matter now." Chris began walking again.

She followed. "I'm sorry."

"Don't be. Sometimes it wasn't all that great."

"But you must miss it," she said, coming up even with him.

He looked at her quickly, then away. "It's the least of what I miss." He saw her shake her head out of the corner of his eye.

"God, I'm sorry, that was thoughtless of me," she said.

"Don't worry about it." He tried to lighten his tone. "At least I'll never be a 'has-been'... Although," he continued with mock consternation, "I suppose I already am."

"Well, but that's not your fault."

"No, it's no one's fault. It just happened. I hardly even think about it anymore, really." He kept his gaze forward, but could tell she was watching him. "I don't usually tell people about it."

"Why not?"

"It's all pointless, now. None of it matters. It's not who I am anymore."

She inclined her head. "Okay. I won't tell anyone."

"Thanks."

"Did you tell Michael?"

"No, it never came up." Chris tried to think of a way to turn the conversation away from himself. "Is that his house down the road from yours?"

"Yes. It's a lovely house. Well, it was. It's a shame he doesn't keep it up. We do what we can to keep it from going to ruin, but we haven't the time for two places."

"He has no family here?"

"No family at all, except us. He didn't tell you?"

Chris shook his head. "Never came up."

"They all died in a car crash, in—let's see—'94, I guess it was."

"Oh. So, not in an outbreak?"

"No, we've hardly had any of that around here. We've been very lucky. Only a bit at the start, nothing in the last few years."

Chris was quiet. He suddenly understood her hospital comment on the day he arrived. *She's never seen anyone die of the plague.*

Pauline went on with the story about Michael. "They'd been up to London to visit him, his Mum and Dad and brother. His brother was a good deal younger. He was a luv. Michael was going to come back with them for a few days, that was the plan, but he changed his mind at the last minute. They were all killed on the way home. Michael would have been, too. It was dreadful, horrible. He didn't take it very well, of course."

"Huh."

"That was the first time he disappeared, just after the funeral. We were all worried out of our minds. We thought he'd done something drastic. He showed up eventually, took care of all the paperwork, all that stuff, you know. He let the farm, after that. It gave him a little income. Nice people, but they didn't stay, when all the chaos started. We don't know what happened to them. It's odd, really. It would have been safer for them to stay, I'm sure."

"Likely they went looking for family," Chris said.

"Yes, I suppose. Michael's never been back, to stay. He's visited, but never for long. We're his second family. He leaned on Dad a lot, back then. It was another blow to him when Dad died."

"He puts on quite an act, doesn't he?" Chris asked, wondering if he did it with them.

She nodded. "Yes, he does. Did you know it was an act, in Portsmouth?"

"I didn't really think about it."

She was looking at him, and he braced himself.

"You don't let yourself get close to anyone, do you?"

He inhaled. "Not anymore. It's safer."

She didn't reply, and he exhaled in relief.

They turned left at the crossroads where the lorry had dropped him, cutting through an abandoned petrol station. The village began in earnest soon after with a row of stone houses on each side of the street. Not too far along was another crossroads and the square. Chris saw the pub, post office, grocer, and butcher, with a few empty shops among them. Some houses were well-kept, some obviously abandoned. Two old men sat on benches near a dry fountain. They watched Pauline and Chris, but Pauline turned into the door of the Post Office before they were close enough to have to greet the men.

Three young women were already in the place, and turned expectantly as Chris and Pauline entered. They smiled brightly.

"Hey, Pauline," one of them said. "Is this your hired help?"

Pauline made an exasperated noise. "I told you I'd be bringing him to register. And I asked you to stay out of it."

The women ignored her.

"I'm Diana," said the one who'd already spoken. "This is Claire, and Janice."

Diana had loose blond hair that bounced on her shoulders. She wore a tight blue jumper with a low neckline. Claire kept her dark hair shorter. Her figure was less curvy, more muscular, but Chris thought her face prettier than Diana's. Janice had tied up her brown hair with a ribbon, and had selected an impractical pink blouse and skirt set for her trip to the Post Office. She'd left one button too many undone, showing modest cleavage.

"Nice to meet you." Chris tried to be polite without being friendly. Their attitudes bordered on desperate as they tried to out-smile each other.

"And you're Chris, right?" Diana said, licking her lips and tossing her hair a bit. She moved to stand in front of Claire, who slid her eyes briefly at her rival and sidestepped to remain in full view.

"I told you his name earlier," Pauline said. "Clear off, ladies. He has to register."

"Just trying to be friendly to the new man in town," Claire said. She directed another smile at Chris. "We'll get a chance to talk at the pub sometime, right?"

"Ah, perhaps," Chris said, edging away from them toward the counter.

"Clear *off*," Pauline said again.

Chris wondered if she would have to shoo them like chickens or ducks.

"Bye, Chris," they all said in various sing-song tones, and exited as a group, fluttering fingers at him.

Pauline screwed up her face. "Sorry."

"Huh," Chris said, and Pauline grinned.

A deep voice spoke up from behind the counter. "You're the most exciting thing to happen around here in years." The man sat at a desk behind the counter. He pushed himself out of his chair with a wry look. He appeared older than George, weatherworn, but not as old as Grace.

"Hello, Mr. Percy," Pauline said. "This is Chris Price, our boarder."

"Friend of Michael Cooper's, I hear," Mr. Percy said. He pulled out a drawer and rummaged.

"Um, yes."

Mr. Percy grunted. Chris raised his eyebrows at Pauline. She smiled back and rocked on her feet.

"Visit or relocating?"

"Extended visit," Chris replied, stepping up to the counter.

"Don't have a form for that. Fortnight visit or relocating, take your pick. If you want coupons, you're relocating."

"Relocating, then."

The postmaster shoved a two-page form at Chris, then pulled a pen tied to a string out from under the counter. "You've got a valid card?"

"Yes, sir," Chris said, reaching for his back pocket. Mr. Percy waved it off.

"Good enough. I'm supposed to ask you some bloody questions, but they're all on the form. There's no carbon, so do both copies." He turned and sat down at his desk again.

Chris stood at the counter and filled out the two identical forms. He signed them, and cleared his throat.

"I think that's everything," he said.

Mr. Percy looked over the papers. "Right. Looks official." He picked out a rubber stamp from a box and thumped each copy with vigor. "You need some interim coupons?"

"No, actually. I brought a book along from my last place."

"Good job," Mr. Percy said, and nodded. He eyed Chris with pursed lips. "You might ask Michael to let you have his place. He's not using it. Good land. You could do well with it. You're young enough to start a family."

Pauline drew a breath and stood up straighter. Chris felt a tickle in his throat, and made a show of coughing.

"Well," he said when he'd recovered his breath, "I'm not planning to stay, as I said. I'll be moving on in a bit. Thanks." He motioned vaguely at the forms on the counter.

Mr. Percy continued to eye him.

"Thanks for your help," Pauline said. She turned for the door. Chris beat her to it, and held it for her. They escaped into the sunshine.

Chris expected the trio to be waiting, but the street was empty except for the old men by the fountain.

"Wow," Chris said.

"I'm sorry," Pauline said.

"Not your fault."

"He's got a daughter, in case you hadn't guessed. Her fiancé was in the military, and never came home."

"Are there no other men in this town?"

"No, actually. No single men of the right age. They're married, or older, or um, not eligible."

"Holy crap."

"I'll tell them to leave you alone, but I don't know what good it will do."

Chris dredged up memories of the crowds of girls and women who would follow the band and compete for whatever they could get. The worst of it had only lasted a couple of years. The breakup and his move to New York had put an end to it. It had been an ego boost at the time. Now he found it distinctly discomforting.

"I expect I can put them off easily enough."

They walked on in silence until they reached the church.

"Let's just stop in here for a moment, okay?" Pauline said outside the lychgate of the churchyard. They passed through the dark wood structure on the stone path, then she veered off into the grass. She made her way past crooked, worn markers to the edge of the graveyard, and stopped by a small, bright white stone. Chris followed, saw the name and date: Paul George Anderson, born 1931, died 2000.

"That's Dad. I hate the stone, but at least we got a stone."

Chris's throat tightened up, and he stood back from her.

"It was a stroke," Pauline went on. "We couldn't take him to hospital, and there were no doctors."

Chris had heard all this before. Cooper told him, one night after lights-out, the two of them on separate sides of their shared dormitory room. Cooper had rambled on night after night about his friends the Andersons, but sometimes Chris hardly listened, never imagining that he would ever meet them.

Pauline squatted down and pulled a few weeds, then stood up again. "Those are my grandparents." She pointed to an ornate gravestone next to the plain, newer one. "That stone cost a small fortune."

"You've always lived here?" Chris asked, having found his voice again, thinking that he should make an effort at polite conversation, and not just stand around uncomfortably.

"God, no!" Pauline said with a wave of her hand. "Grew up here, yes. I left to go to University. No intention of coming back. I thought I hated it here. I was a modern, independent woman, y'know. I came back when all the chaos started."

He nodded. She turned and headed back out of the churchyard. Chris looked again at the stones, then walked after her.

She glanced back, slowed her pace so he caught up.

"So, tell me about New York. Did you live right in the city?"

"For a short time, yes. Bought a house and moved to the suburbs when I mar—got married."

"I always wanted to go there. Never managed it."

"I wouldn't recommend it now," he said, and she half grinned.

"No, I think not." They walked on up the road, and she got serious. "You were there, when it all started?"

"Yes."

"Was it awful?"

Chris took a deep breath. "Yes."

"I'm sorry. I always ask too many questions. It's my nature. Used to make a living at it."

"I know. You were a psychologist. Cooper told me."

"What else did he tell you?"

"That you were very good at it."

Pauline smiled at the compliment. "You can tell me to naff off any time."

"All right."

They walked in silence for a few minutes.

"How did you get back here?"

"I worked my way over on a ship."

"Are there ships again, then?"

"Yes. Not like it used to be, but there's some trade."

"And you came in at Portsmouth?"

"No." Chris shook his head. "London. I was there for a couple months before I got another ship to Portsmouth. I'd used up all my money in London, and was trying to earn some more," he said, bending the truth somewhat. "But they stiffed me."

"And you had to work off the jail debt."

"Yes."

"That's awful. They shouldn't be able to do that." They walked on a bit, and she seemed to be thinking. "What's London like, now?"

"It's a stinking hole."

"I used to go up to London on the weekends. Michael had a flat there. I'd go and stay with him. I loved the museums. I loved to watch the Horse Guards come down the Mall. I used to go to Buckingham Palace."

"It's a burnt-out ruin now," Chris said, and regretted it when he saw her pained expression. "Crap, I'm sorry."

She shrugged. "It's all gone, everything, isn't it?" They reached the house, and she stopped and leaned on the wall. Chris stopped, too. "Look at us. We don't even have electricity."

"This is a good place. You have your family, you have food, and you're safe. It's better than a lot places I've been. And you know where your Dad is buried." Chris's right hand went reflexively to his left, caressed his wedding ring briefly.

She looked over at him, did not say anything.

"I'm sorry, I didn't mean to lecture."

"No, I know." She looked away into the distance. "My little brother went missing. Jim. He was traveling. He wanted to celebrate the new millennium someplace exotic." She shook her head. "We have no idea what happened to him."

"Yes, Cooper told me."

"He was a black sheep. A lucky black sheep. Anything he tried turned to gold. Except at the end." She took a deep breath and pushed herself away from the wall and met his gaze. "Sometimes I forget how good we have it. Thanks for reminding me. I don't know what it's like anywhere else. I never go beyond Breton, except into Petersfield for my blood test or shopping. At first it wasn't safe, and then I couldn't bear the thought of it. I don't want to see what's happened."

"It's a hard place, now. But you can still find good people, even in the worst places." He looked away from her, trying not to think of Beryl. "Even in London."

***

They were sitting down to breakfast a few days later when the back door opened, and Wes stepped in, wearing a dripping slicker and holding a fishing pole.

"You're up early today," Pauline said in surprise.

"Do you want to go fishing?" Wes asked her.

"Oh, um, well. I have some things to do this morning. Maybe Chris would like to go?"

Wes's face fell. He looked at Chris with doubt clear in his expression.

"Yeah, sure," Chris said, taking his cue from the pleading look Pauline gave him. "I'll go with you, after milking."

"Do you know how to fish?" Wes asked.

"I've done a good bit of fishing over the years."

"Okay."

"Come have breakfast," Pauline said, taking the pole from the boy's hand. "Give me your slicker."

He shrugged out of it, and Pauline hung it up while Marie got a plate, cup, and fork for him and George pulled a chair over from the other side of the room. They squeezed him in between Pauline and Grace. He ate hungrily, and Chris saw Pauline frowning as she watched the boy. She shifted her eyes to Chris.

"I'll have to find you a slicker, Chris, and some wellies."

"He can use mine," George said. "I've a pole you can use, too."

"There should be some in that closet, in the spare room," Pauline said. It sounded tentative to Chris. She and George exchanged a look, and they both looked at Grace.

"Yes, I believe there are," Grace said, her eyes downcast. Then she looked up at Chris and smiled. "There may be some other clothes in there you can use, as well. Whatever you need. Have a look."

"Thank you." Chris glanced at Pauline, but she was looking at her plate. She seemed to take a breath in relief.

After breakfast, Chris followed Pauline up to the spare room. He sat on the bed unlacing his shoes while she squeezed in through the tiny door and rummaged in the closet. She found the wellies quickly, and handed them out to him to try on. She came out with the slicker as he was putting on the second boot.

"Perfect," he said, standing up.

"Lovely." Pauline held out the slicker. Chris put it on and pulled up the zip. "Good. I thought you were about Jim's size. Anything else you want, just take it."

"I'm not going to rifle your brother's closet. I wouldn't feel right."

"You're as bad as Mum. It's not like he'll ever need them again." She put her chin up a bit as she said it, looked off into a corner of the room.

Chris hesitated, not sure if he should say anything, but then she looked back at him.

"But you're here, aren't you?" she said softly. "And in Bath they all think you're dead."

The way she said it made him take a sharp breath. He put his hands in his pockets, then made a pretense of exploring the slicker.

"I'm sorry," she said. "I didn't mean anything by that. It's just—well, I kept hope alive for a long time. Then I decided it was pointless. No real hope, not anymore. And then you came, and you've been trying to get home all this time, and now you're almost there. And I feel guilty for giving up hope."

Chris's stomach was churning. He didn't say anything. He wanted to escape into the rain with Wes. He shifted one foot backward toward the door. Pauline saw it.

"I'm sorry, I've made you uncomfortable." She shook herself slightly. "I'll find you some things today, then, while you're out, and leave them on the bed. Some trousers, shirts, a couple of jumpers... all right?"

"All right. Thank you."

"Thank you, for going with Wes. I rather put you on the spot, I'm afraid."

"I don't mind. I like fishing."

"Good. I find it unbelievably boring, but he always wants me to go. And it will be easy on your ribs. They're sore again, from the milking, aren't they?"

"It's not bad."

"Make sure he eats the lunch, even if you don't stay out 'til lunchtime?"

"I will do," he assured her. She nodded, and he left her there, arms crossed, staring at the open closet.

Chapter 9

"I was wondering," Chris said, but did not go on.

The sewing basket sat open on the kitchen table between them. Pauline had a pile of mending next to her, Chris a pair of cords and a shirt to mend. George, Marie, and Grace had all gone to the pub. Chris had encouraged Pauline to go too; he felt odd that she was staying home because of him. It was the second time she had stayed home since he had arrived, but she insisted that she had mending to do, and didn't really want to go anyway. She offered to do his things for him, but he assured her that he could do them.

Pauline looked up at him, waited.

"Do you think it would be all right if I stayed through the winter?"

She straightened in her chair. "Oh. I thought you'd want to go on to Bath as soon as you could."

Chris swallowed, concentrated on the rip in his trousers. He took a few stitches. "You know what you said about hope? Last week, when you got me the slicker and the wellies... How you'd given it up, about your brother, because it seemed pointless?"

"Yes," she said softly.

"Hope is all I've had, for years." He took a breath, and went on before he decided against it. "I've got nothing else. In London, I found out that one of my brothers is dead. That was a lot of my hope gone. It was... bad. And I keep thinking, what if I get to Bath and there's no one left? I couldn't take that."

He caught Pauline's eye, then looked back down at the fabric, his vision blurred, taking a stitch with shaking fingers.

"I'm so sorry, Chris, about your brother. But the chance that someone is there, waiting for you, hoping for you to come back—"

"I'm not sure I'm ready to take that chance."

"You're so close."

Chris took a deep breath, and his ribs barely hurt at all. "It hardly seems real anymore. Look, I'll push off if you want me to, I didn't mean to—"

"No, that's not what I meant. You can stay as long as you want, of course, certainly. It's lovely having your help. Poor George has shouldered the burden all by himself for so long."

Chris looked up at her. "You work just as hard as he does."

She shrugged. "We'd love to have you stay on, of course, if that's what you want. You've been a huge help."

"I don't do so very much," Chris protested. "I know you tell George not to let me do anything strenuous. But I'm not ill anymore, and you've got to let me take on more. I want to."

"Michael said you're a hard worker in his letter."

Chris took a few stitches in silence, annoyed at the way she turned the conversation. "What else did he say?"

"That you never smile. That you don't answer questions."

Chris swallowed, kept stitching, did not look up at her. He got to the end of the rip, tied a knot in the thread, reached for the scissors on the table.

"He was wrong about the questions, though," Pauline said. "Where did you learn to sew?"

"Taught myself, I guess. Out of necessity."

"What's your favorite color?"

"Um, red?"

"Why does that sound like you're not sure?"

"Because I hadn't thought about it in a long time."

"Dogs or cats?"

"Dogs."

"Luxury car or economical?"

"I had both."

"Definitely wrong about the questions." She smiled.

Chris grunted, snipped the thread, and tied it off again ready to sew. He switched the cords for the shirt.

"You're not going to use that color thread on the shirt, are you?"

"Does it matter?"

"Yes. Were you really going to?"

"Yes."

Pauline rolled her eyes and reached for the needle in his hand. Chris moved his hand away.

"I'll get you the proper color," she said, but he kept the needle out of her reach.

"I think I can manage."

She left her hand stretched out, then pulled it back. She looked down at her mending.

"Have you always done that?" Chris asked.

"Always done what?"

Chris stuck his needle into the pincushion in the basket, then selected another, and a different spool of thread. "Tried to do everything for everybody." He threaded the needle, tied it, snipped it. *That was rude.* He figured he should apologize.

"Since Dad died," she said before he could. "Since things started going to hell. I suppose it gives me a feeling of control. I'm sorry. I'll try not to."

"I'm not used to it. I'm used to doing for myself."

"Yes, of course."

Chris kept his eyes on the needle, his face warming. "I don't mean to be rude. You don't have to take care of me."

"I know. But I don't mind, and Michael asked me to."

"I don't know why. I hardly knew him."

"He said you seemed to be trying to work yourself to death."

Chris couldn't help frowning, couldn't stop a little anger growing toward Michael. "He doesn't know me."

"He said you were mates."

Chris took little stitches in the shirt where the seam had opened, thinking back. "Not really."

"Because you don't do that, get friendly?"

He couldn't get the needle in the right place, had to keep his hands still. He remembered what had happened to Stew on the road in New York. In London: Beryl sitting close to him, her arm touching his. And Jenny, snuggled in his lap, how she had trusted him to keep her safe, and he had failed. "You've had the answer to that one already."

"Yes, I remember." Pauline tied off the thread she was working with and snipped it. She shook out the dress she had just mended and folded it. "I'm going to get a glass of cider. Would you like one?" she asked, pushing back her chair and standing up.

"Yes, please."

She got two glasses out of the cupboard and went down into the cellar. Chris flexed his shoulders while she was gone. He had been holding himself tensely, and his shoulders were beginning to ache. She tried to make it sound like small talk, but Chris knew she was probing, trying to open him up and see inside. *Don't fall for it.*

She came back shortly, set a glass in front of him.

"Thank you."

"You're welcome," she said easily. She settled herself in her chair and took a few sips before she got back to mending. Chris finished closing the seam of the shirt and stuck the needle back into the pincushion before he took a drink of his cider.

"That's good stuff."

"Yes, I try not to guzzle it," she agreed. "The beer at the pub is good, too."

"Is it? Why don't you go, then?"

"I wouldn't feel right, leaving you here by yourself."

"I don't mind. You should go if you want, really."

"Oh, let's not go on about it again, all right? Next time we'll both go."

He glanced at her with the glass halfway to his lips.

"Don't say anything. Just think about it, okay?"

Chris took a drink, put the glass down. He reached over and took a pair of George's jeans off the mending pile.

"You don't have to—" Pauline started, but then pressed her lips together.

"Would you like to pick the thread color?" Chris asked, straight-faced.

"No, I think you can manage. Here's a patch for that." She smiled at him as she handed him a small piece of denim.

She has a nice smile. Cooper was right about that. He pulled the basket toward him and rummaged for the proper color thread.

"Michael was right about the smiling," Pauline said, as if reading his mind, and he looked up, startled. She saw the look on his face. "What?"

Chris shook his head, and went back to the basket. "Nothing."

"When's the last time you felt like smiling?"

He found a spool, drew out a long piece of thread before he answered. "Wes made me smile when I met him. And I smiled at your Mum the day I got here, I think."

"Oh, well, Mum can make anyone smile. And before that?"

"Not sure." Chris found the triangular tear on the seat of George's jeans, positioned the patch and started to stitch it. He looked up to reach for his cider, and saw her watching him. "What?"

"You never sewed? Before? Didn't do your own mending?"

He shook his head.

"You do that like a pro. I doubt I could do any better."

"Did you do mending, before?"

"Well, no, I guess not." She tilted her head to the side. "No, of course not. I took it to the cleaners. Or I threw it away. Well, sent it off to Oxfam, anyway."

Chris nodded in agreement. "We had Goodwill, or Purple Heart, if you were done with it. For mending, there was a cleaners just down the road. Little old Asian lady. She could fix anything. Five dollars," he said in a high voice, mimicking an accent, holding up one hand with his fingers spread out. "Five dollars."

Pauline smiled, took a drink of her cider.

"She sat at a sewing machine in the front window," Chris continued, remembering, "stuff piled up all around her, sewing in zips and hemming suit pants and doing alterations..." He took another drink himself. "And her husband did shoes. He had a little corner in the other window, tools piled up, and rows of shoes on the shelf above him... Sophie had this pair of red sandals, with all these little straps—"

Chris stopped, his heart flailing, hand gripping the glass. He looked up at Pauline.

Her face was calm. "Go on."

No! He clenched his jaw shut and stared at her, his throat tightening, his breathing getting faster, heat spreading into his face. He wanted to say no, but she just kept looking at him with her calm expression, and he couldn't yell at her, couldn't tell her no, couldn't even look away.

"Go on," she said again.

He had to clear his throat. "Um, the straps kept breaking. Every time she wore them, a strap would break." He had to stop, gather his thoughts, clear his throat again. "And the old man would fix them, each time. She'd take them in and he'd fix the strap, and he always told her not to buy that brand of shoe again." He remembered Sophie, wearing the sandals, modeling the dress she had bought for New Year's, the one she never got to wear, the little tight red dress with a 'V' neckline and three rhinestone buttons on one shoulder...

laughing as he whistled at her... the first time she had gone shopping since Rosie had been born, the first tight thing she had put on in months and months. She had pressed her hands against her stomach and made a face at the mirror, but to him she had looked better than ever. He couldn't see the needle, the thread, the patch on George's trousers. "Dammit," he muttered, wiping at his eyes.

"You've never done that, have you? Talked about her like that?" Pauline asked, her voice even and everyday, as if she were asking him if he wanted eggs for breakfast.

"No." He let the jeans fall into his lap and his head into his hands, resting his elbows on the table. "Oh, crap." He had to take deep breaths.

"You should," Pauline said softly. "It'll get easier."

"Will it?" He didn't believe her.

"It's been nearly five years, hasn't it? You should be able to talk about her by now."

"What the hell do you know about it?" he rasped, and immediately regretted it.

"I know a lot about it."

"Shit, I'm sorry, of course you do." His voice still wasn't right. He pushed back his chair suddenly and stood up, dumping the jeans onto the table.

"Chris—"

"Look, I'm sorry." He rubbed his palms against his trousers. "I'm no good at this." He glanced around, fidgeting, wanting to move, to release pent-up energy. He looked at her finally. "How did you *do* that?"

The calm was gone from her face. Worry had replaced it.

Chris wanted to yell and break something, but he hadn't done that in years, and he wasn't going to start again now.

She clutched her mending in both hands, biting her lip. "I didn't do anything. Sit down, please."

"No, I'm just going for a walk." Chris moved to the door, grabbed the knob. He heard her say, "Take a light," but he was already counting backwards. He wrenched open the door and escaped into the dark, trying not to slam it shut behind him.

Chapter 10

Pauline stared at the door after Chris had gone out, surprised at his reaction. He had done a good job of keeping himself in check, but she wondered if in the past he had resorted to violent outbursts. It seemed he had done nothing to try to deal with his grief and anger. He had simply bottled it up, locked it away, tried to ignore it, and it rattled him when it leaked out unexpectedly. Michael must have sensed it, and so sent Chris to her. In his letter, Michael said Chris was a mate, but Chris had denied it. She frowned, sipped at her cider. It seemed Chris had figured that out, and she wondered if he resented it. She knew she could help him, but he had to want it, it had to be his choice. Resentment of Michael could turn into resentment of her, and that would ruin her chance to help him. She wished Michael would be more truthful with people. He always ended up making people feel manipulated, even when he was trying to do the right thing. She went back to her mending.

Less than half an hour later Chris opened the door and stepped in. He closed it behind him, stood there near it, not looking at her. She waited, but he didn't say anything. She broke the silence.

"I'm nearly done. Shall I finish those jeans or do you want to?"

"I will." He came back to his chair at the table. He found the needle and took a stitch. He noticed his cider, took a long drink, then went back to the mending.

"Are you okay?"

"Yeah." Chris took a few stitches. "Why did you do that?"

"I didn't do anything," she said, her hands still. "We were just talking. You started talking about her."

"I didn't want to, but you—"

"I didn't do anything. You wanted to talk about her, or you wouldn't have."

He shook his head, not looking at her, his eyes on the fabric in front of him, his hands still. Pauline watched him, a little ache in her gut. She didn't want to push him too hard, didn't want him to change his mind about staying, but she felt she had to say something.

"I can help you, if you let me."

Chris took a deep breath. He glanced up at her, then back at the jeans, pulling the thread through. Pauline finished the shirt she was working on, folded it slowly, looked over at him. He was sitting with the needle poised, not moving, oblivious to her, focused inward. His face revealed some of the pain he was feeling. She checked the time; they had probably half an hour before the others came home. She waited, not really expecting anything more from him this evening. She thought it would be a few days before he decided what he would do.

He took another deep breath, and went back to stitching, but he hadn't put the neutral mask back on his face. He tied off his thread, snipped it carefully, pushed the scissors back toward her and folded the jeans. He finally caught her eye.

"Why is it so hard?" he asked, his voice low.

She kept her face calm under his stare. "Probably lots of things. I think you've come to see her death as the reason for your life going all to hell. You never had a chance to go on with a normal life after she died, to see that life can go on as normal, does go on as normal. Was there a funeral?"

"No." He looked off into a corner of the room. "They just came and took her away."

"You don't even know where she's buried, do you?"

"No."

"You feel she was taken from you, and you resent that. You never had a place to leave her." His head jerked toward her when she said that.

"I didn't want to leave her," he said through his teeth.

She thought quickly, chose her words carefully.

"A funeral, a burial, can be an important part of the grieving process. It can help you to accept the permanence of what's happened. It can give you a place where you know she is, where you can go to be with her, talk to her if you need to, and a place where, eventually, you can learn to leave her, and go on without her. You never had that. You never went through the normal grieving process. You started wandering, am I right?"

He nodded. "Yeah."

"You were looking for some kind of normalcy, maybe, even though you knew you weren't going to find it. You decided you had to get back to England, that the only happiness you could ever find was the family that had been here."

He glanced at her, looked away again, nodded slightly. "So why can't I make myself go to Bath?"

"You know that's not an automatic fix, right? Even if they are there, it doesn't mean everything will be fine, that you'll suddenly be happy again."

He blew his breath out. "I don't expect happiness. That's gone forever."

"It doesn't have to be," Pauline said.

Chris shook his head dismissively. "I just don't want to go through what I did in London."

"What did you go through?"

He tensed up and clamped his mouth shut.

"Do you mean when you first found out your brother was dead?"

Chris nodded. "I couldn't... I just..." He shook his head, put a hand to his face.

"It's hard, I know. Try."

"I stopped caring. About anything," he said in a monotone. "I did things—that I regret, now."

Pauline watched him. She would have to get him talking, find out what had happened to him, where he had been, what he had done, in the years since his wife's death. She had the whole winter, apparently. Was that long enough?

"You have to deal with your wife's death first, put that behind you, before you'll be able to deal with what you might find in Bath."

Chris stayed still and silent, then opened his mouth as if to speak, but nothing came out. He tried again, and managed this time, his voice barely above a whisper.

"We had a baby. She died too, of course."

"I'm so sorry, Chris," Pauline said, the ache in her stomach deepening.

"That will never go away."

"No, no it won't. You'll always have an empty place. But that doesn't mean you can't find a way to be happy again. You can be happy again, if you let yourself."

The door opened. Grace, Marie, and George all came in.

Chris shot a quick look at her as he grabbed his cider glass. "I really don't see how," he said under his breath, and downed the remaining drink. He stood and gathered up his clothes, the mask back on his face. He left the kitchen, saying "Goodnight," briefly to everyone as he went.

***

George had gone off to help at the next farm over, so Pauline knew she would be able to talk to Chris without interruption while he did the milking. He had been avoiding being alone with her since their talk over the mending the week before, but she was determined to get him talking.

Pauline made sure he heard her as she went into the barn and leaned with her arms on top of the partition.

"I've only just started," Chris said without stopping, his cheek pressed against the cow.

"I know. You had another nightmare last night."

The rhythm of his milking slowed. "I'm sorry if I woke you."

"It's all right, I've told you. What was it about?"

He stopped milking altogether, then started up again. "London."

"Are they always about London?"

He made noise in his throat, shook his head. "God, no. London is new on my play list. I've a whole collection of golden oldies in heavy rotation."

She thought it a good sign that he could make a joke about it, even if it didn't exactly sound like a joke.

"Do you interpret dreams?" Chris asked her.

"There're a lot of theories about dreams. I never made a study of it, but I know a bit about it."

"Nothing mysterious about my dreams. Completely straightforward."

"You talk in your sleep, you know," Pauline said.

Another pause. "So I've been told."

"I'm glad you don't use that sort of language when you're awake."

"Ah, sorry," Chris said. "I've, um, been among some rough types. It's easy to slip into."

"Who is Beryl?" she asked next.

His rhythm faltered, then evened out. "How long were you listening at my door?"

"Only for a moment. You sounded so distraught. I got up to check on you."

"It's just dreams. They come and go. Don't worry about it, or me."

Pauline pulled a face at the back of his stubborn head. He was good at deflecting, but she was confident she could get him talking, if not today, then soon.

"So who is Beryl?" she asked again, trying to steer him back.

The cow shifted, swished her tail, jerked her head.

"Just someone I met in London."

"What happened to her?"

"Nothing."

"It didn't sound like that." Pauline wondered if she was pushing too hard. Chris stopped milking, his hands still, his whole body tense, his forehead against the flank of the cow. "Was she one of the good people?" she tried.

"What?"

"You said that you could still find good people, even in London. Was she one of those?"

Chris took a deep breath. "Yes." He began to pull on the teats again.

"What happened?" Pauline waited, with only the sound of the milk hissing into the bucket. "Okay, then tell me about the 'rough types'."

Chris finished the cow. He stood up and set the bucket outside the stall door on the floor, and picked up the basket with the cleaning rags. He had to walk around Pauline to get to the next stall. He didn't look at her, settled himself on the stool and started cleaning the second cow's udder. Pauline moved a few steps so she had her arms on the wall of stall he'd gone into.

"Before I got to Britain I worked for a year on the ship docks in Canada, loading ships. Then I was on a ship for a month or so before we finally docked. Rough types on ships. And in Portsmouth, of course, at the Distribution Center, more rough types."

"And London—that was before Portsmouth, wasn't it?" Pauline asked, aware that he had deliberately skipped over it.

Chris finished cleaning the cow, put aside the basket and positioned the bucket. "Yes. I told you already, it's not a nice place." He turned and looked up at her. "You can stop asking about London now."

"Okay. Tell me about one of your other dreams," she said as he got himself comfortable on the stool and started milking.

He was quiet for so long she almost gave up. She thought he might finish this cow as well without saying anything. Then he spoke.

"I'm on my patio, back home, looking in the glass doors. Sophie is inside. She's searching for something. She opens all the closet doors, checks behind the furniture and drapes, under the beds. I can follow her from room to room, which makes no sense, but that's the way it always is. I can follow her, but she can't hear me. I'm trying to get in, calling out to her, but she never hears. I can't get the door open. She gets more and more frantic. And so do I. At the end, she's crying." He grunted, then continued the milking.

Pauline took a breath, a vivid image in her head. "Yeah, pretty straightforward," she said.

"That's the oldest one," Chris said. "I've had that one right from the start. It's always the same. Never changes. Some of the others, well." He finished the cow, stripping the last drops of milk from her, and stood up. "So now I've told you, I'll stop having that dream?"

"You know it's not that easy." She caught his eye. "But it's a start."

"Great," he said, his face tight. He handed her the bucket, glanced at the other one on the floor, then back at her.

"I'll come back for the others when you're done," she said, picking up the second bucket. She looked back at him from the barn door; he was still standing there, staring at the wall, biting his lip.

Later, he sought her out where she was hanging laundry. He paced, arms crossed.

"What is it?" Pauline asked.

"How is this going to work? Are you going to ambush me like that every day or so?"

"I didn't mean to ambush you. I'm sorry. I knew you'd be alone, so I took the opportunity. How would you like it to work?"

Chris paced some more, and Pauline went back to hanging the clothes. She watched him. His expression bordered on angry.

"Cooper had this all planned, didn't he? Did he tell you, in that letter?"

"He mentioned your nightmares, yes. His intentions were good, Chris. Surely you can see that."

Chris huffed and stopped with his back to her. "I need to know how this is going to work."

"Okay. Do you want to set a certain time? Like an appointment?"

"That seems silly."

"Why? That's the way we would have done it before. My office would be the place for opening up, for exploring things that make you uncomfortable."

"*This* makes me uncomfortable," Chris said. "Anyway, you don't have an office now, do you?"

"There's Dad's study, but it's so full of stuff we'd have a hard time squeezing in."

"No," Chris said, and started pacing again.

"Well, then we'll just have to find a couple times a week when we can talk, wherever that happens to be."

"Sure, okay."

"There have to be some rules." Pauline took a step closer to him and crossed her own arms. Chris turned to

119

look at her. The anger had gone, but he narrowed his eyes.

"What rules?"

"This will be pointless unless you want to. You have to want to. Do you?"

He blinked a few times. "Yes."

"Good. You have to trust me."

Chris glanced away, then back. "Okay."

"Everything we discuss will be totally confidential."

He nodded. "I know."

"It won't be easy sometimes. I'll push you if I have to."

Chris swallowed, shifted his feet. "Okay."

"My fees are outrageous," she said, and when Chris jerked his head up in surprise, she grinned at him.

"I've got a fat bank account back in the States," Chris said, his mouth twitching. "It's all yours."

Pauline stuck out her hand. "Shake on it."

He raised his hand up, gripped hers, held on for longer than she would have expected. "Thank you," he whispered.

***

A few days later they met in the garage, just after lunch, wearing coats against the autumn chill.

Pauline patted a silver Polo hemmed in by assorted junk, and coated with a layer of dust.

"My one big purchase in life," she said, with a sigh. "Odd, isn't it? And here it sits. I wonder if it will ever run again."

"Petrol rations go up a bit every year, don't they?"

"Enough to run the tractor. Not enough for a car. George's is up on blocks out behind with a tarp over it. Amazing what we took for granted." She wiped her dusty hand on her thigh.

Chris grunted, and perched on the edge of an old wooden crate, hunched up tight, fidgeting. "Okay, here we are. Have at it."

Pauline sat on the stool by the workbench. "What do you mean?"

"Ask me questions, or something. I don't know what you want."

"I don't want anything. What do you want?"

"I don't know. To be... normal."

"There is no 'normal.' Everyone is different."

"That's a standard 'feel good' line, isn't it?"

"Where do you want to start?"

"I don't know."

"At the beginning?"

"You mean when—? Um, no. Not that."

"Okay, we'll work up to that."

"Fine."

"You've never had any therapy at all, for anything?"

"No. Well, maybe. Yeah, some, maybe."

"Maybe? Tell me about that."

"Brother Luke tried. But I didn't."

"Who's Brother Luke?"

"He was a monk, at the monastery of St Crispin in Wheeling, New York. It was more of a commune, actually, by the time I got there. But I fit right in." He ran a hand through his hair.

"When did you get there?"

"Um, I don't know. It was summer. 2000? No, 2001."

"So you'd been wandering around for some time."

Chris nodded.

"And you chose to join a monastery?"

"Commune, and I didn't choose to join, I just ended up there."

"How?"

Chris hesitated, fidgeted on the crate.

"I got jumped on the road," he said, eyebrows drawn together.

"You'll have to explain a bit more."

"Yeah, okay. I was heading north, toward Canada. I thought I might be able to get a ship there, since I had a British passport. I was traveling with another bloke, Stew. We'd met up by accident. He was a good sort, so we decided to go on together. We were on a road, not paying attention, and a group jumped us." Chris stopped and put his head down into his hands.

"Go on," Pauline said.

"Stew had a gun, a pistol—he'd been in the military—and I thought they would shoot us, but they decided not to waste the bullets. So they beat us. They started with Stew. Beat him with a baseball bat." Chris's voice had gone monotone. "They broke his legs. They laughed while they did it." He took a ragged breath. "I told myself I didn't care if they killed me. I was tired of walking, starving, with no end in sight. Once they beat him senseless, and he wasn't moving anymore, they started on me."

122

Pauline didn't trust her voice to speak. She hid her hand in her lap as she dug her fingernails into her palm and concentrated on keeping a calm face.

"I don't remember much. I guess I tried to deflect the first blow. They broke my arm. They got me good in the head, too. I had a hell of a concussion."

"How did you get away?" Pauline managed.

"Some lorries drove up, just in time. A team from the monastery. They chased off the gang. They had medics with them. They did what they could, but it was too late for Stew. They took me with them. They said I was lucky."

Chris shook his head and paused.

"So, I woke up in their infirmary. Brother Luke took care of me. He had some training in counseling. He tried to help. He pushed religion, though, and that made me resistant. I was pretty angry at God."

"Were you religious, before?"

"No, not really. Mum took us to church when we were kids. It was always in the back of my mind, but not a big part of my life."

"Are you still angry at God?"

Chris thought, chewing on his lip, then looked up. "When I think about it, yes."

Pauline nodded. "Do you think talking with Brother Luke helped at all?"

"I suppose, a bit. He taught me one thing that helps with staying calm."

"What's that?"

"Counting backward."

Pauline raised her eyebrows.

"It's more than that, but that's the main thing. Focusing on that, instead of what's got me angry, or—" He put his head down.

"Hurting?"

"Yes."

"You did that the night we were mending."

Chris nodded.

"I thought you might break something. You were awfully wound up."

He looked up at her.

"You used to, didn't you?" Pauline said. "Break things? Get violent?"

"How did you know?"

"It's not so uncommon."

"Huh."

"Not a good thing, though."

"No."

"How often do you do that? Count backwards?"

Chris shrugged. "Just that once, here. A fair bit before, in other places."

"Like Portsmouth?"

"I was just—well, numb, in Portsmouth."

"Because of what happened in London?"

"Yes. Let's not talk about that, yet."

"Okay, back to the monastery. How long did you stay?"

"Year and a half, about. No, maybe more like two years."

"Doing what?"

"Cows, mostly. I tried all sorts of jobs, but I liked the cows. Not sure why."

Pauline smiled. "That's where you learned to milk."

"Yes."

"You must have made some friends there, besides Brother Luke."

Chris scrunched up his face and shifted on the crate. "At the beginning, yes."

"Tell me."

"Evan. He was driving the lorry that found me. He was in quarantine while I was in the infirmary. We talked. He'd lost his wife." Chris flexed his shoulders and kept his head down. "He stayed on a few months, then went back out with the Outside Teams."

"So you didn't see him much after that?"

"I never saw him again. His team never came back. We never knew what happened to them."

Pauline took a deep breath. "I'm sorry, Chris."

Chris shrugged.

"So you don't get close to people anymore."

"I try not to."

"Who else did you get close to?"

Chris shot her a wary look. "Can I stand up? Move around?"

"Of course. Whatever you want."

He stood up with clenched fists and paced in a small area.

"Did you get close to someone else at the monastery?"

"No, not really."

"Did you get close to Beryl in London?"

He jerked, drew in a breath.

"Not a huge deduction, Chris."

He turned his back and crossed his arms. "Can we be done, now?"

"We've hardly started."

"I wouldn't say that."

"We won't get anywhere at this rate."

"Tomorrow, then. I'm feeling the need to count."

"Okay, just one more thing," Pauline said. "Tell me something about Sophie."

A shudder ran through Chris. He said nothing.

"How did you meet?"

"On an island."

"Tell me a little more."

"It was early spring, March. An island off the coast of Maine. Cold, windy. Usually people only go there in the summer. We'd both gone to get away and be alone. Neither of us knew the other would be there. I was staying at a friend's cottage, she was staying at her sister's. Every evening we watched the sunset together." He wiped at his eyes.

Pauline waited a moment. "I think that went well. Do you?"

"Oh, yeah, it was great. I'm looking forward to next time."

Chapter 11

"Someone's been busy," Chris said, eyeing the new seating in the garage.

"I moved a few things around to make it a little more comfortable. It'll be too cold out here, soon, though. I've been cleaning up Dad's study." Pauline took a seat in a padded desk chair.

"I like the décor." Chris settled himself onto a stuffed chair covered in an old sheet with orange and yellow flowers.

"It's cheerful, don't you think?"

"Was your office cheerful?"

"Hm, neutral, actually."

Chris nodded and shifted, not looking at her.

"Is there anything you want to talk about today?"

"I told you, I'm no good at this."

"Do you want me to ask you questions?"

He chewed on the end of one finger. "I don't know."

"Okay. Tell me about your family in Bath, then."

"They're probably dead, you know."

"Stop that. Do you have more brothers, besides the one in London?"

"One more. Jon. The youngest. He was always reckless, always got in more trouble than Kevin and me. He was the most outgoing. People liked him."

"Are you close?"

"We were, as much as possible, living on different sides of the ocean."

"What about your parents?"

"My Mum. But she wasn't well, back—when it all started. She was frail, needed a lot of help. So I don't think her chances were very good."

"You're so sure there's nothing for you in Bath?"

"If I was sure everyone was fine, I wouldn't be here, would I?"

"Who else?"

"Friends. Brian and Fiona, and their two boys. Brian was my partner, in the band."

"Oh, right. Just him? I thought there were more."

"Yes, Stan was bass, Erik the drummer. The record company always minimized their roles, and that was fine with them. Erik moved to France, I think, a few years after the band broke up. Stan went off to Manchester, searching for new talent with his brother."

"Tell me more about Brian."

Chris gave a sigh and sat looking off into the distance, before he answered.

"We'd been mates since we were eleven. We had a lot in common, but were different in other ways. But we clicked, y'know?"

"How did you meet?"

"I had to transfer schools," Chris said. "We had some classes together. He always told everyone that he ran off some bullies who were about to beat me up, but I don't remember that."

"Did you get bullied?"

"Doesn't everyone, a bit? Sure, I got my fair share. They had reason enough."

"What reason?"

"I was the new kid. I had been a rich kid, but not anymore."

"What do you mean?"

128

"My Dad was an executive with a big company. He was killed, in a car crash, when I was ten. We'd been quite well-off, but he'd not been careful with the money, and left a lot of debt. By the time it all settled out, we hadn't much left. We had to sell our house, move to a flat. Mum had to get a job, of course. No more fancy schools. We were tossed into the pond with the rest of the little fish. That's what Dad used to say, that we didn't have to swim with the little fish, we could swim with the big fish. He was a hell of a snob, I suppose, but I didn't see it that way then. We were happy, until he died."

"I'm sorry," Pauline said.

Chris didn't take any notice. "So suddenly I'm one of the little fish, and missing my Dad. Brian was a good kid; we got on well, got to be mates, and stayed that way, as we got older. Brian was the real musician. I learned to play so I could be in the band, but I liked it, and I had a knack for it. We had all sorts of bands as teenagers, but none of them ever really worked out. But it was always the other blokes who quit, or got sacked. The two of us, we were mates. Some people thought— well, we had a hard time getting dates. It took us awhile to figure it out." He shook his head, thinking about it. "I guess we were a bit naïve. Brian's brother finally sat us down and explained it. God, I remember that. We made it our mission to get girls, after that." He made a little noise; anyone else might have chuckled. He twisted his mouth in a way that didn't look quite like a smile.

"And did you? Get the girls?"

"Yeah, you could say we did. It only took once, and then word got around." He shrugged, looked

129

embarrassed. "But that didn't last too long. I met Laura."

"First love?"

"I thought it was love, anyway. For a time."

"How old were you?" she asked.

"Um, nineteen, I guess."

"That's not so young, for a first love."

"I told you: we had a hard time getting dates. Anyway, it was my twentieth birthday party where we met Stan and Erik. Stan's older brother was in the music business, had a recording studio. Brian got us all together, we played together a bit, and it seemed to work. We recorded a few demos, and got lucky. By the time I turned twenty-one we had a number one single and another moving up the charts. We moved in together to celebrate—Laura and me—and because Brian had married his girl, Fiona. But we weren't quite ready. We set a date, then kept pushing it back." He stared at the floor. "In a few years I was rich again, and didn't make the same mistakes my father had. I hired a good accountant, made good investments..." He trailed off.

"Did you get married, then?"

"No." He looked up at her, then away. "It wasn't really love. We found that out. Went our separate ways."

"Well, it's good to find that out before you marry."

"Fewer legal issues, anyway. I think she'd already met someone else, but she was nice enough to be discreet about it for a few months. The last I heard, she and her husband still lived in Bath. I don't plan to look her up."

Pauline waited while Chris stared at the door handle of the Polo. "That's not so much about Brian," she said.

Chris glanced up at her again. "What do you want to know?"

"I don't know. You seemed to skip over him. You said you were mates, but you didn't have much else to say about him."

Chris stared at her, his face a mask.

"We had a falling out," he said. "I quit the band and moved to New York. I never spoke to him again."

Pauline stared back in surprise. "Oh," she managed. First his father, then Brian, then Sophie, and the rest of them over the years. *No wonder.*

Chris turned his face from her, but she could see that his jaw was set.

"What did you fight about?"

"Money, of course. Isn't it always money? We were in danger of losing our contract, and he was dicking around and wouldn't let them have anything. I told him we had to give them an album quick, or they'd dump us, but he didn't give a damn. He said I only cared about the money, not the music. He said I'd only got that far because of him. He said I wouldn't be anything if it weren't for him."

Chris stopped and inhaled, stared at the ground. His mask had dropped away while he was talking, and Pauline saw again the pain she had seen the night they were mending. Then he shook it off. "Yeah, well, maybe it was more than just money. We weren't the same kids anymore. He'd grown into a serious musician, while for me, it was a job. It *was* about the money. I wanted what I could get, so I didn't end up

131

poor again. I didn't have a back-up plan. We fell into it so young. I knew bands like ours didn't last. Hot, then cold. So yes, I pushed Brian to be less than what he could have been, for the money. We managed to make a second album to suit the label, but the whole process did us in. We just couldn't deal with each other anymore. And as soon as the first round of publicity ended I quit the band. I thought—"

"What did you think?"

"I don't know. I thought if I quit the band, if we didn't have that to fight over, then maybe we could still have some sort of friendship. But Brian took it as a personal attack, I suppose. Stan and Erik took off too, of course, and that was the end of that. The label gave us hell, but we'd fulfilled our contract, so there was nothing they could do." He shook his head. "It was like a divorce. From Brian. There was a lot of joint stuff, you know, with the band. We had a studio, rights, all that stuff. We had to split it all. Brian made it hard." He shook his head again, looked up at her. "We'd been mates for so long. And for Brian to be like that, well."

"You've talked about this before, haven't you?"

"Yeah, with Fiona, Brian's wife. We kept in touch. I used to visit her when I went back to Bath, her and Ian, their son. He was a real cutie. I used to take him on little outings, to the zoo, or just out for ice cream, but Brian put a stop to that." His voice got hard at the end.

"Did you talk about it with Sophie?"

"Sure, of course. She knew all about it. She got the worst of it. I used to rant at her. I'd call him all sorts of horrible names. I couldn't say that to Fiona, of course, so Sophie got the worst of it. I really thought I hated him, for awhile."

"But—?"

"Well, I didn't hate him, of course. If I had it wouldn't have hurt so much, would it? See? I'm not a lost cause."

"I never see anyone as a lost cause, Chris. Certainly not you," she said. "It sounds like you had two kind, intelligent women to help you through all that."

"Yeah," he said softly.

"How do you feel about Brian now?"

Chris looked up at her sharply, his eyebrows together, but did not answer.

"Do you still think about him much?"

"Well, he's in a couple of my dreams, so I suppose I do."

"What are the dreams like?"

"He's angry, and usually there's something between us, like glass, so I can't hear what he's saying."

"What do you think he might be saying?"

"I don't know."

"What do you want to say to him?" Pauline persisted.

Chris seemed to struggle for words. "He's probably dead."

"No, that's not what I asked. If he's not dead, what do you want to say to him?"

Chris stared at her for a long time, eyes narrowed, biting his lip, gripping handfuls of the flowered sheet. His voice came out low when he spoke.

"I want to tell him how much it hurt me."

"Do you? Don't you think he knows that already?"

"I want to say it," he insisted. "I want to say it to him, so I know he knows."

"Do you think that will make you feel better?"

"No."

"Do you think it will hurt him? Is that what you want to do? Hurt him back like he hurt you?" Pauline paused, and when Chris remained silent she went on, pushing now. "You've come this far, across the ocean, struggled so long, so you could find him, and hurt him back?"

Chris was holding himself still, not looking at her. "I can't do this."

"Yes, you can. You need to," Pauline insisted. "Tell me."

"He's probably dead."

"Do you want him to be dead?"

"No!" he snapped. "Of course not! Why would I want that?"

"So it would all be over, and you wouldn't have to deal with it when you go to Bath," she said, keeping a reasonable tone.

"No. God, no," he rasped, shaking his head. "I used to wish he had died, back before, when I was still so angry. I used to think it would have been easier to lose a friend that way. Then it happened, the crash, the plague, and everyone started dying, and I found out it wasn't easier. God, it was so much worse." He crossed his arms tightly and shook. "Everyone thought I hated him, but I didn't. I want to tell him—tell him that I don't hate him. But if he's dead, I'll never have a chance to tell him that." He choked, swallowed.

"You want to fix it with him," Pauline said gently.

Chris nodded. "I tried, after a few years, after talking with Sophie and Fiona. But he ignored everything, never answered. Shit. Maybe I'm just being stupid."

"No, absolutely not stupid," Pauline said, and Chris managed a quick look at her, his eyes wet, his jaw clenched. "He's your one piece of unfinished business. As much as it hurt to lose Sophie, you hadn't left anything unsaid to her, had you?"

Chris shook his head, then let it drop into his hands.

"And your brother in London, more grief, more loss, but you were on good terms, so no regrets there, right?"

Chris wiped at his eyes. "You don't need to go on."

"You've convinced yourself that Brian will be dead, and you won't be able to fix it."

"When I got to London, after so long, I was so sure, *so sure,* that I'd find something at Kevin's flat. A note, a clue, telling me he'd gone to Bath. I knew he'd be fine. He was the careful one. He always made plans. I'd imagined a pristine note tacked on the door: 'We're fine. Gone to Bath. See you soon. Kevin.'" Chris took a deep breath, and went on. "And instead I found the government marks—have you ever seen those? Big red 'X' for the plague, then the number of bodies, and a 'D' for 'deceased.'"

Pauline gave a shake of her head as a shiver went through her.

"He'd been living with his girlfriend and her daughter for almost two years. I knew he'd do everything he could to keep them safe. I *knew* he'd get them out of London. But I was deluding myself. I'd imagined a happy homecoming, with everyone safe and well. And instead I found my brother's death notice painted on his door by a stranger: '3D.' That was it. Someone came in and dragged their bodies out to a truck and dumped them in some mass grave. Or incinerator. Who knows? I don't know. I'll never know." Chris sat hunched over in the chair, breathing hard. Pauline waited. "You don't know what that's like."

"No, you're right, I don't."

"Another part of me, dead. More of me is dead than alive. That's how I feel. I switch off and run on autopilot. Don't think, don't feel. Just coast. Until something finally kills me and I'm done."

"I don't believe that," Pauline whispered.

"Oh, really, *Doctor*? Tell me how I feel."

Pauline ignored the hostility. "You have a lot of grief, Chris. I know that, I understand that. You've let it fill you up until you haven't got room for anything else. You've gathered all this anguish around you, and you let it control you. You hide behind it. You've come to think, for some reason, that it's easier to keep it than to let it go. Well, I'm telling you now: you're wrong. You can find a way to let it go and move on without it."

Chris snorted and didn't answer her or look at her.

"You just said it yourself. You said you want to fix it with Brian. You *want* to leave it behind. You just haven't figured out how."

Chris gripped his head with his hands.

"Have you ever tried to kill yourself?" Pauline asked him.

"When Sophie died, I had a big bag of pills. All the pills in the house. But I couldn't take them. I should have."

"You don't think there could be any reason you've kept going this long, except that you never got around to ending your life?"

Chris lifted his head and eyed her. "Do you mean God has a purpose for me? Brother Luke tried that crap on me. It's bullshit."

"No. I mean the fact that you didn't sit down and give up. You've kept going, overcoming huge obstacles, for years. With one goal: get to Bath. Find out. You haven't given up, ever. Look how far you've come. That was *you*, not God. That wasn't autopilot. That was determination."

Chris put his head down into his hands again and sat shaking. Pauline waited, her own stomach in a knot.

After long minutes, Chris sniffed and wiped at his eyes again. "I'm sorry I was rude."

"I don't take it personally. I'd much rather you get it out, in whatever way it comes, than to keep it all locked up like you've been doing. I know you'll be your usual cheerful, polite self by teatime."

He stared at her with red-rimmed eyes. "Is this how it's supposed to work, then? I can't say I'm keen on it."

"There's no 'supposed to.' Whatever works. Yes, usually it's very emotional. I told you it would be hard."

"Like digging graves."

Pauline caught her breath. "Yes. Now, tell me something about Sophie."

Chris closed his eyes. "She loved cats, but she was allergic, so we never got one. We were going to get a puppy when the baby was older." He looked over at her. "There, kittens and puppies to end with." He put his hands up and wiggled his fingers. "Cute and fuzzy and happy."

Pauline nodded. "Okay." She left him sitting in the chair and went out of the garage, digging in her pocket for a handkerchief.

Chapter 12

A cold November wind chilled Chris's fingers and the tip of his nose. It was getting too cold for fishing. Wes sat huddled in a worn plaid coat with the collar pulled up around his ears.

"Shouldn't you be in school today?"

Wes scowled. "I hate school."

"Huh," Chris said. No big surprise. He would have given the same answer at Wes's age. "Why?"

"It's stupid."

"Yeah, I guess I thought school was stupid when I was your age. But once I grew up, I was glad they'd made me go. It's important, even if you don't think so now."

"Who made you go?"

"Well, my mum, of course. Plus it was the law. All kids had to go. It'll go back to that soon, I expect."

Wes looked incredulous. "The law?"

"Of course. It's very important to get an education."

"What for? I don't need to read stupid stories if I'm going to have a farm."

"You do need reading, and math, if you want to run a farm. Ask George, he'll tell you."

Wes watched him, chewing on his lip.

"Do you think the work is too hard?" Chris asked.

"Nar," Wes said, with a disgusted look. "It's easy, mostly."

"What about your teacher?"

"Ms. Barnes? She doesn't like me."

"What makes you say that?"

"She's always telling me I'm not doing things right. She doesn't let me get out of my seat *at all*, she won't let me eat except at lunchtime, and sometimes she makes me sit with the little kids and read stupid stories. She doesn't like me. She's mean."

"How is she mean?"

"I just told you."

"Well, teachers have to have rules that are the same for everyone."

"I'd rather go fishing."

"Well, sure, but sometimes we have to do things we don't want to do."

Wes hunched his shoulders and stared at the water.

Chris tried another tack. "What about the other kids? Don't you have friends at school?"

Wes's face darkened. "None of them like me either."

"What makes you think they don't like you?"

"They make fun of me."

Chris thought back to his own schooldays. No matter what went on in the world, school would always be the same.

"Have you tried to make friends with them?"

Wes reeled in his line and stood, ignoring Chris's question. He picked his way downstream to find a new spot to cast.

They caught no fish.

"I guess it's too late now," Wes said as they trudged across the field toward the house. "No more fishing 'til spring."

"Back in the States, in New York, people used to go ice fishing on the lakes in the middle of winter."

"The States? I thought you were from Portsmouth."

Chris explained, and Wes's mouth opened, and Chris figured his status with Wes had just gone up a notch. "I never went myself. And I'm pretty sure it has to be a deep lake, and not a shallow river, like we have here."

Wes nodded thoughtfully. Chris pictured the boy falling through thin ice with no one around to rescue him.

"You have to be really sure the ice is strong enough. I mean, it has to be really cold for a long time. I'm not sure it gets cold enough here for the ice to get strong enough."

"Probably not," Wes agreed.

"And no one ever goes ice fishing alone."

Wes quirked an eyebrow at him.

Later, Chris found Pauline in the kitchen, kneading bread dough.

"Do you think you might have some books that Wes would like? Adventure stories, or something like that?" he asked.

"Did he ask you for books? That doesn't sound like the Wes I know."

"No, but he said something about 'stupid stories' twice. I thought maybe something different than he gets at school would get him interested."

Pauline folded the dough over and over. "Hm, no, I can't think of anything we might have. Most of Dad's books are textbooks or history or heavy literature. Mum and Marie have collected a fair number of novels, but I hardly think they'd interest Wes."

"Is there a library in town?"

"No. We always had to go to Petersfield for a library, and I doubt it's still open. You might find some

141

books in the market, though. The school should have a library of sorts."

Chris nodded, leaning against the sink. Pauline lifted the dough into a bowl and covered it with a cloth.

"Is he showing some interest in school?" she asked. "He's a bright little chap. I should think he'd like school, but it's impossible to get him to go every day."

"No. He says it's stupid. He also said most of the work was easy."

"He gets all grumbly whenever I try to push it. He admires you, though. You might be able to get him to go."

"He said the other kids make fun of him."

Pauline frowned. "It might be his clothes. He wears the oddest assortment, sometimes. And he's always ready to scrap with the other kids. I've seen him in action. He brings it on himself."

"Well, I don't want him to get grumbly with me," Chris said. "I'm not going to push him just yet. What about his teacher, Ms. Barnes? He says she doesn't like him."

"Ms. Barnes? She's a dear." The corner of Pauline's mouth turned up. "All the kids love her."

"All but one," Chris said. He pushed away from the sink and went back outside.

***

Pauline was clearing the supper dishes when the kitchen door opened and George came in.

142

"Sorry I'm late. I had a pint with the blokes from McGovern's."

"Really? The old man?"

"No, his son is taking over. The old man didn't even come this year. It was his son and a partner. Nice chaps. Seem to know what they're doing. Fair." He shrugged out of his coat and hung it on a hook. "Feed me, please," he said, kissing Marie as she stood up from the table. He stopped to warm his hands by the stove.

"So, how did it go?" Grace asked.

"I got an excellent price for the hogs," he said.

"That's wonderful," Grace said.

George pulled an envelope from his pocket and handed it to Chris as he sat down at his place.

"What's this?" Chris asked. The envelope had an address scratched out on the front, and felt too lumpy to be a letter.

"Your wages."

"No, you don't need to—"

"You've earned it. You've earned more, actually, but that's what I can afford to pay you." George reached for a baked potato.

"But I'm paying you back—"

"Oh, rubbish. You paid that debt the first month you were here."

Chris started to protest some more, but Grace stopped him.

"Take the money, dear. You wouldn't have worked for free before, would you?"

"I—um, thank you."

"I signed us up to go into Petersfield day after tomorrow," Pauline said.

"Good, I'll do up a list," Marie said.

143

"How did Mr. Thorn do with his honey, this year?" Grace asked George, and the conversation went on around Chris, the question of his wages over and done. Chris sat thinking. He had coupons, and he had money, now.

"How does one sign up to go into Petersfield?" he asked during a lull.

"There's a sheet at the Post Office," Pauline said. "Mr. Hutchins has a passenger van. He'll go any day if he has five or six people signed up. It'll cost you a quid. Our trip is full."

"You can have my seat if you want to go," Grace said.

"No, it's not urgent," Chris said to Grace. "You go with Pauline. I thought I might take Wes to the market."

"Have you asked him?" Pauline said, her eyebrows drawn together. "He doesn't like to. He only goes for his blood tests."

"I was hoping to find him some clothes that fit."

"You'd best be sneaky about it, then," George advised. "He'll run off if he thinks you're trying to take care of him."

"Have you any coupons?" Grace asked. "I'll contribute to that project, if you can pull it off."

"I have some, but more would be good, if you can spare them."

When he went to bed that night Chris had a good supply of clothing coupons tucked into the envelope with the money George had paid him.

***

It turned out all Chris had to do was ask Wes if he wanted to go into Petersfield.

"With you?"

"Yeah."

Wes narrowed his eyes. "What for?"

"Just to check out the market. Everyone else has gone in today. Shall I sign us up?"

"I don't have a quid."

"I have. No worries."

"Okay."

Two days later they shared the back seat in the passenger van. Two older couples took the other seats. Pauline had loaned Chris two rucksacks, and Grace sent along two meat pies and a bottle of water. The van passed through a few small towns and some open country, and pulled into Petersfield after less than an hour.

"Stick with me, okay?" Chris said. "It's my first time here. I don't know where everything is yet. I had to ask Pauline for directions." He headed north out of the square with Wes beside him.

"Isn't the market that way?"

"I need a few things at the Distribution Center first."

"Then are we going to the market?"

"Yeah, sure."

The Petersfield Distribution Center was half the size of the one in Portsmouth. Chris led Wes a roundabout route through the boys' and teen clothes to get to the men's section. Wes lagged behind, scrutinizing the racks of jeans and jackets. He stopped in front of a display of shoes. He scowled, shoved his hands in his pockets, and followed Chris.

Wes slouched nearby while Chris made a show of searching the underwear bins. He then picked out several pairs of socks, and perused the jumpers until he figured Wes was about at the breaking point.

"Well, I guess I have what I need," he said. Wes heaved an exaggerated sigh of relief. Chris took him back past the shoe rack. Wes slowed. "Do you need new shoes, Wes?"

Wes put his head down. "I don't have any coupons."

"I've got some extra." Chris fished them out of his pocket.

Wes jerked his head up. He shifted his eyes from the envelope to Chris's face, and back to the envelope.

"Go ahead, pick a pair, if you want."

"I don't know what size."

"Take off one of your shoes."

The sole of Wes's shoe was worn down to nearly nothing at the back of the heel and coming loose in the front. Chris showed him where the size was printed on the inside of the tongue, then directed him to the shoes one size bigger. Wes tried on three pairs before he decided. He clutched the shoes to his chest and beamed.

"What else?" Chris asked him.

"Um, jeans?"

Chris whipped out a tape measure he'd borrowed from Marie. "Sure, let's do it."

They spent an hour selecting clothes for Wes. Jeans, shirts, underwear, and a nearly-new winter jacket with big pockets. Chris was glad he'd collected extra coupons. Wes would smile, then glance at Chris with eyebrows drawn together, as if he simply could not believe his good fortune.

"Haven't you ever been shopping for clothes before?" Chris asked him.

Wes shook his head. "People just bring stuff. Mostly it doesn't fit."

"I'd noticed," Chris said. "From now on, if you need new clothes, tell someone. Pauline or George, or me. Okay?"

Wes nodded.

They bundled most of the clothes into their rucksacks. Wes put on his new shoes and jacket and strutted out the door with a big grin. Chris led him off to try the next part of his plan.

It took a bit of searching, but Chris found the book stall eventually.

"Hang on," he called out to Wes. The boy turned, saw the stall, and frowned.

"It's just stupid books," he said.

"What have you got for someone his age?" Chris asked the proprietor. The man took them around the side and pointed out some boxes on the ground. Chris squatted down and began pulling out books, looking for something Wes might find exciting, pirates or soldiers or the like. Wes stood with his arms crossed, his scowl back.

"This looks good," Chris said, "and this." He tried to hand the books to Wes, but the boy took a step away and refused to put his hand out. Chris made Wes wait while he took his time with the books. He picked out one he was pretty sure most boys would find exciting, and paid for it. He put it in his own pack while Wes watched. At another booth he bought a spiral notebook and two pencils, one of which had never been sharpened.

"Anything else?" he asked Wes.

Wes eyed him warily, and shook his head.

"You hungry?"

Wes kept quiet while Chris got them fish and chips. He sat on bench next to Chris and ate the food without a word. He licked his fingers and then rubbed them on his trousers.

"Are you gonna make me go to school?" he asked eventually, studying the pavement.

"No, I'm not going to make you, but I really wish you would," Chris said. "Things are changing, Wes. Someday it's going to be more like it used to be, and you might not want to be a farmer anymore. You might want a different job. You'll need to know how to read, how to do math."

"Can we shop some more?" Wes asked, getting up and shouldering his pack.

Wes led off through the market, and apparently knew exactly where he was going. He passed up food stalls and house wares, clothing, baskets, and tools. He stopped to pet some puppies in an open-topped cage, but moved on as soon as the woman selling them tried to talk to him. He stopped at a stall full of crates of machine parts, and began to search the boxes. Chris stood back and watched.

"Here," Wes said after a few minutes, holding up a small wheel on an axel. He brought it to Chris. "Harry needs one of these for a cart he's building. If you buy it for a couple of quid, you can trade it to him."

"Trade it for what?"

"For beer, of course. At the pub." Wes spoke as if Chris was being dense.

"How do you know he needs it?"

"The cart's been sitting in his back garden for months. I was asking him about it just yesterday."

"Why can't you just tell him it's here and he can buy it?"

Wes put one hand on his hip. "You buy it for two, and trade it for a fiver's worth of beer."

Amused, Chris took the wheel from Wes and looked it over. "It says it costs four pounds," he pointed out.

"Bargain for it."

"All right." Chris grinned and pulled two pound coins from his pocket. He held them out to Wes. "Do it." He saw a flash of uncertainty in the boy's face, but Wes grabbed the wheel and the money and marched up to the proprietor of the stall. Chris ambled close enough to hear.

"I'll give you a quid," Wes said to the man, ducking his head and sounding timid.

"Now then, old chap, this 'ere wheel is four."

"I haven't got four. I'll give you one."

"Nar, can't take one. I'll take three."

"Haven't got three, neither." At this point Wes lifted his hand and gazed sadly at the two coins in this palm. "I gots two, is it," he said, and cocked his head at the man. His back was to Chris, but Chris could imagine the pathetic expression on Wes's face.

"Give me the two, then, and off with you," the man said with a frown.

"Thank you, sir," Wes said. He flashed a grin at Chris, and headed out of the stall.

Chris caught up with him two booths down. "That was clever."

Wes handed him the wheel. "Can I have another quid?"

"Another one? Do you think I'm made of money?"

"I'll double it for you."

"Where did you learn this?"

"I watch people. No one ever let me have any money before. Pauline and Marie and Mrs. Anderson all grumble about the prices, but they never try to bargain. I see other people bargaining. Even George won't bargain. Other people do. Why not me? Why not you?"

Chris handed him another pound and held the wheel for him.

This time Wes went into a house wares booth. He rummaged among some utensils and came up with a rotating beater. Next he found a rolling pin, then a long wooden spoon. He added a few other things to his armful that Chris couldn't see. Then he went to the counter and piled it there.

The woman poked among the things. "That's an odd lot for a little chap like yourself," she said.

"For me mum and auntie," Wes said.

Chris pretended to examine a set of glass bowls.

"Two pound fifty," the woman said.

"Huh," Wes said, his voice full of disappointment.

"What have you got, luv?"

"Just a quid."

"Oh, dearie, I can't let you have all that for a quid."

"Please?"

"No, no. I just can't."

"Um, what if I took out these?" Wes selected some of the items and pushed them aside.

"The beater, the roller, and the spoon, then? They're worth more than a quid."

"It's all I have," Wes said.

At this point Chris put the bowls down and left the booth before he started to laugh.

Wes joined him soon after. He held up the three items. Chris shook his head at him, and couldn't help smiling.

"I'll go to school if you promise to let me shop sometimes," Wes said with a straight face. "And we split the profits."

Chris put out his hand. "Deal."

Wes had to juggle his utensils to shake on it.

"So who are those for?" Chris asked him as they walked back to where Mr. Hutchins had parked the van.

"Mrs. James broke her rolling pin last week. Mr. Weeks was sanding off the broken handle of a spoon while Mrs. Weeks was complaining that it wasn't long enough anymore. And Marie was telling one of her friends that she'd make meringue pie for George, except that it took so long to whip the egg whites with a whisk and she wished she had a beater."

"What about that other stuff you didn't get?"

"Oh, I never wanted those. They were just so I had some stuff to take out of the pile."

Chris snorted. "You should consider a future other than farming."

Wes looked at him and grinned.

They ate the meat pies on the ride back to Breton.

Chapter 13

Grace decreed it had got too cold for baths in the upstairs bathroom, let alone the little shower shed tacked onto the side of the house that George and Chris usually used. George brought a big galvanized wash tub from the garage and set it next to the stove. Pauline strung a curtain, and Marie sent George and Chris off to the pub for the evening while the women had their baths.

"Twice a week for the rest of the winter," George said as they headed down the hill. "Mind you, they won't clear out when the men want to bathe. We'll just have to trust they stay in the sitting room."

"I'm used to a cold washhouse," Chris replied. "One place I stayed for a while, there was never enough hot water. They had a boiler, but you had to get up in the middle of the night to be sure of anything but ice cold well water. Wasn't so bad in the summer. But sometimes you'd rather go a couple of weeks without a shower than use that water." Chris gave an exaggerated shiver at the memory of the showers down the hill from the men's dormitory at St. Crispin's.

"Ah, for the days when you had hot water from the tap whenever you had the urge to be clean."

At the pub, George got them both pints, and they wandered into the darts room. Chris had never been any good at darts, so he stood back against the wall while George joined a game. He'd been to the pub several times with Pauline, and a few times with George, but still hadn't got over the feeling that he was being sized up by the residents of Breton.

A few games later, Chris saw a young woman heading across the room toward him. He tried to remember her name, but came up blank. He took a swig of his beer and adjusted his attitude. *Civil, just be civil.*

"Can I have a word?" she said.

"Sure, what word would you like?"

She smiled. "I'm Freddie. I'm Wes's teacher."

"Ah." Chris took another look at her: dark shoulder-length hair, big eyes with long lashes, classic lips. A bulky jumper hid her figure. "The formidable Ms. Barnes." He tried to make it sound light-hearted.

She grimaced. "Am I formidable?"

"Wes thinks so."

"I have to know what you've said to him," she went on. "He's like a different boy. He comes to school, he's usually on time, and he actually applies himself to his studies. It's wonderful."

"Glad to hear it. I didn't want to push too hard, but we made a deal."

"What sort of a deal?"

Chris gave her a brief outline.

Freddie's smile got wider. "He's so bright. I've despaired over him for years. He's just soaking it up, now. I know we owe it to you. He adores you."

Chris noticed the way she tilted her head, blinked her lashes at him, licked her lips. *Oh, hell.*

"He's a good kid." He took a step back, sipped at his glass, kept his eyes averted.

"Wow," Freddie said. "That was loud and clear." She crossed her arms.

Irritation crept out of its hiding-hole. Chris sucked air in through his teeth. He tried to come up with something that wouldn't sound too rude.

She spoke again before he could. "Relax. I'm not on the prowl. I really only wanted to talk about Wes.

I'm hugely pleased that he's coming to school. I wanted to thank you."

Chris slid his eyes over at her. "You're welcome."

"We don't all of us have a one-track mind, you know." She smiled as if she couldn't help it. "The gals were right."

"About what?"

"You. You go all prickly at the first sign of a female."

"Not true." Chris's face grew warm. He wanted to down the rest of his beer. He sipped again.

"Okay, you weren't prickly to start, I'll give you that. But the least bit of flirtation scares the hell out of you."

Chris stared. "Was that a test?"

She shifted her stance. "I guess it was. I'm sorry."

Chris clenched his jaw, counted to ten. He didn't know this woman well enough to get angry at her. He glanced toward the door. Surely bath time was over.

"Oh, don't bolt, please," Freddie said. She put a hand on his arm. Chris resisted the urge to jerk away from her. "Look, I know your story: you lost your wife. I'm sorry, really I am. Can we get past that now? I promise not to flirt if you promise not to bite." She took her hand back.

Chris studied her through narrowed eyes. She had a confidence he used to find attractive. He tried to let go of the tension in his shoulders.

"My bark is worse than my bite," he said.

"I figured that." She stood waiting while he fidgeted.

He gave in. "Can I buy you a drink?"

"Yes, thanks."

They found an empty booth near the back corner, away from the darts room and the front door. Chris nursed what was left of his beer. He didn't think another pint was a good idea. Freddie sipped.

"So. Um. Freddie is an unusual name," Chris said, and realized how it sounded. "But nice," he tacked on and mentally kicked himself.

"It's better than 'Frederica,' isn't it?"

"Ah. Well..."

"Relax," she said and rolled her eyes.

"I am."

"I'd hate to see you tense, then."

"It's not pretty."

Freddie studied him. He felt the warmth rising in his face again, and looked away.

"How much do you know about Wes?" she asked finally, to his relief. "Does he talk to you? I mean, really talk to you?"

"I know what Pauline told me, that he's been on his own since the first outbreak, as far as anyone knows. I asked him once where he came from. He said Portsmouth, but he was lying."

"How do you know he was lying?"

"He wouldn't talk about it. Wouldn't give me any details. I don't know, I could just tell." Chris shrugged. "He doesn't open up easily."

"You've tried?"

"A little, yes. It's like pulling teeth, though. He's got plenty of questions, but not as many answers."

Freddie leaned forward a little, intent now. "What does he ask about?"

"About me. About what things used to be like."

"Has he ever asked you to help with schoolwork?"

"No. I've asked a few times how it was going. He always says it's fine. How is it going?"

"He does very well in mathematics. He's struggling a bit with reading, but coming along. He used to get frustrated easily, but he seems to have more patience, now."

"That's good to hear. What else do you teach them?"

Freddie got a disgusted look on her face and sat back. She took a swig of her drink. "Not much else. A bit of history. A bit of geography. I don't know what it's like other places, but we're taking a big step backward as far as education goes around here."

"The world's changed," Chris said. "Priorities have changed."

"We don't have to slide back into ignorance."

"You were always a teacher," Chris guessed.

"Yes. I'd been teaching for three years when the crash came. We had no school here for two years, then Mrs. Wright and I started it up again. It's been a challenge. But I love teaching. What did you do, before?"

Chris stared at the tabletop. "Nothing so noble," he grunted, and took a drink. Freddie was quiet, turning her glass around in circles on the table.

"You'll keep up with Wes, won't you? Offer to help him, talk to him?"

"Of course, for as long as I'm here."

"Pauline said you don't plan to stay."

"No."

"It's a nice town. The people are friendly. We could use a few more men."

"I have family in Bath," Chris said, gripping his glass.

"So why—" she started, then bit her lip. "Sorry, none of my business."

Someone in the pub was smoking. Chris breathed in the smell. For the first time since Portsmouth, he wanted a cigarette.

"It's a long story," he said, his voice low. He didn't know what else to say, struggled to find something.

"This may be an intrusive question, but have you ever sent a letter?"

Chris blinked, held the glass halfway to his mouth, and stared at her. He took a drink. "Ah, no."

"We do have the post. It gets more reliable all the time. Do you remember their addresses?"

"I don't know—" Chris said, and in an instant, the numbers and roads and even the postal codes leapt forward from the recesses of his mind. Jon's flat and Brian's house. "Um, yes."

"I have note cards and envelopes, if you want to do that. Or you could get them at the Post Office."

"I—thank you. I'll have to think about that." Chris sat back and took a deep breath, trying to slow the thumping of his heart. A letter. Such a simple idea. One that had never entered his head. Brother Luke had once said that the brain was capable of blocking out the strangest things, if someone didn't want to face it. He wondered what Pauline would have to say about it.

Freddie furrowed her brow. "I think I've struck a nerve. I'm sorry. I didn't mean to—"

"No, it's okay. Just surprised me. I really hadn't ever thought about it. I might do, though." Chris fiddled with the little cloth square on the table that served as a napkin and drink mat. He really wanted a cigarette.

Freddie glanced at the clock on the wall. "Gosh, look at the time. I have to go." She downed the last of her beer. "I have papers to grade. Thanks for the drink."

"You're welcome."

"We'll talk some more, about Wes, okay?"

"Sure."

Her eyes flicked over his shoulder. "Um, Diana's just spotted you. You might want to make your escape." She grinned.

Chris found himself grinning back. "Indeed." They both slid out of the booth and headed for the vestibule to get their coats. Chris took Freddie's from her and held it for her while she put her arms in the sleeves.

"Thanks, you're sweet. What a waste." She gave him a mischievous look.

Chris let it pass and put his own coat on. He held the door for her.

"Goodnight, Chris. I'll see you around?"

"I expect so. G'night."

She headed off into town without looking back. Chris watched her, then turned up the hill.

***

Floor-to-ceiling bookshelves lined the study's two long walls. Her father's desk stood in front of the only window in the end wall. Two dark leather chairs with brass studs sat across from each other on an oriental rug. Pauline had always considered the place dark and foreboding, so she draped the sheet with orange and yellow flowers over a pile of boxes and other things in the corner next to the door.

"We were never allowed to come in here as kids," Pauline told Chris as he settled himself in a chair.

"You brought in some cheerful." Chris motioned with his head at the flowered sheet.

"You know what's under there? Electric lamps, the microwave, the stereo, phones. Dad's computer. The coffee maker."

"Oh, coffee...." Chris gave a mock groan and leaned his head back against the leather.

"I've got used to herbal tea, but I do miss coffee," Pauline said.

"They had real tea in London," Chris said. "But no coffee."

"Oh? Tell me. What kind of tea?"

Chris stiffened. He clutched the arms of the chair with fingers gone white and stared at the books on the wall above her head. Pauline could see his chest rise and fall.

"Relax. Nothing horrible. Just tea. Go on."

"I only had it once when I first got there. Only the Big Four got tea, usually."

"Who were the Big Four?"

"They ran the place. Not all of London, just the group I happened to—"

"To what?"

"End up with."

"How?"

"How what?"

"How did you end up with them?"

Chris went into his hunch. "You said nothing horrible."

Pauline wasn't sure how to reply to that. She waited.

"They picked me up on the street. After—after I'd been to Kevin's flat. And I was—just wandering around."

"Okay. And they gave you tea?"

"Next morning. For breakfast. I think Marcus—"

Here Chris stopped and took several deep breaths. He pushed himself out of the chair, paced, then sat back down. "I don't want to do this."

Pauline waited.

"I think the leader wanted to impress me with the tea. So I'd stay. Not that I was in much shape to leave."

"Why not?"

"I'd been beaten up. I was upset about Kevin, and didn't pay attention, and got jumped just as it was getting dark."

"They jumped you and beat you, then gave you tea?"

"No." Chris clenched his fists. "No. A different gang jumped me. Marcus's gang came along and saved me." He stared at the floor. "They had a nice racket going. Blackmail, black market, 'protection.' They'd taken over a boarding school. Posh place, hot showers, plenty of food. I got—drawn in. Some of the chaps were nice enough. It's easy to justify your actions when the alternative is starving, or being killed, right?"

"I don't know. Is it?"

"You've never been in that situation, have you? It never got that bad here. You never had to worry about what you might eat the next day."

160

"We had to be very careful with food for several years before George and I really knew what we were doing."

"Not what I mean," Chris said, watching her with his hands in fists. "You've never gone for days without food. You've never wished for a crumb of something to use as bait for a squirrel or a rat, because all the dogs and cats had already been eaten."

Pauline didn't know what her face looked like. She didn't feel calm. She wondered if Chris could see her shaking. She had to clear her throat.

"Did you eat rats, Chris?"

He leaned forward in his chair. "When you're cold and starving—not hungry, *starving*—it's just meat."

Pauline put a hand up to her mouth; she couldn't help it.

Chris hung his head and cursed under his breath. "I'm sorry. I shouldn't have done that." His voice shook. "I'm sorry. Crap. That was uncalled for."

"It's okay. Maybe I need to learn a thing or two."

"There are things I don't remember. Long stretches of time. After I left Archie's cabin, before I got to St. Crispin's. There used to be people—before winter came, that first year, when it was so bad—that weren't right in the head anymore. They just wandered around, dirty, stinking like shit, crying sometimes." Chris ran a hand through his hair.

"Go ahead," Pauline told him. "Tell me."

"Stew used to call them zombies. I think I might have been like that, for a while. I don't know. I got pretty dirty, I think. And then I just remember this man, talking to me, giving me food. He locked me in a room, I think, in a house. But it was warm, and he kept giving

161

me food. And he used to sit with me and talk to me for hours. After awhile I started talking back. He made me clean myself up. He showed me how to find food. We made plans. And then one morning I woke up and he was dead."

Pauline stifled a sob and blinked rapidly. "I'm sorry. What was his name?"

Chris shook his head. "I don't know. If he told me, I don't remember."

Pictures wheeled in Pauline's mind of hungry people, crying children, huddled around fires. Of Chris, dirty and shivering, lying on a floor, watching the rats hungrily. Something touched her shoulder, and she jerked a little. Chris stood next to her.

"I'm sorry. Are you okay?"

She looked up and saw worry in his face. "I told you it might be hard sometimes." She wanted to reach out and take his hand.

Chris stuffed his hands into his pockets and stepped away. "Sophie was kind, like you," he said. "She always wanted to help people." He turned for the door and left the room. It sounded like he took the stairs two at a time.

Chapter 14

The days grew shorter, and frost glittered on the ground in the mornings as Chris went out to do the chores. George taught Chris how to harness the two draft horses to the wagon, and they drove down the road past Cooper's house and into the woods to cut trees. George had borrowed a chainsaw, but he only used it for felling. They used axes as much as they could to save on petrol. They took two loads of logs to a sawmill north of Petersfield and came back with two loads of lumber. They cleared off the concrete floor of an old barn that had burned down when George and Pauline were both away at University. George's father had never felt the need to rebuild it. George hoped to have a good start on a new hay shed before the weather got too bad.

For several evenings they sat at the kitchen table and discussed plans for the shed, referring to a couple of how-to books George had found in the market. Other nights they sat with the women in the sitting room, a cheerful fire in the grate, sipping cider. George taught Chris to play chess.

"Finally, someone other than Paulie to play with," he said as he set out the pieces on the board.

"Finally someone you can beat, you mean," Pauline said from her seat on the couch.

Chris remembered the basics from his teen years when his grandfather had tried to teach him. After his first few games with George, Pauline pulled up a chair, sat beside Chris, and explained strategies. Chris enjoyed it more than he had thought he would.

The framework of the new shed rose up. A couple of older men from town lent their experience to the project. It was usually dark by the time Wes got out of school, but he came on Saturdays and Sundays to help however he could.

The nightmares came less often.

Sometimes Chris missed the calm rhythm of milking now that the cows were nearly dry. He took up brushing the horses instead, in long, steady strokes, while they shifted in contentment and snuffled at his shoulder.

"Hey, it's snowing!" George said one evening as they prepared to head back into the house. "Paulie will be pleased."

"Do you get much snow here?" Chris asked.

"No, usually we just get cold rain. A few little snows a year, at most, and never this early, before Christmas."

Chris followed him across the yard to the house, his head down, eyes half-closed against the wind. The snow was coming down thicker by the time they reached the back door.

"We should bring in wood, eh?" Chris suggested.

"Yeah, probably a good idea," George agreed, and Chris veered off to the left toward the woodpile. "I'll get a light," George called after him.

Chris fumbled in the dark at the woodpile and managed to get an armful. George passed him with the lantern as Chris headed back to the house. He was about to thump at the door with his foot when it opened and Pauline stood there, putting on her coat, a big grin on her face.

"We can manage the wood," Chris said, but she only grinned wider.

"Oh, I want to be out in the snow!"

Chris turned to watch her in the light from the back door, skipping out into the yard, throwing her arms wide, putting her head back so her face was open to the snow.

"Isn't it lovely!" she exclaimed, laughing. Chris shook his head, went in with the wood. He carried it down the stairs into the cellar, dumped it in the box there, and went back up, passing George again as he came in with a load.

The lantern sat on a stump next to the woodpile. Pauline was there, getting a load.

"We can manage," Chris said to her again, but she tossed her hair back from her face.

"I don't mind. I told you, I want to be out in it."

By the time they had filled the cellar woodbox, each of them having made several trips, there was a liberal coating on the ground.

"I'll get the lantern," Pauline said to George, and then, to Chris, "Walk with me."

He had already begun to stamp the snow off his boots, but he followed her back out without a word, pulling the door shut behind him. He put his hands in his pockets and hunched up his shoulders as the snow settled on his neck. She turned to look at him, but he didn't think she could see much in the dark.

"You're not scowling, are you?" she asked.

"No."

"You don't like snow?"

"I've had enough of it."

"Where?"

"Upstate New York. Months of it, snow on top of snow."

"Oh, it sounds wonderful," she said.

He snorted. "Maybe for the first week. You'd get tired of it, trust me."

They reached the woodpile, but instead of picking up the lantern, Pauline brushed the snow off a stump and sat down. The lantern lit her face; the snowflakes drifted down and whirled around.

"Where were you?" she asked.

"It's dark and it's cold and it's snowing," he pointed out. He pulled his hands out of his pockets long enough to turn up the collar of his jacket around his neck and button it tight.

"It's the first snow. Don't you just want to enjoy it for a little bit?"

"It will be here tomorrow, I expect."

"Oh, it could warm up and be raining by then," she said. "Don't spoil it for me."

He made an exaggerated sigh and stood where he was.

"So, where were you?"

"I told you, upstate New York."

"What does that mean, 'upstate'?"

"Not in the city. North of that, in the mountains."

"Oh. When?"

His heart was suddenly beating. "Um, after it all started."

"Go on."

He stared at her in the dim light, trying to decide what to say. She sat with her hands in her lap, her face neutral. Snow gathered on her hair.

"I was at a friend's cabin, in the woods, on a mountain. It was a weekend getaway type of place. Posh, all the comforts, few of which worked because the electricity had gone. But we had a woodstove, and a septic system, and a well, so we were okay."

"Who was "we"?"

"Um, Archie, who owned the place, and his girlfriend… and me."

"So it was after your wife died?"

"Yes." Chris didn't like the way she tossed out things like that into the conversation, like tossing rocks at him, making him flinch.

"Go on," she said again.

"About what?"

"About the cabin. What was it like?"

He couldn't think of anything to say. "Boring, mainly." The snow came down and stuck to his jacket sleeves.

"Why did you go there?"

"I had to leave my house," he said, and instantly regretted it, because he knew what the next question would be.

"Why did you have to leave?"

Chris hunched up against the snow coming down, took a few steps in a small area.

"There was a fire. The house was going to burn. I had to leave."

"I'm sorry."

"Yeah, well. I wanted to stay there; I was hoping I'd get sick and die, in my own bed, in my own house.

But I didn't get sick. And I didn't want to burn." He watched her face. She was good at keeping a calm face. Lots of practice, he supposed. He'd only rattled her once, with the rats, and he hadn't meant to do that.

How could she be so naive? Because the plague hadn't settled in here. Because she hadn't left this safe haven, hadn't seen what really went on in the world. Her patients in the past had probably wrestled with things like self-esteem and depression because they didn't like their job or had suffered one too many failures in life. What did she really know about the horrendous things that could happen to people? Things *people* could do to each other. Things like torture and starvation and murder and rape.

An image of Jenny in London came into his mind. *Shit, no, not now.* How could he tell her about London, ever, when the idea of having to eat rats had brought her so close to tears? She'd need her own psychologist, if she ever got the details about London out of him.

He glanced over at her, sitting there waiting, being the doctor, in the dark, in the snow.

"So you went to the cabin, and your friends were there. What did you do?"

"We sat around wondering what the hell was going on in the rest of the world."

"And it snowed a lot?"

"Yes, every few days, and I had to spend hours out in it, collecting wood so I wouldn't freeze."

"Archie didn't help?"

"No, he left to try to find out what the hell was going on, and never came back."

"So then it was just you and the girlfriend?"

Ouch. "For about a week, yes. Then she killed herself. With the bag of pills I had saved for myself," he said, tossing his own rock. It must have hit, because she was quiet, and looked down at her shoes. *Yes, add that to my list of guilt, doctor. I supplied the pills that killed her. It all piles up, like snow, and suffocates you.* "Can we go in now?"

"Sure." She stood, picked up the lantern, and headed toward the house. "It'll be rain by morning," she said over her shoulder. "It never really snows this early."

Did she change the subject like that for her benefit or for his?

"That's what George said. Never before Christmas."

She stopped outside the door, blew out the lantern. "Listen."

Chris stood still, straining his ears. He heard only the wind.

"It's always quiet, now there're no cars, but it's even quieter in the snow. Quiet, calm."

She looked at him, but he had nothing to say. She reached for the doorknob, and he followed her in.

During the night the snow turned to rain. It woke him; he could hear it drumming on the roof. He felt a little disappointed, but did not know why. He went back to sleep and dreamed about the cabin in the woods, the snow drifting down in huge feathery blobs, covering the woodpile, burying everything, turning his world white and silent. The axe made no sound as he chopped the wood. When he dumped the pieces into the box next to the stove they made no noise. And when he opened her door and found her dying on the bed, the silence

169

buffeted him, and he couldn't hear himself screaming at her....

***

The market in Petersfield was more crowded than Chris was used to. As he threaded his way through the people, he couldn't help wondering who—if any— among them might be carrying a deadly germ. This was how outbreaks started. All it took was one person. Every year, Pauline had told him, as the outbreaks decreased, the market got a little bigger, a little more crowded, especially before Christmas.

Half the booths had some sort of faded plastic decorations or shabby tinsel garland strung around. Quite a few had vintage ornaments or tired-looking fake trees for sale out front. Finding wrapping paper was harder. After hearing Pauline complain to Grace about the state of their wrapping paper supply, Chris had decided to surprise her with whatever he could find. He asked at numerous booths with no success.

A lady wearing a limp Santa hat smiled at him from her chair as he stopped for a quick look in her booth.

"How can I help you?"

"I'm on the hunt for Christmas wrapping paper and having no luck."

She jumped up. "Your luck just changed." She pulled a flat packet from where it was half-hidden under some ornaments. "Some people don't like the creases, but I have this."

The outer plastic was dingy and ripped. The paper inside was folded in fours, but unused. Three sheets, the label stated, in assorted designs.

"Perfect!" Chris handed her the money without trying to bargain.

He had barely got the paper into his rucksack when he heard his name, turned, and found Pauline nearly at his elbow, smiling.

"I've found you. How are you doing?"

"Mission accomplished," he told her, zipping his pack, hoping she hadn't seen the paper.

"Lovely." She turned to the woman in the booth. "Hello."

The woman looked from her to Chris and back again. "How can I help you, dear?"

"Um, Jerry, a few booths down, said you might have some Christmas wrapping paper?" Pauline asked.

Chris, standing just behind Pauline, shook his head slightly at the woman, hoping she'd catch it. She gave no indication that she noticed him, but smiled gently.

"Eh, sorry, luv. Some bloke got it a just a while ago. Wanted to surprise his sweetheart, I think." She winked at Pauline.

"Oh, bother," Pauline said. "That's the second time today."

"It's getting harder to come by. Hang on a minute, eh?" She turned and stuck her head through the curtain at the back of her booth for a muffled conversation with the proprietor of the booth backing hers. She reached an arm through, and brought out a roll of paper about fifty centimeters long, crumpled on the ends. "Here we are, luv. This is rather nice." She untied a bit of string holding it, and unrolled the paper. "Four different pieces. The edges are a bit wonky, but the centers are good."

Pauline smiled, looking at the papers carefully. "They are pretty, aren't they?" She ran her fingers over each piece. Chris watched her profile. "How much?" she asked, but frowned at the price the woman gave. "I've spent so much today."

"Have you any jam?" the woman asked. "I recognize you. You've had lovely jams before, haven't you?"

"I do." Pauline brightened, and slipped off her pack to rummage. She brought out a jar, held it up. The woman named her price with the jam included. Pauline began to reach into her pocket. Chris already had a pound coin ready and put it on the table. "Oh, no, Chris—" Pauline started, but he didn't let her go on.

"I've got it."

The woman smiled knowingly. She scooped up the coin and took the jam that Pauline held out to her. She fished in her pocket for change.

"Have you any ribbons?" Chris asked. Pauline glanced at him.

"Hm, I've a bit of red here somewhere, I think," the woman said. She poked around under the table. She held up a small bundle of red ribbon.

"Throw that in?" Chris said in a bargaining tone.

She raised an eyebrow, and sighed. "Yeah, all right, handsome." She rolled the ribbon up in the papers, tied it all with the bit of string, and handed it to Pauline. "You two have a happy Christmas."

"Happy Christmas to you," Pauline said cheerfully. Chris gave a brief nod and a "Ta."

They pushed off through the crowd.

"Thank you, Chris." Pauline flashed a smile at him. "These are lovely. All our papers have got so tired, used so many times. It will be nice to have a few new ones this year."

"I want a bit of the ribbon."

"Oh, of course. You take the ribbon. You paid for it."

"I just need a bit."

"Ah," Pauline said. Her tone made Chris look at her, and he saw a little smirk on her face.

"What's that for?"

"You." She slid her eyes toward him. "You've got some sort of secret, don't you?"

Chris shrugged. "I bought that ornament that your mum was so taken with earlier."

Pauline stopped and turned to him with her mouth open. "It was you! I went back there to get it and it was gone!" She laughed.

"Oh, sorry. Do you want it?"

"No, no, of course not! You bought it, you give it to her. I have something else, anyway. That was sweet of you."

Chris took a breath. "I haven't done Christmas since—well—you know."

Pauline put a hand on his arm. "It's nice, isn't it?"

"Yeah, it is." He tried to smile. "Shopping's harder, though."

Pauline grinned again. "We have to be more creative," she agreed. "No more gift cards." They started walking again.

"No more credit cards," Chris said.

"No more overspending on useless things."

"Um, well, I think I overspent on that ornament," Chris confessed.

"You seem to know how to bargain," Pauline said, and then, almost without pause, "No more department stores."

"No more personal shoppers."

Pauline grimaced. "You didn't have a personal shopper, did you?"

"No, no," Chris assured her. "But I knew people who did."

"Where's Wes?"

"He'll meet us at the van."

"Is that safe? To leave him alone?"

"For him? I think so. For the stallholders? I'm not so sure."

Pauline snorted.

Chapter 15

Pauline wore a skirt and festive jumper from the back of her closet for the Christmas party at the pub. She'd used the last of the shampoo from Michael, and tied up her hair with a green ribbon. Chris made noises about staying home, but Mum persuaded him to come along.

"There'll be music and dancing," Pauline told him on the walk down. "Mr. Weeks is a jolly good fiddler."

"I don't dance."

Pauline thought Chris drank his first beer too quickly, then she figured he must feel uncomfortable in such a crowd. A couple of beers to loosen him up couldn't be a bad thing.

All the booths and tables were full, but Pauline managed to find a seat for Mum. She spent some time greeting and chatting, and lost track of Chris. Music started up in the darts room. She headed that way, along with a good bit of the crowd.

Laughter and the stamp of feet mixed with the fiddle to fill the air. Pauline found herself drawn into the dancing, clasping hands most often with other young women, doing a quick turn with a grinning older man. The first few dances were slower, more hesitant, as people remembered the steps and loosened up. Someone started beating on a pot from the kitchen, and the music got faster. The steps became less important. Skipping circles collided and re-formed as someone shouted instructions. Pauline broke away finally, panting, to find her beer and push up her sleeves, wishing she'd worn a lighter top. She caught sight of Chris in the corner, watching.

Freddie approached him, put a hand on his arm. He scowled and shook his head. Freddie stayed a moment more, then turned away as he said something short to her. Chris turned the opposite direction and moved toward the door. Pauline pushed through the crowd and met him in the doorway.

He scowled at her, too.

"I'm not going to ask you to dance," Pauline said.

"You're the only bloody one, then."

"Are you okay?"

Before he could answer, Diana's cheerful voice nearby called out, "We've got a couple under the mistletoe!"

The music and dancing went on in the background, but the people nearby all turned toward them expectantly, calling out encouragements and laughing.

Pauline's eyes went up to the little bundle of leaves above them. She gave Chris a little grin and a shrug, but he wasn't smiling. His face had gone hard; he stood still, leaning away from her. The laughter died away, but everyone stood watching, wondering what would happen next. Chris grunted and walked away into the main room.

Pauline turned to Diana.

"What's wrong with you?" she said, her face hot.

"What? It's mistletoe. I would have said it whoever was standing there."

"But you know what he's like."

Diana tossed her hair. "Well, I figured if he'd kiss anyone it would be you."

176

Of course it was just a silly misunderstanding. Pauline tried to keep her anger in check.

"Maybe you should just leave him alone," Pauline said. She imagined people watching her as she returned to the table where Mum was sitting with her friend Helen.

She spent an hour sipping a half-pint, deflecting questions about Chris, waving off a few apologies, exchanging Christmas greetings with those folks she didn't see often. She scanned the crowd for Chris, but didn't see him. George and Marie came in from dancing to take Mum home. Pauline went in search of Chris. In the darts room they said he'd left a few minutes before. She got her coat and went out into the cold night.

He was leaning against the wall across the road, arms crossed, staring at the ground in front of his feet. The bright moon and the light from the pub windows gave just enough illumination. He had his jacket on, his hood up. He didn't move as she approached.

"What are you doing out here?" she asked.

"Needed some air."

"I'm sorry about that whole mistletoe thing."

"Caught me off-guard," he said. "I didn't mean to embarrass you. Sorry."

"It's okay, I know. I wasn't embarrassed. I know it bothered you."

"I could have handled it better than that. I just…."

"You weren't expecting it." She shrugged.

He looked up at her then, stared too long without saying anything.

"What?" she said finally.

"I'm a little drunk."

"Do you want to go?"

"Sure, let's go." He pushed away from the wall, heading into the darkness. "So is it just some sort of game to them?"

"What?"

"Us. As a couple. Are we or aren't we? I wouldn't be surprised if there were bets running. It's like they think they can keep pushing us together until we hook up like toy trains or something."

"What do you care what they think?"

"I don't, generally. I told you, I'm drunk. Everything matters more."

"Does it?"

"No, but it feels like it does. Haven't you ever felt that way?"

"Maybe."

"You've never seen me drunk, so you don't know," Chris mumbled.

"Know what?"

"What I get like."

"What do you get like?"

"I get morose. I get depressed. I'll be hell to live with for the next couple of days."

"Oh, I doubt that," she said.

He was quiet, and they walked on for a few minutes.

"I should have just kissed you," he said eventually. "That's what anyone else would have done, right? A peck on the cheek. Why couldn't I just do that and laugh it off? Instead I had to make a bloody show of not kissing you."

"It wasn't a show."

"It doesn't bother you?"

Pauline pursed her lips and thought before she answered. "Michael always caused a good bit of speculation and gossip. We were on and off so much, there was always someone talking. I'm used to it. There's not much entertainment around here. We used to be able to gossip about famous people. Now it's just our neighbors. It's not malicious. Usually."

Chris grunted. "Michael's a fool," he said under his breath.

"I don't think so. We're just too different. He simply isn't able to—" She stopped. "I'm sorry. I shouldn't bore you with my professional opinion of Michael. Not proper, really."

"I suspect I'm "simply not able to" either," Chris said in a low voice.

"You've been through a long time of grief and shutting people out of your life. You can change that if you want to—and I think you do want to. I think you've made progress since you got here."

"Thank you, doctor."

A woman's laughter carried up the road from the pub. Chris turned his head back at the sound, but did not stop.

"What do you want for Christmas?" he asked her, out of the blue.

"Hm," Pauline mused, stalling for time. A couple of answers popped into her head, but they seemed heavy, weighted. "A pizza!"

"Huh. You could make a pizza if you really wanted to, couldn't you?"

"Well, maybe I could, but that's not what I mean. I want to go out to a little pizza place and order one, and sit at a cramped little table with bad music playing in

179

the background, and have them bring it to me, too hot to eat at first, with lots of gooey cheese and hot sausage and pepperoni and black olives."

"Green pepper and onions," Chris said.

"Green pepper, okay, but no onions, because they really ruin your breath," she said, and laughed.

"Oh, so this is a date, then?"

"Wouldn't have to be a date, but it would be nice to share it with someone. Better than eating alone."

"Who?"

"Do you like pizza?"

He didn't answer for awhile, and she thought maybe she'd said the wrong thing. When he finally spoke his voice was soft.

"There was a place Sophie and I used to go to—Carpelli's. Little place stuck between a bakery and a card shop in a strip mall. Some of the best pizza I've ever had. Something about the sauce. There were only four booths on one wall, two tables for two, and a little counter where two people could sit. And you could get take-away, too. Sometimes there would be a queue on Friday or Saturday night. We'd go every couple of weeks, usually just the two of us, but sometimes with friends. She liked pepperoni, I liked onions, so we'd get a half-and-half. And if she had to work late at the office, I'd stop and pick up a pizza, and take it in, and we'd eat it at her desk." He paused. "I really miss that."

Pauline wanted to put her arm through his, but after what had happened in the pub, she decided against it.

"I was thinking about her, so I just kept drinking. Stupid."

"It's okay," she said. "It happens. I understand." They walked on in silence for a few minutes. "So, what do you want for Christmas?"

Chris took a breath and exhaled. "I want to be able to enjoy it, and not ruin it for everyone else."

This time she did put her arm through his and squeezed a little. He didn't react, kept walking. When they reached the front gate, he pulled his arm away and opened the gate for her. They went around to the kitchen door. His longer strides got him there first.

Chris stopped with his hand on the doorknob, then turned to face her. He reached up and pushed back his hood. Faint light from the lamps in the kitchen came through the curtains, lighting his face. His dark eyes were on hers.

"I should have just kissed you," he whispered. "Would have given them something to talk about, eh?" He slipped one hand around her waist and pulled her close. Surprise made her draw a breath. She put one hand on his arm, waited, then rested the other on his hip, not quite an embrace. Her heart beat fast; her face warmed. Chris licked his lips, swallowed. He breathed out faint puffs into the cold air. He touched her hair lightly, his face close to hers.

It's the beer, she thought. *Did I have that much? I need to stop this.*

"Oh, crap," Chris said, and pushed her away gently. "I'm sorry. I'm drunk. I shouldn't have—"

"It's okay," Pauline said automatically, stepping away and putting her hands into her pockets.

"I'd never—" Chris started, but he didn't go on.

"It's okay," she repeated, confused, wondering why she felt disappointed.

181

"It won't happen again, you needn't worry. Goodnight." Chris wrenched open the door and went in without waiting for her.

***

His hangover lasted the entire next day, and Chris hoped no one had heard him puking into the toilet in the middle of the night. At least no one mentioned it. He ate only toast for breakfast. Pauline kept *looking* at him, in a way that made him feel like a guilty child. He ignored the beaming headache and pushed the familiar depression aside. He tramped through the field across the road to cut holly branches for Grace. He crawled up a ladder into the attic and handed down the boxes marked "Christmas" to Marie while George and Pauline went off to cut a tree. He even agreed—though he regretted it later—to go to church with the family on Christmas Eve when Grace brought up the subject.

"I'll find you a nice shirt and trousers," Grace said, and Chris knew he wouldn't get away with what he'd worn to the party at the pub.

He sat and brooded while the rest of them decorated the tree in the sitting room. The tangled strings of electric lights had gone back in a box and right back up to the attic. George was employed to put a few ornaments on the topmost branches, then the women took over. George retired to his favorite chair to smoke a pipe.

"George doesn't really care what the tree looks like," Grace said. "But if you'd like to help, Chris, you're more than welcome."

Autopilot. "No, don't worry about me. I used to do the lights, but Sophie never let me touch the ornaments. She had boxes of antique ones from her mother. It all had to be just right. I enjoyed watching her do it, because she enjoyed it so." His head pounded. The women smiled at him.

He went up to his room after tea. He'd got the red ribbon from Pauline, and carefully folded the wrapping paper around the gifts he had purchased: the glass bird ornament for Grace, a pair of leather work gloves for George, a magazine of crossword puzzles for Marie with only two puzzles started by someone in the past. He'd erased the penciled-in words. He didn't plan to wrap the black-and-white football he'd found for Wes. He tied a piece of red ribbon around it.

For Pauline he'd bought a tortoiseshell hair clip. He used what he considered the most elegant of the wrapping papers on it, folding the extra carefully so it wouldn't be wrecked. He tied it with a piece of gold cord he'd snagged from one of the boxes of decorations.

Two days later, Chris found himself scrubbing up after supper with a bucket of hot water in the bathroom while the women bathed downstairs. He shaved and frowned at his hair in the mirror. Too late to do anything about it now. He put on the clothes Grace had laid out for him: black trousers, white shirt, red tie, and a heather-green v-neck jumper. At least it wasn't a suit. He didn't think he could handle a suit. She hadn't forgot shoes, either. They were a bit tight, but Chris figured he could stand them for the evening.

He carried his packages down and added them to the small pile under the tree. He remembered another Christmas: the twinkling lights, baby toys, little dresses, a bath towel with yellow ducks on it. He'd bought Sophie a cream silk blouse and an expensive watch. She'd never worn either. They were still in the boxes under the tree when he left the house.

"Are you okay?"

Chris spun around with a gasp. He hadn't heard Pauline come down the stairs. She wore a simple dark green gown with a black belt and glittery black necklace. She'd pulled her hair back from her face.

"You look nice," Chris managed.

"Thanks. Wow, look at you. Mum did good."

"The shoes are a bit tight." Chris held up one foot and wiggled it.

"It's just for tonight." She leaned forward a bit and cupped her hand around her mouth. "I vetoed the suit," she said in a mock whisper, and smiled.

"Thank you." Chris rolled his eyes.

"Are you okay?" she asked again.

He nodded. "It's good and bad. More good, though."

The vicar stood at the door and welcomed everyone with a handshake as they came into the church. Chris had never been inside before. Candles in sconces lined the walls. Chris stood aside, letting the women enter the pew first, and managed to get the end seat next to George. He thought about Brother Luke, how often he'd encouraged Chris to come to church, even though Chris had always refused. He'd spent two

Christmases at the monastery playing cards in the dormitory, or working in the barn while the services went on up the hill in the church. Brother Luke would be pleased to see him now.

He let the singing wash over him. When was the last time he'd sung? That little gig in September, at the bar with the bad spotlight that kept going out. Jon had been there. Is Jon in church right now, too? Sitting next to Mum, holding the hymnal for her? Chris found it hard to breathe. *Happy Christmas, Mum.*

No, they weren't. They would have answered his letter. Crap. *Nine thousand, nine hundred and ninety-nine; nine thousand, nine hundred and ninety-eight; nine thousand, nine hundred and ninety-seven…* on and on.

Then it was over, and Chris was making his way out of the church, saying "Happy Christmas" again and again, while his shoes pinched his feet.

If he dreamed that night, Chris didn't remember it. He did the chores before breakfast, before George got up, even. He stood out in the yard under a lead-grey sky and watched some little birds pecking around in the dirt. They fluttered away when he roused himself to go inside.

After breakfast, they opened presents.

Pauline exclaimed at the new wrapping papers. She smoothed them out carefully after she'd thanked Chris and clipped up her hair. Everyone chuckled when Chris and George opened their gifts to each other at the same time and both found leather work gloves. Chris put on the hat Marie had knit for him, and Marie's mouth opened in delight as she paged through the puzzles. Grace hung her bird on the tree and stooped to give

Chris a peck on the cheek while she handed him her gift: a small leather wallet containing a nail clippers, file, and scissors.

"I do like a man with neat nails," she said, and winked at him.

Pauline passed him a gift done up like a Christmas cracker. He untied the red and gold cords and unrolled the foil paper, smoothing it out the way Pauline had done. Inside a cardboard tube he found a carved ivory chess piece: a castle, intricate and ornate, with little towers and windows, and vines snaking up the walls.

"I found it in a box of junk in the market. Bought the box, picked that out, and left the rest behind. Imagine what the whole set must have looked like."

"It's brilliant, thank you," was all Chris could say. He passed it around for everyone to ooh and ah over.

"It'll fit in your pocket, that," Pauline said, and looked away.

Wes showed up. He opened his gifts—a knit cap, mittens, and a bag of peppermint sweets—and took Chris outside to try out the ball. George and Pauline came out soon after, and the four of them spent a happy hour kicking the football around the yard until it started to rain.

Games in the sitting room, tea, chores, and supper rounded out the day. Wes seemed ready to stay, so Pauline fixed him a bed on the couch in the sitting room. Chris was about to head to bed when she stopped him at the bottom of the stairs.

"Can I talk to you? In the study?" She carried a lamp.

"It's Christmas," Chris said. Did she really want to wrestle more painful memories out of him?

"I know. Just for a minute."

He followed her in and shut the door. She set the lamp down, but didn't sit, so neither did he. She bit her lip.

"What is it?"

Pauline pulled something from her back pocket and held it out to him. He saw red writing and realized what it was.

"I've had them since the day before yesterday. Mr. Percy gave them to me. I didn't want to ruin your Christmas."

Chris took the envelopes from her. Each one had a diagonal line through the address, and underneath, in red letters, was scrawled "Abandoned." The line went right through Jon's name, and appeared to underline Brian's.

"Huh," Chris said. The hand holding the letters had gone numb, like it didn't belong to him anymore. Pauline was talking to him, but he didn't listen. He stared at the word. *Abandoned.*

Pauline took his arm. "You know that, right?"

"What?"

"It doesn't necessarily mean they're dead." She held his gaze with her own. "Right?"

"You're always so optimistic," he whispered. "I wish I could be. But you haven't seen what I've seen."

"Do you want to talk about it?"

"No." He felt bad for her. She had known for days, kept it from him to give him the best chance of a good Christmas. He put his arms around her, kissed her cheek—the way he should have done at the pub—and held her. "Thank you, for everything," he said into her hair. "You've made this the best Christmas I've had in a long time. I'll treasure all the gifts your family has given me." He released her, touched her hair—such pretty hair, the way it gleamed in the glow of the lamp—and went upstairs to bed.

Chapter 16

The New Year's Eve party at the pub was more subdued than the Christmas party. Fewer people came, perhaps due to the snow coming down steadily since midday. Chris had tried to politely decline, but Pauline managed to convince him to go.

"I'll laugh at you when you slip in the snow in those wellies and fall on your arse," he said to her while they were getting their coats on.

"I would hope you would kindly grab my arm and keep me from falling," she replied.

The walk to the pub was accomplished without incident. Chris waited in the vestibule while Pauline changed into the shoes she'd carried along.

"Did you have a huge closet full of shoes, before?"

"I shudder when I think about how many shoes I owned," she said. "That's what you did when you went out shopping with your girlfriends. You bought shoes. I wore most of them, I suppose. But you can't complain if I don't want to wear wellies to a party."

"I'm not complaining. They're simply divine, *dahling*."

"You won't be so grumpy tonight, will you?"

"Don't let me drink too much, okay?"

Chris followed Pauline as she made her way through the crowd, greeting and smiling. The tortoiseshell hairclip nestled among the hair at the back of her head. He wondered if she had chosen it to go with her outfit, or if she had chosen the outfit to go with the clip. She drew him into short conversations he would otherwise have stayed out of. She didn't touch him, but to Chris it seemed as if the people they talked to viewed them as a couple, as if Pauline were hanging onto his arm and casting loving glances at him. Maybe it was just his imagination. Maybe he needed a drink. *No, don't think like that.* A drink would be *nice*, but he did not *need* a drink. He slipped off to the bar and got himself a pint and her a half.

"I owe you one," she said as he handed it to her.

"Not at all."

The music started, Mr. Weeks warming up with an easy step, accompanied by the scrape of chairs and tables as they cleared more space in the darts room. Pauline and a few others headed that way.

No one asked Chris to dance, which suited him fine. He avoided the archway between the main room and the darts room with its insidious bundle of mistletoe still hanging there, and instead found a seat at the end of the bar and nursed his second—last?—pint.

Freddie approached him, her face neutral. He tried to look approachable. She inched closer.

"I'd like to apologize for my behavior," Chris said to her.

"In advance?"

"I'm sorry, Freddie. I was drunk, which isn't an excuse, but...."

"Apology accepted. Buy me some crisps."

"Is that what I've been smelling?"

"No one let you in on it?"

Chris gave her a coin and she was back soon with a small bowl heaped with crisps and a stool. Chris moved his stool to make room for her. When she settled herself her thigh pressed against his. She didn't seem to notice.

"They're still warm. They're best this way," Freddie said, munching.

"I haven't had these in years."

Harry brought them beer.

"Last one tonight, okay?" Chris said to him.

Harry winked. "Lay off the crisps, then, old chap."

"I saw you in church," Freddie said.

"Grace asked me to go. I couldn't say no."

"You didn't look very comfortable."

"My shoes were too tight."

"That's not what I mean."

Chris sipped. "Yeah. No."

"How was the rest of your Christmas?"

"Um. Up and down. But mostly up. You?"

"Very nice," she said, not meeting his eye.

"Wes came up and spent the day."

"Good. He needs that sort of family thing. He brought his ball to school this week. That was a brilliant gift, by the way. We all had a grand time kicking it 'round the schoolyard."

"Good. Is he getting on with the other kids better?"

"Yes, I think so. I was thinking that we should get the school field back in order this year, maybe after planting. It'll take some work. We could have games, get the community involved."

"That's a great idea. I'll help."

Freddie eyed him. "I thought you might be gone by then."

"Ah. Yes. Well." Chris stared into his beer, then reached into his back pocket. "Maybe you should see these." He slid the letters toward her on the bar.

Her eyes widened and she drew in her breath. She picked up the top one, the one to Jon, and looked at the one underneath.

"Oh, I'm so sorry, Chris." She put a hand to her mouth.

Chris took them back a slipped them into his pocket again. "It doesn't necessarily mean they're dead, you know."

"No, no. Of course not."

"I wish I believed that."

"But you'll still go, to find out."

"Not in the snow."

Freddie looked into her glass, then crushed a small piece of crisp that had fallen on the polished wood of the bar top with her fingertip. "Do you wish you hadn't sent them? It was my idea. Maybe I shouldn't have—"

"It was a good idea," Chris said, putting his hand on her arm briefly. "Don't worry about it, okay? It's done. It doesn't really change anything."

She drank down the last of her beer in one swig, and pushed the rest of the chips closer to Chris. "Look, I'm tired, and I'm not good company tonight, so I'm off. Happy New Year, and all that." She slid off the stool.

"Wait—" Chris said. He glanced toward the darts room. "Should I walk you home? It's just that—"

"No, no. You came with Pauline, I know. It's not far at all. I'm fine. You stay."

"I didn't come 'with' Pauline," Chris said, not sure why he felt the need to clarify that.

"Yes, yes, I know," Freddie said. She was already moving away. "Good night." She disappeared into the vestibule.

Chris felt a scowl coming on and slouched onto his stool. Now what had he done? He wanted to guzzle the rest of his beer and order another. No. He sipped, and nibbled a crisp.

Pauline appeared next to him, laughing, breathing hard.

"Oh, I need a drink!" she said, climbing onto the stool Freddie had vacated. "Harry! Please?" She turned to him. "Are you behaving?"

"I think so." Chris could feel her thigh pressing against his like Freddie's had, but Pauline's was warmer, from the dancing.

"Did you have a nice chat with Freddie?" she asked, pulling the bowl of crisps towards herself.

"I'm not sure. She left suddenly. I don't think it was me."

"Well, the holidays can't be easy for her, either."

"What do you mean?"

Pauline looked him, eyes wide. "She didn't tell you?"

"No, apparently. What?"

"She lost her husband. In the Bad Winter. He'd taken a job in London. She was to join him in the spring."

He gripped his glass hard. "Holy crap."

"I figured you knew."

"How would I know that?"

"I assumed she'd tell you. You've been chatting her up for weeks."

"I have not. We've talked about Wes a few times, that's all, because she's his teacher."

"Okay, don't get upset. I'm sorry."

"Shit, I'm an idiot. I never thought—"

193

"Never thought that someone else might be having as bad a day as you?"

"Let me find a stick and you can beat me with it."

Pauline put her arm around him and squeezed a little. "There, there," she said, "you're not the first man to be self-centered and oblivious."

"Thank you very much," Chris said. "Should I go after her?"

"Do you want to?"

"Does it make me more of an ass if I don't?"

"Oh, dear." Pauline sighed and leaned against him. She still had her arm around him.

That feels good. Crap.

"Here's a pretty pair of lovebirds," a slurred voice growled close by.

*　　　　*　　*

Pauline sat up straight and turned on her stool at the sound of Rob's voice behind them. Chris did the same as she pulled her arm away from him.

Rob Warren—when had he showed up?—sneered at her.

"Hello, Rob. I didn't know you were here tonight. Happy New Year," Pauline said. She put on what she hoped was a polite smile.

"Michael Cooper should be here to see this," Rob went on, ignoring her greeting.

"Yes, it would be nice if Michael could be here."

"*He* wouldn't think so," Rob said, jerking a thumb at Chris.

"What the hell—?" Chris said.

Damn, I thought Rob had got over me. Pauline tried to keep her anger in control, tried to treat Rob as if he were still her patient.

"Maybe you've had a little too much to drink, Rob." She was relieved to see a couple of men edging closer, Malcolm and Walt, whom she could count on to help, if necessary. Rob rarely got violent, but he was bigger than Chris, his bravado propped up with too much beer. And she didn't know how Chris would react to this sort of situation.

She felt Chris brush against her as he slid off the stool behind her, so she stood too. Rob backed up a few paces. The crowd had moved away, leaving a clear area around them, with the bar at Pauline's and Chris's backs.

"Did Michael know he was sending you a bed-warmer?" Rob said to Pauline. "Or are you shagging this skinny behind his back?"

"Rob, what's wrong with you? Why would you say such a thing?"

"Push off," Chris said.

"Why don't you push off?" Rob sounded angrier now, more than just drunk. "I live here. I belong here. You don't."

"Give it a rest, Rob," someone in the crowd said.

"I'll go when I'm ready," Chris said.

"Maybe I'll make you go sooner." Rob stepped closer.

"There'll be no fighting in my place," Harry put in sternly from behind the counter. "Someone take Rob out back and cool him down."

Malcolm and Walt edged forward. Rob brought fists up and set his feet in a warning stance. "Back off!" He turned to Chris. "Let's go, Price."

Chris put his hands on Pauline's shoulders and pushed her to the side. "Get back," he said to her, keeping his eyes on Rob.

"Don't fight him," Pauline said as she stepped away. Chris shook his head a little, but the look on his face belied that. His whole demeanor had changed; he was relaxed, light on his feet, his hands not quite fists, but ready.

A few people tried to talk Rob down, but he ignored them, teeth bared as he glared at Chris.

"Outside," Chris said.

"Sure," Rob replied. He started to turn, then lashed out.

Pauline gasped as Chris moved. He stepped into the blow, deflecting with one arm. He twisted his body and got Rob in a choke hold. Rob gurgled as Chris kicked his legs out from under him and dropped him to the floor. The whole thing ended in seconds with Chris kneeling on Rob's back, gripping Rob's hair with one hand and wrenching Rob's arm back with the other. Rob groaned.

"Holy shit," someone said into the sudden quiet.

"Next time I will fight you," Chris said, thumping Rob's face against the floor once, "and you'll be worse off than you are now. Do you understand?"

Rob nodded as best he was able.

Chris leaned close to Rob's ear. "Don't fuck with me." He thumped Rob's head once more, then released him and stood. Rob stayed on the floor. No one else moved. Chris turned for the vestibule.

"Good job," someone said, to a round of soft agreements. Chris didn't seem to hear them.

Pauline went after Chris. He had grabbed his coat and was already out the front door. She had to get into her wellies and jacket. Outside, it had stopped snowing. She hurried to catch him up.

"Wait!"

Chris turned his head back. He didn't stop, but he slowed as he zipped his coat.

"That was brilliant," Pauline said as she reached him.

Chris hunched his shoulders and shoved his hands into his pockets. He strode on without acknowledging her.

"Where did you learn to do that?"

For a few moments Pauline thought he wasn't going to speak to her at all, then he stopped abruptly and turned to face her.

"If he'd done that in London he might be dead now."

Pauline's stomach turned over. She tried to keep her voice calm. "You'd have killed him?"

"No, not me," Chris said, running a hand through his hair. He took a few steps in a small space, as if to release tension. He pulled his knit cap out of his pocket and put it on. "Stupid drunks who pick fights don't last long. If you want to survive in this world you need more brains than that. And if you've got enough brains, you learn how to fight."

"We've all got on fine without knowing—"

"This isn't London!" Chris cut her off, rounding on her, stepping closer. "This isn't Portsmouth, or Halifax, or New York. You people have no idea. What the hell does it matter who might be screwing who? It's not like you have to worry that someone might kill you today!"

"Chris, calm down. Come on, walk with me. Talk if you want to." Pauline started up the road into the darkness toward home. She heard him behind her, and the beam of a torch came on and lit the path they had made through the snow on the way down. Pauline remembered the black torch she'd seen on the chair in the spare room on the day Chris arrived.

She thought they might make it to the house in silence, but when she reached the wall Chris said her name. She turned to face him.

"I wouldn't kill anyone," he said, his voice strained, barely above a whisper. "I wouldn't hurt *anyone*. Please believe me."

"I know. Of course I believe you."

He lurched to the wall with a groan, put both hands on it, leaned over. "I think I'm gonna be sick."

Pauline waited while he panted, then moved closer. She put a hand on his back. He was shaking. He handed her the torch.

"What happened in London?" she asked him.

"No, I can't—"

"Okay." Pauline moved her hand in circles until his breathing evened out. "You're okay."

Chris pushed away from the wall, away from her hand. He paced again. "I'm sorry. I didn't see that coming. I should have—"

"What?"

"I should have handled it differently."

"I think you handled it brilliantly."

"Do you think that will be the end of it? I don't. I've ticked him off."

"Rob can be—um—unstable at times. Especially if he's drunk. However much of this he remembers, he'll likely ignore. I think you made your point. He can't beat you. I don't think you have to worry about it happening again."

"You know him pretty well, do you?"

"He was my patient, for a while. He used to be on medication. No medications, now. We try to make allowances for him."

"Is he Michael's friend?"

"No, not particularly."

"Then why does he care about—"

"Whether we're a couple?"

"That's a nice way to put it, yes."

Pauline paused. "I had to stop working with him. He'd fixated on me. He started having—um."

"Fantasies?"

"Unhealthy expectations."

"He fell in love with you?"

"No, he fixated on his therapist."

"Which was you."

"It could have been anyone. It happened to be me. Someone was listening to him, taking him seriously, caring about him. He twisted that into something it wasn't."

"Huh," Chris said.

Pauline held the torch pointing down into the snow. It reflected just enough light to see his face. "I couldn't be his doctor anymore under those circumstances."

"No, I suppose not."

"It happens. Female patients fall for male doctors. Sometimes men fall for their male doctor, and women for their female doctor."

Chris gave her a piercing look.

"Yes. It wasn't anyone here. I'd just started to practice. I had to stop being her doctor, too."

"Huh."

"It's important to keep a distance."

"So, having your patient living in the same house probably isn't a good idea."

"I didn't say that."

"Distance. Got it."

"Right..." Pauline said faintly.

Chris turned and headed for the house without another word. Pauline followed, slipping a bit in the snow.

Chapter 17

Chris waited at the front of the school yard, and in a few minutes a group of kids burst out of the doors and hurried toward the gate. Some of them eyed him warily as they passed.

"Chris!" Wes called. "What are you doing here?"

"I came to see your teacher, actually," Chris said.

"About me?"

"No, not about you. Is she inside?"

"Down the hall on the right," Wes said, and headed off toward town.

Chris peeked in the doors until he saw her sitting at a desk in a classroom. He knocked softly.

She looked up and smiled. "Oh, hello. What brings you here?"

"I thought I might owe you another apology?"

She shifted some papers, fiddled with her pen, and turned her chair toward him. "No, not at all."

"I should have walked you home. I was about to go after you—"

"I heard about what happened with Rob Warren."

Chris leaned against the doorframe. "Yes, that."

"I wish I could have seen it. He's an ass."

"Pauline says he can't help it."

"Yes, she can see it as a medical issue, but some of us find it hard to be so charitable." She swiveled the chair back and forth a little.

"This may be not be my business…" Chris started, and she looked up at him. "Pauline told me about your husband. I'm sorry. I didn't know."

"It's hard to talk about. But I don't expect people to walk on eggshells around me."

"You don't wear a ring."

She shook her head. "I realized I was too attached to it. Am I still married to him because I wear the ring? No. He's dead. I'm not married anymore. Simple as that."

Chris couldn't quite feel the doorframe against his arm or the floor under his feet. Some part of his brain wailed in alarm. He couldn't speak. Freddie looked him up and down.

"I still love him. I always will. But he wouldn't expect me to shrivel up and die with him. I wished that, for a while. I hoped I'd die. Does this sound familiar, Chris? I'll bet it does."

Part of him wanted to tell her to stop. Part of him wanted her to go on. She watched him, her face neutral, matter-of-fact.

"Why are you here?" she asked him.

"To talk about the playing field."

"That's just an excuse."

"Do you think you know?"

"I'm not sure, actually. Couple of possibilities."

Freddie stood, dropped her pen onto the desk, and took the few steps to Chris. She came too close, but Chris resisted the urge to step back. She put her hands on his hips, tilted her head back, looked into his eyes.

"Now's your chance," she whispered.

A hundred footballs careened about in Chris's stomach. His lungs had stopped working. How long before he suffocated? How long would she wait? Would kissing her make this whole thing better, or worse? This had to be a no-win situation.

"Well, I think that answers that," Freddie said, and stepped away.

"I don't know what—" Chris started.

Freddie gave a little smile. "What you want? I know you don't. Some day, you'll figure it out. I really don't think I'm it. That's okay, because I'm not willing to get left behind, and at some point you'll be leaving."

All Chris could say to that was, "Yes."

"Poor you," she said, and Chris heard real sympathy in her voice, not sarcasm. "You're in for a rough ride, if my hunch is correct."

Women. Chris shook his head and managed to breathe normally.

"So, now we've got all that out of the way. Friends?" She stuck out her hand.

Chris took it. "You're willing to put up with me?"

"Oh, I'm going to put you to work, strong man. Come look at the state of our playing field."

***

Chris went into Petersfield in late February for his blood test. He hardly hesitated when he filled in the lines on the form for "place of residence." He sat in the waiting room with an assortment of nervous-looking people, all of them as far from each other as possible, each one heaving a sigh of relief when the girl stepped out holding a green card and called their name. He wondered what he'd do if his test came up positive. How often did that happen? He'd never seen it. He didn't feel particularly nervous. Why was everyone else? The whole thing was a sham anyway, a game to make people feel like the government was doing something to keep them safe. He could be negative today and positive next week, but his card wouldn't reflect that.

The girl came out with a green card and called his name.

"Ta, luv," he said to her as he plucked it from her fingers.

He had time before he had to be back at the van, so he wandered the market. It had shrunk considerably since Christmas. Stallholders huddled next to fire barrels, or sat in their stalls wrapped in blankets. Chris looked over the seed packets that heralded the coming of spring, but Pauline and Marie picked out the seeds for the garden. He saw a football in one booth, but since Freddie had discovered a stash of all sorts of balls in a bin in the basement of the school, he passed it by.

Chris realized there was nothing he really needed. He bought a meat pie to eat on the way back to Breton.

In the evenings, Chris and George talked endlessly about plans for spring plowing, harrowing and planting. Chris had never realized how much preparation was needed, how much work was involved. George drew up charts with weather contingencies. On their twice-weekly pub trips on bath nights they made plans with other men in the town for labor sharing. Chris volunteered for various jobs. He pushed aside the thought that he had planned to leave for Bath in the spring.

During the first week of March Pauline brought it up. Their talks in the study had dwindled to once a week. Chris did not tell her things that made her go silent. He did not talk about London, or the dark days in the States before he reached St. Crispin's. He didn't tell her about Portsmouth. He talked about the band, life on the road, accosted by screaming fans outside hotels. It was as if he was talking about a different person, not himself, and it made her laugh. That was better than making her cry. It was good to hear her laugh.

It became easier to talk about Sophie. He smiled when he remembered little things he hadn't thought of for years, like the robins that nested in a topiary on the back patio, and how Sophie would put out bits of string and yarn for birds building their nests in the spring.

"It's nearly spring," Pauline said. "We'll be starting some seeds soon, in trays."

Chris knew what she was referring to. "Things have changed. Do you want me to go?"

"I don't *want* you to go, no. How do you feel about it? What things have changed?"

"Everything's changed," Chris said, avoiding a specific answer.

Pauline put on her practical face. "Not really. You still don't know what you'll find in Bath."

"The chances are slimmer, though. All that's left is to check their doors for the marks like I found in London and make it official."

"Not necessarily," Pauline said. "I left my flat, came here, stayed here. I didn't leave a forwarding address."

Chris gave her a quick look. "Where would they have gone? Brian in particular. He had a big house with a big garden in a nice neighborhood. His would be the place to escape to, not escape from."

"You can't know," Pauline said. "So many things could have happened that you know nothing about."

"Well, I know he's not there, and I don't know where to start looking."

"There must be other people in Bath that you both knew. You could ask them."

Chris had pushed Bath into a hazy future. Yes, at some point he planned to go. Of course he did.

"There's so much to do here," he said. "George can't do it all himself."

"I helped him last year."

"You have the garden."

"We managed last year."

Chris shifted in his seat. "I promised to help Freddie with the playing ground."

"Yes, you've made all sorts of arrangements, I know. Why?"

"Because... people need help. I can help." His voice came out louder than he expected. Pauline raised an eyebrow at him, something that always annoyed him because it meant she didn't believe what he was saying. She folded her hands in her lap, sat back, and *looked* at him. She'd wait now, with her patient look, silently, with the corners of her mouth turning up just a little the way they did, until he dredged up something she deemed worthy. Crap, it was exasperating when she did that.

Chris crossed his arms and glared at her. What did she want to hear?

"I'm not ready," he said.

"Okay."

The temperature dropped that night, and it was snowing hard in the morning. It snowed for three days, piling up in drifts against the doors, filling the paths Chris and George shoveled twice a day. They stayed home on bath night, holed up in the study with the door shut, discussing petrol rations and crop rotation.

Then the sun came out, the temperature went back up, and within a week the snow was gone, and the rain came. Cold drizzle turned the yard to mud. Chris and George spent a week in the barn and garage, tuning the tractor and getting the machinery ready.

In the kitchen, little green sprouts pushed up from the soil laid out in trays on tables set up near the windows. Spring came, and with it the long days of hard work in the fields and gardens. Chris rarely saw Pauline except at breakfast and supper. They had no time for talks in the study. Some days Chris found himself working alongside men and women he hardly knew, but a sense of community, a sense that all this work was for the good of everyone, satisfied him in a way he hadn't felt since he'd left St. Crispin's. Once he ended up working in the same field as Rob Warren. They exchanged cool nods in greeting, but did not speak. It didn't happen a second time.

Before he knew it, May was mostly gone, and Chris had spare time for the playing field at the school. Freddie organized a couple of work days when all the kids came out to help. Pauline came sometimes, and the parents who could spare the time.

"It won't be world-class for a few years," Chris said to Freddie one day, "but you could have some decent games later this summer, maybe."

"Should I bother to ask you to help coach the kids?"

"I don't know," Chris said, and Freddie nodded, and did not ask.

***

Chris sat still, staring at the bobber on the water, listening to raindrops pattering on the hood of his slicker. He had managed a few fishing trips with Wes once planting was finished, but Wes no longer looked for a reason to skip school. A rainy Saturday had brought the boy to the house early with his fishing pole, and Chris had been glad to join him. Wes usually plied Chris with questions, but today he had been nearly silent. Both of them had caught several fish, and Chris decided it was almost time to head back.

Wes, who had found a place further down the bank, reeled in suddenly, stood, and made his way back toward Chris through the wet grass. He stopped a few meters away and sat himself down on a rock. He cast out again. Chris glanced at him. Wes's eyebrows were drawn together.

"Can I ask you something?" he said, not looking at Chris.

"Sure."

Wes flicked his line around a bit. "Are you going to marry Pauline?"

"Um, why do you ask that?"

"I heard Mrs. Bainbridge talking," Wes muttered.

"Hm. What did she say?"

"She said she thought something was going on. She said she didn't believe all that talk about you leaving because you haven't yet, and don't show any sign of it, and what else would be keeping you here except Pauline because you haven't shown any interest in any of the other ladies." Wes stopped, chewed on his lip, then went on. "She said she hoped Pauline was smart enough to make you marry her before she let you into her bed, or you'd just end up being another Michael Cooper, and she'd be heartbroken again."

"Anything else?" Chris tried to keep his tone light, a sinking feeling in the pit of his stomach.

"The other lady said that after Michael Cooper, of course Pauline had already let you in her bed because she's not the sort to hold out."

Chris gripped his pole as Wes trailed off. He'd known there must be some gossip, but he had never imagined it would be quite so succinct.

"What does that mean?" Wes asked. "Who is Michael Cooper?"

Chris sighed. "There's a lot to explain, Wes. You don't know Michael?"

"I don't think so."

"He's an old friend of the family. He grew up here, so everyone in town knows him. He was... um, Pauline's boyfriend for a long time. But not anymore."

"Oh, him. I guess I met him once. Do you know him?"

"Yes, I do. He's why I'm here. I met him in Portsmouth, and when I got ill, Michael arranged for me to come here to get well."

"Why did she say you were leaving?"

"Well, I do plan to leave, Wes. I have family in Bath, and I plan to go find them."

Wes looked stricken. "When?"

"I don't really know," Chris said, looking out at his line, reeling it in slowly. "I didn't plan to stay much past spring, but I'm still here."

"Because of Pauline? Are you her boyfriend now?"

"Um, no." Chris had to take a deep breath. "It's not like that, Wes."

"But you like her, I can tell. You talk all the time, and she's not married, and neither are you, so you could get married, couldn't you? And then you could stay."

Wes might as well have whacked him on the head with his fishing pole.

"Now, hang on a minute," Chris said. He tried to collect his thoughts. "People don't just get married because they like each other. Of course I like Pauline. I like you, too, and George, and Marie, and Grace. But I have family in Bath, I grew up there. At some point I'll go and find them."

Wes sat stony-faced. "So why have you stayed this long?"

"It's kind of complicated, Wes."

"Because you're in Pauline's bed?"

Chris thought he must look like a stranded fish. "I'm not 'in her bed.'"

"Mrs. Harrington thinks you are. And Mrs. Stone, and—"

"Okay, I get it," Chris interrupted him. *Crap, crap, crap.* "That's just ugly gossip."

"Why is it ugly? People who are married sleep in bed together."

"Well, yes, but sleeping is not what she meant by it," Chris said, his eyebrows drawing together. He could see where this conversation was going, and he wasn't sure he was the one who should be having it with Wes.

"What did she mean, then?" Wes asked.

***

Chris left his fish in the kitchen with Grace. He found Pauline in the barn, brushing down one of the horses. She looked up as he approached.

"Ah, did you catch anything?"

"A couple small ones," he said. "Wes and I had an interesting chat."

"Oh? What did you talk about?" she asked, brushing out the horse's mane.

Chris crossed his arms. "Sex."

Pauline's eye flew open and her mouth formed a little "o."

"How did that come up?"

"He asked me. Hasn't anyone ever talked to him? Hell, he didn't know anything."

"He's only thirteen—"

"I knew all about that stuff by the time I was twelve."

Pauline fidgeted. "Yes, you're right, of course. I should have thought of it, had George deal with it. But at least he felt comfortable enough with you to ask. Thanks for taking care of it." She chuckled. "Well, not what you planned on, eh?"

Chris would have found it amusing if it weren't for what else they'd talked about. He didn't smile. Pauline caught his mood.

"What is it?" she asked, trying to get serious.

Chris looked hard at her. "He told me some gossip, too."

"Oh. About?"

"Us, of course. Mrs. Bainbridge hopes you're smart enough to make me marry you before you let me into your bed."

"Damn her," Pauline muttered. "I'm sorry, Chris. I'll have a word with her."

"But Mrs. Harrington and Mrs. Stone and several others apparently feel you're not the sort to hold out."

Chris saw the pink creeping onto her cheeks before she turned her face away.

"Look, if me being here is going to cause problems for you—" Chris started, but Pauline cut him off.

"Don't be ridiculous," she said. "Why should I care what silly old ladies gossip about? It's just talk. I'll set them straight." She returned to brushing, her face set hard, her strokes bordering on vicious.

Chris watched her until she looked up at him.

"What else?" she asked, as if steeled for something more.

Chris considered, and decided to take the plunge.

"They said Michael broke your heart. Did he?"

Surprise flitted across her face, and she tossed her head with feigned indifference.

"More than once. He's a good friend, but a lousy boyfriend." She pretended to concentrate on a tangle in Molly's mane. "Eventually, I stopped feeling sorry for myself and accepted whatever he had to offer. More's the pity. Took me far too long to get a spine." She took a deep breath, stood up straighter, and looked at Chris.

A few ugly thoughts about Cooper gave way to the thought that her eyes got darker when she was angry, and the way she pursed her lips in determination was undeniably attractive. Chris blinked, cleared his throat.

"All right," was all he could manage, and he left her there and went to clean the fish.

Chapter 18

"Freddie asked me to coach the kids," Pauline said to Chris one sunny July afternoon while they worked in the vegetable garden, weeding and picking.

"That's great. You're going to, aren't you? You'll be good at it."

"Did she ask you?"

"No."

Pauline straightened her back and stretched. "Why not? You've been to all the practices, and the kids like you. You're good with kids."

"My temporary situation," Chris said. "She said it wouldn't be good for the kids when I go."

"Oh. Have you been thinking about that?"

"I'm always thinking about that."

They moved down the garden, one row apart, at a steady pace. Chris enjoyed the Saturday practices at the school. Nearly all the kids participated, and some of the adults. Each week more people came, bringing chairs or blankets to sit on—and picnic lunches—to watch the fun. Each week more people joined in.

"We had games at St. Crispin's, too," Chris volunteered. Their talks had moved out of the study, to wherever and whenever they happened to have a few private moments.

"What games?"

"Sometimes it was football. Sometimes it was American football, but without all the equipment, a watered-down version. They called it 'flag football'. And they had basketball, too."

"Did you play or coach?"

"I played sometimes. The teams were always different. Anyone could play. They had kids' games in the morning, and adults after lunch."

"Were there a lot of kids?"

"Yes, quite a lot. They had an orphanage. The outside teams were still collecting them when I left."

"Outside teams?"

"The groups that spent a lot of time on the road, foraging. They called it collecting. Anything useful, including people. They always looked for orphans."

"That's wonderful, to do that, give them a home."

Chris thought of Wes. "Yes, well, some of them turned into problems. Some of them were older, they'd been on their own a couple years, and they didn't like the rules. Some stayed and caused problems, others just left."

"The older boys, eh?"

"Not just the boys. Some of the girls, too. They'd learned how to get by, figured out what they had that men wanted, and that really caused problems."

"Oh, that's sad," Pauline said, glancing up at him, making a face.

Chris shrugged. "Oldest profession," he said. "It's everywhere, really. If you were starving, really starving, it might not seem such a bad option."

Pauline was quiet, looking a little distressed, the way she often did when he told her about what it was like now in the rest of the world, the world beyond Breton.

"It was an outside team that found me," Chris said. "On the road, half-dead."

"And took you to Brother Luke," she said, nodding. "Did you stay friends with him after you left the infirmary?"

"I saw him occasionally, yes. We talked now and then. He stitched up my elbow, once. I tore it open on a nail in the barn." He stepped closer to her, through a gap in the pea plants, and showed her the scar.

"Uh, that's huge!" she said, grimacing.

He twisted his arm around to look at it. "Yeah, it was impressive. Bled all over the place. They were worried I'd get tetanus. They didn't have any vaccine. But I didn't. Just can't kill me, I suppose."

"You've been very lucky," Pauline said.

"More like unlucky, wouldn't you say?"

"Well, if you're going to be a pessimist." She smiled. "So, why did you leave? It wasn't something awful, was it?"

"No. Their security was excellent. They had good people in charge of it. The place is probably still going strong. God, I hope so. It was the way the rest of the world should be—utopia. But that can't exist, can it? No such thing as utopia, isn't that how the story always ends? Because there are always enough people who won't want to follow the rules, no matter how reasonable those rules are, people who will never be content with everything ticking along smoothly." He grunted.

"But that's not what you asked. No, I had to go. It just wasn't home, it wasn't England. I just couldn't give up trying to get here." He stopped before "trying to find my family." He was so close now, he was closer than he'd ever been, Bath was in reach, but the despair of London, the proof of one brother dead, still gnawed at

216

him, a wound that opened without warning, like the gash on his elbow, spilling blood, making him catch his breath in pain. The thought of the same thing again in Bath still stopped him cold. Better to stay here, with a sense of purpose, in a place where his help was undeniably needed, at least for a while longer.

Pauline stopped and sat back on her heels, wiped at her forehead under her straw hat, and looked at him. He met her gaze.

"I never would have believed you if you'd told me six years ago that I would be content here," she said. "Back then, I thought I hated this place. Now I can't imagine living anywhere else."

"But would you feel that way if the world hadn't gone all to hell?"

"What does it matter? The world *did* go all to hell, and I *do* feel that way."

"Then you can't ask for better than that, can you?" He carried a bucket of peas and a basket of weeds off to the end of the row. He dumped the weeds in the wheelbarrow, left the peas, and brought back an empty bucket. He did the same with Pauline's basket and bucket.

"Thank you," she said, and went back to weeding.

Chris watched her. An odd sensation infused him, a pull, something stronger than he'd felt at St. Crispin's, something more than contentment. He shook his head, went back to his row, back to picking peas, but then he stopped and fingered his wedding ring. It was almost a relief to feel the little stab in his heart, to know it was still there, that it still mattered, that the ring was still important. If he let himself think about it long enough, he knew the little feeling would swell into something that made his throat tight, his shoulders tense, something that made him grieve for the pictures he used to have, the pictures that had been lost in London. It was the only thing he could do for her. He hadn't got home in time, he hadn't been able to help her, he hadn't been able to do anything to save her, but he could still save her memory, keep it as something he would never betray. It was the only thing he could do for her, for Sophie.

"You're coming to the pub tonight, right?" Pauline asked, and he had to stop and look at her, clear his head, bring himself back.

"It's a *dance*," he said.

"Would it kill you to dance? To loosen up, have some fun?"

"Suppose I did. Suppose I danced with you, or with Freddie. Then the rest of them would descend like vultures."

Pauline gave a little snort.

"Just when I've got them to leave me alone, they'd be at it again. I'll have to throw rocks at them."

"You can't really blame them, Chris. They're lonely. There are no men here—well, no available men. You're it. Of course they're going to hang around, try to get your attention." She shrugged. "And you're good-looking."

He shot a glance at her, saw her trying not to smile.

"I'm not available."

She got serious. "They don't see it that way. You keep saying you're going to go, but you're still here."

He had nothing to say to that.

"There are worse things to have to put up with," she said, moving down the row, pulling her basket with her.

A nice quiet evening at home would suit him just fine, he figured, sitting on his arse in the sitting room by himself.

***

Pauline had just stood up to clear the supper dishes when George raised his head and said "Quiet, what's that?"

Chris heard the sound of a motor on the road. The noise got fainter, then stronger again. Someone had come up the driveway on the other side of the house and driven into the yard. George beat Pauline to the back window, pushing aside the curtain.

"It's someone on a motorcycle."

Pauline crowded in to see. "It's Michael!"

Chris tried to quell the sudden annoyance, reminding himself that Michael had every right to be here. He'd said, on that last day at the Distribution Center, that he'd try to come in a month or so. That was—when—October? That long ago?

George pulled open the door and went out to greet their visitor. Pauline stayed inside. She looked over at Chris. He couldn't read her face. Did she think he should jump up to greet Michael, too? The more he'd heard about how Michael had treated Pauline, the less friendly Chris felt toward him. Grateful, sure. Indebted, yes. But friendly? Not so much.

The motor went quiet, George's voice took its place, and soon Michael came in ahead of George, shrugging a rucksack off his shoulders.

"Did I miss supper?" he asked, with a big smile on his face. He looked the same: dark, curly hair, intense blue eyes, and gleaming white teeth. Crap, had the man managed to find a *dentist* while the rest of the population was struggling to grow food? He wore a natty leather jacket. George came in carrying a motorcycle helmet.

"Paulie!" Michael said, putting his arms out. "You look smashing!" He grabbed her in a big hug and tried to kiss her, but she turned her face at the last moment and he had to kiss her cheek. He pulled back and seemed a little confused, but regained his happy face. He released her, and moved to hug Grace, who had stood as he came in. "Mum, you look lovely, as always."

"It's so wonderful to see you, dear," Grace said.

Michael caught sight of Chris. His mouth dropped open. "Price, what are you doing here?" He held out his hand. Chris stood up and leaned across the table to shake it. "They've been taking good care of you, obviously. Good to see you. You looked half-dead the last time I saw you."

"Good to see you, Cooper," Chris said.

"Marie," Michael said with a smile, turning to her, bending to give her a little kiss on the cheek.

"What brings you all the way out here?" Pauline said. She had her arms crossed, tried to look disapproving, but a little smile showed through.

"Santa sent me." Michael grinned, and went to pick up his rucksack from where he had let it fall. "I know I'm late, but only by what, six months?" He brought the pack over to the table, pulled out the chair Pauline had vacated, and sat down with the pack between his feet. He looked up at Chris and frowned. "Santa did not say you would be here."

"Oh, Michael, c'mon," Pauline said. She picked up a few empty dishes from the table. "Did you eat?"

"A bite, yes, but I would never refuse anything cooked by you, as you know." He tried to grasp her hand as she reached for the plate in front of him. She pulled it away and smacked at his. He ignored it. "Right, what have we got in here?" he said, rummaging.

Chris gathered dishes at his end of the table and took them over to the sink. He reached it the same time as Pauline. He caught her eye. She shrugged at him, got a clean plate, and went back to the table, where she dished up the small amount of leftovers for Michael and set the food in front of him. Chris scraped off the plates into the scrap bucket.

"George," Michael was saying, "you still fancy a pipe now and then, don't you?" He handed George a small bag. "Tobacco, and quite smooth, too. Oh, and somewhere I have some petrol coupons for that tractor of yours. Are you keeping it running?"

George grinned. "Just barely." He opened the bag and smelled the tobacco. "That's fine stuff. Wherever did you get it?"

"There's a lot of stuff coming in these days, my friends," Michael said. "Way out here in the country, you never see it. Mum, I know you were always partial to a good sherry." He pulled a bundle out and unrolled it, revealing a slim bottle. "I've had some of this, and it's excellent." He handed it to her.

"Thank you, Michael, dear."

"Now, Marie," Michael said, "I know you would love to get your hands on some cashmere yarn I saw the other day, big bags of it, terrific soft stuff, but I didn't have room in my sack for it. I got you this instead." He handed her a flat block of something wrapped in white paper, about the size of a paperback book.

"What is it?"

"Smell it," Michael hinted.

She did, and her eyes flew open wide. "Is it chocolate?"

There were amazed exclamations around the room.

"Thank you." Marie shook her head. "Oh, what should we make with it?"

"Cake is always good," Michael suggested. "Now, Paulie." He looked up at her, his hand inside the rucksack. "Come over here, luv."

Chris leaned against the sink and watched as she went. She stood about a foot away from Michael.

"You must have used up the stuff I sent with Price by now, eh?" He pulled a bottle of shampoo out of his pack. It was bigger than the other one had been. "Pretty hair needs good shampoo." Pauline took it with a smile. He pulled out another bottle. "Different scent. And of course, soap. I know how much you like pretty-smelling soap." He handed her two bars of soap.

"Michael," she said softly, shaking her head. "This must have cost you a fortune."

"Don't worry about that, my dear. Ah. Here you go, Price." He pulled a pack of cigarettes out of the bag and tossed it across the table toward the sink. Chris caught it.

"I don't smoke, Cooper," Chris said. "But thanks."

"They're as good as money, most places," Michael assured him. He looked around at everyone. "There's more, but this is calling to me." He pulled his chair up to the table, grabbed a fork, and began to eat.

Chapter 19

Michael insisted that George, Marie, and Grace should go to the dance at the pub as planned.

"I'm knackered after that ride," he said. "You go and have fun. I'll be here a day or two. Plenty of time to catch up."

He did not push Pauline when she said she wouldn't go. He watched her as she moved around the kitchen, putting away dishes, brewing some herbal tea, and getting a small plate of biscuits.

"Have you got some of that delightful cider?" Michael asked, snagging a biscuit as soon as she set the plate down.

"I'll get it," Chris said, pushing his chair back. He took a pitcher and went down the cellar stairs. Why did he find Cooper so annoying? He was the same as he'd been back in Portsmouth, but for some reason, Chris wanted to smack him. Now that Chris knew some of his background, his manner seemed even more fake.

As he came back into the kitchen, Chris saw Michael pulling his hand away from Pauline's. *Not my business.* He got glasses and poured, then took his seat again, at the opposite end of the table from the two of them.

"Thank you, Price." Michael took a long swig. "Ah, this always did rival Harry's brew."

Chris had to keep himself from guzzling. He needed a good buzz.

"It's not a problem if I spend a night or two, eh?" Michael said to Pauline. "My place is in a hell of a state. I'd no idea it could go so bad in a couple of years." He shrugged, as if it were no great consequence.

"Chris is in the spare room," Pauline said.

Ha, it's the couch for you, Cooper. Chris rested his chin on one hand and turned his glass around on the table with the other, trying to look uninterested.

"I could bunk in with you, Paulie." Michael gave a light laugh, as if it were a joke.

Chris shifted in his chair; he couldn't help it. Michael's eyes flicked over at him, then went back to Pauline. She watched Michael out of the tops of her eyes with her chin down. Chris knew she was angry. Apparently Michael didn't, or didn't care. She shook her head.

"I did the last time I was here," Michael said, cocking his head to one side.

"You can have my bed," she said. "I'll sleep with Mum."

"Oh, come on, Paulie, don't be mad," he said. So, he did know.

Pauline rose, her chair scraping the floor. "I'll just get that ready for you." She left the room. The stairs creaked.

Michael leaned back in his chair, his attention on the doorway where she had gone. He sipped at his cider, turned back to Chris, ran his tongue over his teeth. "Well, well."

"You blew it with her a long time ago," Chris said. "You told me that yourself."

"That I did." Michael tapped on the tabletop with his fingers. "I didn't think you'd still be here. What happened to your quest? What happened to Bath?"

Then he sat up straighter. "Have you been and come back?"

"Not yet, no."

Michael narrowed his eyes at him. "Do you bunk in with her, then?"

The question made Chris's stomach contract. "No. Not that it's any of your business."

"You're right, it's not," Michael said. "It's just she's always been happy to see me, before now."

"She seemed happy enough to see you."

"You know what I mean."

Indeed I do, Cooper.

Michael gave him a hint of a smile. "You're working on it, though, aren't you?"

Chris stared at him without changing expression.

Michael stabbed a finger at Chris. "You need to take that wedding ring off your finger."

Chris was sitting with his chin in his left hand. He pressed the smooth band of gold against his lip. "Maybe."

"If you've got any chance with her, Price, you're a fool to pass it up. Time to move on, mate; your wife's dead, but you're not."

"That's enough, Cooper." Chris sat back in his chair, crossing his arms.

Michael put up his hands. "End of discussion. I suppose if I'd gone to the dance I'd have the pick of any number of fun-filled beds for the night. But now she's gone to the trouble of changing the sheets, I guess I'll have to stay."

Chris took a long drink.

"Don't look at me like that, Price. I'm not so bad, and you know it. I have enough manners to keep my

226

visits to a minimum and behave myself while I'm here. I'm sure you've had the whole story by now. This is my family, you know."

***

Chris heard a quick knock on his door, just before he put out his lamp. He opened it a crack. Michael stood there.

"Truce, okay? I have something for you."

Chris stepped back and let him in.

"Look, I've been hearing some talk," Michael went on, keeping his voice low. He closed the door. He had a small bundle in his hand. "There are trouble spots, not around here, closer to London, but you never know."

"What do you mean?"

"Gangs. Taking what they want, generally causing trouble. Here, take this." He unrolled the bundle, a scrap of rag, exposing a small black handgun. He held it out. "You've been around, Price, I know. Hell, you spent time in London. You never wished you had one?"

Chris fought the rush of adrenaline. "I did have." He took the gun. It fit into his hand in a comforting way, easier than the last one. "A SIG-Sauer. Brilliant." It was obscene: this brutal thing in this gentle house. He checked the clip for bullets.

Michael grinned. "You never cease to surprise me, Price." He fished in his pocket, dropped a number of bullets into Chris's hand.

Chris counted them. "That's all?"

"Best I could do. Enough to get you out of a tight spot, maybe."

"Thanks."

"Come in handy on your trip to Bath, eh?"

Chris eyed him.

"You're still planning that, aren't you? You seemed bent on it, back in Portsmouth," Michael said.

"Yeah, I suppose."

"Or have you given it up in favor of greener pastures?"

"Not entirely."

Michael gestured at the gun. "Right, well, I wouldn't let on about that."

"No," Chris agreed.

"'Night, then." Michael went out and closed the door.

Chris stared at the gun, then wrapped it up in the rag again and put it in the top dresser drawer. He lay in bed a long time before he went to sleep, thinking about London, the faded red X and "3 D" scrawled on the door of his brother Kevin's flat, the weeks of despair, the depths he'd fallen to, and the deadly end of it.

***

"Paulie," Michael said as they were clearing the breakfast dishes, "come and take a walk with me."

Pauline's first inclination was to say no, but her mum smiled at her.

"Go on, dear," Grace said. "I'll finish up here."

Michael held out his hand to her as he stood by the back door. She ignored it, instead getting a light jacket off a hook on the wall, and putting it on as she went out the door ahead of him. George and Chris had already gone out, and Chris was just dragging open the big door on the barn. He looked over as they came out.

"We won't be long," she called to him. Michael looked sideways at her.

They walked around the house, through the garden, to the road, and strolled in the direction of Michael's house. Pauline waited to see what Michael had to say.

"Things are looking good around here," Michael started. "Your place is picking up. You've got more veggies this year, eh?"

"Yes, we planted a bit more."

"Is that a new shed out back?"

"Yes, but we can't find shingles for it. George doesn't think he can afford to pay someone to make wooden shingles."

"I'll have a look around, see what I can come up with."

"Don't get in trouble over it," Pauline said, but Michael waved it off.

"And you, you're not having to work as hard?"

"What are you getting at, Michael?"

"Is Chris planning to stay, then?"

Pauline had to smile. As she suspected, Michael was jealous of Chris. She did not answer right away, just to see what else Michael would say.

"Is he the reason you slept with your Mum last night?"

"No, Michael, you're the reason I slept with Mum last night."

"Paulie..." he said, shaking his head.

"Michael, we've already had this conversation, two years ago, the last time you turned up and wanted to pick up where we left off, like you always do. Two years, Michael. It's been almost two years!"

"I've been busy—"

"You could have been dead, for all I knew. At least before, when you disappeared, I figured I'd hear about it if there was going to be a funeral."

Michael rolled his eyes.

"But now," Pauline went on, "I wouldn't ever know. You'd just disappear forever, and I'd never know what happened. Just like Jim."

"Paulie, you're being dramatic," Michael said, trying to take her hand.

"No, I'm being fed up, is what!" she said, pulling her hand away. "Just because it suits you fine doesn't mean it suits me fine. I'm serious, Michael. We're done. I'll be your friend, I'll always be your friend, but that's it." She turned around and started walking back toward the house.

"Paulie, wait," Michael said, and she stopped. "I'm just worried about you."

She screwed up her face at him and put her hands on her hips. "You have got to be kidding. You show up here after almost two years without so much as a letter, and you're worried about me? Piss off, Michael!"

"I sent a letter," he protested. "I sent one with Price."

"Oh yes, thank you for that very informative scrap."

"You don't know this bloke, Paulie."

She stood with her mouth open. It took her a moment to take in what he had said. "And you do? Are you actually trying to tell me that you know him better after two months than I do after nine? I think I've come to know him quite well, actually. No, shut up," she said when he tried to interrupt. "You have no right, Michael, to say anything like that. You have no idea what's going on here—which, by the way, is nothing!"

"I just mean that he's got a lot of baggage."

"Excuse me, but I'm the one with the degree, remember? You lasted how long at University? One term? Of course he "has baggage," as you so eloquently put it. He lost his wife and baby, quite horribly, and a whole lot of other people as well. He's seen far more horrible things than you. He's come a long way in the time he's been here. Hell, you sent him here, remember?"

"He said he just needed to get well enough to go on to Bath."

"Maybe he doesn't think he's well enough, yet. He can stay as long as he needs, or wants."

"You'd like that, wouldn't you?"

She stared at him, trying to control her anger. It always ended like this with Michael. He always pushed it too far. As if he could dictate to her. As if she had to run her life through him. Usually they could have a good week together before things fell apart. This time they hadn't even had twenty-four hours.

"Don't be mad, Paulie," he said. "Look, you've seen him at his best. I've seen him at his worst."

"What the hell does that mean?"

"I saw him nearly beat a man to death. I helped pull him off."

231

An image of Chris taking down Rob Warren with lightning speed popped into Pauline's head. She clenched her fists. "What are you talking about?"

Michael looked as serious as she'd ever seen him. "It was on the lorry docks. Some bloke shows up with a gun, and grabs one of the gals—Kay—who was one of the supervisors. Puts the gun to her head, says he's going to kill her, that he wants to see Chris Price. Chaos, of course, and no one knows where Price is, not that we'd let the guy shoot him, but you know what I mean. Well, along comes Price, out of nowhere—someone must have told him—walking right toward the guy. He aims the gun at Price, of course, and starts screaming at him, that it's all his fault, that he's going to shoot both Price and Kay."

Michael stopped, took a deep breath, as if it really bothered him to remember this, to talk about it. "Price never stopped, just walked right up to him, grabbed the gun out of his hand and beat him with it. Dropped the poor bugger like a stone, and then just kept beating him until we pulled him off. Never said a word. Sat in the corner with blood on his hands until they decided not to charge him with anything. Everybody figures he saved Kay's life, right? They carted the other bloke off to hospital. Don't know what ever happened to him."

Pauline stared at Michael. Her stomach twisted, sending a nasty taste up into her mouth. "Why did you tell me that?"

"I just thought you should know," he said. "This guy knew him, Paulie, knew Chris, and hated him enough to want to kill him. It must have been something to do with the time he was in London. I just want you to be careful. I think you've fallen for him."

Pauline kept her face calm, but her heart flip-flopped. Had Michael said that about her falling for Chris just to annoy her, because he was jealous, or had he seen something in the way she interacted with Chris? She had tried so hard to keep it strictly friendly, and now she wondered if she had failed.

"Why did you send him here in the first place, if you're so worried about it?" she asked then, steering the conversation away from his last statement.

"I'm not so worried about it. I think he's a good chap," Michael said. "I really do. I like him. I owed him. He covered for me a couple of times when he didn't have to. He needed a break. I don't think he's had many breaks in this whole bloody mess. And that had happened the first week he was there. Nobody really knew him yet. Everybody left him alone, of course, after that. And then he was—well, you know, quiet, no expression. I never saw him even raise his voice the rest of the time we were there. He talked in his sleep, though."

"Yes, he did that here, too."

"I wasn't worried about him coming here. He said he was going to get over that cough and head to Bath. I figured that would be the end of it. When he did talk, that's what he talked about, going to Bath, finding his family. I never dreamed he'd still be here."

"He's afraid to go to Bath," Pauline said.

"You've worked your magic with him, have you, Doctor Anderson?"

"A bit, yes. He's afraid they'll all be dead. He's not sure if he can stand that. And that's the only reason he's still here, Michael. It's got nothing to do with me."

"Ah, that's where you're wrong, Doctor," Michael said quietly. "Once again, your patient has fallen for you. Maybe you should work a bit more magic, send him off to Bath to find out what's what."

Pauline's heart flopped again, but she dismissed what Michael had said about Chris falling for her. He didn't show the slightest sign of it. "You just want him gone, Michael. You don't care about him at all."

"I care about *you*, Paulie. Every time I see you I wonder why the hell I stayed away so long." He took a step closer, tried to look sincere.

"Oh, piss off, Michael," Pauline said, pushing him away. She started walking again, back toward the house.

She didn't let him get her alone again, didn't let him try to talk to her. Later that afternoon he packed up his bag, said his brief goodbyes, and drove off on his motorcycle. He promised to come back soon.

Chapter 20

"Michael told me something," Pauline said as she used the hatchet to chip kindling. Chris was splitting logs a few meters away. He stopped, rested the axe on the ground, wiped his sleeve across his forehead. He looked over at her, waited. "About when you were working on the lorry docks."

His mouth became a hard line. He hefted the axe, took a swing, and split a log balanced on a stump. "He told you what happened with Kay and Marcus."

Pauline nodded. "He didn't know the man. He said the man knew you, though."

"Yeah, I knew him," Chris said, his voice hard. "He deserved it."

"Michael said he pointed a gun at you, and said he was going to shoot you, and you walked right up to him."

"He'd have shot Kay if no one did anything. I took a chance." Chris set another log on end on the stump.

"And you beat him unconscious."

"He deserved it."

"Michael said they had to pull you off, that you were going to kill him."

"If I were going to kill him, I would have used the gun. I almost did. Maybe I should have." He swung the axe hard. It stuck in the log, and he worked it loose. Pauline chipped away at her piece of wood.

Chris took a few more swings, grunting with each one. Then he threw the axe down.

"Is that what he took you off to tell you? I'm still here, so he decided he had to warn you about me? Something bad enough so you'd send me packing?"

"No, he just—"

"Michael doesn't understand. I knew Marcus. I'd seen him do things, heard him bragging about other things—things that give decent people nightmares." He stopped, staring at the ground. "I don't know if I ever mentioned him. He was the leader of the gang in London. He killed people, Pauline, like you butcher chickens. You want to know what happened to Beryl? Marcus ordered her execution because she was helping me, trying to get me out of there. We escaped, but while we were running, she was shot. My fault. That's what those nightmares are about: Beryl dying—in pain—because of me."

Chris glared at her, as if defying her to contradict him. Pauline didn't know what to say. She wasn't a detached therapist anymore. She wanted to go to him and hold him and soothe him. All this was a mistake. She should never have brought this up.

"Marcus followed me to Portsmouth. That's the kind of person he was. He couldn't bear that I got away, that he'd lost control of anything. He couldn't just let me go. He had to kill me. But I knew he'd hesitate. I took the chance.

"I'm not proud of what I did to him, but I'd do it again. He deserved it. He would have killed Kay." Chris paced among the stumps, saw the axe, bent to pick it up. He held it, stood still again, and put a hand to his face. "In a way, I did kill him. He got an infection when he was in hospital and died there." He kicked a piece of wood off a stump and sat down suddenly, his back still to her. He let the axe fall.

"How do you know?"

"Kay told me. I don't think Cooper knows."

"But it was self-defense—"

"Right, whatever you want to call it."

"It doesn't change anything. I knew there were things you didn't want to tell me. Of course I wouldn't expect you to go because of that."

Chris pushed himself up and turned to her finally. "Cooper's been lucky. He has no idea what goes on in some places. He thinks he does. He thinks he's clever. But shampoo, tobacco, an extra petrol ration... That's nothing, Pauline. Pointless shit. He has no idea. I hope he doesn't fall in with people like Marcus, because it will be the end of him. He gets by on fawning and fakery and petty bribes. He brought me a gun—did you know that? I suppose he has one, too. But it will only get him killed if thinks he can flash it about. He hasn't got the balls to use it because he's never had a gun pointed at his head by a man who doesn't give a damn about anyone."

Pauline took a deep breath, hoping to calm her stomach. "Okay, calm down. Let's go inside, to the study, get a little calmer, and talk this out. Okay?"

"No."

"There's more. I know there's more. You can tell me. I think it will help." She dropped the hatchet she was still holding and stood, taking a step toward Chris.

Chris was shaking now, holding himself stiffly. "I can't be your patient anymore."

"Why not?"

"Don't you see it?" His voice quavered. "I don't want to be the stupid drunk picking fights in the pub with the unlucky chap who happens to sit next to you."

"You're nothing like that—"

"We're done, Pauline. We have to be. I can't tell you anything that might upset you, because seeing you upset hurts me too much. I despise Cooper for the way he treats you. He shows up once a year and expects you to welcome him into your bed, as if that's enough for you. I know that's not enough for you. I want to hurt him because he hurt you. Do you see what's happened? I thought I could ignore it. I'm good at ignoring feelings, right? I've spent the last five years perfecting the art. But Cooper saw through it, even if you never did. Did he tell you that? Did he point out that I've fixated on you?"

It was like a blow to her gut. She had to catch her breath.

"I never saw any sign of that, not in you," she said. "I don't believe it."

"He did tell you. He saw it."

"He's jealous of you, that's all."

Chris barked a humorless laugh at that. "Look, you tried to warn me. You did your best. It doesn't make you a bad doctor." He stopped and swallowed. "You really helped me, I know that. I appreciate that. But we're done now. You know what happens next."

"No, I don't." Was that her voice, sounding so forlorn?

He had his jaw clenched, staring at her, but he didn't look angry. He looked desperately sad. He shook his head at her and turned away, stripping off his work gloves. He walked away down the driveway, out to the road, and kept going.

***

When Chris came back he found Pauline in the barn, mucking out a stall.

"I'm sorry. I'll do that," he said.

She jerked her head up as if she hadn't heard him come in. "I'm nearly done. It's okay." She bent to the task. "You missed tea."

"I was with Freddie and Wes. I wanted to say goodbye."

Pauline stopped, held still, then faced him. "Are you sure?"

"Don't look at me like that. You know I have to go."

"Maybe we should talk about it more."

Somehow, the vault he'd built had cracked open, rusted through, worn away with time and talk and comfort. He couldn't lock it anymore. He couldn't close the door and spin the dial and keep everything unseen, unfelt. He wanted that back. He'd got used to not feeling anything. Now it just hurt.

"What's to talk about? I was always going to go. I should have left in the spring. I shouldn't have stayed this long. All I've done is hurt people."

"You haven't hurt anyone. How can you say that?"

"I've hurt Wes. He tried to act tough, but he'll cry when he's alone."

"Because he cares about you."

"I've hurt you, haven't I?"

"If I hurt, it's because of how I feel, not anything you've done."

I've hurt myself.

"Look, I've thought about it, about what Michael told you, and why he told you. I was wrong, before. I said he only told you so you'd be... suspicious, or scared. But, no. He told you because he really is worried about you. He really does care. I know that. He thought it was the right thing to do. I'd have done it. If I were in his place, I'd have warned you. You should know what I'm capable of. I should have told you."

"I already know. You're capable of standing up for what's right. Of defending yourself and others you care about. Of feeling, caring, and *loving* other people."

He was too close to her, an arm's length. He stepped farther back. "And making a hash of everything."

"No. Don't say that. We can work this out. Stay— awhile longer anyway—and work it out."

"How, Pauline? I can't be your patient anymore. Can't you see that?"

"Not as my patient, then."

"As what? Your pathetic, besotted pet? Do you know how many—what did you call them?— 'unhealthy expectations' I've had the last few months? How many times I've had to resort to counting backwards in bed at night because I couldn't stop thinking about you? How *jealous* I was when Cooper walked in that door and hugged you?"

Her breathing had got short and choppy as he spoke. She blinked.

And then she was in his arms. He didn't know if she moved first or he did. He hugged her as hard and as tight as he dared, his face in her hair, his eyes shut tight. Her body pressed against his, and set off a raging heat he'd been denying for too long. He must have groaned, or made some sort of noise, because she said "It's okay," muffled against his shoulder.

"How is it okay?" he protested. This was everything she had warned him against. Besotted, yes, that's what he was, drunk on her smell, her skin, the small of her back and her breasts and her hair. Despair fought with elation. Elation won, and he kissed her lips, just as soft and sweet as he'd imagined them. He explored her mouth with his tongue, explored her body with his hands. He was falling past the point of no return. The only way to stop was to hold her tight, crush her against him, count backwards until his pounding need subsided.

"Oh, crap," he whispered when he was able.

"Don't go," she said. "Stay."

"I can't think now," Chris said. Somehow he let her go, stepped away, kept his eyes off her. "I can't think. Go away and let me think."

"Will you come in for supper?"

"I—okay. Yes. Just go away now, please."

She tried to touch him again, a hand on him, but he sidestepped it. She left him, wiping at her eyes.

Chris went into the little tack room. He sat at the bench where George mended the harness, put his head down on his arms, and tried to bring Sophie back.

241

Chapter 21

The clanging of the supper bell roused Chris from something close to a trance. His eyes hurt. He stood, overwhelmed with fatigue, and made his way out of the barn. He pumped water and washed his hands and face at the tub, taking longer than he needed. He stood with his hand on the doorknob. *Autopilot.*

Grace and Marie were putting the dishes of food on the table. Pauline did not look at him.

"Here he is," Marie said.

"Sorry, I had a wash outside," Chris said, and took his place. Grace said a quick blessing, and they began the meal, passing the various dishes around the table. Chris went through the motions, disconnected from the everyday conversation happening in front of him. The food had no taste. He kept glancing at Pauline, but she never looked at him. Her silence stood out to him, but it did not seem as if anyone else noticed. When they were nearly done he put his fork down, took a deep breath. Grace looked at him.

"Is something wrong, Chris?" she asked. "You've been quiet."

He spoke quickly before he lost his resolve, staring at the water pitcher in the middle of the table. "Something Coop—Michael said started me thinking, and I've decided it's time for me to go to Bath. I need to know about my family. I thought I'd go tomorrow."

He could tell they were looking at him, except for Pauline. She was staring at her plate.

"Well, this is sudden," Grace said gently. "But of course we understand, Chris. We hope you find them well and happy."

"Thank you. I can't begin to tell you how much I appreciate the way you've taken me in," Chris said, his voice catching in his throat. "I won't forget it."

"Well, we certainly hope you'll have a chance to come back and visit us sometime," Marie said. She glanced at Pauline.

"How will you go?" Pauline asked, her voice not quite a monotone.

Chris made himself look at her. "Michael said there was a bus route about eight miles from here." She did a good job of keeping a normal face. He hoped he was doing as well. "I might be able to take buses most of the way."

"You don't want to take a few days to plan things out?" George asked.

"Well, I need to get there before my card expires in a fortnight," Chris said. "I'll get a new one there. I don't want to cut it too close."

George nodded. "You don't want to get caught without a valid card."

"So we have just this evening to get you ready," Marie said, and started to clear the dishes.

"I don't have much to pack."

"We're not sending you off with nothing, dear," Grace said. "We'll have to get some food together for you, and a few other things."

"Thank you," Chris said softly. He sat at the table, his hands in his lap, staring at the knife and fork crossed on his plate, until Pauline's hand came to take it away. She put her other hand lightly on his shoulder, briefly, as she leaned in. He caught the scent of her hair, saw the gleam of it out of the corner of his eye, the dark blue of her shirt, and then she moved away.

Chris stood, pushed his chair in carefully, and left the kitchen. He stopped at the bottom of the stairs, glanced into the sitting room, where they had all spent so many cozy evenings, where George had taught him to play chess, where Marie had tried to teach him to knit, where he had come to think of Grace almost as his own mum. Then he thought of his own family: his mum, and Jon. He thought of Brian, and Fiona. He went up the stairs to his room to pack his duffle.

The tiny room held little that was his. He remembered the day he arrived: Pauline leaning against the doorframe in jeans and a pale green shirt. He shook his head, got down and fished around under the bed until he found his duffle. It had become dusty in the time it had been under there. He brushed it off and put it on the bed.

He got the bundle Michael had given him out of the top dresser drawer, and the old towel he had arrived with, that Pauline had rolled her eyes at, then washed for him. It had been in the drawer ever since. He re-wrapped the gun in the towel and put it in the duffle, carefully wrapped the bullets in the piece of rag and put them in too, and a few pairs of clean underwear and socks.

From the second drawer two shirts, an extra pair of cords, and a jumper—the clothes he had arrived with—filled most of the space in the duffle. He gathered the rest of his things: his torch, dead now, but maybe he'd have a chance to re-charge it, his journal and pencil, his penknife, comb, the pack of cigarettes from Michael.

The manicure set from Grace made him smile, and the knit hat from Marie. His work gloves were outside somewhere. He stood with the ivory chess piece from Pauline in his hand. His castle, his stronghold of memories. He tucked it inside the cap to protect it.

The top drawer was empty. He looked again, felt a small stab of panic. Something was missing. He opened the second drawer, took out the clothes Pauline had given him—Jim's clothes—laid them out on the bed, put them all back. He didn't find it. Then he unzipped the side pocket of the duffle, and there it was: a small, soft, pale yellow animal that he had long ago concluded must have been intended to be a horse. It had been Rosie's favorite thing in her short life. She had sucked on the nose of the poor creature enthusiastically, her little fingers grasping the soft loop coming out of its back. He'd lost the pictures somewhere in London, but he still had the little horse. He fingered it briefly before zipping up the pocket.

Chris sat down on the bed. It had taken him all of fifteen minutes to pack.

He glanced down. He kept a few books stacked under the chair next to the bed: a couple of novels and a book on the Conquest of England he had found on the shelves in the sitting room. The novels had been forgettable, and he'd never finished the Conquest. He picked them up to take them back downstairs.

He encountered Pauline coming up the stairs. He stood aside to let her pass. She had some things in her hands.

"I hope you have plenty of room," she said, with a wry face. "Mum and Marie are planning big. This is just the start."

He followed her back to his room, where she put the things she was holding on the bed: two plastic bottles of water, a small box of matches, two candles, an empty tin can, a spoon, fork, and knife, and his ration book.

"My bag's almost full," he said.

"They're worried you might have to camp out overnight, or something. They want you to be prepared. And who knows," she continued softly, "what you might find once you get there. You might need some things."

"I'll put these back, and I'll go see." He hurried downstairs, slipped the books into the bookshelves in the sitting room, and went into the kitchen, where he argued good-naturedly with Grace and Marie about what he could and could not fit into his duffle. They reached a compromise, and he went back up to his room.

As he passed her door he glanced into Pauline's room. She was sitting on her bed, digging through a shoebox of photos. Back in his room, Chris put the things she had brought up into the duffle. He took out the jumper, which made plenty of room for the food he had agreed on with Grace, and put it back in the dresser drawer. Pauline came into the room.

"Here, I found this for you," she said, and held out a picture to him. He took it. She was sitting at a table, smiling at the camera. She wore a black sleeveless top, and a bit of make-up.

"Ta," he said.

"It's the most recent one I have, I think. It's from the summer before it happened."

"I like it." Chris got his journal out of the bag and slipped it inside the front cover. "I don't have one to give you. I'm sorry."

She shrugged. "That's okay. Are you packed already?"

He put the journal back into the bag. "Except for my toothbrush and the food." He sat down on the edge of the bed. "I left Jim's clothes in the drawer."

"You can take them. It's okay."

"I don't have room."

"Do you want a bigger bag?"

"No, really. I'm okay."

She bit her lip and fussed with the hem of her shirt. "Just a minute," she said, and left him. She came back shortly, holding out a small sheaf of clothing coupons. "Here, I hardly use them, I don't need them."

"No, I don't need them. You keep them."

"I kept a few, for shoes," she said. "That's the only thing I might need. I don't wear all the clothes I have. When you get there, you can get yourself some more clothes. Or maybe you'll find another orphan."

Chris took a deep breath. "Okay, thank you." He put them into his journal, with her picture.

Pauline folded her arms and leaned against the doorframe, stared off out the dark window, in the exact same position as on the first day he had arrived. He remembered how on that day he had seen her the way Michael's description had influenced him to see her.

"You're really going?"

"Yes."

"Come downstairs."

He went down after her, and they sat in the kitchen for awhile. George found some maps among his old

247

papers, and they discussed possible routes to Bath, and the most likely places to have bus service. Chris went out with George to do the evening chores and close up the barn for the night. Grace had gone to bed when they came back in, and Marie was knitting at the kitchen table. Pauline sat doing nothing, something Chris had rarely seen.

"Can I talk to you, Pauline?" Chris asked. She followed him into the study.

Chris took a seat in one of the chairs, just so she'd know he didn't plan to kiss her again. Pauline lowered herself into the other. They didn't have to pretend now, like they'd been doing in front of the others. Her face nearly made him weep.

"I was with Laura for almost five years," Chris began, "but in the end, it wasn't love." Pauline sat with her hands clenched together in her lap. "Sophie was different. I know I loved her. I still love her." Chris couldn't go on if he kept watching her, so he focused on the carpet at his feet. "Look at our situation. I was lost, I was sinking. You saved me. You listened, you cared, you showed me goodness and hope when I'd about given up. How could I *not* end up feeling the way I do? And you. You've been here, in a place with no opportunities, no available men. Michael broke your heart, and you've had no other chance to move on, and I showed up. It's understandable—logical—that you feel the way you do. It's circumstance, Pauline. It's two people grabbing desperately at what's closest."

"How do you know?"

"I don't know. Oh, crap, I don't." Chris put his head down into his hands.

"So you'll just run away?"

248

"Don't say that to me. I was always going to go. I'd never planned to stay. You know that. The whole point of all this was for me to get well and go to Bath. You know that. Be fair."

"Yes, okay. I'm sorry. You're right about that, anyway."

"If we stand back from it, give it some distance... Maybe that will make it clearer, to both of us."

"Out of sight, out of mind?"

"Why do you want to make this harder for me? Don't you think it's hard enough?"

"I'm sorry, I'm sorry," Pauline said, her voice catching. "Maybe I want to be angry so it doesn't hurt so much."

Chris had no reply. He knew all about that. He couldn't blame her.

"Will you come back?" Pauline asked, her voice barely more than a whisper.

"If I find my family, I'll stay with them."

"You could still come back. They'd understand."

"After all this time? All this time apart, each of us thinking the other is dead? You want me to find my mother and my brother, and then turn around and walk away again? Just like that? How could I do that? Would you leave here like that?"

"I... no."

"It's not like it used to be. No phones, no email. No hopping in the car for an afternoon visit. Family is more important now, when so many have died. I know you understand that. You, all of you, are so much like family to me, now. But I have to know. I have to find out about my real family, and be with them, if they're alive. I know you can understand that."

"My head can, yes. It still hurts."

Chris knew. "I'm sorry this happened the way it did. I wish it all could have been different."

"How?"

"I wish I could have met you as a normal person, not so…damaged."

"We wouldn't have met. The only reason we met is because you were damaged, and Michael knew it, and sent you to me."

"I know. He has good intentions. I know it. I'm trying not to dislike him so much."

It seemed there was nothing else to say. They sat for awhile longer, silently. Chris pushed himself up from the chair.

"Good night, Pauline."

"Wait." She stood, too, stepped close to him, reached out a hand to touch his face. "Stay with me tonight."

He wanted to. It surged through him with force, a hunger, a need, a nearly overwhelming urge to grab her and not let go. It had been too long. He had done it to himself. He fought it.

He put his hand up to hers and kissed her palm. "No."

"Don't you want to?"

"Of course I want to. But how could I leave tomorrow if we did? No. I'm sorry. No." He had to keep saying it to convince himself.

She pulled her hand away. Chris fled to his room before he changed his mind.

***

He had the dream again, the one with Sophie searching the house. He followed her through the halls and rooms, pressed against the glass of the patio doors, calling out to her, while she checked all the usual places without hearing him. And then finally, as the dream was fading, she seemed to hear him, and she turned around, but it wasn't Sophie anymore. It was Pauline, and the blackness crept in and swallowed her.

Chris awoke sweating. It wasn't light yet, but he heard birds chirping, and knew morning wasn't far off. He got out of bed and went to the window, put his forehead against the cool glass, and watched the light come. There was no sunrise; the sky was overcast and grey. Fog hung in the low spots in the field across the road, as it had the first morning he had awakened in this room. He closed his eyes and tried to think about Bath, but kept seeing the door of Kevin's flat in London.

Chris went to the loo, and then downstairs. There was no one in the kitchen yet. He went out to the barn, began the chores. After a while he heard someone coming quickly, and Pauline ran in through the door. Her eyes were big and she was slightly out of breath.

His heart lurched. "What is it?"

"I thought you'd left," she said, and turned away from him.

Her tone pierced him. "I wouldn't do that," he said. He wanted to touch her, but stood where he was.

"I'll get the eggs." She left the barn without looking at him.

George came as he was finishing. "You were up early," he said, and they went in together for breakfast.

Breakfast was almost as hard as dinner had been the night before. He tried to enjoy the food; it might be his last good breakfast for days, maybe longer. He tried to smile, tried to compliment Grace and Marie on the food. He tried not to keep looking at Pauline. It was over too soon. They all sat quietly for a short time, lingering over a bit of water left in their glass, or one last bite of muffin.

"I should get going," he said finally, pushing back his chair. He started to gather his dishes.

"Just leave them, Chris dear," Grace said. "We'll take care of it later."

"I'll just get my bag," he said, and went up. He half-expected Pauline to follow him, but she didn't. He wanted her to. He wanted some time alone with her, even if it was just a few short minutes. He got his duffle, looked around his room, then brushed his teeth, and went back down.

They had the food ready for him, and helped him fit it in. It was time for goodbyes. He hugged Grace and Marie, shook George's hand, hugged Pauline. He knew he said all the right things, but wasn't really sure what it was he was saying. He picked up the duffle, and they all went out into the grey morning.

Most of the fog was gone. The birds had quieted some. A heavy dew hung on the grass and bushes. They walked as a group around to the front of the house.

"I'll write, let you know how it goes," Chris said. He turned to Pauline. "Do you want to walk down the road a bit, see me off?"

"Sure," she said lightly, pretending, and shook the hair back from her face.

Chris waved back at George, Marie, and Grace as he went through the gate. Pauline latched it, and they walked down the road, their hands in their pockets.

As they passed the church, Chris reached a hand out, and she took it, and squeezed hard. They came to the crossroad that would take him to the bus route. They stopped and stood, near to each other, but not as close as either of them wanted to be. They avoided looking at each other. Chris glanced down the road he would take, Pauline toward the village. Then he turned to her, and she to him. He dropped his duffle, and they closed the gap between them, grabbing on tight. Why couldn't it just be this, with nothing else to think about?

Chris loosened his hold. "It'll be okay," he whispered. "Don't cry, please."

"I can't help it," she said. Chris felt her hands clutching at his clothing.

"I have to go. I'm sorry."

"I know," she said into his chest. "I'll be all right. I really will." After a few minutes her shaking subsided, and she pulled back a little and looked up at him, her face wet. "See?"

He took her face in his hands and brushed at the tears with his thumbs. She licked her lips, and he kissed her, for a long time. He didn't want stop. But he pulled away finally.

"I have to go," he said. She grabbed him again for one last hug.

"Come back," she said softly into his ear, and let go.

Chris picked up his duffle, slung it over his shoulder, and walked away on the road toward the bus. He had told himself he would not look back, but he couldn't help it, and he turned. She put up a hand to wave at him, and he waved, then kept walking. The road curved to the right, along a wall and some bushes, and he knew she couldn't see him anymore, but he knew she was still standing there, watching the place where he had left her sight.

Chapter 22

Sunlight leaking in through the window curtains on the wrong side of the bed woke Chris the next morning. He squinted, blinked, trying to sort out what he'd dreamed and what was real. The room was too big, and he sat up to confirm it: the bigger room, the double bed, the window on the left side instead of the right... and the picture of his family on the bureau. Not some agonizingly vivid dream, then. He thought back to his room in Breton: the single bed, the chest of drawers half-full of someone else's clothes, the bar on the half-size closet door where he'd hung his towel. He'd left some of his clothes there, with no room in his duffle to carry them. It felt like he'd left other pieces of himself there, too. He wondered if he'd ever wake up in that room again, then shook off the thought. He got out of bed, put on his brother's clothes and laced his shoes.

It still amazed him that the loo actually flushed. He washed his face with water from the taps, not a bucket. He lingered at the top of the stairs. A window looked down on the yard at the back of the house, where he'd reunited with Jon the evening before. He saw a neat vegetable garden on the right. A worn path led off through the fields to the next farm. Cows and a few sheep dotted the pastures, and away on the left a square church tower stuck up through the trees. After a few minutes he went down the stairs and into the kitchen.

Fiona and the boys sat at the big table.

255

"Good morning, Chris." She smiled, getting up from her chair. "Did you sleep well?"

"Yes, very well, thank you. Someone should have got me up."

"Jon wanted to let you sleep. Have a seat. I have eggs for you." She indicated a place set for him.

Chris hesitated. He did not want her to have to do everything, but he also did not want to intrude. "Can I help?"

"No, no," she insisted. "Sit, really."

Chris sat. "Good morning, chaps."

The boys mumbled good mornings back.

"Everyone else is off at the moment," Fiona said. She carried Chris's plate to the Aga. "Jon and Simon go over to Mr. Dealy's—that's the farm behind us—every morning to help with the cows. Brian's off with the road crew. Alan and Vivian have gone to church. Laura and David, I'm not sure, they may have gone to church, too."

"Oh, right, it's Sunday, isn't it?"

She turned and grinned at him. "Yes, Sunday. Not much of a day of rest, though, not around here." She got him two pieces of toast that had been keeping warm. "I'm sorry about last night," she said softly as she bent near to put the plate in front of him.

"Oh, never mind," he said, and "Thank you," for the toast.

"Pass Chris the butter and jam," Fiona said to Ian, and he leaned over to push them wordlessly from his place near the end of the table. Preston watched Chris silently.

"Ta," Chris said. He looked at Ian as he spread up his toast. "So what's road crew?"

"Um, we have to fix the roads to keep the bus service. There's a different crew each week."

"They'll be out all day," Fiona added, breaking two eggs into a pan. "Scrambled okay?"

Chris nodded, chewing. "The jam is wonderful. Did you make it?"

"Laura does jams, actually, and Vivian. I mostly do vegetables."

"Are those for today?" Chris asked, indicating some preserving jars and large cooking pots lined up on the counter.

"Oh, yes. The garden's going all out, we put up as much as we can. Plenty of laundry for today, too."

"I've done that, I can help."

"Laundry or preserving?"

"Either." Chris shrugged. "Some of it's my laundry, anyway."

"You've done preserving?"

"Sure, on the farm in Breton."

Fiona brought the pan over and scraped the cooked eggs out onto Chris's plate, smiling. "Generally we keep the men out of the kitchen."

"Thank you." He took a deep breath through his nose over the plate of food. "Gosh, that's nice. I haven't had a hot breakfast in more than a week."

"What did you have for breakfast?" Preston asked.

"Hm, whatever I could come up with," Chris said. "I've been on the road."

"Did you really walk for a whole week?"

"Most of a week, I did."

Preston looked suitably impressed. "Your hair sure is long," was the boy's next observance. "Dad showed us some pictures last night, but your hair was short."

257

"Do you think I should cut it?"

"Aunt Laura cuts my hair. She cuts everybody's hair."

"Goodness, Preston," Fiona said. "Let Chris eat his breakfast." Preston went back to his porridge. "I'll be right back," Fiona said to Chris. She went out toward the stairs.

"Dad says you're very sad," Preston remarked. Ian nudged him and made a face at him.

Chris took a bite of eggs so he would not have to answer right away.

"Are you sad?"

"Sometimes," Chris said.

"Why?"

Chris knew it was coming, but he felt no sudden grief, not any more. It had shocked him, in Breton, that moment in the barn—was it really less than a fortnight ago?—when he had discovered just how much it had faded, without him realizing it. He had come to accept its waning importance since then. In some ways, it was a relief, but not in others.

"My little girl died, and her mummy, too." His voice worked just fine. A year ago he would not have been able to say that.

Preston frowned a bit and nodded. "Yes, Dad was very sad when his little girl died."

This gave Chris a start. "*Your* Dad's little girl?" He glanced at Ian, who sat watching silently.

"Yes," Preston said brightly. "He found her in Frome, and she didn't have a Mummy or Daddy, so he brought her home to live with us, but she got sick and died, and now she's in the churchyard with Anthony and Bettina. Her name was Alice."

Alice was Brian's mother's name. What had he said to Brian at the bus station? 'You look like you've got it easy.' A wave of unexpected guilt washed over Chris. Anthony and Bettina were Colin's children, if he remembered right. The happy family picture was beginning to fall apart. He began to think about the holes, about who was missing.

Fiona came back into the room in the silence that followed. "You boys can get started on your chores, now. Dishes in the sink, please."

Preston complained, but Ian got up wordlessly, gathered his dishes and took them to the sink. Preston followed him out.

Fiona sat down on the edge of the chair next to Chris. "I hope they didn't bother you."

"No, not at all." Chris wondered if he should mention what Preston had told him. But he forgot about it as Fiona held out her hand.

"I thought you might like to have this." She held a small, framed photo. Chris reached out to take it. The rest of the world slowed and stopped as he stared at the trio.

It was a studio shot, taken when the baby was about two months old. She wore a frilly white dress embroidered with tiny roses. Sophie, holding her, wore a pink sweater that also had a pattern of roses. The Chris in the photo smiled down at his daughter as the baby grasped his finger. His sweater was maroon, and the background a deep blue. Sophie was the only one looking at the camera. Her smile radiated happiness and contentment. Chris inhaled a shallow breath and stared at her face, trying to burn it into his brain, trying to replace the image that most often intruded into his thoughts, the image of her as he left her for the last time at the airport, cradling little Rosie in a carrier against her chest, stroking the soft, silky hair with one hand as she held onto his hand with the other, trying not to cry. As if she'd known something would go wrong.

"I sent you this?" Chris said, pulling himself back before he sank too deep.

Fiona nodded. "Yes, the last thing I heard from you, I think, just before that last Christmas. I was always so glad that you and I kept in touch."

"They died right at the start," Chris said, and gave her a brief summary of those days. "By the time I got home, Rosie was gone. They must have caught it at the airport. I was with Sophie at the end, but I don't know if she knew it."

Fiona laid her hand on his arm. "I'm so sorry, Chris."

"It was a long time ago, now. I've learned to deal with it." He kept staring at the picture. "Gosh, look at her. Thank you for this. I haven't any other."

"I thought you mightn't."

"I did have some pictures, and other things, but over the years, things got lost."

"Jon should have some, shouldn't he?"

"Yes, he mentioned it. He gave me a picture of us boys and Mum last night. I'll have to ask him." He put the portrait down, pulled his eyes away from it. "My eggs are getting cold." He took a bite.

Fiona got up from the chair. "Do you want some tea?" she asked, and added, "The local stuff, not the real stuff. We're saving the real stuff for a proper tea this afternoon."

"Just water is fine, thanks."

Footsteps sounded on the flagstones outside, and then Ian burst into the kitchen, more animated than Chris had yet seen him.

"Jon's coming with the constable," he said to his mother. Preston followed him in, and they both looked over at Chris, apparently wondering what sort of trouble he might be in, if the constable was coming.

Fiona shooed them back out the door, both of them protesting, and turned to Chris with a furrowed brow. "You'll need your card, I expect."

"I have it."

He finished his eggs before they came in. Fiona went to the sink, began washing the boys' dishes, and did not go to the door to greet them.

Jon came in first. The constable followed: a tall, thin man, not the burly type one would expect. He wore tweeds—no uniform or hat—and his thinning hair stood out in a fluff about his head. He carried himself rigidly, and had an air of self-importance.

"Ah, good, you're up," Jon said to Chris with a half-smile. "The constable here has come to have a word with you. Constable, my brother, Chris Price." He made an exaggerated sweep of his arm in Chris's direction. Chris chewed and swallowed while he stood. He pulled his green blood test card out of his back pocket and held it out to the constable.

"Thank you, sir," the man said, stepping forward to take it. He turned toward Fiona. "Mrs. Wolcott." Chris thought he would have tipped his cap if he'd had one.

"Constable," she said, her face expressionless.

The man scrutinized Chris's card the way the bus driver had done, and seemed almost disappointed when he could find no fault with it. He handed it back to Chris.

"Pleased to meet you, sir." He pulled out a small notebook and pencil. "I just have a few questions. What was your last place of residence?"

"Really, Mr. Stokes, it's Sunday," Fiona said. "He only just got here last night. He can see the Registrar tomorrow, can't he?"

Mr. Stokes turned to look at her. "It is within my line of duty to make inquiries of new arrivals." His tone did not invite discussion. Fiona turned back to the sink.

"Now then, Mr. Price, your last place of residence?"

"Breton, near Portsmouth."

The constable made a note. "And how long were you there?"

"About nine months."

"Was there an Outbreak in Breton during that time?"

"No."

Mr. Stokes nodded, jotted something down. "Good. Now, is this a visit or do you plan to relocate?"

"Relocate," Jon said, as if there should be no question, and after a glance at his brother, Chris nodded.

"You don't have any illegal or contraband items, such as drugs or firearms, eh?" the constable asked.

"No," Chris said, aware of Jon's eyes on him.

"That will do, then. You'll need to see the Registrar tomorrow, and you'll need another blood test in a fortnight." He tucked his pencil and book into a pocket.

"Why would he need another test?" Fiona asked.

"I can request one if I feel it's necessary," the constable said. "And in view of past... incidents, I am doing that."

Fiona pressed her lips tightly together and looked away.

"It's not a problem," Chris said. "I'll get another test in a fortnight. Do I need to go into Bath for that?"

"Frome or Westbury will do as well. I'll send the registrar up to see you in the morning. And perhaps you would be good enough to keep to the grounds here until your next test, eh? I'll not impose a strict quarantine on you. I'm sure that's not necessary."

Jon drew in his breath as if he were about to say something, but Chris cut him off.

"Might I visit the churchyard?"

"Ah, well, yes, I suppose that would be all right. Avoid Sunday services, if you would?"

"Yes, sir," Chris said. "Of course."

"Thank you for your time, then. I'll be off." The constable nodded at Fiona. "Mrs. Wolcott." She did not reply, and Jon walked him to the door, and almost slammed it after he left.

Chris could tell that Fiona wanted to say something, but she bit her lip and stood at the sink with arms folded.

"Sorry about that," Jon said to Chris. "He takes his job over-seriously."

Chris folded his own arms. "In Portsmouth they locked me up for a fortnight. That's why I didn't register in Bath." They both looked at him with mouths open. "It's a lot different in other places. Some places won't let you stay at all. Makes no difference if you're someone's relative or not."

The door opened. Alan and Vivian came in. They had changed into work clothes. Vivian had an apron over her arm.

"What did the constable want?" Alan asked.

"He very kindly did not put Chris in quarantine," Fiona said.

"I should think not!" Vivian said. "He can't do that, can he?"

"Of course he can, Viv," Alan said.

"I'm not supposed to wander about," Chris said.

"Some welcoming committee, eh?" Alan said, shaking his head.

"Chris says some places lock you up for a fortnight," Jon told them.

"That's still going on?" Alan asked Chris.

Chris nodded. "Oh, yes. They nabbed me in Portsmouth. And I got run out of a town on my way here, just last week. I had a valid card and coupons and money, but they wouldn't sell me any food, and ran me out of town."

"Suspicion and fear and ignorance," Fiona said, shaking her head. "And it gets worse again every time there's an outbreak somewhere."

"Is that often?" Chris asked. He knew there'd been an outbreak in Portsmouth a few months before he'd arrived, but that was all he'd heard of.

"There are small ones every few months," Alan told him. "We hear about them on the radio, but there hasn't been anything around here for a couple of years."

"Do you remember at the beginning, how they said it would run its course, then disappear?" Chris said. "Were they saying that here? They said that in the States."

"Yes, they said that here, too," Jon replied, with some bitterness in his voice. "The advice was to stay where you were, avoid contact when you could, ration your food to survive, and in the spring everything would be okay."

"And we've still got it," Alan said. "You never know where it will hit next."

"But at least it's not like that first winter," Fiona said.

"They never had much of it at all, in Breton, apparently," Chris told them.

"Did they take drastic measures to keep it out?" Alan asked.

"I don't know, didn't talk about it that much, really."

"Chris says he knows all about preserving," Fiona said, pointedly changing the subject. "And laundry." She grinned at him.

"Ah, I said I could *help*," he corrected her. "Actually, once I was well enough for the heavy work, they kicked me out of the kitchen."

"How were you ill?" Jon asked him. Everyone else seemed interested, too.

"Bronchitis, or some sort of chest infection, I suppose. It was going around the warehouse in Portsmouth where I worked. I coughed so hard I cracked a rib or two."

"And someone there sent you to Breton?" Fiona asked. "They weren't worried about catching it?"

"Well, I'd seen a doctor, wasn't contagious... just needed some time to rest up and let the ribs heal."

No one said it, but Chris saw it in their faces: 'Why didn't you come sooner?' He'd explained it to Jon, but it seemed a weak excuse, without the longer, deeper, darker reasons. 'I was in therapy'? No.

The boys came in then, saving him from further inquiries. Ian carried eggs in a wire basket like the one in Breton. They all trooped out to the garden to pick vegetables.

Not unexpectedly, Jon stuck close to Chris. While everyone else worked more or less independently, Jon was never more than a few steps away. Chris asked him questions about the workings of the farm, but Jon always countered with a question of his own about Breton.

"So, are there a lot of places without electricity, still?" Jon asked, pausing with a bucket of beans in hand.

"They didn't have it in Breton. I don't know how widespread it is. Some places I passed through on the way here had it, some didn't. Portsmouth had it, and Petersfield. London did, of course."

"I see crews working on the lines between here and Frome. Always jobs to be had, I hear."

Chris glanced up. "Have you tried to get a job? Or are you happy farming?"

Jon grunted. "Not much call for an estate agent anymore. I worked in an office for a while a few years ago. Endless lists of properties taken over and emptied out by the authorities. Inventories of personal belongings unclaimed and sent to Distribution Centers, all written out by hand in triplicate, because our office didn't rate a precious manual typewriter. It started to give me nightmares."

Yes, I know all about nightmares.

"I looked into other things," Jon went on. "No openings here in Hurleigh. The bus costs too much to get a job in Frome, or Bath. And I don't want to get a flat by myself." He shrugged. "So I work on the farm. There's plenty to do. I don't hate it."

"Would you do something else if it were closer? What would you do?"

"I don't know. What about you? I can't see you loving farming, but you've been at it for the better part of a year, haven't you?"

Chris had to think about that. Would he have stayed so long in Breton if not for Pauline? If it was only a matter of helping out with the work, and nothing else? He remembered the satisfaction he'd got from working alongside others in a community, and seeing the crops greening the fields.

"I like farming," he said.

Jon went back to the beans. "What about music? Do you ever wish you could do that again?"

"No. What use is it now?"

"You were good at it."

"I was lucky at it."

"You loved it."

Chris sighed. "I liked being successful. It was fun, sometimes, being on stage." He straightened and caught Jon's eye. "It kinda screwed up my life, didn't it?"

Jon narrowed his eyes, and Chris thought he would bring up Brian, but he didn't. He went back to picking.

"Do you do road crew?" Chris asked, remembering why Brian wasn't home.

"Sure, everyone does, in rotation. There's a hard day's work. Hell, I used to come home from a 'hard' day at the office. I'd have driven clients around to see properties, sat at the computer for a couple hours, made some phone calls. And I thought I was tired."

"Is there a pub in town?" Chris asked to change the subject.

"Yeah, the Ram. The beer is good."

"They had great beer in Breton."

"I'll take you, when your restrictions are over."

After lunch, they walked around the grounds of the house. Jon pointed out the solar panels on the roof, showed him the greenhouse with its rows of vegetables, the well house, the garage. They went into the barn.

"That's a nice tractor," Chris said. He climbed up to check out the enclosed cab. He supposed it always started with a quick turn of the key, and never leaked oil from degraded seals. "George would love this."

When he jumped down, Jon was watching him with the unsettled expression Chris had seen on his face a few times already.

"What?"

"Hell, you've changed," Jon said. He didn't smile.

"Everything's changed. But I'm still your brother."

"We should get back to work."

Jon worked several rows away for the rest of the afternoon.

Chapter 23

Preston came to tell them it was nearly tea time.

"Mum says you should wash and put on a clean shirt."

"I'll have to borrow another," Chris said to Jon. But when he went up to his room he found his laundry neatly folded on his bed. He took his turn in the loo and went downstairs.

"You have to let me fold my own laundry," he said to Fiona, who was whipping cream in the kitchen.

She grinned at him. "We all have our jobs about the place. You'll settle in."

He gave her a stern look, but she only reached her foot out to nudge him.

Chris figured he could worry about laundry some other time. He looked over the plates of food on the table. "This looks amazing."

Laura came in from the sitting room. "Shall I put the water on to boil?"

"Yes, I think we're about ready," Fiona said to her, testing the consistency of her whipped cream. "Brian's not back yet, but let's get started anyway."

"Brian's not here?" Chris said.

"He's usually back by tea. I suspect he stopped off at the pub. He knew we had a tea planned. After the way he acted last night, it would serve him right to miss out."

Laura picked up a plate of cakes and gave Chris a glance as she carried them out to the sitting room.

"Can we wait for him?" Chris said.

Fiona straightened up and met his eye. "If you like."

"There's no point in punishing him," Chris said in a low voice as he heard the boys thumping down the stairs. "I don't want to make it all worse."

"Of course." Fiona smiled and turned as the boys came into the kitchen. "Boys, run out to the gate and look for Daddy on the road. Tell him to hurry, we're waiting."

Vivian came in from the sitting room. "Is Brian late?"

"Of all days," Fiona said. "Oh, good, that's the bowl I wanted for this cream."

Chris left them to the last preparations and went into the sitting room. Alan was already there, in one of the big chairs, with his foot propped up on an ottoman.

"Did you hurt your foot?"

"Last year. It still gives me trouble sometimes. I rest it when I can."

Jon came in from the stairs. "Here's aspirin," he said, and put the pills into Alan's hand.

"I've got something stronger, if you need it," Chris said. They looked at him with raised eyebrows.

Simon came in and said, "Stronger than the tea?"

"No, pain pills. I found them on the way here. In the same house as the tea," Chris explained.

"It's not that bad," Alan said. "But thanks."

"They're available, should the need arise," Chris said to all three of them.

"Where was this house?" Jon asked.

"Three or four days from here," Chris said. "I forget exactly, but I marked it on my map. It seemed nearly untouched."

"At all?" Simon said with disbelief in his voice.

Laura and Vivian both came in carrying plates of tea cakes. "What was untouched?" Laura asked. They set the plates on a table off to the side of the room with the rest of the tea things.

"A house. Where I found the tea. They'd been living in it since the Bad Winter, that was clear. Oil lamps and candles. All the electric stuff moved out. But they'd been dead well over a year, I figure."

"How could you tell?" Vivian asked.

Chris blinked. He unexpectedly relived that moment when he'd opened the bedroom door, and his gut clenched. "They were upstairs. In bed."

For a long five seconds no one moved or spoke.

"You don't expect to find that, these days," Simon said.

"No," Chris said. "I found a bottle of scotch at the back of a cupboard. I got well and truly drunk."

"The government hadn't been in?" Vivian asked.

"No."

"But doesn't that mean that no one ever missed them? How could no one miss them?" Laura said.

Chris was sorry he'd mentioned it.

"Any sign of my errant brother yet?" Simon said, moving to a window. The others took the cue and said nothing else about the dead occupants of the house, but Laura's expression remained troubled as she arranged plates and silverware and teacups. Vivian went back to the kitchen.

Chris moved closer to Laura. "Where's David?"

"He went back to Frome early," she said, and her pursed lips told Chris he had again brought up an awkward subject.

"Maybe I should just keep my mouth shut," he muttered.

"No, it's all right."

"Here's Brian," Simon said from the window.

Soon they were loading their plates from the elegant display of food on the table. Fiona poured the tea into the delicate china cups.

"Oh, it's been so long since we've used these," she said. "Preston, don't touch. You have one of these." She handed him an everyday mug.

Chris stirred sugar into his tea and watched as the rest of them held their cups under their noses and made happy sounds. He tasted it when he noticed they were watching him.

"Still good," he said, and they all grinned and sipped.

Brian kept to the other side of the room, but otherwise acted normally. Chris tried to steer the conversation away from himself when he could. He kept thinking how much Pauline would have enjoyed drinking tea from fine china, and nibbling on sweet cakes in this grand room. She would have fit in, in her green gown and elegant shoes. He could see her, turning to him with a warm smile.

Fiona was watching him, and raised her eyebrows. He gulped, made himself smile and nod. *Sure, I'm fine.* He concentrated on the conversation.

They all ate so much that supper was a simple affair of bread and soup.

***

272

The next morning the Registrar came to the house after breakfast, a stern little man with the same attitude as the constable. Chris spent a good while sitting at the kitchen table, filling out forms and answering questions.

"Right, that should cover everything," the man said finally, stacking up the papers. "Here's a few odd coupons, but your official book could take some time. You can call in at the Post Office in a fortnight, see if it's come in."

"After my blood test?"

"Yes. After." He gave Chris a look.

Jon was waiting for him outside when the Registrar left.

"I'm surprised he didn't wear a mask," Chris said, watching him hurry off down the road. "He'll wash his hands when he gets home."

"I wonder if he'll go in for another blood test?" Jon said, and they both chuckled.

"How often does the post go?" Chris asked. "I should write to them, in Breton." To Pauline. "Tell them I'm all right." Jon promised to get him some paper and envelopes.

"Look, I have to go over to the Dealy farm for a while," Jon said. "The vet's coming to do some inoculations. He'll need a hand."

"I guess I need to stay here."

"Might be best. I'll be an hour or so."

"I'll find something to do," Chris said, and Jon went off.

Chris wandered around the grounds of the house. He thought he should probably find Fiona and ask what he could do to help, but he wanted to be alone for a

273

little while. The boys were at school. Brian and Alan had gone off to another farm to help out in a labor-sharing arrangement the community had worked out. In a few days men from around the town would be coming to Heaton House. Chris wondered if he would be expected to stay away, since he was unofficially quarantined.

Eventually he came across Laura hanging laundry.

"Preston says you cut everybody's hair," Chris said.

"Would you like me to do yours?"

"You always used to. Do you think it needs it?" He smiled.

Laura cast him a look. "Oh, yes. I'll get my scissors."

Chris hung the last pairs of trousers from the basket while she was gone.

The sun came out. They sat on some stone steps set into a slight incline in what must have been a fancy garden at some point in time, Chris with a towel draped around his neck. He closed his eyes and clenched his jaw against the feel of her fingers in his hair, trying not to remember Pauline's fingers.

"Do you want a trim, or a cut?"

"You might as well make it short."

"You haven't cut it in awhile," she said, snipping. "You used to keep it short."

"Yeah."

She cut in silence for a few moments.

"I'm sorry about Sophie, and Rosie," she said quietly. "Fiona told me."

"Thanks. I'm sorry about Stephen."

"Thank you."

274

"Was it at the beginning?"

"Yes, he died that first winter, in January. He had volunteered at the hospital. They needed people to help, so many were getting ill. I didn't want him to go, but he did anyway. That was before we knew what it was going to be like, of course. I tell myself that if we'd known how bad it was going to get, he would have stayed with me. Once he got ill, he just didn't come home. They wouldn't let me in to see him."

"You can be proud of him, though, stepping up to help."

Laura stopped cutting, and Chris turned his head to look at her. "It was pointless," she said, her voice and her face hard. "They all died, and so did he. I could be proud of him anyway. He was a good man. I'd rather have him alive." She began snipping again, repositioning his head lightly.

"No guarantee of that, even if he didn't try to help."

"Simon had the right idea. Get out fast and stay away. It worked for everyone here."

"Some people just won't ever get it," Chris said. "I've never got it. I've been exposed, over and over."

"Did you volunteer?"

"No. At the beginning I was holed up in a friend's cabin in the woods, away from everyone, for months."

"By yourself?"

"Um, not at first. But later, yes."

"What happened?"

Chris took a breath. "Archie went off to town to find out what was going on, and he never came back. And his girlfriend killed herself."

Laura rested a hand on his shoulder without saying anything. Then she took up cutting again, turning his head this way and that, and the hair fell onto the towel on his shoulders. "How long were you alone?"

"I don't know, a few months." He thought back, but that time was jumbled in his memory, no clearer than when Pauline had asked him. He had not kept the journal for nearly a year. "I don't remember everything."

"My sister came to live with me," Laura said. "She'd lost her husband—you never knew him, did you? But she got ill in the second wave, in late February. She had a job at the Post Office, and she was still going to work, for the paycheck, so we could eat. After that, there was no one left I knew. I went round to Brian's house one day, I was so desperate, but they had gone. About a week later I ran into Brian in the street, and he brought me here. Just in time. If I hadn't chanced across him just then... well." She paused, blew her breath out. "He was looking for Jon. Found him a couple weeks after that." She tilted his head forward, snipped at the back of his neck.

"I guess I owe a lot to Brian," Chris said.

"Are you going to be okay with him?"

"We'll work it out."

"It didn't seem a good start, the other night," she commented.

"That won't happen again," he said. "It's too hard, being angry."

"I never understood how you two, of all people, could fall out like you did." She put a hand on his shoulder again. "You were such mates."

Chris didn't know what to say to that, so he didn't say anything, and Laura continued with his hair.

"It's Simon, really, that we have to thank for all of this," she said after a few minutes of snipping.

"Yes, Jon told me it was all his doing."

"The place you were, in Breton, is it like here?"

"Well, it's a farm, like here, so they grow a lot of their own food, like you do. Not as big. They don't have electricity. No one in the town does. And they have to hand pump their water."

"Fiona said it sounded like you were happy there," Laura said, and paused.

Chris held himself still. "I worked there, is all." He felt her fingers in his hair again. "How did you meet David?" he asked, to change the subject.

"We worked together, in Frome. In a light bulb factory, of all places," she said with a little chuckle. "I still work there. It keeps us in light bulbs."

"Oh."

"I work a week, then I'm off a week," she explained. "This is an off week. When I'm working I stay with David. He has a job with the government, now. That's what he did before, so he's glad to be back at that." She pushed Chris's head to the side and concentrated while she trimmed around his ear. "He wants me to come and live in Frome all the time."

"So why don't you?"

"I like it here," she said, and the scissors were still. "Maybe I'm not ready." She tilted his head the other way and did around his other ear. "He has a nice place, but he depends on his ration book, y'know? He hasn't a place to grow anything. That worries me, I suppose. He says he can get me a better job, though, if I'm there all

277

the time. But there have been two Quarantines in Frome. That really worries me."

"How far is it?" Chris asked, trying to remember.

"Oh, something like seven miles, I think. Bit of a ride, especially if it's raining. We bike it, usually, to save the bus fare. Jon goes on Saturdays, did you know?"

"No, he hadn't mentioned it."

"There's a good market; he trades there. Brian goes into Bath, and Simon goes over to Westbury. There's a little market here in Heaton on Fridays; we have a stall."

"Really?"

"Jams and such. Simon put in quite a few berry bushes. Plenty of extra to trade."

"It's a nice set-up," Chris said. "I'm impressed."

"There," she said, brushing at his head with her hand, and carefully lifting the towel off. She stood up and shook it out, then used it to brush him off more. "All done. You'll probably want to have a wash." She stood back and surveyed him. "Much better."

Chris ran his hand across his head. "Just like old times, eh? Thanks, Laura." He stood up too, and saw her face, gone all pinched, as if she'd heard bad news. "What is it?"

"It's not like old times at all, really." She sat down on the stone step, folded the towel into a fastidiously neat rectangle on her knees.

Again Chris did not know what to say. He had not meant to upset her. "I'm sorry, I didn't mean—"

"We were so young," she said, "we thought everything was going to be perfect. We had so many options." She looked up at him. "And we still managed to screw it up."

Chris stood silently, watching her.

"We were happy, for a time, weren't we?"

"Like you said, we were young."

"And we changed. Everything in our lives changed. It scared me. But we loved each other, didn't we?"

It had been a love of discovery, of togetherness, of intimacy. He had confused a love of what she represented with a love of her. "In a way, we did. For who we were, at the time."

"But not the way Brian and Fiona did. Do still."

"No, obviously."

"Not the way Stephen and I did, or you and Sophie."

"We both got it right the second time," he said.

"Now everything's changed again. But I'm not sure I've changed. Everyone expects me to marry David. They don't understand why I don't jump at the chance to move to Frome."

Chris took a breath in surprise. "I'm sorry if I gave the impression—" he said, but again she interrupted him.

"No, not you, sorry." She didn't look at him. She shook out the towel and folded it again. "I'm sorry, you don't have to stand there and listen to me whinge on."

Chris settled himself next to her on the stone steps, his arm almost touching hers, and waited.

She smiled down at the towel. "Thank you."

"Don't do something because someone else thinks you should," he said. "Not if it's not what you want."

"I don't know what I want." She continued to stare at the towel, smoothing it out with her fingers. "Well, I do know what I want, but I can't have that back."

"It's no good doing that to yourself, Laura."

"I know. I don't, generally. I've just been thinking about—well, things from before, is all. Recently."

"Since I got here?"

"Yes."

"Well, so have I," Chris admitted.

"Brian?"

"Of course."

"We had such good fun, the four of us, didn't we?"

"Yes."

"But we have to take what we can get, now, don't we?"

"No, we don't," he said, and looked hard at her. "We have to make what we want." She chewed on her lip, thinking about it. "I think you do know what you want," Chris went on. He watched her thinking for a time. "What do you want?"

"I want it to stay the way it is, for now," she said, fiddling with a corner of the towel. "I want him to be happy with that. For now."

Chris nodded. "That doesn't sound so hard."

"You don't know David. He wants things his way."

"What you want is important, too."

She sat looking back at him for a time. "What do *you* want?"

He didn't have to think about it, but he had to take some time before he answered her. He looked away. "Home. I want to be home."

"Are you, now?"

"Well, I'd better be. It took me long enough to get here," he said, trying to make light of it, but not sure if he succeeded. She kept looking at him. It had been a long time, but there were still things about her that he remembered. She had been good at seeing through his disguises. From her look, he guessed that she was doing it now. He stared down at his feet, his heart thumping in his chest. She put her hand on his shoulder, moved it toward the middle of his back. He managed not to flinch, but had to draw a deep breath. She leaned toward him, put her forehead on his shoulder, slipped her arm around his waist and squeezed him gently.

"Make what you want, Chris," she said. Then she gathered up her scissors and comb, stood, and went back toward the house.

Chapter 24

The late afternoon sun slanted through autumn-tinted trees. Church Street curved away to the left, bordered by stone walls and hedges in places, a footpath and a row of cottages on the right, their warm stone fronts glowing in the light. Chris walked slowly, hands in pockets. The trees hid his view of the church tower from here. He kept to the footpath until he reached the cottages, then took to the road.

The church could have been the same church in a hundred other small villages nestled across the countryside. The squared-off tower, rounded Norman arches, the drunken gravestones covered with lichen, looked nearly the same as its counterpart in Breton. The blue and gold clock on the side of the tower did not have the correct time.

Chris ambled among the old stones, reading names and dates. Birds chirped, a gentle breeze brushed his face. The grass here was kept mowed, soft and green, but the foliage all around was starting to turn dry, piles of leaves gathering under the bushes.

In another part of the churchyard, all the gravestones were new. Chris found a seat on a stone wall, near three small markers placed close together. He did not need to read the names on them. He tried to keep his thoughts superficial. He had practiced it for years, thinking of nothing important, resting.

But thoughts of Pauline kept intruding, in short, vivid scenes: kneading bread dough at the kitchen table with her hair clipped back; working in the garden in her mucky cords and wellies; laughing as she scooped up a snowball to throw at him while he shoveled; putting her arm around him at the pub.

He remembered their encounter in the barn the day before he left Breton, and the feel of her lips against his. He dropped his head into his hands.

He remembered her face as he walked away and left her on the road.

Chris had spent the journey to Hurleigh trying to forget all of it, but he couldn't do it. How long would it take? He fingered his wedding band, but the hurt was not from the loss of Sophie. He had let her go somewhere in Breton, and he couldn't get her back.

The sun sank lower. The shadows from the gravestones reached across the ground. Another shadow moved into his sight.

When he looked up, Chris was startled by how close Brian had got before he'd noticed.

"I didn't mean to sneak up on you," Brian said.

Chris sat up straighter. "I was just thinking."

Brian eyed the three graves. He came closer, leaned against the wall where Chris sat, with an arm's length between them. He looked out over the whole space. "No one you know here, is there?"

"I don't think so."

Brian pulled a brown beer bottle from his pocket. He unscrewed the top, held the bottle out to Chris. "I stopped by the pub."

"Cheers," Chris said as he took it. "It's not sacrilegious or something, is it?"

Brian pulled another one for himself from his other pocket. "They have wine in church." He shrugged. "A toast?"

"All right." Chris held his up in front of him. He thought for a moment. "To loved ones lost," he said, and moved his bottle toward Brian.

Brian had raised his bottle too, but he stayed still, gazing out over the churchyard. He turned to look at Chris.

"And found." He touched his bottle to Chris's.

Chris nodded, and they drank.

The first taste brought back memories of days long ago, when they had sat up drinking late into the night, so serious, thinking themselves invincible, believing that once they hit it big the world would be theirs, and they could make it better. The future had seemed a bright adventure, and they believed they had control, when really they were just specks in a sea of humanity, caught up in an immense wave rushing towards a crashing, chaotic dissolution.

Now they were cast together once more. Chris took a deep breath, and said into the silence, "I never hated you." *There, done.*

"You had every reason to."

Yes. But I didn't. I loved you.

Brian took a long drink. "When I think back about the way I treated you…. I don't know why. I'm sorry. I'd take it back, if I could."

"I didn't come looking for an apology. I don't need it, not anymore. It's over, it's done. Everything has changed."

"No, I do know why." Brian put his head down, eyes squeezed shut. He hugged himself, one hand holding the bottle.

Chris waited. Is this how he had looked to Pauline? Is this how she had felt, curious, but unsure if she really wanted to hear it?

"I didn't think I could be successful by myself," Brian said. "I depended on you. I didn't know how I'd go on without you. I thought I was finished, a failure. I blamed you. So I did what I could to hurt you."

"You had all the talent."

"I might have had more musical talent, but you had everything else. You knew how to deal with the label, the execs, the publicity, the fans. I didn't know shit. I was scared. I'd never had to do anything without you to turn to. And suddenly I had to do it all."

"Huh."

Brian tipped his bottle back again. "Holy shit."

"Therapy. It's a bugger, innit?" Chris glanced over at Brian. "I've just been through nine months of it."

Brian gave him a questioning look.

"Long story. Never mind." He raised his beer in Brian's direction. "To starting over."

"Starting over," Brian repeated, and they drank together again. "It can never be the way it was, can it?"

Chris regarded the plain brown bottle in his hand. It had no label. The glass was scratched. It had been used over and over, saved and refilled. "No, but I knew that was never in the cards. I just couldn't leave it, though. If you weren't dead, there had to be something better than the way we left it."

"If nothing else, I've learned that the people you love are what's important in life. I'm glad you're here."

"Me too." Chris stared ahead, and his eyes settled on the three gravestones in front of them. Brian shifted his feet.

"I'm sorry, Chris, about Sophie and Rosie. I should have said it before now."

"No, it's okay," Chris said. "I'm sorry about all of them: the kids, and Colin, and Emily. Preston told me about the little girl."

Brian nodded. "He never knew her, of course."

"Tell me."

"I found her in a house. She was the only one left. Her parents and a brother were all in their beds. She was waiting for someone to come and help them. She thought I was there to help." Brian shook his head. "Of course there was nothing I could do. I was just foraging, not looking to help anyone. When she told me her name was Alice, I couldn't leave her." He looked over at Chris. "I couldn't leave her there, to die alone. I brought her home."

"Did you know she was ill?"

Brian took a drink and stared at the ground before he answered.

"Yes. And I risked everybody, and brought her home anyway. Somehow I convinced myself that it would be okay. Simon had got over it. He got it when he went to London to get Colin's kids. I knew a few others who had got over it. At least I wasn't stupid enough to bring her into the house."

"We have to try, don't we?" Chris said. He shuddered as an image of Jenny came into his mind. He hadn't been able to tell Pauline, but Brian would understand. "In London, there was a girl. She was fourteen. She'd been kidnapped, and they'd traded beer for her, and couldn't decide who got her first. I managed to convince them to give her to me. I kept her safe for as long as I could, but when they realized that I didn't want her for—for sex, one of them broke into my room and raped her."

"Shit," Brian whispered.

"I tried to kill him. Nearly managed it. Too many of them, though."

"So you had to leave."

"That's the short story, yes. There were a few good people in London, caught up in a bad situation. They got the girl away, got her home."

"At least you know she's safe."

"Yes, at least."

"I'd kill to defend my family, if it came to that."

Chris nodded. "I hope you never come to it. It's harder than you think." He looked up. "London is hard to talk about."

Brian nodded. "Okay."

"I know I didn't handle it so well, on the bus."

"I didn't, either." Brian took a drink, then a deep breath. "I'm glad you're here, Chris. We all are. If there's any place in this screwed up world you belong, it's here."

Chris ran his hand across his hair. He wasn't sure of that at all.

"Or is it?" Brian asked.

Chris didn't answer. He gazed away toward the church. The clock's hands had not moved. He drank the last of his beer, handed the bottle back to Brian, still without looking at him.

"Jon is here," Chris said finally.

"Right. Well," Brian said, pushing away from the wall. "We should get back. Supper will be ready soon, I expect."

Chris jumped down lightly. He put his hands in his pockets, and followed Brian as he made his way through the gravestones toward the road.

***

After dinner Jon took Chris up to his room.

"I've got some boxes of stuff here, from my flat and Mum's. You should have a look, take what you want."

Several cardboard boxes sat on the floor and a couple on the bed.

"They're yours, Jon. You saved them."

"I don't need it all. It's family stuff. Your family. You should have some of it."

His hand shook as Chris opened the first box on the bed.

"That one on top is the picture album I made after that trip in September, when Mum and I came to visit you."

"You sent me one."

"Yeah, I made three. One for Mum. It's in one of those boxes on the floor. That's Mum's stuff, this is mine."

Chris picked up the dark green album and opened the cover. The first picture took up the whole page. It was another shot from the same studio session as the one Fiona had given him. They were all three smiling at the camera. He stared at it, heart pounding, then turned the pages, one after another. The book was filled with candid shots of Chris, Sophie, Rosie, and Mum, some in black and white, some in color.

"These are a little different from the ones I had, I think," Chris said.

"I made them all just a bit different, yes. Here, this is from your shows that month, at that little bar in Soho." He handed Chris a black book.

Chris flipped through it, then put it back in the box. "I don't need it."

"It's fun to remember, isn't it?"

"I want to see the albums when we were kids."

They spent the evening going through the old albums and boxes of photos, laughing and remembering. They talked about Kevin. Chris swallowed past the tightness in his throat and gave Jon more details about London: what had happened after he went to Kevin's flat, how he'd got away. He told him about Marcus, mentioned Beryl, but didn't tell him what had happened to her, or Jenny. He didn't want to travel down that dark path again just yet. Some other time.

Later, Laura knocked softly and stuck her head in the door. "It's late, boys," she said, and grinned.

"Oh, do we hafta go to bed already?" Jon said in a mock whine.

"Haying tomorrow," Laura said. "Goodnight." She pulled the door closed.

Chris gathered up the small pile of photos he had set aside. "Thanks, Jon, for these."

"We'll do this again," Jon said, putting stuff back into boxes. "You've got so much to tell me. I want to hear it all."

"I want to hear about you, too."

"I have nothing to tell. I've been here. Milking, planting, harvesting. Dull, dull, dull."

"It's not so dull," Chris said. Jon shrugged.

Lying in bed, Chris couldn't get the images of Jenny and Beryl out of his head. He'd done his best, just as Brian had done. Had it been failure? No. The little girl Alice hadn't died alone, and Jenny knew someone cared enough to try to keep her safe. She knew that not all men were bad. In the end, she'd got home safely. Beryl had known the risks. It wasn't his fault. But what if—?

No. No more 'what ifs.' Focus on the now. Did Jon find his life so dull? Did that mean he might want a change? Of location, if not occupation? Plenty of opportunity for a single man in Breton. And then Pauline invaded his head, holding him hard, crying. *Come back.*

Chris gasped, sat up. A dream? He hadn't been asleep, had he? His heart pounded, and other parts of him, too. *Shit.* How had he managed before now, year after year? *You didn't let yourself fall for anyone, much less a beautiful, intelligent, caring redhead, that's how, you idiot.*

Chris curled up, clutching his pillow, and counted backward.

Chapter 25

Chris came down the stairs hearing an odd noise. For a moment he couldn't place it, then it struck him what it was, and he looked into the sitting room in amazement.

Laura was hoovering. She had her back to him, and was working her way across the floor evenly. She was getting close to a small table next to the couch. Chris stepped in and picked up the table for her. She flashed him a smile and pushed the vacuum under the legs. He set it down, and tilted the couch onto its back legs so she could get underneath. They did the whole room that way, with never a word between them. She turned off the vacuum when they had finished.

"Thank you," she said. "Hoovering is such a chore. That made it much easier."

"Happy to help," Chris said.

She wound up the cord while watching him.

"What?"

"Oh, nothing really," she said. "You never did that, before, you know."

"Didn't I?"

"No." She smiled.

"I haven't seen anyone vacuum in years. It must have been the shock." He smiled back at her.

"David would never have thought to do that."

That seemed the sort of remark best left unanswered. "Is there anything else I can help with?"

"No, no," she said, with a wave of her hand. "Don't you have to go out, with the rest of the men?"

"I've been politely asked to find something else to do."

"Oh, that's just ridiculous. God, these people and their stupid blood tests!"

"You can't really blame them. It is a matter of life and death."

"But it's all for show. You know that, right? The damn card is pointless after a week."

"I've seen people go down in a day, and dead the next."

She blinked. "Yes, of course. Sorry."

"Anyway, it gets me out of the hard work. I get to help the ladies." Chris grinned at her to lighten the mood.

"You're no stranger to hard work, from the looks of you. You look good, Chris. Healthy."

"Chopping wood for cooking and heat, shoveling muck, pitching hay. Not as many machines as you've got here, I expect." He curled his arm with a mock serious expression.

"You must have killer abs."

Chris grinned again and pulled up his shirt. Laura's mouth dropped open.

"Oh, my. Where's that cute little pudgy belly I remember?"

"Starvation took care of that," Chris said, without thinking about it.

Laura's expression changed, and guilt washed over Chris.

"Sorry, I shouldn't have said that," he said.

"When were you hungry, Chris?"

He couldn't get Pauline's expression out of his mind, that day he'd told her about the rats. He didn't want to do that to Laura, too. "Never mind. It doesn't matter."

"You've had a hard time of it, haven't you?" she said, and got the same look on her face—the distressed look—that Pauline would get.

He didn't move, didn't say anything, tried to decide what he should tell her.

"It might help, to talk about it, don't you think?"

He sighed. "I have done. There was someone I could talk to in Breton. I'm okay, really."

She stood there, crossed her arms, and drew her eyebrows in. "Who did you talk to?"

Nearly any question still made him want to clench his jaw and take a step back. He'd worked hard to get over that in Breton. Apparently it didn't transfer to here, to Hurleigh, to this room and this woman he'd lived with so long ago. No reason to keep secrets, though, right? Deep breath. "A psychologist. I was in therapy, basically."

Surprise showed in her face. "Oh. Good. Man or woman?"

"What does it matter?"

"A woman."

"Yes. Pauline." Deep breath.

"George's sister. She lived on the farm you worked on."

"Yes." Right, he'd mentioned all that the night he arrived. She'd always had a good memory.

"Did you have a relationship with her?"

"No. That's not proper."

"Why are you so tense?"

"Why are you asking me all these questions?"

"Don't get cranky."

Chris took a step back and turned away from her. "Stop it."

"Stop what?"

"You're doing what you used to do. You're trying to figure out what I'm thinking, what I'm feeling, so you can tell me what to feel instead. So you can tell me what I'm doing wrong. So I'll start thinking what you want me to think."

She didn't reply, and Chris turned back to her. She stood gripping the handle of the vacuum, her knuckles white, her eyes big.

"That's not what I—is that all you remember? *That?*"

Chris sagged, rubbed at his face. "No. I'm sorry. I didn't mean it like that. Crap."

"Something's wrong," she said. "I know you well enough—"

"No, you knew me a long time ago," Chris cut in. "I'm not the same person. At all. You don't know me." He started to turn away toward the door.

"Wait—" she said. "Please."

He turned back. "What?"

Laura stepped close to him, hesitated, then put her arms around him.

"I'm sorry. Let's not fight. I don't want that."

"I don't, either," he said, and hugged her back.

"You're hurting, Chris. Aren't you?" She loosened her hold just enough to look up into his face.

Chris was ready to end the hug, but she didn't let go. He'd feel like an ass standing with his arms at his sides while she held him, so he kept them around her. He avoided her eyes.

"You need something. Someone."

Why was she always right? How could she know that? A thought struck him. Chris looked at her face, her dark eyes, her lips. They'd been so close for so long. She'd known him so well. Hell, she still did.

Distance, he'd said to Pauline. Distance might make it clearer. And what else? Someone else? Is that what he needed to get Pauline out of his mind? Did he need to let someone else in?

Laura put a hand up behind his head, pulled it down to hers, and kissed him. Like she used to. There'd never been anything wrong with the sex. Chris pulled her close. Kissed her back. It was good. But... *wrong*.

"Stop," he gasped, disentangling himself. "What about David?"

Laura stood breathing hard. She licked her lips. "It's been iffy for a while. I've been afraid to leave him."

"Afraid of David?" A little surge of anger started in Chris's gut.

"No, no." She shook her head. "No. Afraid of being alone again."

Chris blinked. "I'd be a nice substitute, is that it?"

Laura put her hand up to her face and moved to one of the chairs. "No, it's not just that. Really." She sank down and took ragged breaths. "We were so happy, once, you and I. I remember that. I want that back. I want to be as happy as I was with Stephen."

"I'm not Stephen."

"I know."

"I'd be a substitute."

She looked up at him from the chair, her eyes wet. "Couldn't we at least try?"

Chris couldn't be angry at her. He couldn't blame her. Circumstance. *Again, dammit.*

"No. I'm sorry, Laura."

She turned her face away, nodded.

"You're right, though, about one thing. I do need someone. But not you. I'm sorry."

She nodded again, wiped her eyes, looked back at him. "Pauline?"

He held himself stiffly, and didn't answer.

"Why did you leave, then?"

"To find Jon, and Brian. Like I said. I had to know."

Laura sat up straighter, and her mouth opened, as if she'd had a thought. "Are you going back? Is that why—?"

"How can I leave Jon?" Chris said, his voice hard.

She saw it all, then. Her eyes opened wide again, and she stood. "Do you think you have to choose—?" she started, but Chris didn't want to hear it, didn't want to have to explain.

"Forget it, okay?" he said. "Please, just let it go." He left her, went to find Fiona so she could give him a job to do while the rest of the men worked the fields.

***

He ended up working all morning in the kitchen with Fiona and Vivian.

"We got behind in preserving yesterday, with so many pickers, and all those cakes to make for tea," Fiona said.

Chris did odd jobs around the kitchen: moving large pots of water and baskets of vegetables, peeling and slicing, hauling peels and cut bits out to the hogs. Laura came in just before lunchtime, and went out to the field with a big basket of sandwiches. Fiona went along with two clean buckets of cold water. Chris offered to carry them.

"No, someone might report it to the constable," she said, with a frown.

After lunch Chris did chores in the barn, then Fiona took him to the greenhouse to pick tomatoes.

"Just the biggest, nicest ones you can find," she said. "I've got a buyer coming later. He only wants the best." They nestled the tomatoes into flat crates that stacked.

"Who does he buy for? The produce I saw in the grocery in Bath was on the grotty side."

"I'm not sure. He's cagey. He's willing to pay extra, so I don't ask."

"Huh."

"Did you grow tomatoes in Breton?"

"Outside. They don't have a greenhouse. Not as nice as these."

"Was it all for home use, or did they sell any?"

"They trade some of everything, yes. George sells off quite a few hogs in the fall."

"George is married, right?"

"Yes. Marie is his wife. His mum is Grace. Pauline is his sister."

"She's not married?"

"Fiona." Chris straightened up and gave her a look.

"We used to be able to talk."

"I know. What did Laura tell you?"

"Nothing I wasn't starting to suspect myself."

Chris tried to keep his tone light. "I've been here five days. What on earth have I done to make you so suspicious?"

"It's what you haven't done. Laugh, smile much, or take that ring off your finger."

He glanced down, fingered it like he used to do so often. "It's still important to me."

"There's a solution to every problem, Chris. Two brains might be better than one."

"I'll remember that. And I'll try to smile more."

"I mean it."

"Okay."

They picked in silence for awhile.

"Did you assume I'd try to take up with Laura again?" Chris asked her finally.

"No. Do you want to?"

Heat rose to his face, and Chris busied himself behind a particularly leafy bush. "I don't think it would work, for all kinds of reasons."

"I agree. Though it would be… tidy, I suppose."

"Life's not tidy. Especially not anymore."

"No. It's not. But you don't have to fight it."

Chris grunted. "Fight what?"

"The untidiness. So you've got some clutter, so what?"

"You've lost me," Chris said, putting two tomatoes into the crate.

"I think you're looking for a solution that will make everyone else happy, without taking into consideration what you want. Talk to Jon."

"Okay."

"I mean it."

"I promise."

"Lovely. Now, take that stack to the kitchen, would you, please? I'll find a few more and bring this one."

Chris carried the stacked crates of tomatoes out of the greenhouse toward the kitchen. The clouds had thickened and a breeze had sprung up. Rain wasn't far off.

A group of men came in through the back gate, some with rakes over their shoulders. Chris stuck close to the wall around the garden. When his restrictions were over, how long would it take before they stopped viewing him as a stranger? In Breton, they had welcomed him with little reserve. The suspicions seemed higher in Hurleigh. Was it because Hurleigh was closer to bigger cities and had more experience with the plague?

Soon, a honk sounded outside the gate. Chris helped Fiona carry the tomatoes out. The sight of the delivery van sent a rush of adrenaline through Chris. The vans in London had been nearly identical. The little man who got out to greet Fiona with a big smile was nothing like the Londoners, however, and put Chris more at ease.

"Oh, such beauties!" he said, lifting one crate off the stack. "Mrs. Wolcott, my dear, you never disappoint."

Chris loaded the tomatoes into the crowded van. He caught sight of other large and perfect produce. Fiona got her envelope, and the van drove off.

The rain picked up as Chris did chores with Brian in the barn before supper. They ran across the yard and had to wait inside the kitchen door while Fiona brought them towels. She made them stand by the Aga then, until they dried some. Jon and Simon were even worse off when they got home from the Dealy farm after the trek though the back field. Fiona sent them upstairs to change.

After supper they gathered in the sitting room. Ian and Preston took turns playing the piano, getting up and bowing after each piece with silly grins at the applause from the adults. Brian left the room and came back with a pitcher of cider and a stack of glasses, and poured for everyone. Brian took his glass and shooed the boys from the piano bench. A smile warmed Fiona's face as Brian settled himself on the bench and took a few thoughtful sips of the cider.

"C'mon, Dad, play!" Preston demanded.

The first few notes were careful, hesitant. Chris did not recognize the piece. It stayed slow, hollow and haunting, and trailed off abruptly. Brian started something else, this one lighter and faster, then launched into an old familiar tune from many years ago, a song crowds used to cheer for. Jon smiled broadly, but Brian stopped suddenly with an exaggerated groan.

"God, not that one!" he exclaimed with an eye-roll, and started something else. He played for the better part of an hour, some things that Chris recognized, some that he did not. Chris spent most of the time focused on a worn spot on the arm of the couch, afraid to meet anyone's eyes, his heart pounding, trying to keep his expression casual, taking occasional sips from the glass that Brian had handed him with a faint "Cheers."

When he finished, Brian took the boys up to bed, and soon after Chris excused himself and went up to his room.

He lay on his back on his bed, still hearing the piano in his head. That Brian could coax such beauty and emotion from the keys still amazed him. What had he said to Jon, about music? *What use is it now?* Well, there it was. Brian had spoken to him, to all of them, through the music he'd just made. He'd always been able to do that. Chris couldn't come close.

Chris smiled. And now Brian was passing that on to his children. Preston could mimic the notes, but he was young. Ian showed promise already. If he kept at it, he could play like his father, someday.

His gut clenched. *Oh, Rosie. What would I have given you? Everything, if I could have.*

Someone knocked softly on his door.

Chris sat up, sniffed, wiped his eyes. "Come in."

Fiona opened the door a crack and put her head in. "I'm not disturbing you, am I?"

"No, not at all."

"Are you okay? You left suddenly."

"It's been a long time since I've heard him do that."

"He did it for you."

Chris took a deep breath.

"He told me you'd talked. You'll be okay, the two of you, won't you?"

"Yes."

"Good. It always hurt him, you know, after he thought you must be dead. He never said, but I could tell."

"God, why do we keep blundering through life hurting the people we love the most?" Chris said.

Fiona came into the room and sat down next to him on the bed. "Hopefully we can learn from our mistakes, and fix them."

"I've fixed the one thing I thought I needed to fix, but now I've made an even bigger mess."

"You can fix that, too."

"What happened with Jon's girl?" Chris asked.

Fiona looked as if she had expected something else, but she nodded.

"It was last year. He'd told us he was going to ask her to marry him; he'd got a ring in Frome. He was so happy. We all were. She's younger, but we all liked her very much. She said yes, but when they told her mother, well, she wouldn't have it. They had a huge row, the three of them. She'd always wanted Susan to marry another chap, a friend of the family. He and Susan had grown up together. Susan said she thought of him more like a brother." Fiona stopped and shook her head. "It was so hard for Jon. In the end, Susan couldn't go against her mother. She married the other chap, just a fortnight later. I don't think Jon's over it yet."

"No," Chris agreed.

"He wouldn't talk to you about it?"

Chris shook his head. "Are there other possibilities? Once he gets over her?"

Fiona wrinkled her nose. "I don't really think so. It's been a bit of a problem. We've plenty of men around here, not so many women."

Chris made a noise in his throat. "It's just the opposite in Breton."

"Have you told him that?"

"If he's not over her yet, the prospect of single women on the hunt would not be a positive."

302

"You're probably right." Fiona was quiet for a time, then laid her hand on top of Chris's. "You could bring her here, you know."

Chris groaned. "She wouldn't come. She wouldn't leave her family. They need her. She works so hard. It made it easy to stay, doing the outside work so she could do Grace's work and Grace could have a rest."

"It sounds like you've already found a family, Chris."

"I promised Jon I wouldn't walk out on him."

"Talk to him. Tell him. Explain it."

"Yes, all right. I'll try."

Fiona put her arm around him and gave a little squeeze. "Good night, then."

"Good night. Thank you."

After awhile, Chris got up off the bed and peeked out his door. The house was quiet, the loo empty. He brushed his teeth, washed his face. As he turned off the tap his gaze fell on his wedding ring. He stood still at the sink, his hand on the knob, and stared at the gold band on his wet hand. He grasped it with the fingers of his right hand, tugged at it, but it didn't come off. He turned the water back on, put some soap on his finger, and tried again, working at it, easing it past his knuckle, until it slid off his finger, and lay in the palm of his right hand.

It was easier than he had thought it would be.

Chris rinsed and dried his hands, keeping a careful hold on the ring, and then went back into his room. He stood with his back against the door, then picked up the picture of the three of them—himself, Sophie, and Rosie—from the bedside table, and took it to the bureau. He opened the top drawer, and put the picture

303

in. He put the ring on top of it, and closed the drawer with a deep breath.

It was easier than he had thought it would be.

He sat down again on the bed, stretched his hand out toward the bedside table, grasped the picture he had left there, face down, under the edge of a book from a shelf in the sitting room. Pauline had seemed a little embarrassed about it when she had brought it into his room as he was packing. He stared at it. The first stirrings of euphoria tickled his stomach. He got a piece of paper out of the drawer, and a pen, and wrote a letter to Pauline.

***

Dear Pauline,

This letter is just for you. I've been thinking, the past two days, how you will get that first letter I sent, the one with all the this-is-what-happened stuff for everyone, and you'll read it out loud, and pretend to be happy for me, but really you'll be gutted because it means I won't be coming back. I couldn't let you go on feeling that way.

The distance thing isn't working, is it? But I've gone and promised Jon I wouldn't walk out on him. When I realized that I had to come back to you, I figured I could just bring Jon with me. But he's firmly entrenched here. He got all grumbly (as you'd say) when I mentioned the vague possibility. I'll work on it. Find out what's got him tied here. I think it must be a woman.

God, I miss you. I'm straddling a fence of razor wire, you on one side, Jon on the other. Whichever way I go it will cut me to ribbons. Will you take me, cut and bleeding, if I fall your way? But I can't walk out on him. I can't.

Please write to me. God I wish we had a phone and could ring each other. I want to hear your voice.

But I'd rather feel your breath against my skin. I want to kiss every part of you. I want you to kiss every part of me. I want to hold you and not let go.

I have to stop now, or there won't be enough numbers to count backward through.

I miss you. I love you.

Chris

Chapter 26

"How big is the school here?" Chris asked Jon as they loaded boxes of jam and produce into the wagon in the damp dawn before breakfast.

"I'm not sure. There are about twelve in Ian's class. They lump classes together. They've got four teachers, I think."

"We started a weekly football game in Breton, mainly for the kids, but some of the adults joined in. Have you got something like that here, for the kids to do?"

Jon stopped with a box in his arms. "I don't know." He gave Chris a neutral expression. "Who was 'we'?"

"Freddie, one of the teachers at the school. It was her idea, I just helped her with getting the field in shape. I went to the practices and games, too, until I left."

Jon put the box onto the wagon and lifted the back gate into place. "I'll harness the horse after breakfast," he said, and turned toward the house.

Breakfast conversation was dominated by market talk. Simon volunteered to go along to get the booth set up.

"You could help with milking if you like, Chris," Simon said. "I had a talk with Winston and he said it would be fine. He won't report you."

"Sure, happy to," Chris said.

Everyone rushed their breakfast and the washing up. The boys grabbed their book bags and headed off to school. Fiona, Laura, and Vivian gathered their bags and lunches and went out to the wagon where Simon was harnessing the horse.

Jon motioned to Chris. "We're running late." They set off through the field.

Chris was glad of the time with Jon. He hoped to start the conversation he had promised Fiona. But it was clear Jon was stewing over something. Chris mulled possible openers. Jon made that unnecessary.

"You did more than just work on a farm in Breton," Jon said, without looking at Chris.

"I made some friends. I pitched in where I could. They're good people."

"Good people here, too."

"I know," Chris said. "Can I tell you something?"

"Sure."

"Fiona told me about Susan."

Jon stopped in his tracks and turned to face Chris. "You could have asked me."

"I did ask you. You wouldn't tell me."

Jon put on his stubborn face. "And?"

"It's a shit situation, I know. I'm sorry."

"What else?"

"So, I was just wondering... if there're other possibilities, once you're feeling less—"

Stubborn changed to annoyed. "What difference does it make?"

"Doesn't it make a difference to you? Don't you get lonely?"

"You've already been on about that. What do you really want to know? Prospects for yourself?"

"No, not at all." Chris took a step back and put up a hand. "I just wonder about you, is all. I suppose I'm worried about you."

"Are you worried about Simon, too?"

"He's not my brother."

"Yeah, well, stuff it, would you?"

Chris stared at him, taken aback, unbalanced, with no idea what to say. He had planned to tell Jon about Pauline, but now he didn't know if he should.

"I'm tired of it," Jon went on, "you and everybody else. 'Oh, poor Jon. We have to find Jon a new girl.'"

"I'm sorry, I won't mention it again."

"Good. Is that it, then? Or did you want to grill me about anything else?"

"Grill you? When have I ever grilled you?"

"Just now."

"No, I'm just—"

"I'm sorry," Jon broke in. He crossed his arms and half turned away. "Look, go ahead. You might as well. I know you've got something else to say. Let's get it over with."

"It's not about you," Chris said.

"About you, then? What?"

"It's about Breton."

"You want to go back," Jon said, making it sound accusatory.

"It's a good place. I think you'd like it there."

"I like it here. I live here. This is my home. Why would I want to leave?"

"Why do you want to stay, Jon?"

"Everything I've had—every*one*—for the past six years, is here. This is my family now, don't you get it?"

"I'm your family, too."

"And to keep you I have to give them up and come with you?"

"I never said that, Jon. Be fair. I made you a promise. But can't you give me a chance? Can't you just hear me out?"

"We're late," Jon said abruptly, turning away, striding off through the grass toward the Dealy farm.

Mr. Dealy could have been any age over sixty. His leathery, creased skin bespoke a hard life out-of-doors. He grinned, showing yellow teeth, and shook Chris's hand with an iron grip.

"Good to meet you, lad," he bellowed. "Done a bit o' milkin', have you?" He plunged in among the cows still milling in the outside pen, shoving and hollering, until they ambled into the barn.

"Tough old bugger," Jon said Chris. "And a bit deaf."

Chris had started his third cow when Mr. Dealy stopped outside the stall to watch.

"Jon! You're going to have to pull faster to keep up with your brother!" he yelled. "Should we let him have a tug at Queen Anne?"

Later, Jon grinned as Chris rolled up his trouser leg to inspect his shin.

"I don't think it's broken," Chris said, kneading it gingerly. "Holy shit, that cow is evil."

Jon appeared to be stifling a laugh. "Did she head-butt you, too?"

"More than once. I may have to take to my bed. You carry the damn milk."

"At least none of her calves show the same tendencies. She's been around a few years. She won't last many more, I expect."

They headed back across the field, Jon carrying the milk can, Chris exaggerating his limp.

Jon smirked. "I did warn you."

***

On Saturday everyone got up early again. Fiona packed lunches. Brian, Ian, Simon and Jon all headed out to catch their buses, rucksacks full of things to trade. Chris did the milking with Mr. Dealy, who took pity and dealt with Queen Anne himself. Back at Heaton House, Chris got Preston to help him with other chores in the barn, then spent some time kicking a football around the yard with him. Lunch was a quiet affair with only Fiona, Laura, Preston, and Chris.

"When do I get to go in to the market?" Preston asked, dunking a piece of bread into his soup.

"When you're older," Fiona said.

"Charles at school gets to go in sometimes."

"Charles is a year older."

"So, next year?"

"We'll see."

Preston finished and went outside to play.

"Have you talked to Jon?" Fiona asked Chris.

"Tried." Chris glanced at Laura and rested his head in his hand. "He's fed up with everyone trying to find him a new girl, he said. Quite forcefully."

"I know two lovely women at the factory in Frome. I tried to introduce him when he went in to market. Once." Laura shrugged.

"Too soon," Chris said.

"So enticing him with the abundance of single ladies in Breton is right out," Fiona said.

Chris grunted in agreement. "He can be stubborn. It's going to take some time. I think everyone else should just let me handle it."

"Yes, of course," Fiona said.

In the afternoon, Preston asked Chris if he wanted to see the loft. He led Chris upstairs to the little door between the boys' room and the loo. He opened it and parted the clothes hanging there, revealing a staircase. Chris had to duck under the bar.

"Ian used to play up here a lot with me," Preston said as they reached the top.

The attic was full of boxes and furniture and unrecognizable items draped in sheets. At one end, a wooden chair sat next to the window, and a pair of binoculars rested on the ledge.

"We can see down the road. I saw you with Dad and Ian last week and told Mum." He offered the glasses to Chris.

"Wow, this is a great view."

Preston pulled another chair over. "I suppose you'll start going into Frome with Jon next week." He put his hand out, and Chris surrendered the binoculars.

"I expect so."

"One of the kids at school said you probably had the plague."

"I don't have the plague, Pres. I had a blood test just a few days before I came here."

"I told him that. Do you still play the guitar?"

"I haven't done, in years."

"Dad's got a bunch of them. Some up here, some in his cupboard." Preston jumped up and gave Chris the binoculars. He pulled back one of the sheets. Three guitar cases were stacked neatly. "This one's blue, this one's red, and this one is wood color."

"Huh."

"You could play guitar while Dad played piano."

"Um, maybe. Sometime."

"Dad said when I'm older he'll teach me to play guitar. He says I have to learn piano first." The boy arranged the sheet to cover the black cases again. "They say that a lot. When you're older. When you're older."

"That always ticked me off when I was a kid," Chris said.

***

Vivian came into the barn late on Tuesday afternoon.

"Chris, you've got a letter," she said and held it up. "I'm just back from town."

The brush fell out of Chris's hand at the end of the stroke. He pushed past the horse and fumbled with the latch on the stall door. His mouth had gone dry. He snatched it from her with a shaking hand.

"Thank you," he managed. He stared at the handwriting, at Pauline's name in the corner.

Vivian winked at him and left without another word.

"One of your friends in Breton?" Jon said from the next stall.

"From Pauline," Chris said, glancing up at him. Jon pursed his lips and went back to brushing.

Chris latched the stall door and went out of the barn. He walked for a few moments, holding the letter,

312

trying to calm his racing heart. He reached the fence, leaned against it, and pulled out his penknife. He slit the envelope open along the top, folded the knife blade, put it back in his pocket.

Deep breath.

"Dear Chris," the letter started. "We are so glad to hear that you are safe and have found your brother, and Brian and his family." It went on in that vein, newsy and cheerful. Impersonal. The harvest was going well. Wes was chosen captain of his football team. One of the cows had gone lame. The big rooster disappeared for two days and they feared a fox had got him, but he came back, only a bit bedraggled. Michael had brought shingles for the new hay shed. He'd got a job driving a lorry for a warehouse in Portsmouth. A few other things. They hoped to hear from him again soon. Cheers, Pauline, Grace, George, and Marie.

Chris folded the letter back into the envelope and walked a few paces along the fence. He pulled out the letter and read it again, this time imagining Pauline's voice and expression with each sentence.

Not a single personal statement. No "I miss you." What did it mean? He groaned. He knew what it meant. She wrote her letter in the same style he'd written his first letter. He glanced at the date, worked it out in his mind. She wrote it the day after he'd written his second letter, so she couldn't possibly have got that one yet. Okay.

Deep breath.

His vision blurred. Holy crap, that first letter must have hurt her. *Was I that impersonal?* Impersonal might be a kind way of phrasing it. Chris calculated again. She would have the second letter by now, most likely.

She could be writing a response already. She might even have *mailed* a response already. In two days, he could have another letter from her, and he'd know how his second letter was received.

Chris read the letter through a third time, and actually processed the news. Good for Wes. Grace would make a poultice for the cow. Damn rooster was better off in a fox's mouth. He hoped Pauline didn't plan to climb on the roof to help with the shingles. No, George wouldn't let her; he'd get Walt or Malcolm to help. Wait, Michael came back already? Chris frowned.

"Everything all right?"

Chris jerked his head up at Jon's voice. "Yes," he said, folding up the letter. "Everyone's fine. Lame cow. Best milker, of course."

"It's always the best milker." Jon peered at Chris, crossed his arms.

Chris waited, but Jon just shook his head and went back to the barn.

At supper, he shared his news with everyone, and told Ian and Preston about Wes and the football games. Jon did not join the conversation.

***

"Did Jon already go to milk the cows?" Chris asked Preston as the boy kicked the ball in Ian's direction the next day after school. It was a tad early, but Chris had checked the barn and not found him. He'd been around only a short time earlier, digging in the garden by the kitchen.

"Nar. Out behind the barn," Preston said with a mischievous grin.

Chris wondered what Jon could be doing behind the barn, then remembered that several old pieces of machinery were stored there. Maybe he was looking for a part. Chris crossed the yard and went through the gap between the end of the barn and the wagon shed. One step beyond the corner gave him a clear view of Jon.

He wasn't alone.

He had a girl pressed against the back wall of the barn. He was working at the buttons of her shirt. She'd got his belt unbuckled and fumbled with his fly.

Chris had no intention of interrupting, but his foot, still moving forward, hit some piece of metal hidden in the tall grass. Both Jon and the girl jerked their heads toward him at the sound. Susan shrieked. Her hands flew up to the front of her shirt.

"Shit!" Jon said, and glared at Chris.

Chris stood frozen until Jon turned his head away, then retreated back the way he'd come. The boys were still kicking the ball around the yard, so Chris went into the barn. He grabbed the top of a stall door and squeezed his eyes shut. Disappointment tinged with anger welled like blood from a puncture wound. He'd never imagined Jon would stoop so low. How long had he been hiding it? Why hadn't Chris guessed? *Have you gone back to the lying, Jon?* He sensed more than heard Jon come in a few minutes later, and turned to face him.

"Don't even think about trying to give me some lame excuse," Chris said.

"It's none of your business," Jon said, fists clenched.

"How long has this been going on?"

Chris thought Jon wasn't going to answer, then he sagged against the wall and put his head down.

"I ran into her in town a few days ago. She kissed me. Said she wanted to talk. I said I didn't know. She showed up today. I didn't mean—it just happened—I wouldn't have—"

"Like hell you wouldn't have. You were just about to. Is that what you really want? A quick upright behind the barn every week or so? Is that what's keeping you here? Seriously?"

"Shut up! I loved her! Can't you understand that?"

You're the one who doesn't understand love, Jon. Chris let it pass.

"Your girl married someone else. It sucks, but it happens all the time. Get over it."

"You're a fine one to talk—"

"Shut up and listen. How bloody stupid can you be, Jon? If she ever loved you enough to marry you she would have done. Mum says no? So what? If she loved you enough *she would have married you.*"

"You don't know—"

"Yes, I do. I do know. How old is she? She looked about twenty, at the most."

"She's twenty-two."

"She's young, Jon." The anger was draining away. The disappointment remained, a black stain. Chris heaved a weary sigh. "She doesn't know what she wants. She still needs Mum's approval. Sure, she might think she still loves you, but it's because she can't have you. Jon, step back and look at the situation. Hell, you're *cheating* with her. What if her husband finds out?"

"She said—"

316

"Forget what she said. Forget everything she said. Of course she said it. It doesn't *mean* anything, not to her."

Jon lifted his chin, gathered up what remnants of defiance he had left. "What makes you an expert?"

Chris lifted his hands and let them fall. "Jon. Holy shit." He paced, tried to order his thoughts. "It's not real. You can't have anything *real* with her. Life is too short, too... too *precious*, to waste it on that. I thought you really felt you belonged here. I believed you really thought of these people as your family, like you said. I understood that, I respected that. But now I find out what's really keeping you here is some fantasy you've dreamed up with her. It's not *real*, Jon. She married someone else. You know it's a fantasy. Yet you expect me to give up the life I want so you can keep pretending."

"I asked you, the night you got here, if there'd been anyone else since Sophie, and you said no. You still wear your wedding ring."

Chris held up his left hand to show Jon his empty finger. "I was hiding behind it. I'd convinced myself that to love anyone else would be a betrayal of Sophie. I was wrong. When I—" Chris stopped at what he was about to say. He hadn't spoken the words, had hardly even thought them, but it was true. He started again.

"When I fell in love with Pauline, I told myself it wasn't real, it was only because she was my therapist, and broken people fall in love with their therapists. I told myself that if I just put some distance between us—me and Pauline—I'd realize it was just circumstance, not love. I told myself that of course my brother was more important. So I promised you I

317

wouldn't leave. But I was wrong. Now I've realized that as much as I love you, my brother... I *need* her. She completes me. I promised you I'd stay, Jon. But if you want me to be happy, truly happy, you'll release me from that promise, and tell me I can go back to Breton."

"And just leave me here?"

"I want you to come with me. I think you can be happy there. I don't want to leave you. After everything—" Chris choked, had to stop. He took a deep breath. "We shouldn't be apart. Not anymore. Come with me."

Jon stuffed his hands into his armpits and would not look at Chris. "I don't know. I don't know how to give her up. I can't."

"You can. You have to. I'll help you. Just like before."

Jon's head jerked up and anger flashed in his eyes. "You can't compare Susan to cocaine, damn you."

"She'll ruin you, just the same. Jon, you were about to *screw* her. Another man's *wife*. You wouldn't be able to respect yourself. And how could I?"

"I need some time." Jon put a hand up to his face and turned away. "I need some time."

"How much time?"

"I don't know. I don't know."

"One month."

"No. Stay through Christmas."

"No. I want to spend Christmas with Pauline."

"'Til December, then. 'Til the start of December."

Hardly daring to breathe, Chris nodded. Three months. *Too long*. But at least he had a commitment from Jon. And what passed for an agreement. Surely this would be easier than the other time. He'd convince Jon to leave sooner than December. "And you'll come with me? I want you to come with me."

"I don't know. I'll have to see what—how I feel then."

"Okay. Sure."

"Please don't tell anyone else," Jon said.

"Of course not," Chris said, keeping his voice low. "You know I'm trying to help you, right? I don't want to see you hurt. I want to see you happy. I never thought I'd be happy again, Jon. Pauline helped me see that I can be. I want it. For both of us."

"I want it, too."

"You won't lie to me, will you?"

Jon looked him in the eye and shook his head. "No. *No.*"

"Good."

"I don't want another girl, Chris. So don't think that's going to fix it."

"You feel that way now, I know. Hell, Jon. Haven't you talked to *anyone* about this? Fiona? Laura? Anyone?"

Jon shook his head.

"You're as bad as me. You need a good therapist. And I happen to know one. But I guess you're stuck with me."

"You did all right the last time," Jon said.

"Don't do that to me again."

Jon shook his head.

Chris moved toward the door. "It's time for milking."

"Are we okay?"

"Of course," Chris said, catching his brother's eye. "As long as you promise to try."

"I promise."

***

The second letter from Pauline came the next day. Chris handed Ian a coin after breakfast and asked him to stop by the Post Office on the way home from school, then made sure he was waiting by the gate when the boys got home. Ian handed him the letter with a roll of his eyes.

Chris managed to get through it without whooping out loud.

"Absence makes the heart grow fonder," Pauline had written, and "I look forward to kissing every part of you, too." She went on from there. It was enough to drive a man to drink.

"What was in your letter today?" Fiona asked at supper.

Chris nearly choked on his peas. He mumbled something about hogs and football and wondered why the room was so bloody hot.

"Have you sent her a picture?" Jon asked. He brought one into Chris's room later that evening. "This one. Suitable for framing." He dropped it on the desk.

"That's from years ago," Chris said, covering up the letter he was writing in reply.

"How many photo studios have you run across lately, brother? Film and chemicals are still hellish expensive. When I can afford it again, you and she will be my first subjects."

320

"Thanks. Now go away."

"After your blood test Saturday we'll go to the pub and get pissed."

"Bloody fantastic. Now *go away*."

Chapter 27

"There, that's it," Pauline said to Michael, pointing out the windscreen into the waning light as they rounded a curve and saw the whole house and the stone wall in front of it, just the way Chris had described it. *Chris, I'm here!* Her stomach fluttered. A smile stretched her face.

Michael had arrived in Breton toward the end of October, on a cold morning with a hard frost glittering in the first rays of the sun. He pulled up in the road in front of the gate in a white lorry and tooted the horn. He apologized for not being able to give her any warning, said his run was going to take him right through Hurleigh, and that she could ride along if she could be ready to go in half an hour. She had rushed upstairs to pack a bag, her heart pounding.

"Nice place," Michael said, pulling the lorry over closer to the edge of the road and putting on the brakes. He did not turn off the engine.

"You don't want to come in, say hello to Chris?"

Michael shook his head. "No, I don't think so. Tell him for me, eh? I'll be here day after tomorrow, okay? Morning; like, eight or so, right?"

"I'll be ready," Pauline said, opening the door.

He smiled at her. "Have a great time, Paulie."

"Thank you so much, Michael." She squeezed his hand.

"I'll wait, just to be sure."

Pauline beamed back at him as she climbed down from the cab with her rucksack slung over her shoulder, and the tote in one hand. She shut the door and turned around.

A boy appeared, standing behind the gate. Ian.

"Hello," Pauline said. "This is Hurleigh House, isn't it? I'm looking for Chris Price."

The boy nodded. Pauline took a step forward, and another boy ran up, younger, with darker hair. Preston. Close behind came a woman, holding her unbuttoned coat shut. Pauline guessed it might be Fiona, but wasn't sure.

"Hello," Pauline said again. "I'm looking for Chris Price."

A smile broke over the woman's face.

"He didn't know you were coming, did he? You're Pauline, aren't you?" She pulled the gate open. "I'm Fiona."

"It's lovely to meet you," Pauline said, smiling back, a little breathless. "Yes, I'm Pauline, and no, he doesn't know." She turned and waved at Michael in the cab of the lorry, gave him a thumbs up. He revved the engine and drove away. The boys watched him go with mouths open.

Pauline stepped in through the gate. "A friend of mine," she explained. "He gave me a ride. I hope I'm not imposing."

Fiona waved her hand. "Don't be silly, of course not! I'm delighted you've come! Chris will be thrilled. What a surprise! Come in, come in."

The boys pushed the gate closed and Pauline walked with Fiona across the yard toward the house.

"Chris is off at the next farm right now with Jon, but he'll be back soon," Fiona said as they walked. "We could send Ian over to get him, if you'd like, or just wait until he comes. Half hour at most."

"Oh, let's just wait, surprise him, shall we?"

The door opened just before they got to it. Pauline knew who it had to be.

"Brian," Fiona said, "this is Pauline!"

They took her into the warm kitchen, big and inviting and smelling wonderful. Brian helped her out of her coat. She met Vivian and Alan, was introduced to the boys, and Simon came in, too, having heard the lorry.

"How long can you stay?" Fiona asked.

"My friend is coming day after tomorrow to take me back," Pauline said, putting her tote up on the table. "Here, I've brought some things. I understand it's polite these days to bring food when one visits." She unloaded the tote: a loaf of bread, some of Marie's apple butter, dried apricots and apricot jam, red potatoes, two big jars of yellow wax beans, walnuts. Except for the bread, she had tried to pick things that were different from what they already had, according to what Chris had told her in his letters. They all exclaimed in delight, especially over the apricots.

Fiona took her off to the loo to "primp" as she called it. Pauline grinned as she turned on the taps and the water came out. She hesitated before she flushed, she wasn't sure if it would really work, even though Chris had told her it would. She almost laughed as the water whooshed into the toilet.

When she came back out she told them about the ride. Brian and Simon asked her about the state of the roads, the number of other lorries or cars she had seen. Fiona and Vivian asked what the towns she passed

324

through had been like. The boys sat listening in rapt silence.

Fiona stayed near the sink, where she had a view out the window. She glanced out every few moments, keeping watch for Chris and Jon.

"Here they come." Fiona turned and smiled.

Pauline's heart thumped in her chest, and she stood up from the chair, eyes on the door. Muffled voices came from outside.

The door opened. Jon entered first. Chris was behind him, laughing at whatever his brother had just said, already unzipping his jacket, not paying attention to who waited in the kitchen. Pauline found she had to concentrate on controlling her breathing. They were both shrugging out of their coats, both with big smiles on their faces. Tears filled her eyes, in spite of the smile on her face. She wanted to stop time and stare at this relaxed, laughing Chris, his hair cut short, so different from the solemn, ragged man who had come to them last year, different even from the much-healed man who had walked away on the road a few months ago. She'd had some idea, from his letters, of the change, but to see him now, laughing, was almost overwhelming.

Jon hung his coat on a hook, and turned toward them as Chris was hanging his. He spotted her, cocked his head, and said "Hello, who's this—?" Then recognition swept across his expression. Chris stopped a step behind his brother, his face still alight with mirth, and caught sight of her. The mirth changed to surprise, and he stood, frozen, staring into her eyes.

Jon elbowed him. "I say, she's *waiting*," he said in a mock whisper.

Chris rushed forward then, and Pauline did too, done with waiting, done with uncertainty. A few steps each brought them together.

"Pauline—!" Chris grabbed her and held her tightly. She made some sort of little noise, but no words came. She couldn't get enough of him into her arms, couldn't hold him tight enough, couldn't take in enough of his warmth or his smell. She wanted the embrace to last forever, wanted to feel this safe and complete and *certain*, forever. He pulled back enough to look into her eyes again.

She smiled. "Hello."

"How did you get here?"

"Michael brought me in his lorry."

"Hell, Chris, she's come all this way," Jon said. "Aren't you going to kiss her, at least?"

Everyone was watching them. Chris kissed her with confidence. He grinned at her. Her heart thumped at the look. Then he glanced over at Fiona, who had a big smile on her face.

"Did you know about this?"

"No, I didn't!" She laughed, throwing her hands up.

"How long have you been here?" Chris asked Pauline.

"Not long at all."

Fiona added, "Less than a half hour. We knew you'd be along any minute, so we thought we'd let you be surprised."

"So you've all met," Chris said, but he kept his eyes on Pauline's face, and continued to hold her close.

"Well, we've not been introduced," Jon pointed out, and he stepped up to take the hand that Pauline held out to him. "Lovely to finally meet you, I'm Jon."

Chris eventually turned her loose with another little kiss, but kept hold of her hand. "How is everyone? Is everyone okay?"

Pauline assured him that everyone was just fine.

"Why didn't you tell me you were coming?" He ushered her into a chair, and sat next to her, on the edge of his seat, staring at her face, her hand grasped in his.

"I didn't know," she said. "Michael came by this morning and said he was coming right through here, and asked if I wanted to ride along." She stopped and licked her lips. "He'll be by the day after tomorrow to take me home."

Chris's smile faltered. "Two days," he said softly, then blinked. "This morning?"

"It's only about seventy miles."

Chris shook his head, looked away from her, and Pauline knew he was remembering the long journey he'd had getting to Hurleigh.

"Well, you chaps need to get washed up," Fiona said. "Supper in about half an hour. Chris, why don't you take Pauline's things up?"

They went hand in hand up the stairs, Chris carrying her bag. In his room he put it down and they stood with eyes locked. Then Chris pulled her close and kissed her for a long time.

"That's even nicer than I remembered," Pauline said.

"It is. God, I can't believe it," he said, his hands in her hair, gazing at her face.

"You've changed. You found what you were looking for."

He nodded. "I suppose I did. And I realized what I was missing."

"You didn't tell me you cut your hair." She ran her fingers through it, and he looked embarrassed. "I like it. I like you happy."

"Oh, I'm happy now," he assured her, and kissed her again. Eventually he stood back. "I suppose we should go down." He picked up her bag and set it on the bed. "Um…"

"What?"

"Will you share with me?" He nodded toward the bed.

"Oh, yes, please."

"Good." He ended up kissing her some more.

"I thought you said we should go down."

Chris rarely let go of her hand the whole evening, even while they ate dinner. The other women wouldn't let her help, so she sat with Chris and told everyone the latest Breton news.

Brian served wine in the sitting room after washing up and homework and more chatting around the kitchen table.

"What have you heard in Breton about telephone service?" Simon asked Pauline.

"Michael said that areas of Portsmouth have it, and they plan to expand. Rumors are that we should have it by next year."

"Meaning January?" Chris asked.

"More like this time next year, I gather," she said. "What have you heard?"

Simon nodded. "It's spreading. They've got lines between quite a few major cities. Adding phones all the time. They seem to envision neighborhood phones in a central location for a year or so. But the government plans phone service to every house that wants it within two years."

"That's so exciting," Pauline said. "Now, if we could just get electricity."

"That's not far off, either. BEC is hiring as fast as they can, all over, repairing the lines. I predict you'll have it within the year."

"I feel like I've been out in the middle of nowhere," Pauline said.

"You have," Chris replied, and nuzzled her. "Do you know they're playing music on the radio now? The BBC is actually broadcasting again, several hours a day."

"Television?"

"Did you keep yours?" Fiona asked.

"Carried out to the garage, I think. Home to generations of mice, I've no doubt, by now."

"We pulled ours out a few weeks ago, but couldn't get a signal."

"Give it a few more months," Simon said. "We'll all be back to watching bad sitcoms."

***

"Finally," Chris said after Brian and Fiona had gone upstairs, the last of the crowd to suddenly decide to retire early. He moved closer on the couch. "I thought they'd never leave." He pulled Pauline into him for a long kiss.

"I feel like a teenager," Pauline said.

"Me, too. Here, feel."

"Oh, I like the feel of that."

"Then help me… take this… *off*."

"Chris—upstairs—bed—door that locks—*please?*"

"Yes, yes. Okay."

He tried to kiss her all the way up the stairs. "Jon's just one over," he warned her as he closed the door and followed her down onto the bed.

"I'll try to be quiet."

"I'm not sure I can promise that."

***

Chris's bare shoulder and bicep had to be one of the nicest things to wake up to, Pauline thought. A little tugging at the bedclothes revealed more nice things to look at.

"Stop that," he murmured, his mouth twitching.

Pauline couldn't resist kissing that mouth. "Good morning."

"Good morning." He reached out a hand to touch her face.

"Someone's up downstairs. Do you have to get up for chores?"

"Not today. Jon said he'd take care of them."

Pauline smiled a little more and shifted closer to him under the covers. "Good."

Chris grabbed her and pulled her partly on top of him. She kissed him for a while before settling down with a sigh, her head against him, feeling his warmth all along her body. She caressed his chest lightly.

"Did you sleep well?"

"Definitely," Chris said. "Did you?"

"Oh, yes."

His arms tightened around her. "This is just about perfect."

"What would make it perfect?"

"If you didn't have to leave tomorrow. If we were in Breton. If we were home."

"We'll get to that."

Her fingers found their way to his left shoulder. She traced the blemish in his skin she'd found the night before, but never had a chance to ask about.

"What's this?"

"Scar."

"I can see that," she said, making a face at him. "How did you get it?"

He hesitated. "A knife fight. They nearly killed me. Remember I told you that Marcus and his group came along and saved me in London?"

The words seared through her. She put her face down onto his neck.

"There's a lot you don't know," Chris said.

"It doesn't matter," she said. "I know enough." She lifted her head and kissed him firmly.

He gazed at her, lips parted, with an intensity that made her heart pound, her stomach fluttery, her arms weak. She was keenly aware of every part of him pressing against her.

"There are some things I should tell you. You should know everything," he said. "Before you decide."

"Decide what?"

"About me. About us."

"I've already decided," she whispered, putting her lips to his, seeing his eyes close, feeling his arms tighten again. "But I'm here to listen to anything you need to tell me."

He squeezed her tight. "I don't want to ruin this, not right now. I just want... *this*."

"I understand." She ran her fingers across his skin. "Whenever you're ready."

He was ready for something else, and so was she. They missed breakfast.

Fiona was the only one in the kitchen when they finally went downstairs. She gave them a cheerful "Good morning!" as they sat at the places set for them, and she served them ham and pancakes with jam.

Later, they walked hand in hand through the bent over, wilted grass, happily quiet, occasionally glancing at each other. Chris had given Pauline his gloves. Her nose ached. Their breath hung in the air.

"It's so cold, for October," Pauline said.

Chris led her down a slope and through a stile in a wall. They came to a stream sheltered by trees dressed only in the rags of their former leafy glory. Ice edged the water where it pooled. She imagined it must be cool and green in the summer.

"Over here," Chris said, and showed her a large rock that looked like a bench set into the bank, with a flat part to sit on, and a back to lean against. They settled onto the seat, arms around each other.

Pauline laughed. "Ooo, it's a little cold."

"Yeah, it's nicer when it's warm, but I wanted to show you."

"It's lovely."

"Ian says there're flowers in the spring."

They sat in silence, listening to the water. She leaned into him, and his arms squeezed her gently. He nuzzled her hair.

"I was thinking…" he said.

"About?"

"Maybe I should just go home with you tomorrow."

"Oh, Chris. I'd like that, of course, but you told Jon through November."

"I know. I always hoped to make it sooner."

"Anyway, I don't think Michael can take a third person in the lorry. Maybe I can visit again."

He kissed her. "I hope so." He fished in his pocket. "I have something for you. Um, I found it. I hope that's okay." He handed her a small puff of flowered tissue tied with a bit of ribbon.

"Of course it's okay."

"It made me think of you when I saw it."

She took off the gloves to untie the ribbon, carefully opened the tissue. Inside was a necklace: a slim chain with a little gold heart pendant about the size of her thumbnail. Set into the heart, off-center, glittered a tiny diamond. "Oh! It's beautiful."

"I don't know if it's a real diamond."

"I don't care. I love it."

Pauline opened the clasp and put it on. He held her hair up off the back of her neck while she hooked it. She adjusted the collar of her jacket and felt for it. It hung just in the hollow of her neck, the perfect length. Chris watched her, smiling.

"Thank you," she said. "But I didn't bring anything for you."

"Yes, you did." He kissed her again. They sat holding each other for a few more minutes.

"Chris?"

"Hmmm...?"

"My butt's cold," she said with a little shiver, and he laughed, like she'd hoped he would.

When they got back to the house, the boys were home from school and everyone was gathered in the yard.

"We're just having a game of football," Simon called out to them. "Would you like to play?"

"Oh, yes!" Pauline said, and they hurried over.

They lined up along the garden wall. Ian and Preston stood out in the yard as captains. Ian picked first.

"Uncle Chris."

Chris seemed a bit surprised, left Pauline's side, and trotted over to stand with Ian.

Fiona leaned a bit closer to Pauline. "Ian knows Pres would pout if Ian chose Brian," she said.

"Dad!" Preston called out with a grin, and Brian went to stand with him.

"Pauline is good," Chris suggested to Ian, but Ian pulled a face at him.

"Uncle Jon," Ian said.

Brian was bending over and whispering something in Preston's ear. Preston looked unconvinced, but finally said, "Pauline."

334

Chris gasped and shot an astonished look at Brian as everyone chuckled and Pauline went to stand with Preston and Brian. Chris put a hand to his heart, but she could see he was laughing too. She blew him a little kiss.

"Uncle Simon," Ian said quickly.

"Mum!" Preston said with a smile.

That left Alan and Vivian. Ian stood chewing his lip. He glanced over at Brian, who looked significantly at him.

"Aunt Vivian," Ian said after a pause, and Preston excitedly said "Uncle Alan!" and the teams were complete. Simon put his hand on Ian's back.

"Good job," he said, grinning. "We've got 'em!"

"I wouldn't be too sure," Chris said. "Pauline's good. She grew up playing with boys." He looked over at Brian. "No mercy, Brian!"

Chapter 28

The game ended in a draw when it was time to get tea. Alan and Vivian went off to the gatehouse, the rest trooped into the kitchen.

"Oh, that was such fun!" Pauline said, hanging her coat on top of Chris's.

"We used to do that in hotel lobbies if it was raining or cold outside," Chris said.

Brian laughed. "Remember that one place in Kansas that tried to kick us out?"

"It's too bad Laura isn't here. She has great tour stories," Fiona put in.

"I would have liked to meet her," Pauline said. She sat down next to Chris at the table.

"Next time," Chris said.

The boys wanted to hear more about the band and the tour from so long ago. Pauline chimed in with them, so the tea conversation was all about their antics backstage and at hotels. Pauline watched Chris, Brian and Jon all trying to outdo each other in the eyes of the boys.

"Were you along for the whole tour, Jon?" Pauline asked him.

"Most of it. I was in charge of cleaning up their messes." He grinned.

"No, no, no." Chris wagged a finger at him. "We were tame, compared to some bands. We had fun. We were never destructive."

"The fire extinguisher in the vending machine?" Jon put in.

"That was Stan. He paid for it," Brian assured Pauline.

"They were out of hot tamales," Chris said.

"What on earth—?"

"A kind of cinnamon-flavored sweet."

"Is that what those were? I always thought they were foul," Brian said.

"Did you demand all sorts of odd things in your contract?"

"No, only that we never took our shirts off or kissed gorgeous models in the videos," Brian said.

"Golly, I hadn't even considered videos," Pauline said, eyeing Chris.

"We were *tame*," he insisted. "They all had that 'games and sports' theme."

Brian got up from the table and disappeared into the sitting room. He returned in a few minutes with a stack of CDs. He set them in front of Pauline, pushing aside her empty plate.

"Oh, I remember that," she said, picking up the first one called 'Good Match.' She smiled at the picture: the two of them—impossibly young—posed as if in the stands of some sporting event, watching intently. "My flat mate owned this, but I don't think I ever did."

Brian gasped in mock disappointment. "I'm crushed!"

"This was the big one, right?" Pauline said. She checked the track listing on the back. The two songs that Chris had mentioned to her that day long ago in Breton were there. "Play this one."

"Later," Chris said. He turned the CD over to the front again and pointed to one of the other "fans" in the

337

bleachers. "Look, there's Stan, he was bass. That's Erik, our drummer, and that's Wyatt, our manager. And here," he pointed to two girls who were sitting below them, looking not at the game, but at Chris and Brian, their faces partly obscured, "that's Fiona and Laura."

Pauline glanced up at Fiona, who rolled her eyes.

"It was all terribly exciting at the time," Fiona said.

Pauline picked up the next CD, "No More Games." The picture was the two of them on a tennis court, with the net between them. They stood apart, arms crossed, each with a racket, staring at the camera with dark looks on their faces. Instead of tennis whites they both wore black.

"Hmm, bit of a departure there."

"There's an understatement," Brian said. "Our thinly veiled message."

"No one got it," Chris said. "Well, not right away."

The third CD had only Brian's name on it. It was titled "Divergence." It showed a darkly shadowed road that split off into two directions, with a stone wall between them. One direction led toward the sunset, the other led off into darkness.

"Oh, subtle," Pauline remarked, and glanced at Brian.

"It didn't seem so childish at the time. I thought I was being clever."

"All sorts of people tried to reason with him," Fiona said, "but he was a stubborn lout."

Brian put his hands up. "Guilty as charged."

The next two were rather plain, architectural, devoid of symbolism. One was predominantly white, the other grey.

"Alan's influence, there," Brian said. "Thank you, Alan."

Pauline shifted them off the stack. Chris drew a breath, and his arm tightened around her. He glanced up at Brian.

"You've got mine?" he said, eyebrows drawn together.

"Of course," Brian said, leaning back in his chair. "Good stuff. What, you didn't have mine?"

"I did. They're excellent."

Pauline examined the CDs. The first one, "Hit The Road," showed a distorted figure on a deserted highway.

"Is that you?" she asked Chris.

He shook his head. "Nah. Just a picture." He flipped it over. The back showed him on a small stage, lights across the top, the heads of the audience in the foreground. He held his guitar and leaned toward the microphone. His eyes were closed.

"You're fat," Pauline said, and snorted.

"I was *not*," he protested. "I had a little extra padding, maybe. Hell, everyone did. You're just used to the new and improved version."

The second one had a close-up of his face. It was called "Home."

"That's the good one," Chris said.

"I liked 'Someone For Me' best," Brian said.

"Play it," Pauline said, and tried to hand the CD to Brian, but Chris took it from her.

"No."

"Play it for her, Chris," Brian urged. "It's brilliant."

"Not right now," Chris said. He put the CD on the bottom of the stack, his eyebrows drawn down. Brian looked at him strangely, but let it go. He went back into the sitting room.

"I've never heard any of this, except that first album," Pauline said to Chris.

He leaned in to kiss her cheek. "Some other time, okay?"

Brian came back with a big photo album. He grinned. "I've got pictures!"

***

Chris kept hold of Pauline's hand and led her across the yard in the dark to the gatehouse where Alan and Vivian lived. He knocked on the door.

Alan answered. "Ah, good evening sir, madam. Your table is ready."

He stepped aside to let them into the main room of the little house. Only one lamp was lit. Some furniture had been pushed back to make space for a small table with a candle and cutlery for two. Alan helped Pauline with her coat.

Pauline's mouth watered at the smell in the air. Chris was grinning.

"What is this?" she asked under her breath.

"You'll see."

"Right this way," Alan said, and ushered them the five paces over to the table. He held the chair for Pauline.

"Thank you," she said, smiling. "I take it we're not having supper with the others?"

"Nope. Just us," Chris said.

Alan produced a bottle of wine and gave it to Chris to pour. He inclined his head. "Your dinner should be ready momentarily." He turned on his heel and went through another door, presumably into the kitchen.

Chris's eyes sparkled in the candlelight. "Wine, my dear?"

"What is it I smell? It's fantastic. What is all this?"

"Do you remember last year, after that disastrous Christmas party at the pub? When I should have kissed you? Hell, I can't believe how much time I wasted not kissing you."

"After the party?" Pauline prompted. Bits and pieces of Christmas came to her in a jumble.

"We were walking home, and I asked you what you wanted for Christmas, and you said—"

Pauline laughed. "A pizza!"

"Well, it's taken me nearly a year, but you're going to get your pizza. Happy Christmas, Paulie. Early."

"I can't believe you remembered that."

"And no onions, because I plan to breathe on you later, heavily."

"I'm looking forward to that as much as the pizza."

"Wow, I'm not used to this," Chris said, and shifted in his seat.

"Used to wha—? Oh." Pauline put a hand to her mouth. "Sorry."

"Not at all. Bloody fantastic. I may go insane when you leave tomorrow."

That made Pauline's heart lurch. "Don't let's mention that, okay?" She picked up her wine glass and held it up. "To tonight."

"Tonight," Chris echoed, and clinked against hers.

***

Pauline snuggled closer to Chris under the covers, moved her leg against his, ran her fingers along his chest.

"That was nice, tonight," she said.

"The pizza?"

"Yes, but I meant tea. The picture album. The stories."

"Yeah, it was."

"I could see it, that you two were mates."

"We were."

"I can see why you missed him so much."

"I think I blew all that way out of proportion," Chris whispered.

"No, you didn't," she assured him, and kissed him gently. "Why wouldn't you play me that song?"

He turned his head toward her in the dark. "It was Sophie's song. She was in the studio when I recorded it. I never sang it unless she was in the audience."

"Oh."

"I'm sorry."

"No, I understand," Pauline said. "It's all right. Brian doesn't know that, does he?"

"No, I don't think so."

Chris got his arms around her, held her close.

"Someday I'll write you a song," he said.

"And will you sing it to me, too?"

"I'll try. Don't know if I still can."

"I'll let you practice if you need to."

"I'd like to practice something else, now."

"Yes, please. Practice makes perfect," Pauline murmured.

"You're already perfect, my darling."

***

Pauline woke up slowly. There was just enough light to see Chris next to her, still sleeping soundly. She smiled to herself, regarded his face in the dim light, then slipped out of bed and went to the loo. She smelled breakfast cooking downstairs. When she got back he was awake.

"I didn't mean to wake you," she said, sliding back in beside him.

"I expect we'll have to get up soon."

"Someone's up and cooking already."

His hand found hers beneath the covers. His eyes stared into hers. "Michael's coming today."

"I know."

"I don't want you to go."

She caressed his face. "They need me at home."

"I know."

"Anyway, you seemed quite content before I got here," she half-joked.

"Well, yes, but I didn't know what I was missing," he said, pulling her closer, kissing her neck, her shoulder, her throat.

Someone knocked on the door.

"Hey, you two," came Jon's voice, "it's gone seven. Sorry."

"Yes, thank you very much!" Chris called out, and continued grazing. He unbuttoned her top. Pauline stifled a giggle.

"All right," she said, "don't get yourself all in a stew."

"Too late. I'm thoroughly stewed."

"We have to get up," she insisted, and tried to roll away from him. He grabbed her tight, threw a leg over her.

"No, wait." He kissed her lips, pulled her to him. "Ten minutes. We can take ten minutes. Please, don't get up yet."

She didn't really want to get up. Michael likely would be late, anyway. She snuggled against him and kissed him back. They took twenty minutes.

***

It was half-eight when they finished a quick breakfast and everyone stood and said their goodbyes. Pauline got hugs from everyone, including Ian, who was nudged forward by his mum, but did not seem at all reluctant.

"Come any time," Fiona urged her, and Pauline agreed to try. Chris helped Pauline on with her coat, got his own, took her hand. He picked up her bag, and they went outside together to wait for Michael.

She walked close to him on the little garden path, through the gate and across the yard. They went out to stand by the road, out of sight of those in the kitchen, and Chris put her bag down, and turned to her. He took both her hands in his, looked into her eyes.

"I don't know if I can wait another month," he said.

"Don't be silly. Of course you can."

He nodded, but didn't say anything.

"And I'm sure I can come visit again."

"That will keep me going." He kissed her.

"Oh, don't make it sound so horrible," she said, and tried to grin. "People have been getting through this kind of thing forever."

"Not me."

"It's only a month," she chided him. "And we can write to each other."

"You sound like you won't mind at all," he said, nuzzling her neck, but she knew he was joking.

"Oh, I put up a brave front, that's all," she said, her fingers in his hair. "I'll ache for you. You know I will."

"You'll be okay?"

"Of course, now I know you're happy. Now I know you're mine."

He nodded, put his cheek against hers. "I'm yours. I love you, Pauline."

"I love you, too, Chris," she said, her heart pounding, and the words almost caught in her throat. She slipped her arms around him and hugged him tight, her face against his jacket, and he hugged her back just as hard. They stood there until she became aware of a noise in the distance.

"Damn," Chris muttered. "He's coming."

"Yes, I hear it." She looked up at him. He kissed her long and hard, holding her tight, and she didn't want it to end, but he broke away from her when the lorry rounded the corner and came into view. "No reason to cry this time," she said to him above the noise of the engine as Michael pulled up next to them. He held her hand, looked at her, and he shook his head, smiled just a little.

The lorry squealed to a halt. Chris stepped forward and reached up to open the door.

"I'm a bit late!" Michael called down from his seat. "But I don't expect you mind, eh?"

Chris helped Pauline up into the cab, then got her bag, and stepped up to hand it in. She took it and put it behind her seat. Chris stood there, gripping the handle of the open door, looked at Michael, held out his other hand.

"Thanks, Cooper," he said, and Michael smiled and leaned over to shake it.

"I reckoned I owed you one," Michael said lightly.

"Can we do it again?" Pauline asked him.

"We'll have to see," Michael said. "I'll have a word with Kay. She's pretty accommodating if she's in a good mood. And of course, she'd do almost anything for you, Price." He grinned wide and winked at them.

"Tell her thank you, too," Chris said.

"I will indeed. She has a job for you any time you want one, you know."

"Not a chance," Chris said, and looked at Pauline. "Tell her thanks, but I have other plans." He took her hand in his and squeezed it.

"Well, I hate to have to rush, but I do have a schedule to keep," Michael said then.

Pauline put a hand up to Chris's face, smiled at him. "I'll see you soon," she said, and he nodded, swallowed. His eyes flicked in Michael's direction

346

briefly. He looked like he wanted to kiss her again, but instead he used his free arm to hug her close.

"I'll miss you," he whispered into her ear.

"Me, too. It won't be too long," she whispered back.

He let her go. "Drive safe," he said Michael, and then he was jumping down and closing the door. She leaned her forehead against the glass, watching him standing there. He blew her a kiss and mouthed "I love you." She did the same, a lump in her throat.

Michael shifted and the lorry started to move, and Chris got smaller behind them, standing with his hands in his pockets, alone by the side of the road.

When he was out of sight she turned and sat facing forward in her seat, blinking.

"You okay?" Michael asked.

She nodded.

Michael was quiet while they went through the little town of Hurleigh.

"You had a good time?" he asked finally.

"Oh, it was wonderful," she said, having got herself back in control. "Thank you, Michael... I had a *shower*."

"That's the most memorable thing?" Michael said with a grin.

"That I can talk about, yes," she grinned back.

"I'm happy for you, Paulie, I really am," he said. "But look...."

She turned to him when he did not go on. "What?"

He bit his lip. "There won't be any more visits. I'm sorry."

"Why not?" she said, her stomach hollow.

"They've decided we all need a second, a guard. No more solo runs. No more passengers. I'm sorry, sweetie. I didn't want to tell Chris. I'm a coward, I suppose."

"Has there been trouble?"

"Not around here. Closer to London, yes. We're safe, don't worry. But they don't want to take any chances."

"No, of course not," she said, thinking of what she had just said to Chris: 'I'm sure I can come visit again,' and how he had answered: 'That will keep me going.' She took a deep breath. "Well, rules are rules."

"He said he'd come the end of November, right? It's only a month."

"He'd have come today if there'd been room. Yes, only a month. He'll be okay."

"What about you, sweetie? Are you going to be okay?"

"Of course. I'm used to it." She cast him a look. Michael rolled his eyes. "Anyway, we have the rest of our lives," she said, and a warmth spread through her as she thought about it.

Michael didn't say anything, kept his eyes on the road, but he reached over and took her hand and squeezed it.

Chapter 29

A week later Chris sat at the kitchen table writing a letter to Pauline. Brian had already put the boys to bed and taken Simon into the little office next to the pantry to go over some paperwork.

"Hey, there's an Outbreak Warning!" Jon called from the sitting room, where he had turned on the radio to try to find some news.

"Where?" Chris asked without getting up.

"I think you should hear this."

Something in his voice made Chris drop his pen and join his brother. Jon turned up the volume.

"… have declared Epidemic Emergencies," the announcer said. "Ports are closed in the following counties: Norfolk, Suffolk, Essex, London, Kent, Sussex, Hampshire, Dorset, Somerset, Devon, Cornwall, and Gloucestershire."

"Hampshire."

"That's just ports," Jon said, still staring at the radio.

Brian and Simon came in, followed closely by Fiona.

"Where is it?" Simon asked, and Jon shushed him as the announcer continued.

"The contagion is still unconfirmed at this time, but citizens should take every precaution to aid in containment. A strict quarantine has been issued for the following counties: Norfolk, Suffolk, Cambridgeshire, Hertfordshire, Essex, London, Kent, Sussex, Surrey, Hampshire, Dorset, and Somerset."

"So many," Fiona said.

"Hampshire," Chris repeated. "That's Breton."

"Shhh!"

"… reported in Ipswich, Colchester, Chelmsford, London, Southend-On-Sea, Maidstone, Dover, Folkstone…" The announcer droned on, city after city, while Chris fought back a rising sense of urgency. He heard "Portsmouth" and flinched as if punched.

"I have to go," Chris said.

"Chris, there's a quarantine, you can't," Jon said.

"I don't care. I have to go."

"How will you get there? The buses will be stopped," Simon pointed out.

"I'll take a bloody bicycle if I have to!"

"Have we enough petrol for the car?" Brian said, and they all looked at him.

"We haven't run the car in years," Fiona said.

Simon shook his head. "I doubt if it will even go."

Brian nodded at Chris. "Alan can get it going."

Chris looked at him, hope starting.

"There'll be roadblocks. You won't get through," Simon said.

"I'll get through."

Simon crossed his arms. "It's crazy."

"Will it be safe, by yourself?" Fiona asked.

"I'll go with you, of course," Jon said, as if it were obvious.

"All right," Chris said. "Brilliant. Can we be ready by morning?"

"I'll go get Alan," Brian said, and left the room.

"What will you need?" Fiona asked them.

"You'll need a good map," Simon muttered, turning back to the radio to listen.

"I've got maps," Chris told Jon.

"I'll pack some food," Fiona said.

Chris took the stairs two at a time up to his room and pulled out his duffle. He shuffled through his maps, found the one he thought would be most useful. He had made a few notations on it during his walk from Breton. He sat holding the map, remembering the walk, how long it had taken. *Not this time.* It should only take a few hours in the car. He checked his torch, made a mental note to replace the batteries.

Jon came in with a brown rucksack. "Here, you'll never get everything into your duffle."

"Thanks."

Chris dumped the duffle out onto the bed. There wasn't much in it, just odd things he hadn't needed since he'd got to Hurleigh.

"Keep that handy," Jon said, gesturing at the rolled towel that hid the black handgun. "We may need it."

Chris caught his eye. "You don't have to come."

"Yes, I do. Of course I do. I want to." He slapped Chris on the back.

"Thanks, Jon."

"I'll go pack." Jon left him with a little salute.

Even the bigger rucksack was too small to fit everything in. Chris eyed the pile of clothes he'd laid out on the bed, pared it down to essentials, and put the rest back into the drawers, as he'd done when he left Breton. He felt no need to travel with more than just one bag. The things would be there if he ever needed them. He got his journal from the desk, the castle chess piece, the picture of Pauline—framed now, thanks to Jon—and the small bundle of letters from her. *I'm coming*, he thought as he put them in the bag, wishing

351

for maybe the millionth time that he could simply ring her up on a phone. He remembered the little black leather box he'd found in the Frome market, just big enough for the picture of Sophie and Rosie, the little toy horse, and his wedding ring. He couldn't leave that behind. He tucked it into the rucksack. He put the pistol handy in a side pouch, the bullets into his trouser pocket. His stomach ached. He closed up the pack, turned to the door.

Simon came into the room with a small bundle in his hand. "You might run into trouble on the road. Take this." He opened the rag, exposing a handgun.

Chris stared at it with his mouth open.

"It's okay, we can spare it," Simon said, holding it out to him.

"I don't need it." Chris showed Simon his own gun in the side pocket of the rucksack.

Simon smiled, nodding. "I should have known you'd be prepared."

"I didn't realize you were quite so prepared."

"Oh, very prepared." Simon put out his hand, and Chris shook it.

"You might give it to Jon," Chris said.

"He has his own. And don't worry; he knows how to use it." Simon winked, wrapped up the gun again, and left Chris standing in the doorway.

Chris carried the pack downstairs and switched out the batteries in his torch. He got his coat, and went out and across the yard to the garage, where the door was open and the lights on. Alan and Brian were tinkering under the bonnet of the car. They glanced up as Chris joined them.

"You should try to get some sleep, Chris," Alan said. "We'll see to the car."

Chris shook his head. "I couldn't sleep."

"Still, you should try," Brian agreed.

Chris shook his head again, then stood still. "Listen." He heard something out in the night that he couldn't quite identify. "What is that?"

Alan cocked his head. "That's a lorry."

"At this time of night?" Brian said. They went out into the yard.

The lorry was clearly getting closer, and soon they saw its lights in the road. It pulled up in front of the gate, the engine cut off, and the door opened.

"Price, are you there?" a voice said as Chris recognized the lorry.

"Cooper! Is Pauline with you?" His heart pounded in his chest.

"No, it's just me."

Brian fished the key from his pocket and unlocked the gate. Michael came into the yard, shook Chris's hand, nodded at Brian and Alan. "Have you heard the news tonight?"

"About the outbreak, yes," Chris said. "I'm going to Breton. We're trying to get the car going."

"Forget the car, I'll take you. They might let me through with the lorry where you'd never get through with a car. But we have to hurry, before they have time to get all the roadblocks in place."

"I'm already packed," Chris said.

"Brilliant."

"How did you get here so fast?"

"I heard about it this afternoon. Luckily, I was at the other end of my run, in Bristol. It's a quick drive between here and there. I've rather 'borrowed' the rig. You haven't got any diesel to spare, have you?"

Chris looked at Brian, and Brian blew out a breath.

"Possibly," Brian hedged, just as Simon joined them, coming quickly from the house. "Can we spare some diesel?" Brian asked Simon. "Cooper here is going to take Chris to Breton."

Simon hesitated. His eyes traveled from Brian to Chris to Michael. "A few liters, perhaps."

"Look, never mind," Michael said suddenly. "I shouldn't have asked, sorry. I have a bigger allowance, of course. I know a place not too far down the road. I think we can get some there. We'll manage." Michael shrugged. "Can I use your facilities before we take off?"

Jon looked up from the table as they trooped into the kitchen. He had spread out a map. His pack rested on the floor next to Chris's. Fiona and Vivian came in from the pantry. Chris introduced Michael all around.

"Jon was going to come along," Chris told Michael.

Michael shook his head. "I'm allowed to have a second in the rig, but not three. It could cause problems at roadblocks. Better if it's just the two of us."

Chris turned to Jon, held up his hands helplessly. Guilt choked him. He had spent nearly two months convincing Jon to move to Breton, and now he had to leave him behind. At least it was Cooper's lorry, Cooper's decision.

"You might need some help," Jon said.

"True, but not if we can't get there," Michael said. "It's no good if I can't at least appear official."

"I'm sorry, Jon," Chris said softly, and Jon nodded.

Simon took Michael off to the loo, and the girls finished packing a bag of food to take along. The rest of them bent over the map and traced out the area of the Outbreak from what they remembered of the list of places on the radio.

"It seems awfully big," Chris said.

"It is big," Simon said, coming back into the kitchen. "Biggest one in years."

Chris found himself staring at the little dot representing the village of Breton, an easy drive back when cars and petrol were readily available, when the roads were maintained, before outbreaks and quarantines and roadblocks. Michael re-joined them a few minutes later.

"We'll try this," he said, running a line with his finger. "Avoid the bigger towns, of course."

"How long will it take to get there?" Chris asked.

"It depends on what we run into. A good few hours, certainly. Even some of the big roads are going bad. But I know that area pretty well."

"I've got some fairly good maps," Chris told him.

"Mine are updated. Have you got a torch?"

"With fresh batteries."

"Good, you can navigate. Let's get going, then."

It struck Chris all at once that he was going to have to say goodbye. He hadn't even thought about it while he was packing. He looked around the group, and it seemed from their faces as if most of them—except for Jon—hadn't thought about it either. And it wasn't a 'have a nice time, come back and see us soon' kind of goodbye, either. It occurred to him that they thought there was a definite possibility that none of them would ever see him again. He turned to Fiona next to him.

"I can't thank you enough," he said, and hugged her.

"Be careful, Chris," she said, and kissed his cheek. "Give our love to Pauline."

"Of course." He hugged Vivian, too.

"I haven't finished your jumper," she said. "I'll send it along when I do."

"Do you have the address? I'll write it down."

She turned to get a pen while Chris shook Alan's hand.

"Maybe I'll just get that car running anyway," Alan said.

Chris took the pen from Vivian and jotted the address on the edge of the map. "I'll write to you as soon as I can, let you know how things go. Hopefully the post will still go." He thought of something else. "Say goodbye to Laura for me, would you? Tell her I'll write to her."

"We will," Fiona said.

"And the boys. Tell them—well, tell them I wish I could have said goodbye."

"I'll explain it to them," Fiona said.

Chris shook Simon's hand.

"Good luck, old boy," Simon said. "Be careful."

Brian was next. Chris turned to him, had to swallow, didn't know what to say. It could be the last thing he ever said to Brian.

"Good luck, Tag," Brian said. The old nickname made Chris smile; he'd nearly forgotten it. "Be careful. Come back and visit."

"I will do." Chris shook Brian's hand.

"Don't wait so long this time," Brian said softly.

He and Brian exchanged a look, and Chris shook his head, and figured he didn't need to say anything else. He turned to look at Jon.

"I'll walk you out," Jon said, and picked up the bag with the food. Michael went out the door; Jon followed.

Chris lifted his rucksack and put one strap over his shoulder, then stood, eyes on the floor. He looked up and around at them all standing there in the kitchen, and they all said 'goodbye' again, or 'good luck,' or 'be careful,' but he couldn't say anything. He raised a hand, turned, and went out into the night, following Jon and Michael to the lorry. Michael got in, and Jon handed the bag of food up to him, then took Chris's rucksack off his shoulder and handed that up. Michael stowed it behind the seats. He pulled his door closed and started the engine.

"I wish I were going," Jon said.

"I wish you were, too," Chris said. "Come and visit, when the Quarantine lifts."

"I'll come to stay, of course."

Chris nodded. "Of course. I think you'll like it there."

"This looks like a bad one, Chris."

"I've never got it yet."

"There's a first time for everything."

"I'll be okay," Chris said. He wished he felt as sure of it himself as he said it.

"I'm here, if you need me."

Chris nodded.

"Be careful, please," Jon said then.

"I will do. You too." Chris hugged his brother, and they walked around to the passenger side, and Chris climbed up.

"Good luck," Jon said, reaching up to shake Chris's hand.

"You'll hear from me," Chris assured him. Jon stepped back, and Chris swung the door closed. Michael released the brakes, and the lorry moved off. Chris saw Jon in the rear-view mirror, bathed in the red glow of the tail lights, standing in the road with his hands in his pockets. Then he disappeared into the dark. *Am I doing the right thing?*

"Two of your chaps offered me a gun," Michael said, and it sounded to Chris like he was grinning.

"Simon offered me one, too. I'm a little surprised."

"What, a place like that? They had better be ready to defend it. I'd be surprised if they didn't have a decent number about the place."

"It appears they do. Did you take him up on it?"

"No need, Price. We're both covered, right?"

Chris fished in his pocket for the bullets, turned around in the seat, and found his gun in the rucksack. He dropped out the clip, clicked the bullets in, and shoved it back into place with a satisfying clack. "Ready to go."

"Excellent."

The road unwound ahead of them in the inky darkness.

"We'll make it," Michael said.

"I know."

Chapter 30

Less than an hour after they left Hurleigh Michael pulled into a darkened petrol station and tooted the horn.

"I know this chap," he said.

A light came on, and the proprietor came out grumbling. Michael got out and talked with him, and convinced him to part with some fuel in spite of the hour. He climbed back up and rummaged in his rucksack by the light of a torch. He handed the man a few items, along with the coupons and money. Chris didn't ask what. When the tank was full they drove off through the dark town. Chris shifted in his seat, chewed on his thumbnail, impatient with the slow speed, but he kept his mouth shut.

"It's not like the old days," Michael said. "You never know what you'll find on the roads. If we want to get there in one piece, we have to take it a bit slower than you'd like, especially in the dark."

"Yeah, I'm a little anxious…"

Michael picked up the pace a bit once they reached a divided highway.

"I won't need a navigator for another hour, at least, if you want to try to get some sleep."

Chris didn't think he'd sleep, but he closed his eyes and gave it a try, and he did doze some. Michael woke him when it was time to get off the highway. They crept along black roads at low speeds, Chris following their progress on the map. The roads here were more deteriorated, and at times they lumbered through deep ruts. Chris had to brace himself against the dash as the lorry bounced and tossed.

Michael slowed even more as they came to a small village, completely dark. The first few houses looked overgrown. The road narrowed. Michael eased the lorry around a tight curve, with a high old stone wall on one side, and a timbered house right against the road on the other. He cursed and braked suddenly. In front of them stood a makeshift barrier of crates and boards.

"What a bloody stupid place for barrier!" Michael exclaimed. "Damn, how am I supposed to back up—?"

"Cooper—!" Chris grabbed his gun and cocked it.

Michael cursed again. "It's a fucking trap, isn't it?" He shifted into reverse and checked the mirrors. "Mine's in my pack, side pocket!" He started to back up, the lorry beeping a warning. Chris got Michael's gun out and reached over to put it in his lap.

The lights of the truck illuminated the roadblock in front of them, lit up the walls close on each side. Chris saw movement behind them in the mirror: a man with a club of some sort, in the glow of the reversing lights. "Keep going!" he said, thinking that no one was going to go up against a moving lorry with just a club. Then he saw the others in front of them, one with a shotgun, one with a pitchfork, one with what appeared to be some sort of spear. Chris watched the one with the shotgun. He did not aim it at them.

Michael tried to back up with just the mirror. "Damn! I can hardly see!" The cab jolted. A grinding came from the rear. Michael hit the brake.

"Damn!" he said again. "That's it, we're stuck."

Another man appeared next to the lorry, on the driver's side, in the small space between the rig and the wall. He held a pistol, and he put it up close to the window and aimed it at Michael, yelled at him, but Chris couldn't make out the words.

Chris unbuckled his seatbelt. "Open the window a bit."

"Are you daft?" Michael said tightly. He had his gun ready, but kept it low, like Chris.

"Do it!"

Michael cranked the window down just a few centimeters.

"Get out of the lorry!" their assailant yelled.

"The rig is empty, we've got nothing," Michael said.

"It's the rig we want."

Michael grimaced. "Not a chance."

The man jumped up onto the step, grabbing the door handle with his free hand. "Get out!"

Chris brought his gun up suddenly, right in front of Michael's face, aimed at the man on the other side of the glass. Michael pushed himself back into the seat.

"Price! For God's sake!"

"Get back!" Chris stared at the man outside, who flinched. His eyes went from determined to unsure. The man kept the gun up, but his hand shook, and his mouth opened as his breathing quickened.

"Get back!" Chris yelled again, leaning in that direction just a bit.

The man outside the window leaned back.

"Get ready," Chris said to Michael, hardly moving his mouth. The peculiar calm he'd felt a few times in London had dropped down over him like a cloak.

"For what?" Michael said through his teeth.

"Check my mirror."

Michael moved his head to see. "He's coming up slowly. He's got a club."

Chris leaned over more, put his gun right up against the window. "Get off the fucking lorry!"

The man outside Michael's door abruptly stepped down.

"He's yours, now," he said quietly to Michael. "Get ready."

Michael gripped his gun in his lap.

Chris had been holding onto the door handle next to him. Now he turned and threw himself at the door. Michael brought up his gun as Chris opened his door with his weight against it, knocking the man with the club to the ground. Chris was out the door and on top of him in an instant. The man dropped the club, threw up his hands and yelled as Chris shoved the barrel of his gun into the man's face. He grabbed one of the man's wrists and twisted his arm around. The man gasped.

Chris looked up at the others, who stood aghast, squinting in the harsh glare of the headlamps. "Move the barrier, or I'll kill him!"

He hoped Michael was holding steady. The others all turned to look toward the one on the driver's side, the one Michael was covering.

"Move the fucking barrier! Do it now!" Chris screamed at them. "I have a round for every one of you shitheads!"

After another tense second of immobility, they all dropped their improvised weapons and started to drag aside the crates and boards.

"Get up," Chris said to the one on the ground, and hauled him to his feet, keeping the muzzle of the gun pressed against his neck. He twisted the man's arm up behind his back. The man retched, doubling over. Chris had to hold him to keep him from falling. Sweat glistened on the man's face.

The lorry's engine revved, and it crunched forward, pushing the last of the crates out of the way. The three men in front of the truck moved away on the driver's side. Chris dragged the last one with him for a few meters, trying to stay even with the cab door as the lorry moved slowly forward, then let go and gave him a kick in the guts for good measure. The man collapsed onto the ground against the wall, clear of the tires.

Chris hauled the door open and jumped in. "Get out of here!"

Michael gunned the engine as much as he could, and they lurched away through the little village. Chris tried to put on his safety belt again, but his hands shook too much. He braced himself against the dash, gulped air.

"God damn!" Michael said hollowly. He loosed a string of colorful curses. "What the bloody hell was that? Were you trying to get us killed?"

"His gun wasn't loaded," Chris said, trying to sound sure of himself.

"How the hell do you know that? Are you some kind of psychic now?"

"The one with the shotgun never even pointed it at us. And he just didn't act like it was loaded."

Michael's mouth fell open. "Didn't *act* like it was loaded? What if he'd blown our bloody heads off?"

"What were you going to do, Cooper?" Chris turned on him, anger welling. "Offer him a pack of fags and a chocolate bar? Do you think that would have worked out better?"

Michael was quiet.

Chris grabbed the safety belt and buckled it. "I intend to get to Breton. I'll do what I have to do."

Michael gripped the wheel with white knuckles. "Would you have killed him? The one you had hold of?"

"Not that one. He's already got it. He'll be dead in a couple days, most likely."

"You're a piece of work, you are, Price. Where the hell are we? Find us a bloody road, would you?"

Chris got his map and torch out. "Just keep on a bit."

They drove in silence for a few minutes, and passed a road sign. Chris found where they were. He directed Michael to turn a few kilometers later, putting them back on a bigger road. After he'd negotiated the turn, Michael finally spoke.

"Look, Price, you were right. I wasn't thinking fast enough. I guess you saved our asses back there. Thanks."

Chris stared out the window. "You're welcome. It might have gone different if they hadn't been a bunch of stupid wankers who didn't know what they were doing."

Michael shook his head. "But you knew they were. You've done that before, haven't you?"

The scene was already playing out in Chris's mind: the lorry pulling up to the roadblock they had put just on the far side of a tight curve deep in heart of London, the lorry trying to back up, Marcus jumping up onto the step on the driver's side, the shots, the bodies falling out of the cab... and Marcus, standing over Tahir, threatening to shoot him.

"I wasn't in the lorry," Chris said eventually. He continued to watch the blackness beyond the headlamps.

"You are a piece of work, Price," Michael said. "God, I need a drink. But I suppose water will have to do." He pulled the truck over, and they both got out to relieve themselves, then had water and a couple of scones from the food bag. Chris didn't say anything, and Michael left him alone. They were back on the road only a few minutes later.

Eventually Michael looked over at him. "Were you a cop? You know, before?"

"No. Not even close."

"Usually, I don't ask. I don't see how it really matters, now, right? But you, Price—you have me beat. You have a Jekyll and Hyde thing, you know?"

Chris did not look at him.

"So, not military, then?"

"God, no."

"You know how to handle a weapon," Michael pointed out.

"I've had occasions to pick that up, over the years."

Michael seemed to be thinking. "Did Pauline tell you what I did?"

"She said you dabbled in lots of things."

Michael sighed. "Ah, Paulie. Always kind. You could have called me a professional screw-up. I like to think that doesn't matter now."

Chris grunted. "No, I suppose not."

"So, you're not going to tell me?"

"Pauline didn't tell you?"

"It never came up."

Chris glanced at him. "It doesn't matter now. You wouldn't believe me, anyway."

"Wouldn't I?" Michael said thoughtfully. "Well, I've said it before, Price: you never cease to surprise me."

"Shut up and drive."

"Yes, sir," Michael replied, with a little salute.

Soon after, they encountered an official roadblock. Two men in army uniforms stood by with weapons ready while a third flagged them down. They all wore masks.

"Do you think *theirs* are loaded?" Michael said, shoving his pistol into his bag.

"Quite possibly," Chris said, doing the same.

The man in charge checked Michael's license and delivery papers.

"You're not supposed to be on the roads," he grated.

"I'm trying to get back to my warehouse in Portsmouth."

"Portsmouth? You're joking."

"It's on the papers," Michael pointed out.

"They're dropping like flies in Portsmouth. I'd go back if I were you."

"It's further to go back than to go on."

The man glowered at Michael, then handed the papers back. "Head south here, then take the M27 around Southampton. You won't get through the flooding, otherwise."

"Got it, thanks." Michael gave him a little wave as they pulled away.

Chris was already consulting the map. "We don't want to go that far south, do we?"

"No. We'll turn east on Petersfield Road soon. It's a straight shot from there."

Chris tried to relax. They were less than twenty miles from Breton now, in familiar territory. Soon he would be with Pauline, holding her. He envisioned bursting in the kitchen door, her face lighting up as she saw him, running to him, kissing him. He considered the time. It was the middle of the night. She'd be in bed, asleep. Even better, he could join her.

"Shit," Michael said, interrupting his thoughts. Another road block loomed in the headlights, blocking a right fork in the road. "That's where we want to go."

A uniformed soldier tried to wave them onto the left fork, his white mask standing out in the dark. Michael brought the lorry to a stop and wound down his window.

"We're headed to Petersfield," he said, trying to hand the soldier his papers.

The man kept his hands on his rifle and shook his head. "Petersfield is under Quarantine."

"Is it? We need to get off the roads, I know. We just need to get to Petersfield."

"Sorry. I have orders. No one gets through. Now, push off." He put his chin up and squared his shoulders.

"It's the middle of the night," Michael tried. "Where else can we go? They're expecting us."

Chris fought the urge to jump into the conversation, even though he was shaking with impatience. He figured Michael probably had far more experience with this sort of thing.

The soldier stood his ground, his eyes hard above the mask. "Push off."

"Look, I can make it worth your while."

"If you are suggesting a bribe, I have the authority to arrest you both and confiscate this rig and its contents," the soldier snapped.

"Ah, right. We'll be off then." Michael cranked up his window and shifted into reverse. "Bloody pigheaded..." he muttered, trailing off as he negotiated their change in direction. "We can head northeast for a bit, then take another road back down."

Chris checked the map. "Shouldn't be much more than a few kilometers."

The road, when they reached it, was solidly blocked by a rusting school bus. They continued on, finding one obstacle after another.

"We'll be in London if this keeps up," Michael grumbled after an hour of nosing carefully northeast.

"We haven't actually got very far," Chris said, and directed Michael onto a road heading south. "This looks good... should take us back to Petersfield Road."

Ten minutes later Michael brought the lorry to a halt. They sat silently gazing out at the road where it ended abruptly in an expanse of black water. Chris wanted to pound his clenched fists on the dash. Michael took the map from him and made a notation in red.

"We'll just go back and try again."

Chris wasn't sure how long they spent scouting around the countryside looking for passable roads. Michael wasn't willing to risk the rig on some of the lanes Chris wanted to try.

"If we get stuck, we're screwed," he would say, and Chris grudgingly conceded. He knew Michael wanted to get to Breton almost as badly as he did. More than once Chris was sure they were hopelessly lost.

The sky was greying in the east when Michael gasped and trod on the brake.

"This is it!" He turned onto a maintained road heading due south. "If the bridge is okay we've made it!"

The road dipped down toward the river, and Chris breathed a sigh of relief as the bridge came into sight. He recognized it; he'd crossed it when he'd left Breton.

They'd be getting up soon, he realized, Pauline and George would be starting the morning chores. Grace and Marie would be cooking breakfast. Unless... *No, Chris thought, they've never had it here. They won't have it now. Please, please, not now.*

The lorry crawled up the final hill in low gear, Chris fidgeting impatiently. Michael shifted, and eased the lorry around the final turn into the village.

"Oh, shit," he said.

Chapter 31

An improvised barrier stood in the road ahead, hardly visible in the dim grey pre-dawn. Whoever put it there had made no attempt to actually block the road. They'd simply set out two chairs with a board across them. Another board with a large red X painted on it leaned against that.

"Oh, god," Chris said, his fears realized.

Michael brought the truck to a halt.

"I'll move it," Chris said. He jumped down, and approached the barrier. The door of the house nearest opened, and a man stepped out.

"Turn back! We've got the plague here! Can't you see the sign?"

"Harry, it's me, Chris Price."

Harry squinted at him for a moment. "Well, so it is."

"Do they have it at the Anderson place?"

"Don't know, son," Harry said. "I haven't seen any of them in days."

Now that Chris looked more closely, he could see that Harry was ill. He stood unsteady near his door.

"How bad is it?" Chris asked him.

"Hard to say, yet. Seems nearly everyone's got it."

Chris's stomach contracted. "How many dead?"

"No one yet. Give it a couple days, I would guess."

Chris grabbed a chair and pulled it out of the way. "We're going up the road, Harry."

"If you're smart, you'll turn that rig around and get out of here while you can."

"I can't do that." Chris motioned to Michael, who eased the lorry past on the narrow road. Chris put the chairs and boards back into place.

"Well, good luck, son," Harry said. He turned and went back into his house. Chris climbed back into the cab.

"How bad is it?" Michael asked.

"Bad. He says nearly everyone's got it. No one dead, yet."

"Yet," Michael said grimly. "Damn, damn. Pauline?"

"He doesn't know."

Chris sat tensed on the edge of his seat, heart pounding, while the Michael drove slowly through the deserted village, and made the turn at the church. He shifted to climb the hill to the house. Chris kept a grip on the door handle. Before Michael came to a full stop Chris had the door open, jumped down, and ran.

"Pauline!" He sprinted around to the back of the house into the empty yard. "Pauline!" He threw open the back door.

She was pushing herself up from the kitchen table. She burst into tears when she saw him.

"No! Don't come in! We've all got it!"

Chris ignored her words, crossed the kitchen with giant steps, and folded her into his arms.

"It's okay, luv. I'm here now."

She sobbed against his chest, grabbed onto him. Chris held her tight to him, eyes screwed shut, legs suddenly weak. After a moment he loosed his hold. He brushed the hair away from her face, put his lips to her forehead. Her skin felt hot, and she shook in waves. Chris rocked her gently, made soothing noises. The house was cold, the table and sink were stacked with dirty dishes. A bucket sat on the floor next to the table, where she had been sitting. Chris could smell it. Michael came in.

"She says they all have it," Chris told him.

Michael dumped the rucksacks on the floor. "I'll go up." He headed for the stairs.

"I'm scared," Pauline said. "Chris, I'm scared!"

"I know," he said. "I'm here now. Michael's here, too. We'll take care of everything. It's okay, now." He stroked her for a moment more. "You need to be in bed. C'mon, luv, I'll put you to bed."

"The fire's gone out, there's no more wood," she said as he walked her toward the stairs.

"I'll take care of it."

"There's nothing to eat."

"I've brought some food, don't worry about it."

He helped her up the stairs.

"How did you get here?" she asked halfway up.

"Michael brought me."

"Michael's here, too?"

"Yes, we'll take care of everything," he said, trying to stay calm.

Her bed was in disarray. The room stank of vomit. A basin on the floor hadn't been emptied, and dirty clothes and towels were piled near the closet door.

"Do you want to change?" he asked her, but she crawled into the bed in her clothes with a little mewling noise. He pulled the covers over her, brushed the hair away from her face.

Michael put his head in the door. "They're all doing okay. How is she?"

"Exhausted. Ill."

"Wes!" Pauline said suddenly from the bed.

Chris sat down next to her. "What about him?"

"He came to help. I told him not to come in the house. He was staying in the barn. But I haven't seen him since yesterday."

"Okay, I'll see to him. Go to sleep now. We'll take care of everything."

"Don't go," she whimpered, clutching at his hand.

"I'll be back in just a bit."

"How's Mum?" she asked.

"Mum is fine, she's doing well," Michael said from the doorway. "Everybody is doing fine."

"Go to sleep, luv," Chris said. "I'll be back."

He tucked her hand under the covers and stood up, with a glance at Michael. He bent to pick up the basin from the floor.

"The place is a mess," Michael said in a low voice. "I'll get started up here, you go see about Wes."

Chris dumped the basin in the loo, but the flush bucket stood empty. He left the bowl and went down, Michael right behind him.

"Where would they keep more buckets?" Michael asked.

There were two by the outdoor pump. Michael worked the handle while Chris went on to the barn.

"Wes?" he called out as he pushed back the door. "Wes, are you here?" He squinted in the near-darkness. Wes had made himself a bed in a hay pile with a couple of old blankets. He shifted and made a noise. Chris knelt down, felt his forehead: hot and dry.

"Who are you?" Wes said.

"It's me, Chris."

Wes rubbed his eyes and looked again. "You came back."

"Yes, I'm here to take care of you."

"I think Pauline is ill." Wes tried to sit up.

"I know."

"Everyone in town was getting ill, so I came here."

"I'm going to take you inside, Wes." Chris scooped him up out of the hay. Wes put his arms around Chris's neck, rested his head on Chris's shoulder. His clothes smelled bad, but at least he had several layers and a heavy coat and knit cap to keep him warm.

"She said not to go in the house," Wes said.

"It's okay now."

"I took care of the animals."

"You did a great job," Chris said as he carried the boy across the yard. He took him into the house and up to the spare room, stripped him down and put him to bed.

"I'm thirsty," Wes said.

"I'll get you some water." Chris figured everyone else would probably need some, too. He went down to the kitchen, but there didn't seem to be any drinking water left. The stove was barely warm. He rummaged in his rucksack and came up with a bottle of water, a clean tee shirt, and a pair of underwear for Wes. He got a cup and took it all upstairs.

Michael was dumping another bowl into the loo.

"There's no drinking water," Chris told him. "I've got this one."

"There's another in my pack."

"I'll get the stove going, boil more," Chris said, and took a clean bowl with him for Wes.

374

Chris got the clothes on Wes. They were too big but better than nothing. He gave him a small amount of water, and left a little more in the cup on the chair. He looked in on Pauline; she was asleep. He went into Grace's room.

"Chris, dear," she said from the bed. "Michael said you were here."

"Hello, Grace," he said, sitting down next to her. "Do you want some water? Are you keeping anything down?"

"I think I'm actually a bit better than yesterday," she said. Chris poured a small amount into a cup from her bedside table and handed it to her. He held her head up off the pillow while she drank it. "Thank you, dear. Is Pauline still all right? Thank heavens she didn't get ill."

"Um, she's awfully tired. I put her to bed. Is there anything I can do for you?"

"No, I'm all right for now." She grasped his arm. "I'm so glad you're here to help now."

"We'll take care of everything," he said, with a hand on her shoulder.

Marie and George were both asleep. Michael was on hands and knees, scrubbing the floor next to George's side of the bed. Chris left the water with him and went down to the kitchen.

Chris filled the empty woodbox from the pile outside, and got the fire going in the stove. He pumped more water and put several pots and the kettle on to boil. He took the bucket from the floor in the kitchen, washed it out with plenty of soap, and put it on the stove to heat. He looked around, found another bucket on the stairs down to the cellar. He took it and the now-heated and hopefully disinfected bucket from the stove outside and filled them at the pump. He carried them both upstairs.

"We're going to have to change some sheets," Michael said, washing his hands in the basin.

Chris nodded. "I have to wash Wes's clothes, too." He handed him the heated bucket. "Here, this water is a little warm. I'll have some boiling soon. You're using plenty of soap?"

"Hell, yes."

Chris took a clean bowl into Pauline's room, set it on the floor, and stood there, next to the bed. The hair around her face was damp with sweat, her eyes crusted in the corners. Chris got a flannel and a small bowl of warm water. He sat down next to her and wiped her face clean carefully. She made little noises, shifted around. A sense of helplessness flooded through Chris. He stood up, stared a moment more, then went out into the hall. He leaned with his head against the wall outside her door, his stomach a deep pit with howling creatures writhing at the black bottom of it. He kept seeing Pauline in the bed, looking the way Sophie had looked when he had finally got home from the airport.

Michael came out into the hall. "Keep it together, Price."

Chris took a deep breath, nodded. "It's too late for masks, now, isn't it?"

"I'd say so."

"I've never got it yet."

"I have. I wonder which of us is safer."

"I should have kept her in Hurleigh," Chris whispered.

"Don't do that to yourself, Price. This is her home. And if you had, who would have been here to take care of the rest of them?"

"Yeah," Chris said, fighting back the clawing crowd trying to climb up his throat.

"It'll be okay, Price."

"What if it isn't?"

"No 'what ifs.' It's going to be okay. C'mon, get moving. Don't think."

"Yeah, okay."

Chris went downstairs. He gazed around the kitchen. Dirty dishes covered the table, filled the sink. Muddy footprints tracked across the floor from the door to the woodbox. The scrap bucket was full. Chris carried the bucket of wasted food out to the pigs in the barn. He dumped it into the trough, and the familiar old despair ballooned as he imagined Pauline cooking the food that no one was eating, on top of everything else she had to do. The thought of her pushing herself, doing pointless work in a haze of confusion and exhaustion made him groan. He checked all the animals, and collected more than a dozen eggs in the chicken house. He stood in the yard and breathed the cold air before he went back inside. He poured the boiled drinking water into shallow pans to cool quickly, put more on to heat.

Michael came down for more water while Chris was starting the washing up.

"Pauline's fine," he told Chris. "She's sleeping."

"I should have been here," Chris said, gesturing around at the mess.

"Don't," Michael said, frowning. "You're here now."

It took Chris a long time to get all the dishes cleaned and put away. He went up and checked on Pauline, then got Wes's dirty clothes and scrubbed them in a washtub on the kitchen floor, rinsed them in the sink, hung them on a folding rack near the stove. Michael came down again, this time with a bundle of bedsheets.

"I've changed Mum's and Pauline's sheets," he said. "I might need some help with George and Marie's."

Chris held out his hands for them. "I'll wash them."

"Let's take a break," Michael said, tossing the pile onto the floor. "I have a treat for us. I was going to save it, but God, I need it." He rummaged in his rucksack. "Here it is," he said, pulling out a paper sack. "They must have a coffee pot somewhere around here, eh?"

"Coffee pot? What for?"

"This, my friend, is coffee. You remember what that is, don't you?"

"Are you serious?"

"Never more so. Let's get brewing."

"Where the hell did you get it?"

"Connections, Price, connections. I know a chap."

Chris found the coffee pot and got the coffee brewing. His mouth watered at the smell. "Oh my God," he said, standing near the stove, breathing in the aroma. "Do you know how long it's been since I've had coffee?"

"Hell of a long time, I'd guess," Michael said. "The smell alone is enough to keep me going. Quite an improvement on what I've been smelling the last several hours."

In a few minutes they each had a steaming mug in front of them.

"There's sugar, but the cows have gone dry," Chris said.

"Black," Michael said, and sipped carefully. He closed his eyes and sighed. "That takes me back. How about you? You feeling better?"

Chris looked up at him. "Did you see the mess? Did you see the food? She just kept cooking food that no one could eat."

Michael nodded grimly. "Confusion. It's not uncommon. I've seen it before."

"She was alone, trying to do it all by herself." Chris started chewing on his thumbnail.

"Relax, Chris," Michael said. "Look, I've seen a lot of plague. I worked in a hospital for a few weeks, once. This isn't like what I saw there. They're getting better, all of them. It's changed, or something. Mutated. I don't think we're dealing with the same thing as before." He took another sip of coffee. "I think they're all going to be fine, I really do."

Chris looked at him, took a deep breath, and nodded.

"What have we got to eat?"

Chris rummaged in the food bag, thinking about what Michael had said. He had seen a lot of the New Plague, and this *was* different, but it was hard to put aside past experiences. He had seen too much death from the plague to be able to feel comfortable about this outbreak. "Quite a few tins, jars of veggies, potatoes…" he said to Michael. He pulled out a loaf of bread wrapped in waxed paper, then some muffins, and a jar

379

of jam. "I got some eggs earlier. Want me to fry some up?"

"This is good for now," Michael said, taking a muffin. Chris got a knife for the jam, spread up one for himself, and handed the knife over to Michael.

Michael dipped into the jam. "So what was that nickname your mate called you? Tag?"

It took Chris a moment to even remember that Brian had called him that. "Oh, that. It's from a long time ago. I don't answer to it." He gave Michael a look.

"What's it stand for?"

Chris bit into his muffin and did not answer.

"Oh, c'mon Price, spill it."

"Not a chance. You'll have to figure it out yourself." Chris got up and took his coffee and muffin with him. "I'm going to check on Pauline," he said over his shoulder, and went upstairs.

Chris moved a hard chair close to Pauline's bed. He finished his muffin and sipped at the coffee. She slept fitfully, moving around, making little noises. He reached out to push hair away from her face. He got the helpless feeling again; his stomach churned with the addition of the muffin and the coffee.

Pauline began to retch. She rolled over and leaned out of the bed. Chris grabbed the bowl and held it under her face, but nothing came up. He held her head and tried to soothe her. She continued to retch for a few minutes, then hung off the bed, whimpering. He eased her back onto the pillow, wiped her face with a damp cloth. She calmed, and fell asleep again. Chris waited to make sure she was sleeping soundly, then stood up. He wanted to stay with her, but found himself sinking closer to panic, in spite of what Michael had said. He had to keep busy. He knew there was still a lot of work to do. He went back downstairs.

"She okay?" Michael asked. He bit into another muffin.

"She was retching. We'll have to keep an eye on her." He pushed up his sleeves, went over to the washtub. "I have to keep busy or I'm gonna lose it."

"You're not going to lose it, Price," Michael said. He jumped up and grabbed one handle of the tub, and together they dumped it in the sink. Chris looked at him as the water poured out, but didn't say anything.

Chapter 32

"Cooper, you should get some sleep."

Michael sat across from Chris at the kitchen table with his forehead in his hand, his eyes closed, his hand around a mug of coffee.

Chris wondered what time it was. The clock in the kitchen, left unwound, had run down and stopped. The overnight drive, the stressful day of work, and the early autumn sunset had thrown off any sense of how much time had actually passed. He had cooked eggs and fried potatoes when Michael mentioned that he was hungry, the first time either of them had sat down since their one coffee break.

"What about you?"

"I got a bit on the drive," Chris said. "I'll stay up." He figured he probably had more experience at going without sleep than Michael.

"I wouldn't mind, that's what," Michael said, lifting his head. "I'm knackered."

"The couch isn't bad. I put a blanket and a pillow in there."

"All right, I'll take you up on that." Michael nudged the mug of coffee across the table. "Here, you have it." He pushed himself up with an effort and went off toward the sitting room.

Chris finished his own coffee and picked up Michael's, then hesitated. They were in the middle of an outbreak. Had Michael drunk from it? He hadn't noticed. The rich smell of the coffee drifted into his face. He thought about the basins and buckets they had been dumping and cleaning, the dirty sheets and towels and Wes's stained clothes. They had not been wearing masks.

It was *coffee*. He wasn't going to waste it. He added sugar, took a sip and savored it, then stood up with the mug in his hand. He glanced around. The kitchen was mostly tidied up, the woodbox full, the stove going well, the jugs filled with drinking water. Drying laundry and towels festooned two racks and the backs of several chairs. The few dishes on the table could wait until morning. He took the mug upstairs.

Wes was coming out of the loo.

"Hey, Wes. You okay?"

"I had to pee," Wes said, and padded back down the hall to the spare room. Chris followed him.

Wes hiked up the underpants. "Where are my clothes?"

"I washed them," Chris told him, setting down his coffee and helping Wes back into bed. "They're drying. How do you feel?" A lamp on the bureau cast a soft glow.

"I'm hungry."

"Are you?"

"I smelled eggs cooking. I'm hungry."

"I'll get you some toast to start, how about that? If you keep that down you can have an egg."

Chris took the water bottle down and filled it while he toasted a thin slice of bread. He put a little bit of jam on it, took it back up on a plate. Wes finished it almost before Chris could pour him a cup of water.

"Can I have more?"

"Let's see how you get on with that," Chris said. "You were puking this morning."

Wes handed back the plate and drank the water.

Chris pulled the covers up over him. "Now go back to sleep, okay?"

"I'm glad you're back," Wes said.

Chris smiled. "Me too."

"I knew you'd come back. I saw you kissing Pauline, the day you left."

"Did you?"

"I hope you don't get sick."

"I haven't ever, so far," Chris said. "Now, go to sleep. I have to check on the others."

Michael had left a lamp lit in each room. Chris looked in on George and Marie—still asleep—then Grace. She turned her head on the pillow to look at him.

He stepped into the room. "You okay?"

"I had the strangest dream. I dreamed I smelled coffee brewing."

Chris smiled and held up his mug. "Michael brought some."

"Oh, how wonderful. You boys had better not drink it all up before I'm well enough to have some," she warned, shaking a finger at him. Chris assured her that he would save some for everyone.

"Can I do anything for you? Get you anything?"

"I've got water here," she said, gesturing to the bottle and cup next to her cn the table. "I'm not sure I'm ready for anything else yet, but I may want breakfast in the morning."

"I'll make you breakfast, then," Chris said, "with coffee, if you want it."

"How's Pauline?"

"She's sleeping."

"She got ill, didn't she?" Grace asked, and Chris couldn't lie to her again.

"Yes, she was ill when we got here this morning. She's doing okay."

"She worked so hard, the first two days. She never got any rest. You need to get your rest, Chris, so you don't get ill."

"I will do, Mum. Michael's sleeping now, and then I'll take a turn."

"How are George and Marie?"

"They're doing fine, sleeping. I may be making you all breakfast. Wes just had a piece of toast."

"Wes is here? Thank heavens. I was worried about him."

"He'll be up tomorrow, I think," Chris said. "He's doing great. Now, you go back to sleep, okay?" He tucked the covers in around her and went out, across the hall, into Pauline's room.

She had thrown off the blanket. He started to cover her, then hesitated. She still wore the clothes she had been wearing in the morning, and from the look of them, she had been wearing them for days. Chris turned up the lamp, and opened her bureau drawers until he found some soft pajamas. He sat down next to her on the bed and tried to wake her. She opened her eyes a bit, but didn't seem to recognize him, and tried to roll over.

"Pauline, luv, let's get some comfy pajamas on you, okay?"

She seemed to wake up a bit while he was changing her trousers, slipping on the pajama bottoms.

"Is that you?" she asked, squinting at him.

"Yes, it's me. I just wanted you to be more comfortable, okay?"

"That's nice."

Chris got her to sit up, and pulled off her shirt over her head. She had another one under it. He took that off too. He put on the pajama top like a cape, buttoned it up, then reached under and unhooked her bra, slipping it down off her shoulders and arms. He put her arms in the sleeves. She was wearing the pendant he had given her.

"There you go, is that better?" he asked her, and she leaned forward and put her arms around him.

"Don't go away again."

Chris hugged her tight. "Never. I'm here to stay, darling."

"I think I'm going to puke," she said dreamily.

She didn't puke, but she did retch some more, hanging off the side of the bed again, with Chris holding her.

"I'm thirsty," she said when he had put her back onto her pillow. He gave her a few sips of water, wiped her face again. She looked at him with sleepy eyes. "I just want to get better."

"I know. You are getting better. You'll be okay. Go to sleep, now."

Chris turned down the lamp and settled in the armchair in the corner of the room. He spent the long night trying to keep dark thoughts at bay, getting up occasionally and making the rounds of the house, checking on everyone, stoking the stove, refilling his mug, chasing away the sleep that kept creeping up on him.

***

386

Chris awoke with a start in the chair in Pauline's room, his heart pounding. The blackness had been invading the house, reaching for Pauline. He stood up, trying to dispel the dream's images from his head. He swayed a little; the room danced. He looked out the window at the lightening sky. Pauline slept quietly. He used the loo and had a wash, and went downstairs. He woke up Michael, then went in to stoke up the stove and start more coffee.

"You can manage to make breakfast if anyone wants some, can't you?" he asked when Michael finally came in, his hair damp from a quick wash upstairs.

"Absolutely. I am a man of many skills. Who's going to want breakfast?"

"Wes will, he had toast last night. Mum said she might, too."

"That's good news," Michael said. "How's Pauline?"

"Sleeping better this morning."

"Good. You're going to bed?"

"I have to do the chores in the barn."

"Couldn't I do them?"

"Do you know what they are?"

"Um, well, it's been a few years, but I could probably figure them out," Michael said, and shrugged.

"I'll do them. I dozed some." Chris took off his shoes and put on George's wellies, got his jacket, and went out.

When he came back in Michael had folded all the laundry, washed up the dishes from last night, and had the coffee ready. Chris put the eggs on the table.

"They usually take some down to the village to trade, but I don't suppose there's much of that going on.

387

We may as well eat them." He shrugged out of his coat. "One of the cows is off its feed. And one of the hens is missing. I don't know if they ate her or if she's setting a clutch somewhere."

Michael gave him an odd look.

"What?"

"Okay, Farmer Price. You have cow shit on your trousers, by the way. You want something to eat?"

"I do," Wes said from the doorway, holding up the underwear that was too big for him.

"You'll want your clothes first, I expect," Michael said, and got him his trousers, underwear, socks, and shirt.

"How do you feel?" Chris asked him.

"I'm hungry," Wes insisted, getting dressed by the stove. "I want scrambled eggs and toast. With jam."

"I'm on it," Michael said. "Chris, what can I make for you?"

Chris sat down at the table, exhausted. "Nothing for me. Come here, Wes."

Wes hesitated, then went over to him. Chris reached out to feel his forehead.

Wes pulled away. "I'm not ill anymore."

"I just want to feel for a fever."

"I'm not ill."

Chris gave up. "Well, you don't seem so."

"Did you think we were all going to die?" Wes asked him.

Chris straightened up in his chair, and Michael stood still with a frying pan in his hand. They stared at Wes.

"Um, well, no, of course not," Chris said, with a glance at Michael.

"Usually people die when they get the plague, right?" Wes said.

"I've had it, and I didn't die," Michael told him.

"But mostly they do," Wes said to him. "My mum and dad died, and so did my sister, and my uncles."

"No one here is going to die," Chris said to him. "Lots of people do die, and it's scary. But not everyone. Okay?"

Wes nodded. "You look tired."

"Yes, he's just off to bed," Michael said.

"I am." Chris heaved himself out of the chair and picked up his rucksack, which was still on the floor where Michael had left it the day before. It seemed heavier than it had. He steadied himself with a hand on the wall. "God, I'm tired."

"The couch is quite nice, you were right," Michael said.

"I'm going up," Chris told him, and Michael glanced at him, then nodded.

"Ah, right. I'll check in on the others once I get Wes fed. Oh, and that nickname? I figured it out." He flashed a grin. Chris was too tired to care.

It seemed to take a long time to get up the stairs. Chris took his pack into Pauline's room, set it in the corner. He went to turn the lamp down, and noticed the pictures she kept there. The one of Pauline and Michael dressed up was gone, replaced by the one he had sent her. He was onstage, flashing a smile at whoever was taking the picture, one hand on his guitar, the other on the microphone. His dark blue shirt contrasted with the red lights behind him. A spotlight lit his face perfectly. He could just make out Ace and Gordy in the background. It was a brilliant shot.

Chris glanced over at Pauline in the bed, turned down the lamp, and dropped his trousers by the closet. He slipped carefully into bed on the other side, settled down onto the pillow, looked over at her for a moment. She didn't wake up, and he closed his eyes and tried to clear his mind of all the worry and fear of the last two days, tried to convince himself that what he had said to Wes was really true, that no one here was going to die. But he had lived through too many outbreaks, and he found it hard to believe. In spite of his exhaustion, sleep was a long time coming.

***

"What are you doing up?" Michael asked as Chris came down to the kitchen. "It's not even two. Is everything okay?"

"Yeah, I was awake, is all." Chris flopped into a chair at the table without getting his shoes. He grimaced at a bad smell in the kitchen. Something must have burned on the stove.

"You've hardly had six hours," Michael said.

"I'm all right."

"You want some lunch?"

Chris shrugged. "Where's Wes?"

"He said he was going to make sure you did all the chores right," Michael said with a grin. "I think he just wanted to look for that hen. You should eat something, you didn't have breakfast."

"I suppose. Is there any bread left?"

"Sure. You want a sandwich?"

"No, just bread, maybe some jam."

Michael got him a plate and cut him a slice of bread. "Coffee?"

Chris reached for the jam and a knife. "Yeah, coffee."

Michael poured him coffee and setting the mug in front of him. "I've got everything under control, here, Price, if you want to go back to bed."

"I wasn't really sleeping."

"You seem a bit off."

"I'm still tired, but I'm all right."

"Mum's up."

"Yeah? Great."

"She's in the sitting room, resting. She helped me make muffins earlier. One thing I never did learn to make properly."

Chris sipped his coffee. "I'll go in and see her in a bit."

"I'm just going out to see what Wes is up to, and get a bit more wood in, then I thought I should scrub this floor."

"Sure, I'll give you a hand."

Michael went out. Chris forced himself to eat the bread. Michael was right, he needed to eat. His head felt muzzy. He wondered if maybe he should go back to bed, but he thought about the series of dreams that had disturbed his sleep. He didn't want to go through them again just yet. He drank the coffee, hoping the caffeine would clear his head. When he finished he pushed himself up from the table and went in to see Grace.

She sat in the easy chair, a blanket over her knees, her eyes closed. She opened them as he came in, and smiled.

"It's good to see you up," Chris said.

"Well, out of bed, anyway. Still not much good, I'm afraid."

"Take your time, don't push yourself."

"Are you all right, dear?"

"I'm a little tired, still," he admitted. "Did you get your coffee?"

She sighed. "Oh, yes, it's wonderful, isn't it?"

The floor tilted. Chris had to take a step to keep from falling over. He reached out for a handhold, but found nothing.

"I'm not used to the caffeine," he said. He sagged down onto the couch. Things in the corners of his vision fell apart into jagged pieces.

"Maybe you should get some more sleep," Grace said.

"I will do, after awhile," he said, putting his head back and closing his eyes. His stomach churned, and the couch began a slow, disconcerting roll. Chris broke into a sweat as kaleidoscope colors wheeled in his brain. *No, no... it's too soon...* He took deep breaths, hoping it would pass, but it only got worse.

"Chris, are you all right?" he heard someone say. It sounded like Grace, but it couldn't be Grace... she was upstairs in bed, wasn't she?

He pushed up off the couch, used the walls and distorted doorways to brace himself, and lurched into the kitchen. The sink seemed a long way off, up a steep slant, past pinwheels of fire, but he made it, just barely, and vomited three times.

Chris hung onto the edge of the counter, found a cup and rinsed his mouth, spit into the sink. His legs had gone to rubber. He didn't think he would make it to the table if he let go of the sink, so he stayed there, shaking. Amazingly, everything in the kitchen—chaos a moment ago—had returned to normal.

The back door opened. Cooper came in with an armload of wood.

Chris gasped as tendrils of black snaked in and coiled around the chair legs. "Close the door!"

"I did," Cooper said. He dumped the wood into the woodbox, brushed his hands on his trousers. "You okay?"

"Where's Jon?" Chris asked, panic growing.

"I think he's ill, Michael," Grace's voice said from the doorway.

"How did you get here?" Chris asked.

Cooper stepped over writhing cables on the floor as if they weren't there. He put his hand to Chris's forehead and glanced into the sink. "Aw, crap. You just lost your lunch, didn't you?"

Chris nodded, blinked. The kitchen had gone the wrong colors. *Jon stayed behind.* "Oh shit oh shit oh shit..." His knees chose that moment to buckle. He collapsed to the floor.

"Chris!" Cooper exclaimed, partly catching him. "Well, I guess we know which of us is safer, eh?"

"It's too soon, isn't it?" *Pauline!*

"Apparently not. You're burning up."

"Where's Pauline?"

"She's fine, Chris."

"I left her behind—"

"No, she's just upstairs. C'mon, let's get you to bed."

"I can't walk." The room seemed to be filling with fog. *Where's Jon?*

393

"Hang onto me. Chris—?"

He couldn't make his arms work either. The fog got thicker. *Pauline... paulinepaulinepauline—* The formless beast hissed and growled, then everything went black.

Chapter 33

"Hello, beautiful." Michael smiled at her from a chair next to her bed.

Pauline blinked to clear the cobwebs, and some of it started to come back to her.

"I'm thirsty."

Michael held a cup for her to sip from. The cool water slid down her throat, the most wonderful thing she could imagine.

"Not too much," Michael said, taking the cup away when she tried to drink it all. "Give it a minute to settle, then you can have some more."

She remembered something even more wonderful, and her heart pounded. "Chris is here!"

"He's downstairs, on the couch."

"Send him up, I want to see him."

Michael hesitated. "Ah, well, I can't, luv. He's going to need a few days."

"He got ill?"

"Intensely," Michael admitted. "But, luckily, our plague seems to have turned into something a good deal less lethal. No deaths in the village, or here either, I'm happy to report."

A sob welled up from deep within her. Worry and fear and relief all mixed together in a storm of emotion she couldn't contain. She put her hands over her face and cried. Michael was there next to her in an instant, on the edge of the bed, patting her shoulder.

"There, there, Paulie, everything's fine," he cooed. "Don't cry, sweetie. Everybody's fine."

She managed to sit up, grabbed him, and he put his arms around her. She wished they were Chris's arms, but Michael's familiar arms would do right now. She cried some more, then calmed herself. Michael handed her a handkerchief from her bedside table.

She wiped her eyes and blew her nose. "I'm sorry. I don't know why I did that."

"You were under a hell of a strain, Paulie." For once Michael looked serious. "You did a great job. I'm proud of you."

"Is Mum okay?"

"She's fine, tucked up in a chair in the sitting room, keeping an eye on Chris." Michael eased her back onto her pillow.

"George? Marie?"

"George is up and about today. Marie is still in bed, but doing great."

"Wes?"

"He was up yesterday. Been a great help."

"He was a big help to me, too."

"I know, he told me all about it."

"Can I have more water now?"

Michael filled the cup again and gave it to her. She sipped it slowly, as much as he would let her drink.

"What about you? You look like hell, Michael."

Michael put a hand over his heart. "Oh, I'm hurt."

"No really, are you getting enough rest?"

"Not at all. Overworked, overstressed. First time in my life, I have to say. And hopefully the last." He smiled.

"Thank you, Michael," she said, more tears coming.

"Good grief, don't start again! Is there anything you need, sweetie?"

"I need to use the loo."

"Well, that's a good sign." He helped her out of bed.

"How do you know about the village?"

"Freddie was here, to check on everyone," he said, keeping a hand on her arm. "Brought us a basket of goodies, in exchange for one of the hens. I gave her some eggs, too. Can you walk?"

"Of course I can walk," she said, but the hallway tilted, and she put a hand out to steady herself. "Okay, maybe I'm a bit dizzy. I can certainly manage in here by myself." She shut the bathroom door firmly. When she came out she went back to her bedroom closet. She got out her warm robe and slippers.

"I take it you're getting up?" Michael said from the doorway.

"I am. I'm going down to see Chris." She stopped in front of the mirror above the bureau, made a face, and worked at her hair with the brush. She and pulled it back and clipped it. While she was doing that Michael had stepped closer. He stared at the pictures, then reached out and picked up the one of Chris, the one Jon had given her, and scrutinized it.

"Great picture. What, was he some sort of rock star, or something?" He gave her a little grin.

Pauline opened the drawer again, and handed the CD Brian had given her to Michael. It was the most famous one, 'Good Match.' Michael's mouth fell open.

"Wolcott Price—holy crap! I used to own this!"

She took it back from him, put it back in the drawer. "Are you coming?" she asked, and went out the door.

***

"Paulie," Michael said, gently shaking her awake. "Wake up, luv." He hated to do it; she looked so peaceful there in the bed next to Chris, but he didn't like the way Chris's breathing sounded.

Pauline took a deep breath and opened her eyes. "What time is it?"

"It's almost noon. You need to have some lunch, keep your strength up."

She sat up, rubbed at her face, and looked over at Chris in the bed. She smiled.

Michael opened a curtain to let more light in. He went back to the bed, sat down next to Chris, and put his hand to his forehead. He tried to keep his face neutral, but an odd feeling changed to a twisting in his stomach.

"What is it?" Pauline asked.

"He's hot again."

"But his fever broke last night." Pauline reached out to feel him, too. "He's hotter than he was."

"Was he breathing like this when you went to sleep?"

"No, it was quiet, regular. Normal."

Chris grunted, shifted, but did not wake up.

"I don't like this," Michael said to her, and she looked at him with worry plain on her face.

"But he was getting better, like all of us."

"Yeah, I thought so, but now... I don't know," Michael said. A little anger swelled in him. Chris should be well on his way to recovery, taking water and broth, getting up to use the loo. It had been three days. He'd even been awake and lucid last night. A second fever and breathing trouble were signs of something much more serious. "Let's go eat something. He's sleeping fine. You can come down for a little while."

He helped Pauline into her robe and slippers, followed her down the stairs. Grace and Marie had put together a hot lunch. George came in with an armload of wood. Wes was already at the table.

"Chris has a fever again," Pauline said, her voice tight. "And Michael thinks he's breathing oddly."

All heads turned to Michael.

"A little setback is all, probably." He tried not to sound too concerned, especially with Wes there. "Let's see how he gets on today."

Pauline kept looking at him while she ate. She hurried through her food.

"I'm going back up," she said.

"I'll be up in a little while, dear," Grace said.

***

"It's colder, isn't it?" Wes said as he and Michael left the barn after finishing the evening chores.

Michael pulled the door shut firmly and latched it. "I believe it is." He gazed up at the wash of bright stars against the black night sky, puffed out crystal breath into the pristine icy silence. A gust of wind cut across his face, invading his lungs when he took a breath in shock. "And windier, too. Let's grab some wood before we go in." They veered off to the woodpile and got an armload each.

"Is supper ready?" Wes asked as soon as they got inside, before he'd even dumped the wood.

"Soon," Marie told him.

Michael went up to check on Chris. At the top of the staircase he paused, his stomach contracting. The sound of Chris's breathing came out of Pauline's bedroom. He hurried in. Grace sat in the chair by the bed.

"Where's Paulie?" he asked her.

"She went to the loo to have a wash."

Michael felt Chris's forehead and neck. Grace had been wiping him down with a cool cloth, but the fever had not abated.

"He's worse."

"I don't like it." Michael wanted to shout in frustration, beat on the wall.

"Is there anything we can do?"

Michael shook his head. "No, not really. Try to get his fever down." He tried to remember what they had done at the hospital. Oxygen, but that was out of the question, of course. IV fluids, again, out of the question. Anti-virals: hopeless. "We could try to humidify the air."

"Boiling water on the stove?" Grace suggested.

"Too far away. Oh, wait, I've got a camp cooker in the rig. We can get a pot boiling right up here. That might help. I'll see to it." He went out the door.

Pauline came out of the bathroom with a towel over her arm. It was dark in the hall, and he could barely see her face.

"He's worse," she said, the way Grace had, but with more worry in her voice.

"Yes." Michael reached out to touch her arm. They had been in this hallway before, years ago, when her father was dying of a stroke, and she had said nearly the same thing. He remembered the tone of her voice, the same fear in it now as then.

"How bad is it?"

Michael didn't answer her, didn't know what to say. Like the other time, he had no good news for her.

"Michael."

"I've seen it like this," he said with a sigh. "It's not good, Paulie."

"What can we do?"

"Not much." He told her about the camp stove.

"We can't take him to hospital?" she asked, as if she already knew the answer.

Michael wanted to hold her. "They won't take him, luv. Not any more."

She nodded, swayed.

"Paulie, why don't you try to get a little nap in the spare room? I'll come wake you in an hour or so."

"No, I'm not leaving him now. I have to get back." Her voice wavered, and she put a hand to her face. A sob escaped her. She stepped forward, put her head against him. Michael put his arms around her.

"Oh, Paulie," he whispered, barely managing to keep his voice steady. She grabbed him and cried into his shirt, trying to muffle her sobs. He closed his eyes, had to take a deep breath. She calmed after a few

401

minutes, wiping at her eyes with her sleeve, pulling away from him.

"This is what happened to his wife. To Sophie. He told me. She couldn't breathe. He held her while she died. Oh, God, Michael…"

"It might not come to that," he said, but he had seen it before, and he felt the anger again. After everything that had happened, everything she had been through, now that she had finally found a chance for a deep and lasting happiness, it was going to be ripped from her.

"What are his chances?"

He stood in the dark, his stomach a tight knot, his mouth dry, his fists clenched. He didn't want to answer her.

"The truth, Michael," she said softly. "From what you've seen, what are his chances?"

"Not good. I'm sorry, but…not good at all."

She sniffed again, rubbed at her eyes. "Thank you for being honest." She turned and went back to her room. Michael stood, watched her doorway, listened to Chris's labored breathing.

He hadn't really thought of Chris as a friend when he'd picked him up in Hurleigh. He had done it for Pauline. If there was anything he wanted, it was for Pauline to be happy. He had never been able to make her happy, not for long; he knew that. Even so, it had startled him when he'd arrived in Breton in July, and Chris was still there. It hurt when Pauline was so short with him. He would have denied being jealous, but looking back, he knew he was, and his interference had caused Chris to leave. Taking Pauline to Hurleigh for a visit had been his way of making it up to the two of them, without having to say anything.

The trip from Hurleigh—the ambush, the way Chris had taken control and done what needed to be done—had shocked Michael at first, but the more he thought about it, the more he realized that Chris was a man who knew his way around this changed world, a man who had finally realized where he wanted to be, and whom he wanted to be with. Seeing Chris once they'd got to the house, taking care of Pauline and Wes, so gentle and soft-spoken, erased any lingering doubts Michael might have had. He had felt a sense of relief knowing Chris was going to be here, in this family, taking care of them. Pauline wouldn't be alone anymore.

Now Michael stood in the dark hallway and clenched his fists, shaking with anger and helplessness. Why did Chris have to be the one person to get the fatal strain? *It should have been me. No one would miss me.*

He turned to go downstairs, and saw Wes huddled on the bottom step. He went down, stopped two steps above the boy, sat down.

"Pauline was crying," Wes said.

"Yes."

"Chris is worse."

"Yes, I'm afraid he is."

"Is he going to die?"

Michael rubbed at his face, took a deep breath. He put out a hand toward Wes's shoulder, but the boy flinched before he even touched him, and moved away a bit, toward the wall. "Aw, Wes," Michael said.

"Is he?"

"I think he might. I don't know for sure, but he's awfully ill."

"When?"

"I don't know. Maybe tonight."

Wes sat silently, arms crossed on his knees, shaking.

"Do you want to go up and see him?"

"No!"

"Are you sure?"

Wes jumped up and ran into the kitchen. Michael followed, and got there as the back door slammed closed.

"Where's he going?" Marie said.

"I'll go after him," Michael said. "I have to go out to the rig for something, anyway."

"How's Chris?" she asked.

Michael turned to her and George, seated at the table. "He's not good," he said, and found he couldn't go on. He shook his head. Neither of them spoke.

Michael got his torch from the shelf, his and Wes's jackets from their hooks, and stepped out into the cold night. He went across the dark yard to the barn. The door stood open a crack, and he squeezed through. He heard Wes crying. He aimed his light into the corner, saw him curled up in a hay pile, on top of a blanket.

"Go away!" Wes wailed.

Michael went over to him. "I brought your jacket. It's cold out here." He draped it over Wes and stepped back. "I'm sorry, Wes. I know it hurts."

"Go away!"

"It's too cold for you to stay out here. If I leave you alone for a little while, will you come back inside? It's nearly supper. Don't you want supper?"

Wes sniffed hard. "Okay."

"Good. Okay, then. I'll see you inside in a little while."

"Leave me alone."

Michael left him in the hay, slipped back out the door, and went around the house to where he'd pulled the lorry into the driveway. He rummaged behind the seats with the torch until he found the camp stove and a can of fuel for it. He locked up the rig and went back inside.

"Did you find Wes?" George asked. He was alone in the kitchen.

"He's in the barn. He said he'd come inside soon. Maybe you could go get him if he doesn't, eh?" Michael opened the cabinets until he found a small pot to boil water in.

"Of course. Do you want some supper?"

"I'll be back down. I'm going to get some water going up there, for moisture. It might help him, some." He held up the stove, and George nodded.

"Marie's gone up with food for Pauline."

"Good. She needs to eat."

"Michael, are you all right?" George asked.

Michael turned. "I don't think he'll make it through the night. I hope I'm wrong. But I've seen this before. Too many times..." He shook his head and went upstairs.

Chapter 34

The wind picked up after midnight. It whistled in the eves, flung itself like a wild thing against the windows, nosed along the doorframes, looking for the smallest cracks. Michael flinched at the worst of the gusts, imagining something more than just the wind, something dark and hungry, seeking an entry. He glanced over at George, in the easy chair on the other side of Pauline's room, his arms crossed, his face fixed. If he heard the wind, he did not show it.

Marie leaned forward in her chair on the far side of the bed, checking the little camp cooker with the pot of water perched on it. Grace sat on the opposite side, in another chair, close to the edge of the bed. Michael had taken a place in the corner by the closet, near to Grace, in an old Windsor chair from her bedroom. They had gathered by unspoken agreement, after Wes had fallen asleep on the couch downstairs, to keep vigil through the night, pooling their strength, facing whatever might happen together.

Pauline was in the bed, propped up with pillows. She held Chris in her lap, wiped his face and neck with a flannel, talked softly to him. His breathing had continued to worsen by the hour, each breath becoming a horrible, rasping fight for life. Except for the labored rise and fall of his chest, he lay limp and unmoving. Pauline would talk to him, kiss his forehead, stroke his chest. She seemed calm and resolved, and did not shed a tear.

Michael sat in the corner and watched her, ached for her. He had been at numerous deathbeds, but they had always been mere acquaintances, or even strangers, at the hospital. This was far worse. He had never cared so much about the person dying, or the person being left behind. He kept his arms crossed tightly on his chest, his jaw clenched. Eventually he had to get up, move around.

"I'll be right back," he murmured, and left the room. He used the loo, splashed water on his face. He didn't want to go back in, but he knew he had to. He tiptoed downstairs to check on Wes. Michael envied him, envied his sleep, but didn't look forward to waking him in the morning. He went back up to Pauline's room, and leaned against the wall outside her door for a moment, in the same place he had found Chris a few days before, when he had told him to keep it together.

"Keep it together, Cooper," he whispered, and forced himself into the bedroom. He took his seat again.

Grace looked over at him, her face full of concern and sorrow. He couldn't meet her eye. He felt like he was sinking down into a black pit, slipping further with every easy breath, while Chris fought for every one of his. Michael began breathing in time with Chris, as if he could help him if they breathed together. It wasn't enough air, he wanted more air, but he kept the cadence in desperate futility, focused solely on Chris's hollow face. Vague forms all around him reeled and canted, faded into nothing, emerged again. He lost his connection to the chair, to the room. His arms and legs became leaden things that pulled him down and kept him from floating up into the dark mist that gathered below the ceiling. Time slowed to a crawl.

And then he wasn't breathing at all. Silence loomed, closed in on him, suffocated him.

"Chris," Pauline said, "don't give up. Breathe for me."

Chris drew a harsh breath. Michael gulped air to clear his head, clenched his fists to try to stop the shaking.

"Again," Pauline said. "Again, darling."

It went on like that, Pauline coaxing, or demanding, and Chris struggling to breathe each time. Another hour dragged by.

Michael reached his breaking point. His frayed nerves propelled him to his feet.

"Paulie," he said, his own voice rasping, "maybe it's time to let him go."

She looked up at him, her eyes fierce. "No."

"He can't go on."

"He can. He will." She dropped her face close to Chris's and whispered something into his ear.

Grace got up from her chair to take Michael's hand in both of hers. "It's all right, Michael. It's up to Chris, now."

He nodded at her, and fell back into his seat. He clutched his head with his hands. He sensed Grace standing next to him, and she rested a hand on his shoulder. Pauline talked to Chris. The water bubbled in the little pot.

Michael wanted to flee, to gather his things, get in the lorry and drive away fast, but this was the one thing in his life he couldn't run away from. He'd run away after his family died. He'd run away after Pauline's father died. He'd run away every time something got too hard. If he left now none of them would ever forgive him, Pauline especially, and he would never forgive himself. Pauline was going to need him, need all of them. He took a deep breath and sat up in the chair.

Marie was leaning over, fiddling with the camp stove. "We need more water."

"I'll get it," Michael said, pushing himself up, glad of something he could to do. He stepped over to take the empty pitcher from her, and noticed that the lamp on the table near her was low on oil.

"Thank you," Marie said, and he nodded back at her.

Michael went down to the kitchen. He stoked the stove, filled the pitcher, and went into the sitting room. Wes stirred on the couch. Michael stood still until he was sure Wes was still asleep, then got the lamp from the table. He carried it and the water back upstairs, gave the pitcher to Marie, and switched the new lamp for the nearly-empty one. He got a match from the bureau to light it.

When he took his seat again in the chair by the closet, he finally let himself look at Pauline and Chris in the bed. Nothing had changed, but at least Chris didn't seem any worse. He still struggled for every breath. Pauline still whispered to him, caressed him lovingly. Michael steeled himself, and the minutes ticked by slowly. Gradually, after another long hour, Michael began to think that Chris might actually be breathing easier. He leaned forward in the chair slightly, stared at Chris, silently willing him to breathe, breathe, breathe.... Against his better judgment, he began to feel a flicker of hope.

After a time, Grace turned in her chair to look at him, questioning him, and he nodded slightly. She put her hands together in her lap, bent her head in prayer. On the other side of the bed, Marie did the same. Michael almost did, but it had been a long time since he had felt the least bit religious, and he didn't think that God would be listening to him after all this time. Sometimes he felt like he believed more in karma, and Chris certainly had good karma. It was not something Michael himself could claim.

By the time the window began to lighten Michael was letting himself believe that this was not a deathwatch after all. Chris's breathing, while not yet easy, was no longer the desperate struggle it had been most of the night. Michael leaned his head back, closed his eyes, totally drained. And this time he did say a little prayer, over and over.

He heard a sniff, and looked over at Pauline. She had her cheek against Chris's head, stroked his hair, and cried silently, the tears leaking out of her eyes. Michael got up and went over to her. She looked up at him.

"You did it, Paulie," he whispered, and smiled at her.

Michael went out into the hall. He found support against the wall. Grace followed him.

"Michael. Is he out of danger?"

"I think so, yes. I can't be sure, of course, but I think so."

"Oh, thank God," she breathed, and put her hand to her face. "Oh, I have grown so fond of him."

Michael put his arms around her and held her. "I know, Mum, we all have."

"You must be exhausted."

"Me? What about you? You've been up just as long, and I wasn't ill a few days ago. You need to sleep."

"Pauline still needs me."

George came out of the bedroom. "He's turned the corner, has he?"

"Yes, I think so," Michael repeated.

"Well, that is a relief. Not a night I'd care to repeat."

"No," Michael agreed.

"I suppose I should do the chores. I'll get Wes to help me. He's had a good night's sleep, even if the rest of us haven't. He'll be glad to hear about Chris. Mum, you should get some sleep."

"We all need to sleep," Michael said.

"Breakfast first. I know if I'm hungry, the rest of you are," Grace said.

"All right, then we're all going to bed," Michael said sternly.

Grace went into the bathroom, George went downstairs. Michael went back into Pauline's bedroom.

Marie was helping Pauline out of the bed, moving Chris gently out of her lap. Michael took Pauline's arm to steady her as she stood. She seemed almost in a daze. He helped her to the bathroom.

Grace, just coming out, took Pauline's face in her hands and kissed her cheek. "I'm going to make us something to eat." She went downstairs.

"He's going to be all right, now, isn't he?" Pauline asked Michael.

"I think so," he said. He squeezed her hand. "I'm sorry I doubted you."

411

She nodded, went into the loo and shut the door.

He went back to the bedroom. Marie adjusted the pillows and covers, making sure Chris was as comfortable as she could make him.

"He's still not breathing well," she said.

"I think it'll get better now. We should try to get a little water in him and keep the pot boiling." A wave of exhaustion washed over him. "Mum is making breakfast."

"You look so tired, Michael."

"We're all tired. It was a hard night. I'll sit with him, if you want a little break."

"As soon as Pauline's out of the loo, yes."

Pauline came back, and Michael settled her in the easy chair in the corner. She stared at Chris in the bed.

"He nearly died," she said softly, and a few tears fell out of her eyes.

Michael took her hand. "It's over now, Paulie. He's going to be okay, now. Because you didn't give up, didn't let him give up."

She laid her head to the side, resting it on the back of the chair. "I'm so tired."

"Mum is making some breakfast for you, Paulie. As soon as you eat you can go to bed and get some sleep."

She had fallen asleep in the chair by the time Grace brought up some muffins with jam and a scrambled egg. She woke Pauline and helped her eat, and then tucked her into bed next to Chris. Pauline was asleep in moments. Michael dragged himself down to the kitchen, ate with the rest of them, then made sure Grace and Marie both went to bed. George went up to doze in the chair in Pauline's room. Wes agreed to find something useful to do. Michael decided he'd taken care of everything he could. He crawled into the spare room bed. As he sank into sleep he realized the wind had died down.

Chapter 35

He wanted to open his eyes, but couldn't manage it. The blackness still had him. It lingered in his lungs; every breath burned. It was going, slowly, but it trickled out in little bits, reluctant to leave him. In his dreams it had seemed like a black cloud, drifting, moving effortlessly, soft and ethereal. But when it finally got into him for real, he found it was not soft at all, it was heavy and hot and sharp. It filled his lungs and kept the air out. He had fought against it for so long, longer than he thought he could, but something had kept him going, some cool presence had stayed with him, and calmed him. He wanted to see that presence. He wanted its cool touch on his skin again.

He groaned in frustration. It got harder to breathe when he tried to move, tried to put a hand to his face to find out why he couldn't open his eyes. He wanted to open his eyes.

Then the presence was there with him again. He could hear it, feel it, soft and reassuring, cool against his face and lips. Something wet trickled into his mouth, and he swallowed, and relaxed, and let himself sleep, so he couldn't feel the burning in his lungs.

He was waking up again; he knew he was because it hurt when he breathed. This time he managed to open his eyes, but something was wrong—he didn't know what. He could hardly see in the dark, and fear surged through him. The blackness was still there in the room, waiting to get back in. He knew he couldn't fight it off again, he was so tired. This time it would take him; he would be defenseless. He made some kind of noise, tried to bring his hands up in front of his mouth, where it always got in.

Then the room brightened, the blackness faded off into the corners. She appeared next to him, smiling at him, and relief washed over him. She leaned in close to him and took his hand.

"I'm here, darling. It's going to be okay."

He couldn't say anything, but he stared into her eyes, and tried to squeeze her hand, and he hoped she understood.

She looked away for just a moment, then back at him. "Swallow this, darling," she said, and dribbled water into his mouth from a spoon. He swallowed. It hurt, but he did it again when she told him to, and a third time. She wiped at his face with a cool, damp cloth, moving it down onto his neck, and he wanted to tell her how good it felt, but when he tried, he couldn't manage it.

"Just relax. Don't try to talk. I know, darling, I know. You're going to be fine, Chris. You need to rest, though." She stroked his forehead with her fingers while she talked to him, and he felt his eyes closing again. "Go to sleep, Chris," he heard her say, and he did as he was told.

***

It had been three days since they sat up the whole night with Chris. He was improving slowly, taking water and a little broth, talking a bit. Michael knew it would be a long time before he was out of bed, even longer before he was fully recovered. The rest of the family were doing fine, getting the work done, resting when they were tired, going to bed early, sleeping late.

Except for Pauline, who spent every waking moment at Chris's bedside, and slept beside him at night. Michael worried about her, but whenever he checked in with her, or gave her a short break, she looked fine. She seemed to thrive on taking care of Chris; she was tireless.

Michael still felt a little stab of something in his heart at times, a sense of loss, when he watched her gently adjusting Chris's pillow, or spooning broth into his mouth, or just sitting beside him, holding his hand while he slept. But he kept telling himself she was better off with Chris. He took on as much of the work as he could, tired himself out so that he fell into bed exhausted at night, slept through without dreaming until morning. And he started to feel that it was time for him to go.

***

"Hey, Wes," Chris heard Pauline say. He opened his eyes and rolled his head on the pillow toward where she sat in a chair next to the bed. She was looking out the door into the hallway. "Do you want to come in?" she asked.

Wes stepped in. He looked over at Chris in the bed.

"Hey, Wes," Chris said. His lungs still hurt when he talked.

Wes stood just inside the door, watching him, twisting his hands together, biting his lip.

"It's okay," Pauline said. "He's going to be fine."

"I'm all right, mate," Chris said.

Pauline stood. "Why don't you sit here for a bit. I'll take a little break." She ushered Wes into the chair, and went out with a little glance at Chris. Wes sat looking at him.

"What's on?" Chris asked him.

"They all thought you were gonna die," Wes said abruptly.

Sudden breaths hurt. "Why do you think that?"

"I saw Pauline crying, and I asked Michael why, and he told me you might die during the night."

In his fragile state, Wes's words were a shock. Chris couldn't think of anything to say to him, could only think of Pauline crying because she thought he was going to die. He swallowed hard, wishing he had a drink of water, but not sure if he could manage to reach the cup on the table by himself. He saw a tear come out of Wes's eye, track down his cheek. Wes sat tensed and pulled in on himself in the chair, and did not wipe it away.

"It's okay, mate. I didn't die. I'm not going to."

"I didn't care when my Dad died, he was always mean," Wes said, his voice shaky. He sniffed hard. "But I didn't want Uncle Mel to die, and he did anyway. I didn't want you to die, either."

Chris motioned with his hand. "Come here." He wasn't sure if Wes would leave the chair; he had never seen the boy let anyone touch him. The only time Chris

417

had ever had any contact with him was when he had carried him in from the barn and put him to bed.

Wes stood, moved to the edge of the bed, and sat down, keeping his arms tight to his sides. Chris opened his hand out where it lay on the coverlet. Wes twitched.

"It's okay, Wes," Chris said, and something seemed to come loose in the boy. He shifted closer, put his head down on Chris's chest and grabbed hold of him. Chris put his arms around him. Wes cried against him, hot choked sobs full of relief.

"It's okay," Chris said again. His own eyes stung.

Pauline was there in a moment, trying to comfort Wes, rubbing his back with her hand. Wes quieted, and she gathered him up and walked him out of the room, talking softly to him. Michael came in soon after.

"Can I have some water, please?" Chris asked.

Michael handed him the cup, sat. Chris drank, then looked at Michael.

"You told him I might die?"

Michael sagged in the chair. "I wanted him to be prepared. I thought I would be taking some bad news back to your brother."

Chris blinked hard. "Pauline…?"

"She had all of us around her," Michael said.

"She was here, wasn't she?"

Michael nodded. "She was right here with you, that whole night, talking you through it. We were all here."

"I heard her," Chris whispered. He remembered the soft words, the coolness of a damp flannel against his skin.

"She kept you going. She wouldn't give up."

It was hard to keep his eyes open any longer. Chris let them close, felt the cup falling out of his hand.

"Go to sleep," Michael said, taking the cup. Chris floated for a moment, and let sleep take him.

***

Michael finished packing his rucksack in the spare room, stood with his heart pounding, sat down on the bed, took deep breaths to calm himself. He did not want to go into Pauline's bedroom, did not want to face them, to tell them he was leaving. He had never been good at goodbyes. He stared at the floor for far too long, then roused himself, and went out into the hall. He glanced in the door of Pauline's room.

"Knock, knock," he said lightly.

"Come in." Pauline smiled. Chris was propped up in almost a sitting position. She had been leaning forward, her face near his, whispering to him.

Michael leaned against the doorframe. "How are you feeling, Price?"

"Better." Chris's voice still sounded rough, he had dark circles under his eyes, but he looked better than he had yesterday.

"I had something I wanted to discuss with the two of you."

"What is it?" Pauline asked.

"It's about my place," Michael said, staring at their entwined hands. "It's a nice house, still salvageable. I want you two to have it."

Pauline's mouth fell open. Chris took an audible breath.

"Look, I'll never do anything with it," Michael went on quickly. "It's not like I'm going to suddenly settle down here again, right? It's going to ruin. But you two will want your own place, your own home. It's perfect. Right down the road. You'll still be around to help out here."

"Are you sure?" Chris said.

"Absolutely!" Michael said, forcing a smile. "I can't think of anyone else I'd want to have it. I'll stop in Petersfield and see what sort of paperwork we'll need to make it all official. I guess they still do things like that." He shrugged.

Pauline got up to give him a big hug. "Thank you, Michael! It's wonderful!"

He hugged her back, closed his eyes for just a moment with his cheek against her neck, then pulled away.

"You may not thank me as much when you see the state it's in," he joked. "Not exactly 'move-in' condition."

Chris grinned, Pauline laughed a little.

"Thanks, Cooper," Chris said, and held out his hand. Michael stepped forward and shook it.

"Take good care of her, Price."

"I will do, if I ever get out of this bed."

"And you, sweetie, take good care of him."

She smiled. "Absolutely."

"Well, I'm off, then," Michael said.

Pauline's smile disappeared. "What?"

"I have to go, Paulie. I've been 'awol' far too long. I have to get that rig back to Portsmouth. I'll be lucky to avoid the lock-up at this point. I'm going to have to grovel. I'm not good at groveling."

"But it's only been a little over a week."

"Closer to two, luv. And I'm not on official business. I told Price, I rather borrowed the rig." He shrugged again. "I might be in serious trouble."

"But—" she started, and Michael shook his head.

"You know I'm not the stick-around type," he said quietly. "My loss, really. Come here, sweetie." He held out his hand, and she took it, and he pulled her to him and hugged her tight, then released her. "I'll come around when I can. I'll try to scrounge up some building supplies, stuff like that."

"Be careful, Michael. And maybe you could write once in awhile."

"That I will do. Absolutely."

"Good luck, Cooper," Chris said. "Say hello to Kay for me. Tell her where you were. She'll go easy on you."

"Oh, she'd go easy on you, Price," Michael grinned. "Me, I don't know. As I said, I'll have to grovel." He stood for a moment near the door, his stomach churning, his hands shaking. "Right, then. I'll push off." He turned and left with a little wave, got his rucksack from the spare room, and went down the stairs to say goodbye to the rest of them.

Epilogue

Breton, April, 2008

Chris straightened up from shoveling compost and wiped at his forehead with his sleeve. He had been working in Grace's rose garden in front of the house on a particularly warm morning. There was extra work to do this year. The roses had been neglected the spring before, when Chris, Pauline, and Jon—who had moved from Hurleigh just after Christmas—were working to fix up Michael's house. Pauline had always taken care of the roses, but she was getting to the point where she couldn't do that kind of work anymore. Chris and Jon had decided to take a few hours and spruce up the garden for Grace. They had left Pauline in the kitchen with her Mum and Marie, stitching nappies.

Jon came around the side of the house with another wheelbarrow full of compost.

"That should be enough," Chris said, but Jon was looking past him, down the road.

"Someone's coming."

Chris turned to look. A man trudged up the road. Chris didn't know him. He reached the stone wall, walked along it toward them. He had a rucksack on his back, and watched them with his eyebrows drawn together, his jaw clenched. He stopped by the gate, hesitated. There was something about him that reminded Chris of something, but he couldn't grasp what.

Chris walked down through the garden toward him. "Can I help you?"

"Ah, don't the Andersons still live here?" the man asked, as if he was afraid of the answer.

"They do," Chris replied.

Visible relief softened the visitor's face. He looked down at the ground for a moment, put his hands on his hips, took a deep breath. He looked back up at Chris. "Who are you?" he asked.

Chris gazed at him, and something about him dispelled any suspicion.

"I'm Pauline's husband," Chris said, pulling off his work gloves.

A small smile changed the man's face as he stood there on the other side of the wall, and Chris suddenly knew why he looked familiar. He recognized the smile.

"Who are you, then?" Chris asked, though he already knew the answer, and smiled in return.

The man smiled more. "I'm Pauline's brother," he said. "I'm Jim."

Made in the USA
Lexington, KY
10 June 2011